TIME TRAVEL: RECENT TRIPS

OTHER ANTHOLOGIES EDITED BY
PAULA GURAN

Embraces
Best New Paranormal Romance
Best New Romantic Fantasy
Zombies: The Recent Dead
The Year's Best Dark Fantasy & Horror: 2010
Vampires: The Recent Undead
The Year's Best Dark Fantasy & Horror: 2011
Halloween
New Cthulhu: The Recent Weird
Brave New Love
Witches: Wicked, Wild & Wonderful
Obsession: Tales of Irresistible Desire
The Year's Best Dark Fantasy & Horror: 2012
Extreme Zombies
Ghosts: Recent Hauntings
Rock On: The Greatest Hits of Science Fiction & Fantasy
Season of Wonder
Future Games
Weird Detectives: Recent Investigations
The Mammoth Book of Angels & Demons
The Year's Best Dark Fantasy & Horror: 2013
Halloween: Magic, Mystery, & the Macabre
Once Upon a Time: New Fairy Tales
Magic City: Recent Spells
The Year's Best Dark Fantasy & Horror: 2014
Zombies: More Recent Dead

TIME TRAVEL: RECENT TRIPS

Edited by
Paula Guran

PRIME BOOKS

For Ann VanderMeer—
with special thanks for
pointing out a couple of these.
₪

CONTENTS

TIME TRAVEL ORIENTATION
₪
Paula Guran

Welcome to the twenty-first century, chrononaut! The stories collected herein were all originally published within the last decade (2005–2014 CE) and reflect what early-twenty-first-century short-form fictioneers imagine (or perhaps know/knew/will know) concerning time travel.

Despite my claim on the back cover, I'm not really sure humankind has always been fascinated with the idea of time travel. The desire to go backward to an earlier era or forward to a future date—or even travel to an alternate timeline—probably requires that one (at least initially) consider time as more or less linear.

Although the subject is currently debated among Egyptologists, there is a school of thought positing that ancient Egyptians considered time as measurable for mundane reasons, but, cosmically, as cyclical, unquantifiable, and not tied to space at all. Ancient Greek philosophers had varying views on time: Antiphon the Sophist wrote, in the fifth century BCE: "Time is not a reality (*hypostasis*), but a concept (*noêma*) or a measure (*metron*)." Parmenides of Elea, who lived around the same time, considered existence as timeless; motion and change were illusions—what our senses told us were false.

The Buddha (c. 563 BCE or c. 480 BCE–c. 483 BCE or c. 400 BCE) said, "Life is ever changing, moment to moment. The only constant is change." Thus, since reality is fluid, possibility is unpredictable, and the past nonexistent—"now" is all there is.

Even in historical Western science and philosophy there are different points of view—the "realist" perspective or "Newtonian time," and the "relational theory" to which Gottfried Leibniz (1646–1716) and Immanuel Kant (1724–1804) adhered:

> [Sir Isaac] Newton . . . did not regard space and time as genuine substances . . . but rather as real entities with their own manner of

existence... To paraphrase: Absolute, true, and mathematical time, from its own nature, passes equably without relation to anything external, and thus without reference to any change or way of measuring of time (e.g., the hour, day, month, or year). [Rynasiewicz, Robert: Johns Hopkins University (12 August 2004). "Newton's Views on Space, Time, and Motion," *Stanford Encyclopedia of Philosophy*. Stanford University.]

Leibniz postulated: " . . . space and time are internal or intrinsic features of the complete concepts of things, not extrinsic... Leibniz's view has two major implications. First, there is no absolute location in either space or time; location is always the situation of an object or event relative to other objects and events. Second, space and time are not in themselves real (that is, not substances). Space and time are, rather, ideal. Space and time are just metaphysically illegitimate ways of perceiving certain virtual relations between substances. They are phenomena or, strictly speaking, illusions (although they are illusions that are well-founded upon the internal properties of substances)... [Burnham, Douglas: Staffordshire University (2006). "Gottfried Wilhelm Leibniz (1646–1716) Metaphysics–7. Space, Time, and Indiscernibles." *The Internet Encyclopedia of Philosophy*.]

Still—I suspect individual human imaginations have always considered going "back" to the past for one reason or another and yearned to take a peek at what "the future" holds.

[Editorial Note: All dates from this point on stated as CE.]

As a fictional theme, time travel is a concept that has existed in English-language literature at least since 1843 when Charles Dickens's character, Scrooge, traveled back and forth in time (was it all a dream?) in *A Christmas Carol*. In one of Edgar Allan Poe's early (and lesser) works of short fiction, "A Tale of the Ragged Mountains" (1844), a character named Bedloe can inexplicably recount being at a battle in India in 1780. Although not a dream, the time travel is ambiguously explained: perhaps "galvanic shock" or mesmerism or even reincarnation is the answer.

Edward Page Mitchell's story, "The Clock That Went Backward"—more easily defined as a true time-travel tale—was published in 1881. But the concept gained a firm grip on popular imagination with H. G. Wells's novella *The Time Machine* in 1895. (It was inspired by his earlier—1888— short story, "The Chronic Argonauts.")

Just a decade later, in 1905, Albert Einstein published his theory of special relativity . . . and time travel (of a sort) suddenly seemed, if not probable, at least possible. The "time-dilation" effect of special relativity (now proven) is most easily and commonly explained with a tiny fiction: There is a pair of twins. One stays on Earth, the other—traveling at close to the speed of light—takes a trip into outer space and back that lasts ten years as far as the Earth-bound twin is concerned. But for the space-voyaging twin, very little time has passed at all. The stay-at-home twin has aged a decade while the traveler leaped ten years into the future and does not age.

And, as we now know but don't really notice, we are all traveling into the future at different infinitesimally small (but real) rates. The universe is structured so that we have to be traveling into the future all the time.

Visiting the past, or coming back from the future—well, that's a different matter. But now, we can now at least consider the possibility, thanks to scientists who—starting in the mid 1980s—have theorized the possibility of "traversable wormholes" in general relativity. Since then, many highly theoretical ways to warp space and time have been proposed . . . and challenged . . . paradoxes noted . . . and countered.

Meanwhile, science has both inspired and been ignored by fiction writers and filmmakers who have never stopped imagining time travel. Nor, evidently, has it lost its allure for the public.

Long a plot point for myriad television episodes and a few series over the years, the concept of time travel was integral to the recent series *Terminator: The Sarah Connor Chronicles* (2008–2009) and *The Fringe* (2008–2013). *Doctor Who*'s time- and space-traveling "Time Lord" and his vehicle, the Tardis (1963–current), are cultural icons.

Time travel has also remained an entertaining, if not always in-depth, consideration in films. Among the recent: *The Butterfly Effect* (2004), *Harry Potter and the Prisoner of Azkaban* (2004), *Meet the Robinsons* (animated, 2007), *The Time Traveler's Wife* (2009), *Star Trek* (2009), *Frequently Asked Questions About Time Travel* (2009, UK-only), *Looper* (2012), *About Time* (2013), *Time Travel Lover* (short, 2014) and *X-Men: Days of Future Past* (2014).

Nor has the (probably) most popular (and possibly the best) time-travel movie been forgotten. The now-venerable film *Back to the Future*, released in 1985, will debut as a stage musical in London's West End in 2015, the thirtieth anniversary of the film's release.

Time travel has remained a theme, if not exactly a staple, of novels. Only two novels—Stephen King's *11/22/63* (Scribner, 2011) and Audrey Niffenegger's *The Time Traveler's Wife* (actually published in 2003, but the 2009 movie has kept it on bestseller lists)—have reached huge reading audiences.

The outstanding *Blackout* and *All Clear* (one novel in two volumes; Spectra, 2010) by Connie Willis won the Nebula, Hugo, and Locus Awards. The duology—part of Willis's fiction involving a mid-twenty-first century time traveler from Oxford, England—has reached a more than respectable readership, but not sold the hundreds of thousand copies King and Niffenegger have.

The same can be said for Charles Yu's *How to Live Safely in a Science-Fictional Universe* (Pantheon, 2010).

The Shining Girls by Lauren Beukes (Umuzi, South Africa; HarperCollins, United Kingdom; Mulholland Books, US; 2013)—which received both high praise and some mixed reviews—has gained considerable readership, but has not yet made a major impact.

The late Kage Baker's historical time-travel science fiction stories and novels of "The Company" (first novel: *In the Garden of Iden*, Harcourt, 1997) have continued into this decade, most notably with the novel *The Empress of Mars* (Tor, 2009), collections *Gods and Pawns* (Tor 2007), *The Best of Kage Baker* (Subterranean, 2012), and—with the assistance of her Baker's sister, Kathleen Bartholomew—*In the Company of Thieves* (Tachyon, 2013). Novella *The Women of Nell Gwynne's* (Subterranean, 2009) won the Nebula and Locus Awards, and was nominated for Hugo and World Fantasy Awards. Baker's work has, so-far, achieved at least a cult-level popularity.

Other notable time-travel novels of the period include: *The Plot to Save Socrates* (Tor, 2007) and its sequel, *Unburning Alexandria* (JoSara MeDia, 2013), by Paul Levinson; *Man in the Empty Suit* by Sean Ferrell (Soho Press, 2013); *The Beautiful Land* by Alan Averill (Ace, 2013) and *Child of a Hidden Sea* by A. M. Dellamonica (Tor, 2014).

Time travel is also a popular theme in the romance genre, but the chronological is considerably outweighed by the carnal (or merely starry-eyed) in these plots, so I shan't delve into them here.

Plotwise, the same is often true with recent young adult titles, but some emphasize adventure and/or intrigue more than romance. A few bestselling titles from the last few years in this latter category include *Revolution* by Jennifer Donnelly (Random House Delacorte Books for Young Readers,

2010), *The Here and Now* by Ann Brashares (Delacorte, 2014), *The Glass Sentence* by S.E. Grove (Viking Juvenile, 2014), and—for even younger readers (8-12 years)—the Newbery Award-winning *When you Reach Me* by Rebecca Stead (Yearling, 2009).

As for the short form—time travel fiction in the current era offers vast variety and a wealth of choices, as I hope this volume helps substantiate. Solid theoretical physics underlies some stories, others eschew the scientific for either the fantastic or the ambiguous-or-only assumed science. Nor is the theme always taken completely seriously. Motivation for chronological wanderings or observations are just as diverse. Thus, in these eighteen stories, you will find the need to acknowledge history combining with political complexity and mixing with theoretical physics . . . an ancestor's heroics inspiring one chrononaut while recording history itself fascinating another . . . only the details of properly dressing time travelers is considered in one story . . . vacations are taken to observe dinosaurs and repair relationships . . . experimental trips taken . . . viewing the past is a struggle to save the world . . . time travel is controlled by bureaucracy . . . love makes a man go back and try to alter the history . . . history is merely recorded . . . a scientific breakthrough is used to learn of a personal past and glimpse one's own future . . . art is saved from destruction . . . the past is sometimes changed and the future altered, or not . . . time travel is one of the many layers of rip-snorting, action-packed, retro-Mars adventure . . . and much, much more.

So enjoy your many journeys, but don't lose track of when you are.

Paula Guran
Bastille Day 2014

WITH FATE CONSPIRE
₪
Vandana Singh

I saw him in a dream, the dead man. He was dreaming too, and I couldn't
tell if I was in his dream or he in mine. He was floating over a delta, watching
a web of rivulets running this way and that, the whole stream rushing to a
destination I couldn't see.

I woke up with the haunted feeling that I had been used to in my youth. I
haven't felt like that in a long time. The feeling of being possessed, inhabited,
although lightly, as though a homeless person was sleeping in the courtyard
of my consciousness. The dead man wasn't any trouble; he was just sharing
the space in my mind, not really caring who I was. But this returning of my
old ability, as unexpected as it was, startled me out of the apathy in which I
had been living my life. I wanted to find him, this dead man.

I think it is because of the Machine that these old feelings are being
resurrected. It takes up an entire room, although the only part of it I see
is the thing that looks like a durbeen, a telescope. The Machine looks into
the past, which is why I've been thinking about my own girlhood. If I could
spy on myself as I ran up and down the crowded streets and alleys of Park
Circus! But the scientists who work the Machine tell me that the scope can't
look into the recent past. They never tell me the *why* of anything, even when
I ask—they smile and say, "Don't bother about things like that, Gargi-di!
What you are doing is great, a great contribution." To my captors—they
think they are my benefactors but truly, they are my captors—to them, I am
something very special, because of my ability with the scope; but because I
am not like them, they don't really see me as I am.

An illiterate woman, bred in the back streets and alleyways of Old Kolkata,
of no more importance than a cockroach—what saved me from being
stamped out by the great, indifferent foot of the mighty is this . . . ability.

The Machine gives sight to a select few, and it doesn't care if you are rich or poor, man or woman.

I wonder if they guess I'm lying to them?

They've set the scope at a particular moment of history: the spring of 1856, and a particular place: Metiabruz in Kolkata. I am supposed to spy on an exiled ruler of that time, to see what he does every morning, out on the terrace, and to record what he says. He is a large, sad, weepy man. He is the Nawab of Awadh, ousted from his beloved home by the conquering British. He is a poet.

They tell me he wrote the song "Babul Mora," which to me is the most interesting and important thing about him, because I learned that song as a girl. The song is about a woman leaving, looking back at her childhood home, and it makes me cry sometimes even though my childhood wasn't idyllic. And yet there are things I remember, incongruous things like a great field of rice and water gleaming between the new shoots, and a bagula, hunched and dignified like an old priest, standing knee deep in water, waiting for fish. I remember the smell of the sea, many miles away, borne on the wind. My mother's village, Siridanga.

How I began to lie to my captors was sheer chance. There was something wrong with the Machine. I don't understand how it works, of course, but the scientists were having trouble setting the date. The girl called Nondini kept cursing and muttering about spacetime fuzziness. The fact that they could not look through the scope to verify what they were doing, not having the kind of brain suitable for it, meant that I had to keep looking to check whether they had got back to Wajid Ali Shah in the Kolkata of 1856.

I'll never forget when I first saw the woman. I knew it was the wrong place and time, but, instead of telling my captors, I kept quiet. She was looking up toward me (my viewpoint must have been near the ceiling). She was not young, but she was respectable, you could see that. A housewife squatting on her haunches in a big, old-fashioned kitchen, stacking dirty dishes. I don't know why she looked up for that moment but it struck me at once: the furtive expression on her face. A sensitive face, with beautiful eyes, a woman who, I could tell, was a warm-hearted motherly type—so why did she look like that, as though she had a dirty secret? The scope doesn't stay connected to the past for more than a few blinks of the eye, so that was all I had: a glimpse.

Nondini nudged me, asking "Gargi-di, is that the right place and time?" Without thinking, I said yes.

That is how it begins: the story of my deception. That simple "yes" began the unraveling of everything.

The institute is a great glass monstrosity that towers above the ground somewhere in New Parktown, which I am told is many miles south of Kolkata. Only the part we're on is not flooded. All around my building are other such buildings, so that when I look out of the window I see only reflections—of my building and the others and my own face, a small, dark oval. At first it drove me crazy, being trapped not only by the building but also by these tricks of light.

And my captors were trapped too, but they seemed unmindful of the fact. They had grown accustomed. I resolved in my first week that I would not become accustomed. No, I didn't regret leaving behind my mean little life, with all its difficulties and constraints, but I was under no illusions. I had exchanged one prison for another.

In any life, I think, there are apparently unimportant moments that turn out to matter the most. For me as a girl it was those glimpses of my mother's village, poor as it was. I don't remember the bad things. I remember the sky, the view of paddy fields from my grandfather's hut on a hillock, and the tame pigeon who cooed and postured on a wooden post in the muddy little courtyard. I think it was here I must have drawn my first real breath. There was an older cousin I don't recall very well, except as a voice, a guide through this exhilarating new world, where I realized that food grew on trees, that birds and animals had their own tongues, their languages, their stories. The world exploded into wonders during those brief visits. But always they were just small breaks in my life as one more poor child in the great city. Or so I thought. What I now think is that those moments gave me a taste for something I've never had—a kind of freedom, a soaring.

I want to be able to share this with the dead man who haunts my dreams. I want him, whoever he is, wherever he is, to have what I had so briefly. The great open spaces, the chance to run through the fields and listen to the birds tell their stories. He might wake up from being dead then, might think of other things besides deltas.

He sits in my consciousness so lightly, I wonder if he even exists, whether he is an imagining rather than a haunting. But I recognize the feeling of a haunting like that, even though it has been years since I experienced the last one.

■ ■ ■

The most important haunting of my life was when I was, maybe, fourteen. We didn't know our birthdays, so I can't be sure. But I remember that an old man crept into my mind, a tired old man. Like Wajid Ali Shah more than a hundred years ago, this man was a poet. But there the similarity ended because he had been ground down by poverty; his respectability was all he had left. When I saw him in my mind he was sitting under an awning. There was a lot of noise nearby, the kind of hullabaloo that a vegetable market generates. I sensed immediately that he was miserable, and this was confirmed later when I met him. All my hauntings have been of people who are hurt, or grieving, or otherwise in distress.

He wasn't a mullah, Rahman Khan, but the street kids all called him Maula, so I did too. I think he accepted it with deprecation. He was a kind man. He would sit under a tree at the edge of the road with an old typewriter, waiting for people to come to him for typing letters and important documents and so on. He only had a few customers. Most of the time he would stare into the distance with rheumy eyes, seeing not the noisy market but some other vista, and he would recite poetry. I found time from my little jobs in the fruit market to sit by him and sometimes I would bring him a stolen pear or mango. He was the one who taught me to appreciate language, the meanings of words. He told me about poets he loved, Wajid Ali Shah and Khayyam and Rumi, and our own Rabindranath and Nazrul, and the poets of the humbler folk, the baul and the maajhis. Once I asked him to teach me how to read and write. He had me practice letters in Hindi and Bengali on discarded sheets of typing paper, but the need to fill our stomachs prevented me from giving time to the task, and I soon forgot what I'd learned. In any case at that age I didn't realize its importance—it was no more than a passing fancy. But he did improve my Hindi, which I had picked up from my father, and taught me some Urdu, and a handful of songs, including "Babul Mora."

Babul Mora, he would sing in his thin, cracked voice. *Naihar chuuto hi jaaye.*

It is a woman's song, a woman leaving her childhood home with her newlywed husband, looking back from the cart for the last time. *Father mine, my home slips away from me.* Although my father died before I was grown, the song still brings tears to my eyes.

The old man gave me my fancy way of speaking. People laugh at me sometimes when I use nice words, nicely, when a few plain ones would do. What good is fancy speech to a woman who grew up poor and illiterate?

But I don't care. When I talk in that way I feel as though I am touching the essence of the world. I got that from Maula. All my life I have tried to give away what I received but my one child died soon after birth and nobody else wanted what I had. Poetry. A vision of freedom. Rice fields, birds, the distant blue line of the sea. Siridanga.

Later, after my father died, I started to work in people's houses with my mother. Clean and cook, and go to another house, clean and cook. Some of the people were nice but others yelled at us and were suspicious of us. I remember one fat lady who smelled strongly of flowers and sweat, who got angry because I touched the curtains.

The curtains were blue and white and had lace on them, and I had never seen anything as delicate and beautiful. I reached my hand out and touched them and she yelled at me. I was just a child, and whatever she said, my hands weren't dirty. I tried to defend myself but my mother herself shut me up. She didn't want to lose her job. I remember being so angry I thought I would catch fire from inside. I think all those houses must be under water now. There will be fish nibbling at the fine lace drawing room curtains. Slime on the walls, the carpets rotted. All our cleaning for nothing!

I have to find the dead man. I have to get out of here somehow.

The scientist called Nondini sees me as a real person, I think, not just as someone with a special ability who is otherwise nothing special. She has sympathy for me partly because there is a relative of hers who might still be in a refugee camp, and she has been going from one to the other to try to find her. The camps are mostly full of slum-dwellers because when the river overflowed and the sea came over the land, it drowned everything except for the skyscrapers. All the people who lived in slums or low buildings, who didn't have relatives with intact homes, had to go to the camps. I was in the big one, Sahapur, where they actually tried to help people find jobs, and tested them for all kinds of practical skills, because we were—most of us— laborers, domestic help, that sort of thing. And they gave us medical tests also. That's how I got my job, my large clean room with a big-screen TV, and all the food I want—after they found out I had the kind of brain the Machine can use.

But I can't go back to the camp to see my friends. Many of them had left before me anyway, farmed out to corporations where they could be useful with medical tests and get free medicines also. Ashima had cancer and she got to go to one of those places, but there is no way I can find out what happened to her. I imagine her somewhere like this place, with everything free and all the mishti-doi she can eat. I hope she's all right. Kabir had a limp from birth but he's only eighteen, so maybe they can fix it. When she has time, Nondini lets me talk about them. Otherwise I feel as though nothing from that time was real, that I never had a mother and father, or a husband who left me after our son died. As if my friends never existed. It drives me crazy sometimes to return to my room after working in the same building, and to find nothing but the same programs on the TV. At first I was so excited about all the luxury but now I get bored and fretful to the point where I am scared of my impulses. Especially when the night market comes and sets up on the streets below, every week. I can't see the market from my high window, but I can see the lights dancing on the windows of the building on the other side of the square. I can smell fish frying and hear people talking, yelling out prices, and I hear singing. It is the singing that makes my blood wild. The first time they had a group of maajhis come, I nearly broke the window glass, I so wanted to jump out. They know how to sing to the soul.

> *Maajhi, O Maajhi*
> *My beloved waits*
> *On the other shore . . .*

I think the scientists are out at the market all night, because when they come in the next day, on Monday, their eyes are red, and they are bad-tempered, and there is something far away about them, as though they've been in another world. It could just be the rice beer, of course.

My captors won't let me out for some months, until they are sure I've "settled down." I can't even go to another floor of this building.

There have been cases of people from the refugee camps escaping from their jobs, trying to go back to their old lives, their old friends, as though those things existed any more. So there are rules that you have to be on probation before you are granted citizenship of the city, which then allows you to go freely everywhere. Of course "everywhere" is mostly under water, for what it's worth. Meanwhile Nondini lets me have this recorder that I'm speaking into, so I won't get too lonely. So I can hear my own voice played back. What a strange one she is!

Nondini is small and slight, with eyes that slant up just a little at the corners. She has worked hard all her life to study history. I never knew there was so much history in the world until my job began! She keeps giving me videos about the past—not just Wajid Ali Shah but also further back, to the time when the British were here, and before that when Kolkata was just a little village on the Hugli river. It is nearly impossible to believe that there was a time when the alleyways and marketplaces and shantytowns and skyscrapers didn't exist—there were forests and fields, and the slow windings of the river, and wild animals. I wish I could see that. But they—the scientists—aren't interested in that period.

What they *do* want to know is whether there were poems or songs of Wajid Ali Shah that were unrecorded. They want me to catch him at a moment when he would recite something new that had been forgotten over the centuries. What I don't understand is, Why all this fuss about old poetry? I like poetry more than most people, but it isn't what you'd do in the middle of a great flood. When I challenge the scientists some of them look embarrassed, like Brijesh; and Unnikrishnan shakes his head. Their leader, Dr. Mitra, she just looks impatient, and Nondini says "poetry can save the world." I may be uneducated but I am not stupid. They're hiding something from me.

The housewife—the woman for whom I have abandoned Wajid Ali Shah—interests me. Her name is Rassundari—I know, because someone in her household called her name. Most of the time they call her Rasu or Sundari, or daughter-in-law, or sister-in-law, etcetera, but this time some visitor called out her full name, carefully and formally. I wish I could talk to her. It would be nice to talk to someone who is like me. How stupid that sounds! This woman clearly comes from a rich rural family—a big joint family it is, all under the same roof. She is nothing like me. But I feel she could talk to me as an ordinary woman, which is what I am.

I wish I could see the outside of her house. They are rich landowners, so it must be beautiful outside. I wonder if it is like my mother's village. Odd that although I have hardly spent any time in Siridanga, I long for it now as though I had been born there.

The first time after I found Rassundari, Nondini asked me if I'd discovered anything new about Wajid Ali Shah. I felt a bit sorry for her because I was deceiving her, so I said, out of my head, without thinking:

"I think he's writing a new song."

The scope doesn't give you a clear enough view to read writing in a book, even if I could read. But Wajid Ali Shah loves gatherings of poets and musicians, where he sings or recites his own works. So Nondini asked me:

"Did he say anything out loud?"

Again without thinking I said, maybe because I was tired, and lonely, and missing my friends:

"Yes, but only one line: *'If there was someone for such as me . . .'*" I had spoken out of the isolation I had been feeling, and out of irritation, because I wanted to get back to my housewife. I would have taken my lie back at once if I could. Nondini's eyes lit up.

"That is new! I must record that!" And in the next room there was a flurry of activity.

So began my secret career as a poet.

Rassundari works really hard. One day I watched her nearly all day, and she was in the kitchen almost the whole time. Cooking, cleaning, supervising a boy who comes to clean the dishes. The people of the house seem to eat all the time. She always waits for them to finish before she eats, but that day she didn't get a chance at all. A guest came at the last minute after everyone had eaten lunch, so she cooked for him, and after that one of the small children was fussing so she took him on her lap and tried to eat her rice, which was on a plate on the floor in front of her, but she had taken just one mouthful when he urinated all over her and her food. The look on her face! There was such anguish, but after a moment she began to laugh. She comforted the child and took him away to clean up, and came back and cleaned the kitchen, and by that time it was evening and time to cook the evening meal. I felt so bad for her! I have known hunger sometimes as a girl, and I could not have imagined that a person who was the daughter-in-law of such a big house could go hungry too. She never seems to get angry about it—I don't understand that, because I can be quick to anger myself. But maybe it is because everyone in the house is nice to her. I can only see the kitchen of course, but whenever people come in to eat or just to talk with her, they treat her well—even her mother-in-law speaks kindly to her.

Her older son is a charming little boy, who comes and sits near her when he is practicing his lessons. He is learning the alphabet.

She makes him repeat everything to her several times. Seeing him revives the dull pain in my heart that never goes away. I wonder what my child would have looked like, had he survived. He only lived two days. But those are old sorrows.

I want to know why Rassundari looks, sometimes, like she has a guilty secret.

■ ■ ■

The dead man has started talking to me in my dreams. He thinks I am someone called Kajori, who must have been a lover. He cries for me, thinking I'm her. He weeps with agony, calls to me to come to his arms, sleep in his bed. I have to say that while I am not the kind of woman who would jump into the arms of just any man, let alone one who is dead, his longing awakes the loneliness in me. I remember what it was like to love a man, even though my husband turned out to be a cowardly bastard. In between his sobs the dead man mutters things that perhaps only this Kajori understands.

Floating over the silver webbing of the delta, he babbles about space and time.

"Time!" he tells me. "Look, look at that rivulet. Look at this one."

It seems to me that he thinks the delta is made by a river of time, not water. He says time has thickness—and it doesn't flow in one straight line—it meanders. It splits up into little branches, some of which join up again. He calls this *fine structure*. I have never thought about this before, but the idea makes sense. The dead man shows me history, the sweep of it, the rise and fall of kings and dynasties, how the branches intersect and move on, and how some of the rivulets dry up and die. He tells me how the weight of events and possibilities determines how the rivulets of time flow.

"I must save the world," he says at the end, just before he starts to cry.

I know Rassundari's secret now.

She was sitting in the kitchen alone, after everyone had eaten. She squatted among the pots and pans, scouring them, looking around her warily like a thief in her own house. She dipped a wet finger into the ash pile and wrote on the thali the letter her son had been practicing in the afternoon, *kah*. She wrote it big, which is how I could see it. She said it aloud, that's how I know what letter it was.

She erased it, wrote it again. The triangular shape of the first loop, the down-curve of the next stroke, like a bird bending to drink. Yes, and the line of the roof from which the character was suspended, like wet socks on a clothesline. She shivered with pleasure. Then someone called her name, and she hastily scrubbed the letter away.

How strange this is! There she is, in an age when a woman, a respectable upper-caste woman, isn't supposed to be able to read, so she has to learn on the sly, like a criminal. Here I am, in an age when women can be scientists like Nondini, yet I can't read. What I learned from the Maula, I forgot. I can recognize familiar shop signs and so on from their shapes, not the sounds the shapes are supposed to represent, and anyway machines tell you everything. Nondini tells me that now very few people need to read because of mobiles, and because information can be shown and spoken by machines.

After watching Rassundari write for the first time, that desire woke in me, to learn how to read. My captors would not have denied me materials if I'd asked them, but I thought it would be much more interesting to learn from a woman dead for maybe hundreds of years. This is possible because the Machine now stays stuck in the set time and place for hours instead of minutes. Earlier it would keep disconnecting after five or ten minutes and you would have to wait until it came back. Its new steadiness makes the scientists very happy.

So now when I am at the scope, my captors leave me to myself. As Rassundari writes, I copy the letters on a sheet of paper and whisper the sounds under my breath.

The scientists annoy me after each session with their questions, and sometimes when I feel wicked I tell them that Wajid Ali Shah is going through a dry spell. Other times I make up lines that he supposedly spoke to his gathering of fellow poets. I tell them these are bits and fragments and pieces of longer works.

> *If there was someone for such as me*
> *Would that cause great inconvenience for you, O universe?*
> *Would the stars go out and fall from the sky?*

I am enjoying this, even though my poetry is that of a beginner, crude, and direct. Wajid Ali Shah also wrote in the commoner's tongue, which makes my deception possible. I also suspect that these scientists don't know enough about poetry to tell the difference.

My dear teacher, the Maula, would talk for hours about rhyme and lilt, and the difference between a ghazal and a rubayi. I didn't understand half of what he said but I learned enough to know that there is a way of talking about poetry if you are learned in the subject. And the scientists don't seem to react like that. They just exclaim and repeat my lines, and wonder whether this is a fragment, or a complete poem.

One day I want to write my poetry in my own hand.

Imagine me, Gargi, doing all this! A person of no importance and look where life has got me!

■ ■ ■

I now know who Kajori is.

I didn't know that was her first name. Even the older scientists call her Dr. Mitra. She's a tall, thin woman, the boss of the others, and she always looks busy and harassed. Sometimes she smiles, and her smile is twisted. I took a dislike to her at first because she always looked through me, as though I wasn't there. Now I still dislike her but I'm sorry for her. And angry with her. The dead man, her lover, she must have sent him away, trapped him in that place where he floats above the delta of the river of time. It's my dreams he comes into, not hers. I can hardly bear his agony, his weeping, the way he calls out for her. I wonder why she has abandoned him.

I think he's in this building. The first time this thought occurred to me I couldn't stop shaking. It made sense. All my hauntings have been people physically close to me.

They won't let me leave this floor. I can leave my room now, but the doors to the stairs are locked, and the lifts don't work after everyone leaves. But I will find a way. I'm tired of being confined like this.

I realize now that although I was raised poor and illiterate, I was then at least free to move about, to breathe the air, to dream of my mother's home. Siridanga! I want to go back there and see it before I die. I know that the sea has entered the cities and drowned the land, but Siridanga was on a rise overlooking the paddy fields.

My grandparents' hut was on the hillock. Could it still be there? The night market makes me feel restless. The reflections of the lights dance on the windowpanes of the opposite building, as though they are writing something. All this learning to read is making me crazy, because I see letters where they don't exist. In the reflections. In people's hand gestures. And even more strangely, I see some kind of writing in the flow of time, in the dreams the dead man brings me. Those are written in a script I cannot read.

I "discovered" a whole verse of Wajid Ali Shah's poem today, after hours at the scope. There was so much excitement in the analysis room that the scientists let me go to my quarters early. I pleaded a headache but they hardly noticed. So I slipped out, into the elevator, and went up, and down, and got off on floors and walked around. I felt like a mad person, a thief, a free bird. It was ridiculous what an effect this small freedom had!

But after a while I began to get frightened. There was nobody else on the other floors as far as I could tell. The rooms were silent, dark behind doors with glass slits. I know that the scientists live somewhere here, maybe in the other buildings. Nondini tells me we are in a cluster of buildings near the sea that were built to withstand the flood. From her hints and from the TV I know that the world is ending. It's not just here. Everywhere cities are flooded or consumed by fire. Everything is dying. I have never been able to quite believe this before, perhaps because of my peculiar situation, which prevents me from seeing things for myself. But ultimately the silence and darkness of the rest of the building brought it home to me, and I felt as if I were drowning in sadness.

Then I sensed a pull, a current—a shout in my mind. It was him, the dead man. *Kajori!* he called again and again, and I found myself climbing to the floor above, to a closed door in the dark corridor.

I tried the handle, felt the smooth, paneled wood, but of course it was locked. With my ear against the door I could feel the hum of machinery, and there was a soft flow of air from beneath the door.

I called back to him in my mind.

I can't get in, I said. *Talk to me!*

His voice in my mind was full of static, so I couldn't understand everything. Even when I heard the words, they didn't make sense. I think he was muttering to himself, or to Kajori.

" . . . rivulets of time . . . two time-streams come together . . . ah . . . in a loop . . . if only . . . shift the flow, shift the flow . . . another future . . . must lock to past coordinate, establish resonance . . . new tomorrow . . . "

The chowkidar who is supposed to guard the elevator caught me on my way downstairs. He is a lazy, sullen fellow who never misses an opportunity to throw his weight around. I am more than a match for him though. He reported me, of course, to Nondini and Unnikrishnan, but I argued my case well. I simply said I was restless and wanted to see if there was a nice view from the other floors.

What could they say to that?

I tried to make sense of the dead man's gibberish all day. At night he came into my dreams as usual. I let him talk, prompting him with questions when something didn't make sense. I had to be clever to conceal my ignorance, since he thought I was Kajori, but the poor fellow is so emotionally overwrought that he is unlikely to be suspicious. But when he started weeping in his loneliness, I couldn't bear it. I thought: I will distract him with poetry.

I told him about the poem I am writing. It turns out he likes poetry. The poem he and Kajori love the best is an English translation of something by Omar Khayyam.

"Remember it, Kajori?" he said to me. He recited it in English, which I don't understand, and then in Bangla—"Oh love, if you and I could, with fate conspire," he said, taking me with a jolt back to my girlhood: me sitting by the Maula in the mad confusion of the market, the two of us seeing nothing but poetry, mango juice running down our chins. Oh yes, I remember, I said to my dead man. Then it was my turn. I told him about what I was writing and he got really interested. Suggested words, gave me ideas. So two lines of "Wajid Ali Shah's poem" came to me.

Clouds are borne on the wind
The river winds toward home

It was only the next day that I started to connect things in my mind. I think I know what the project is really about.

These people are not scientists, they are jadugars. Or maybe that's what scientists are, magicians who try to pass themselves off as ordinary people.

See, the dead man's idea is that time is like a river delta; lots of thin streams and fat streams, flowing from past to present, but fanning out. History and time control each other, so that if some future place is deeply affected by some past history, those two time streams will connect. When that happens it diverts time from the future place and shifts the flow in each channel so that the river as a whole might change its course.

They're trying to change the future.

I am stunned. If this is true, why didn't they tell me? Don't I also want the world to survive? It's my world too. This also means that I am more important to them than they ever let me know. I didn't realize all this at once; it is just now beginning to connect in my mind.

I burn inside with anger. At the same time, I am undone with wonder.

I think the dead man is trying to save the world. I think the scope and the dead man are part of the same Machine.

I wonder how much of their schemes I have messed up by locking the Machine into a different time and place than their calculations required.

What shall I do?

For now I have done nothing.

I need to find out more. How terrible it is to be ignorant! One doesn't even know where to start.

I looked at the history books Nondini had let me have—talking books—but they told me nothing about Rassundari. Then I remembered that one of the rooms on my floor housed a library from the days before the scientists had taken over the building.

I think Nondini sensed how restless I was feeling, and she must have talked to Kajori (I can't think of her as Dr. Mitra now) so I have permission to spend some of my spare time in the library.

They might let me go to the night market tomorrow too, with an escort. I went and thanked Kajori. I said that I was homesick for my mother's village home, Siridanga, and it made me feel crazy sometimes not to be able to walk around. At that she really looked at me, a surprised look, and smiled. I don't think it was a nice smile, but I couldn't be certain.

So, the library. It is a whole apartment full of books of the old kind. But the best thing about it is that there is a corner window from which I can see between two tall buildings. I can see the ocean! These windows don't open but when I saw the ocean I wept. I was in such a state of sadness and joy all at once, I forgot what I was there for.

The books were divided according to subject, so I practiced reading the subject labels first. It took me two days and some help from Nondini (I had to disguise the intent of my search) before I learned how to use the computer to search for information. I was astonished to find out that my housewife had written a book! So all that painful learning on the sly had come to something! I felt proud of her. There was the book in the autobiography section: *Amar Jiban*, written by a woman called Rassundari more than two hundred and fifty years ago. I clutched the book to me and took it with me to read.

It is very hard reading a real book. I have to keep looking at my notes from my lessons with Rassundari. It helps that Nondini got me some alphabet books. She finds my interest in reading rather touching, I think.

But I am getting through Rassundari's work. Her writing is simple and so moving. What I can't understand is why she is so calm about the injustices in her life. Where is her anger? I would have gotten angry. I feel for her as I read.

I wish I could tell Rassundari that her efforts will not be in vain—that she will write her autobiography and publish it at the age of sixty, and that the future will honor her. But how can I tell her that, even if there was a way she could hear me? What can I tell her about this world? My wanderings through the building have made me realize that the world I've known is going away, as inevitably as the tide, with no hope of return.

Unless the dead man and I save it.

■ ■ ■

I have been talking to Rassundari. Of course she can't hear me, but it comforts me to be able to talk to someone, really talk to them. Sometimes Rassundari looks up toward the point near the ceiling from which I am observing her. At those moments it seems to me that she senses my presence. Once she seemed about to say something, then shook her head and went back to the cooking.

I still haven't told anybody about my deceit. I have found out that Wajid Ali Shah and Rassundari lived at around the same time, although he was in Kolkata and she in a village that is now in Bangladesh. From what the dead man tells me, it is time that is important, not space. At least that is what I can gather from his babblings, although spacetime fuzziness or resolution is also important. So maybe my deception hasn't caused any harm. I hope not. I am an uneducated woman, and when I sit in that library I feel as though there is so much to know. If someone had told me that, encouraged me as a child, where might I have been today? And yet think about the dead man, with all his education. There he is, a hundred times more trapped than me, a thousand times lonelier. Yet he must be a good man, to give himself for the world.

He's been asking me anxiously: *Kajori, can you feel the shift in the timeflow? Have we locked into the pastpoint?* I always tell him I feel it just a little, which reassures him that his sacrifice is not for nothing. I wish I could tell him: I am Gargi, not Kajori. Instead I tell him I love him, I miss him. Sometimes I really feel that I do.

I have been speaking to Rassundari for nearly a week.

One of the scientists, Brijesh, caught me talking into the scope. He came into the room to get some papers he'd left behind. I jumped guiltily.

"Gargi-di? What are you doing . . . ?" he says with eyebrows raised.

"I just like to talk to myself. Repeat things Wajid Ali Shah is saying."

He looks interested. "A new poem?"

"Bah!" I say. "You people think he says nothing but poetry all the time? Right now he's trying to woo his mistress."

This embarrasses Brijesh, as I know it would. I smile at him and go back to the scope.

But yes, I was talking about Rassundari.

Now I know that she senses something. She always looks up at me, puzzled as to how a corner of the ceiling appears to call to her.

Does she hear me, or see some kind of image? I don't know. I keep telling her not to be afraid, that I am from the future, and that she is famous for her writing. Whether she can tell what I am saying I don't know. She does look around from time to time, afraid as though others might be there, so I think maybe she hears me, faintly, like an echo.

Does this mean that our rivulet of time is beginning to connect with her time stream?

I think my mind must be like an old-fashioned radio. It picks up things: the dead man's ramblings, the sounds and sights of the past.

Now it seems to be picking up the voices from the books in this room. I was deaf once, but now I can hear them as I read, slowly and painfully. All those stories, all those wonders. If I'd only known!

I talk to the dead. I talk to the dead of my time, and the woman Rassundari of the past, who is dead now. My closest confidants are the dead.

The dead man—I wish I knew his name—tells me that we have made a loop in time. He is not sure how the great delta's direction will change—whether it will be enough, or too little, or too much.

He has not quite understood the calculations that the Machine is doing. He is preoccupied. But when I call to him, he is tender, grateful. "Kajori," he says, "I have no regrets. Just this one thing, please do it for me. What you promised. Let me die once the loop has fully stabilized." In one dream I saw through his eyes. He was in a tank, wires coming out of his body, floating. In that scene there was no river of time, just the luminous water below him, and the glass casing around. What a terrible prison! If he really does live like that, I think he can no longer survive outside the tank, which is why he wants to die.

It is so painful to think about this that I must distract us both. We talk about poetry, and later the next few lines of the poem come to me.

> *Clouds are borne on the wind*
> *The river winds toward home*
> *From my prison window I see the way to my village*
> *In its cage of bone my heart weeps*
> *When I was the river, you were the shore*
> *Why have you forsaken me?*

I am getting confused. It is Kajori who is supposed to be in love with the dead man, not me.

■ ■ ■

So many things happened these last two days.

The night before last, the maajhis sang in the night market. I heard their voices ululating, the dotaras throbbing in time with the flute's sadness. A man's voice, and then a woman's, weaving in and out. I imagined them on their boats, plying the waters all over the drowned city as they had once sailed the rivers of my drowned land. I was filled with a painful ecstasy that made me want to run, or fly.

I wanted to break the windows.

The next morning I spent some hours at the scope. I told Rassundari my whole story. I still can't be sure she hears me, but her upturned, attentive face gives me hope. She senses something, for certain, because she put her hand to her ear as though straining to hear. Another new thing is that she is sometimes snappy. This has never happened before. She snapped at her nephew the other day, and later spoke sharply to her husband. After both those instances she felt so bad! She begged forgiveness about twelve times. Both her nephew and her husband seemed confused, but accepted her apology. I wonder if the distraction I am bringing into her life is having an effect on her mind. It occurs to me that perhaps, like the dead man, she can sense my thoughts, or at least feel the currents of my mind.

The loop in the time stream has stabilized. Unnikrishnan told me I need not be at the scope all the time, because the connection is always there, instead of timing out. The scientists were nervous and irritable; Kajori had shut herself up in her office. Were they waiting for the change? How will they tell that the change has come? Have we saved the world? Or did my duplicity ruin it?

I was in the library in the afternoon, a book on my lap, watching the gray waves far over the sea, when the dead man shouted in my mind. At this I peered out—the hall was empty. The scientists have been getting increasingly careless. The lift was unguarded.

So up I went to the floor above. The great wood-paneled door was open. Inside the long, dimly lit room stood Kajori, her face wet with tears, calling his name.

"Subir! Subir!"

She didn't notice me.

He lay naked in the enormous tank like a child sleeping on its belly. He was neither young nor old; his long hair, afloat in the water like seaweed, was sprinkled with gray, his dangling arms thin as sticks. Wires came out of him at dozens of places, and there were large banks of machinery all around the tank. His skin gleamed as though encased in some kind of oil.

He didn't know she was there, I think. His mind was seething with confusion. He wanted to die, and his death hadn't happened on schedule. A terror was growing in him.

"You promised, Kajori!"

She just wept with her face against the tank. She didn't turn off any switches. She didn't hear him, but I felt his cry in every fiber of my being.

"He wants to die," I said.

She turned, her face twisted with hatred.

"What are you doing here? Get out!"

"Go flee, Subir!" I said. I ran in and began pulling out plugs, turning off switches in the banks of machines around the tank. Kajori tried to stop me but I pushed her away. The lights in the tank dimmed. His arms flailed for a while, then grew still. Over Kajori's scream I heard his mind going out like the tide goes out, wafting toward me a whisper: thank you, thank you, thank you.

I became aware of the others around me, and Kajori shouting and sobbing.

"She went mad! She killed him!"

"You know he had to die," I said to her. I swallowed. "I could hear his thoughts. He . . . he loved you very much."

She shouted something incomprehensible at me. Her sobbing subsided. Even though she hated me, I could tell that she was beginning to accept what had happened. I'd done her a favor, after all, done the thing she had feared to do. I stared at her sadly and she looked away.

"Take her back to her room," she said. I drew myself up.

"I am leaving here," I said, "to go home to Siridanga. To find my family."

"You fool," Kajori said. "Don't you know, this place used to be Siridanga. You are standing on it."

They took me to my room and locked me in.

After a long time of lying in my bed, watching the shadows grow as the light faded, I made myself get up. I washed my face. I felt so empty, so faint. I had lost my family and my friends, and the dead man, Subir. I hadn't even been able to say goodbye to Rassundari.

And Siridanga, where was Siridanga? The city had taken it from me.

And eventually the sea would take it from the city. Where were my people? Where was home?

That night the maajhis sang. They sang of the water that had overflowed the rivers. They sang of the rivers that the city streets had become. They sang of the boats they had plied over river after river, time after time. They sang, at last, of the sea.

The fires from the night market lit up the windows of the opposite building. The reflections went from windowpane to windowpane, with the same deliberate care that Rassundari took with her writing.

I felt that at last she was reaching through time to me, to our dying world, writing her messages on the walls of our building in letters of fire. She was writing my song.

Nondini came and unlocked my door sometime before dawn. Her face was filled with something that had not been there before, a defiance. I pulled her into my room.

"I have to tell you something," I said. I sat her down in a chair and told her the whole story of how I'd deceived them.

"Did I ruin everything?" I said at the end, fearful at her silence.

"I don't know, Gargi-di," she said at last. She sounded very young, and tired. "We don't know what happens when a time-loop is formed artificially. It may bring in a world that is much worse than this one. Or not. There's always a risk. We argued about it a lot and finally we thought it was worth doing. As a last ditch effort."

"If you'd told me all this, I wouldn't have done any of it," I said, astounded. Who were they to act as Kalki? How could they have done something of this magnitude, not even knowing whether it would make for a better world?

"That's why we didn't tell you," she said. "You don't understand, we— scientists, governments, people like us around the world—tried everything to avert catastrophe. But it was too late. Nothing worked. And now we are past the point where any change can make a difference."

"'People like us,' you say," I said. "What about people like me? We don't count, do we?"

She shook her head at that, but she had no answer.

It was time to go. I said goodbye, leaving her sitting in the darkness of my room, and ran down the stairs. All the way to the front steps, out of the building, out of my old life, the tired old time stream. The square was full of the night market people packing up—fish vendors, and entertainers, getting ready to return another day. I looked around at the tall buildings, the long shafts of paling sky between them, water at the edge of the island lapping ever higher. The long boats were tethered there, weatherbeaten and much-mended. The maajhis were leaving, but not to return. I talked to an old man by one of their boats. He said they were going to sea.

"There's nothing left for us here," he said. "Ever since last night the wind has been blowing us seaward, telling us to hasten, so we will follow it. Come with us if you wish."

So in that gray dawn, with the wind whipping at the tattered sails and the water making its music against the boats, we took off for the open sea. Looking back, I saw Rassundari writing with dawn's pale fingers on the windows of the skyscrapers, the start of the letter *kah*, conjugated with *r*. Kra ... But the boat and the wind took us away before I could finish reading the word. I thought the word reached all the way into the ocean with the paling moonlight still reflected in the surging water.

Naibar chhuto bi jaaye, I thought, and wept.

Now the wind writes on my forehead with invisible tendrils of air, a language I must practice to read. I have left my life and loves behind me, and wish only to be blown about as the sea desires, to have the freedom of the open air, and be witness to the remaking of the world.

॥

TWEMBER

Steve Rasnic Tem

Will observed through the kitchen window of his parent's farmhouse as the towering escarpment, its many strata glittering relative to their contents, moved inescapably through the fields several hundred yards away. He held his breath as it passed over and through fences, barns, tractors, and an abandoned house long shed of paint. Its trespass was apparently without effect, although some of the objects in its wake had appeared to tremble ever so slightly, shining as if washed in a recent, cleansing rain.

"It might be beautiful," his mother said beside him, her palsy magnified by the exertion of standing, "if it weren't so frightening."

"You're pushing yourself." He helped her into one of the old ladder-back kitchen chairs. "You're going to make yourself sick."

"A body needs to see what she's up against." She closed her eyes.

He got back to the window in time to see a single tree in the escarpment's wake sway, shake, and fall over. Between the long spells of disabling interference he had heard television commentators relate how, other than the symptomatic "cosmetic" impact on climate, sometimes nearby objects *were* affected, possibly even destroyed, when touched by the escarpments, or the walls, or the roaming cliffs—whatever you cared to call the phenomena. These effects were still poorly understood, and "under investigation" and there had been "no official conclusions." Will wondered if there ever would be, but no one would ever again be able to convince him that the consequences of these massive, beautiful, and strange escarpments as they journeyed across the world were merely cosmetic.

His mother insisted that the television be kept on, even late at night, and even though it was no better than a white noise machine most of the time. "We can't afford to miss anything important," she'd said. "It's like when there's a tornado coming—you keep your TV on."

"These aren't like tornadoes, Mom. They can't predict them."

"Well, maybe they'll at least figure out what they are, why they're here."

"They've talked about a hundred theories, two hundred. Time disruption, alien invasion, dimensional shifts at the earth's core. Why are tsunamis here? Does it matter? You still can't stop them." At least the constant static on the TV had helped him sleep better.

"They're getting closer." Tracy had come up behind him. There was a time when she would have put her arms around him at this point, but that affectionate gesture didn't appear to be in his wife's repertoire anymore.

"Maybe. But it's not like they have intelligence," he said, not really wanting to continue their old argument, but unable to simply let it go.

"See how it changes course, just slightly?" she said. "And there's enough tilt from vertical I'm *sure* that can't just be an optical illusion. It leans toward occupied areas. I've been watching this one off and on all day, whenever it's visible, almost from the time it came out of the ground."

"They don't really come out of the ground." He tried to sound neutral, patient, but he doubted he was succeeding. "They've said it just looks that way. They're forming from the ground up, that's all."

"We don't know that much about them. No one does," she snapped.

"It's not like it's some predator surfacing, like a shark or a snake, prowling for victims." He was unable to soften the tone of his voice.

"You don't know that for sure."

Will watched as the escarpment either flowed out of visual range or dematerialized, it was hard to tell. "No. I guess I don't."

"Some of the people around here are saying that those things sense where there are people living, that they're drawn there, like sharks to bait. They say they learn."

"I don't know." He didn't want to talk about it anymore. "I hope not." Of course she was entitled to her opinion, and it wasn't that he knew any more than she did. But they used to know how to disagree.

He could hear his father stirring in the bedroom. The old man shuffled out, his eyes wet, unfocused. The way he moved past, Will wasn't sure if he even knew they were there. His father gazed out the window, and not for the first time Will wondered what exactly he was seeing. In the hazy distance another escarpment seemed to be making its appearance, but it might simply be the dust blown up from the ground, meeting the low-lying, streaked clouds. Then his father said, "Chugchugchugchugchug" and made a *whooh whooh*ing sound, like a train. Then he made his way on out to the porch.

In his bedroom, Jeff began to whimper. Tracy went in to check on him. Will knew he should join her there—he'd barely looked at his son in days, except to say good-night after the boy was already asleep—but considering how awkward it would be with the three of them he instead grabbed the keys to his dad's pickup and went out looking for the place where the escarpment had passed through and touched that tree.

Will had grown up here in eastern Colorado, gone to school, helped his parents out on the farm. It really hadn't changed that much over the decades, until recently, with that confusion of seasons that frequently followed the passage of escarpments through a region. The actual temperatures might vary only a few degrees from the norm, but the accompanying visual clues were often deceptive and disorienting. Stretches of this past summer had felt almost wintery, what with reduced sunlight, a deadening of plant color, and even the ghostly manifestation of a kind of faux snow which disintegrated into a shower of minute light-reflecting particles when touched.

Those suffering from seasonal affective disorder had had no summer reprieve this year. He'd heard stories that a few of the more sensitive victims had taken to their beds for most of the entire year. Colorado had a reputation for unpredictable weather, but these outbreaks, these "invasions" as some people called them, had taken this tendency toward meteorological unreliability to a new extreme.

Now it was, or at least should have been, September, with autumn on the way but still a few pretty hot days, but there were—or at least there appeared to be—almost no leaves on the trees, and no indications that there ever had been, and a gray-white sky had developed over the past few weeks, an immense amorphous shroud hanging just above the tops of the trees, as if the entire world had gone into storage. Dead of winter, or so he would have thought, if he'd actually lost track of the weeks, which he dare not do. He studied the calendar at least once a day and tried to make what he saw outside conform with memories of seasons past, as if he might will a return to normalcy.

Thankfully there had been few signs as yet of that fake snow. The official word was that the snow-like manifestation was harmless for incidental contact, and safe for children. Will wasn't yet convinced—the very existence of it gave him the creeps, thinking that some sort of metaphysical infection might have infiltrated the very atomic structure of the world, and haunted it.

"Twember," was what his mother called this new mixing of the seasons. "It's all betwixt and between. Pretty soon we're going to have just this one season. It won't matter when you plant, or what, it's all going to look like it died."

He thought he was probably in the correct vicinity now. Parts of the ground had this vaguely rubbed, not quite polished appearance, as if the path had been heated and ever-so-slightly glazed by the friction of the escarpment's passing. The air was charged—it seemed to push back, making his skin tingle and his hair stir. A small tree slightly to one side of the path had been bent the opposite way, several of its branches fresh and shiny as Spring, as if they had been gently renewed, lovingly washed, but the rest with that flat, dead look he'd come to hate.

Spotting a patch of glitter on the ground, Will pulled off onto the shoulder and got out of the truck. As he walked closer he could see how here and there sprays of the shiny stuff must have spewed out of the passing escarpment, suggesting contents escaping under pressure, like plumes of steam. He dropped to one knee and examined the spot: a mix of old coins, buttons, bits of glass, small metal figures, toys, vacation mementos, souvenirs, suggesting the random debris left in the bottom of the miscellanea drawer after the good stuff has been packed away for some major household move—the stuff you threw in the trash or left behind for the next tenants.

The strong scent of persimmons permeated the air. The funny thing was, he had no idea how he knew this. Will didn't think he'd ever seen one, much less smelled it. Was it a flower, or a fruit?

For a few minutes he thought there were no other signs of the escarpment's passing, but then he began to notice things. A reflection a few yards away turned out to be an antique oil lamp. He supposed it was remotely possible such a thing could have been lost or discarded and still remain relatively intact, but this lamp was pristine, with at least an inch of oil still in its reservoir. And a few feet beyond were a pair of women's shoes, covered in white satin, delicate and expensive-looking, set upright on the pale dust as if the owner had stepped out of them but moments before, racing for the party she could not afford to miss.

The old house had been abandoned sometime in the seventies, the structure variously adapted since then to store equipment, hay, even as a makeshift shelter for a small herd of goats. From the outside it looked very much the same, and Will might have passed it by, but then he saw the ornate bedpost through one of the broken windows, and the look of fresh blue paint over part of one exterior wall, and knew that something had occurred here out of the ordinary.

The house hadn't had a door in a decade or more, and still did not, but the framing around the door opening appeared almost new, and was of metal—which it had never been—attached to a ragged border of brick which had incongruously blended in to the edges of the original wood-framed wall. Two enormous, shiny brass hinges stood out from this frame like the flags of some new, insurgent government. The effect was as if a door were about to materialize, or else had almost completed its disappearance.

Once he was past the door frame, the small abandoned house appeared as he might normally expect. Islands of dirt, drifted in through the opening or blown through the missing windows, looked to have eaten through the floorboards, some sprouting prairie grass and gray aster. There were also the scat of some wild animal or other, probably fox or coyote, small pieces of old hay from back when the building had been used for feed storage, and a variety of vulgar graffiti on the ruined walls, none of it appearing to be of recent vintage.

A short hallway led from this front room into the back of the house, and as he passed through Will began to notice a more remarkable sort of misalignment, a clear discrepancy between what was and what should have been.

A broken piece of shelf hung on the wall approximately midway through the brief hallway. It had a couple of small objects on it. On closer inspection he saw that it wasn't broken at all—the edges of the wood actually appeared finely frayed, the threads of what was alternating with the threads of what was not. Along the frayed edge lay approximately one third of an old daguerreotype—although not at all old, it seemed. Shiny-new, glass sealed around the intact edges with rolled copper, laid inside a wood and leather case. A large portion of the entire package bitten off, missing, not torn exactly, or broken, for the missing bite of it too was delicately, wispily frayed, glass fibers floating into empty air as if pulled away. The image under the glass was of a newly married couple in Victorian-style clothing, their expressions like those under duress: the bride straining out a thin smile, the groom stiffly erect, as if his neck were braced.

A piece of pale gauze covered the opening at the end of the short hall. Now lifting on a cool breeze, the gauze slapped the walls on both sides, the ceiling. Will stepped forward and gently pulled it aside, feeling like an intruder.

A four-poster bed sat diagonally in the ruined room, the incongruous scent of the perfumed linen still strong despite faint traces of an abandoned staleness and animal decay. The bed looked recently slept in, the covers just pulled back, the missing woman—he figured it was probably a woman—having stepped out for a moment. Peering closer, he found a long, copper-colored hair on the pillow. He picked it up gently, holding it like something precious against the fading afternoon light drifting lazily in through the broken window. He wanted to take it with him, but he didn't know exactly why, or how he could, or if he should. So he laid it carefully back down on the pillow, in its approximate original location.

Half a mirror torn lengthwise was propped against a wide gap in the outer wall. Beyond was simply more of the eastern Colorado plains, scrub grass and scattered stone, but somewhat smoother than normal, shinier, and Will surmised that the escarpment had exited the farm house at this point.

He found himself creeping up to the mirror, nervous to look inside. Will never looked at mirrors much, even under normal conditions. He wasn't that old—in his fifties still, and as far as he knew, the same person inside, thinking the same thoughts he'd had at seventeen, eighteen, twenty. But what he saw in the mirror had stopped matching the self-image in his brain some time long ago.

He stopped a couple of feet away, focusing on the ragged edge where the escarpment had cut through and obliterated the present, or the past. More of that floating raggedness, suggesting a kind of yearning for completion, for what was missing. His reluctance to find his reflection made him reel a bit. What if he looked down and it was himself as a teenager looking up, with obvious signs of disappointment on his face?

But it was himself, although perhaps a bit older, paler, as if the color were being leached out and eventually he would disappear. The problem with avoiding your image in the mirror was that when you finally did see it, it was a bit of a shock, really, because of how much you had changed. Who was this old man with his thoughts?

He left the abandoned house and strolled slowly toward the pickup, watching the ground, looking for additional leavings but finding nothing. The empty ground looked like it always did out here, as it probably did in any open, unsettled place, as if it were ageless, unfixed, and yet fundamentally unchangeable. Whatever might be done to it, it would always return to this.

He wanted to describe to Tracy what he'd seen here, but what, exactly, had he seen? Time had passed this way, and left some things behind, then gone on its way. And the world was fundamentally unchanged. His mother might understand better, but Tracy was the one he wanted to tell, even though she might not hear him.

He felt the pressure change inside his ears, and he turned part of the way around, looking, but not seeing. Suddenly the world roared up behind him, passed him, and he shook.

He bent slightly backwards, looking up, terrified he might lose his balance, and having no idea of what the possible consequences might be. The moving escarpment towered high above him, shaking in and out of focus as it passed, and shaking him, seemingly shaking the ground, but clearly this wasn't a physical shaking, clearly this was no earthquake, but a violent vibration of the senses, and the consciousness behind them. Closing his eyes minimized the sensation, but he didn't want to miss anything, so other than a few involuntary blinks he kept them open. He turned his body around as best he could, as quickly, to get a better view.

He could make out the top of the escarpment, at least he could see that it did have a top, an edge indicating that it had stopped its vertical climb, but he could tell little more than that. As his eyes traveled further down he was able to focus on more detail, and taking a few steps back gave him a better perspective.

There were numerous more or less clearly defined strata, each in movement seemingly independent of the others, sometimes in an opposite flow from those adjacent, and sometimes the same but at a different speed. Like a multilayered roulette wheel, he thought, which seemed appropriate.

Trapped in most of these layers were visible figures—some of them blurred, but some of them so clear and vivid that when they were looking in his direction, as if from a wide window in the side of a building, he attempted to gain their attention by waving. None responded in any definitive way, although here and there the possibility that they might have seen him certainly seemed to be there.

The vast majority of these figures appeared to be ordinary people engaged in ordinary activities—fixing or eating dinner, housecleaning, working in offices, factories, on farms—but occasionally he'd see something indicating that an unusual event was occurring or had recently occurred. A man lying on his back, people gathered around, some attending to the fallen figure but most bearing witness. A couple being chased by a crowd. A woman in obvious anguish, screaming in a foreign language. A blurred figure in freefall from a tall building.

The settings for these dramas, suspenseful or otherwise, were most often sketchily drawn: some vague furniture, the outlines of a building, or not indicated at all. The figures sometimes acted their parts on a backdrop of floating abstractions. In a few cases, however, it was like looking out his front door—at random locations a tree branch or a roof eave actually penetrated the outer plane of the escarpment and hung there like a three-dimensional projection in the contemporary air.

It was like a gigantic three-dimensional time-line/cruise ship passing through the eastern Colorado plains, each level representing a different era. It was like a giant fault in time, shifting the temporal balance of the world in an attempt to rectify past mistakes. But there was no compelling reason to believe any of these theories. It was an enormous, fracturing mystery traveling through the world.

And just as suddenly as it had appeared, becoming so dramatically *there* it sucked up all the available reality of its environment, it was gone, reduced to a series of windy, dust-filled eddies that dissipated within a few seconds. Will shakily examined himself with eyes and hands. Would he lose his mind the way his Jeff had?

If they'd pulled their son out of school when these storms first began he'd be okay right now. That's what they'd been called at first, "storms," because of their sudden evolution, and the occasional accompanying wind, and the original belief that they were an atmospheric phenomenon of some sort, an optical illusion much like sunlight making a rainbow when it passed through moisture-laden cloud, although they couldn't imagine why it was so detailed, or the mechanism of its projection. Tracy had wanted to pull Jeff out until the world better understood what all this was about, and a few other parents, a very few, had already done so. But Will couldn't see the reasoning. If there was a danger how would Jeff be any safer at home? These insubstantial moving walls came out of nowhere, impossible to predict, and as far as anyone knew they weren't harmful. There had been that case of the farmer in Texas, but he'd been old, and practically senile anyway, and it must have been a terrible shock when it passed through his barn.

Tracy inevitably blamed Will, because in Jeff's case it certainly hadn't been harmless, and then Will had compounded things by being late that day. Will was often late. He had always worked at being some sort of success, even though the right combination of jobs and investments had always eluded him. He'd been selling spas and real estate, filling in the gaps with various accounting and IT consulting. Too many clients, too many little puzzle pieces of time, everything overlapping slightly so that at times his life was multidimensional, unfocused, and he was always late to wherever he was scheduled to be.

He'd pulled up to the school twenty minutes late that day to pick up Jeff. Normally it wouldn't have mattered that much—Jeff liked hanging out in the school library using their computers. And if that's where he'd been he would have probably been okay. But that particular afternoon Jeff had decided to hang out on the playground shooting hoops until his dad came to pick him up. And that's where he'd been when the towering wall came through. One of the teachers who'd witnessed the event said later that the wall appeared so suddenly no one had time to move, and it ran over Jeff much like a runaway truck, looking scarily solid, seemingly obliterating everything in its path as it thundered across the concrete and asphalt.

Will had arrived just in time to see that rapidly moving wall vanishing into a dusty brown mist, bending gel-like, quickly losing resolution as it leaned precariously like some old building coming down in an earthquake, but silently—the roar and the shaking were entirely visual, the trauma entirely mental. He had raced into the last of its shimmering eddies and scooped his drooling boy off the ground.

Will drove the pickup back toward his parents' farm more slowly, and with more care than he had when he left. The ambient light of the day had dimmed only slightly, but the canopy of sky appeared even lower than before, only a hundred yards up or so. The landscape looked flattened, stretched out under the pressure of the low-hanging clouds. He could hear rumbles in the distance, and could see the brief glimmer of escarpments appearing, disappearing, surfacing, diving back into the world. Time escaping, time buried and sealed.

Another pickup approached on the narrow gravel road, identical, or almost identical to his. He held his breath, wondering how he would handle it if he encountered a younger or an older version of himself driving the same pickup on the road. Surely that would still be impossible, even during Twember? And if it did occur, might that not shatter the world?

The pickup slowed as it came up alongside him. He stared at the driver. Because it was Lana Sumpter, much as she'd been when she was seventeen years old—her face so new, fresh, and shiny with a soft-lipped smile cradling her words. "Will? Will Cotton? Is that you?"

Both trucks stopped, his head still shook. "I, I'm not sure," he replied. "Probably not the same one. Lana, are any of us the same one?" He was babbling, just like he used to with her. He'd loved her so much his bones used to ache, making his skin seem ill-fitting. He'd never loved anyone that much before, or since.

Lana gazed at him, cheeks slightly flushed. The dark blue of the truck appeared to fade, to lighten, to whiten. Will blinked, then could see the individual bits of faux snow accumulating, layering the truck with a sugary coating, and the white air looking crisp, brittle, about to break. She laughed, but it wasn't really a laugh. It was like words escaping under stress. "I, I guess not, Will. Not these days. Seems like only yesterday I felt too young. Now I feel too old."

Lana's face still flushed, her eyes looking uncomfortable, her smile struggling to remain. And her lips not moving. She wasn't the one speaking.

Will shifted his head a bit to the side and peered past the lovely young girl to the older woman sitting in the shadows on the passenger side. The woman leaned forward, and although the face was somewhat puffy, and makeup had cracked in not the most flattering ways, there was a ghost of a resemblance, and as if a mask of reluctance had been peeled away, Will recognized her with a jolting, almost sickening sensation.

He felt ashamed of himself. He'd never been one to care much about people's appearances, so why did it bother him that he might have passed Lana—at one time the love of his life—on the street and not even recognize her. It was as if he'd been in love with a different person.

"This is my daughter Julie. Julie this is Will, an old friend. We knew each other when we were kids."

"Hi, Julie," he said, and had to take a breath. "You look like your mother."

"*Everybody* says that," the girl didn't sound as friendly, or as sweet, as Will had first thought.

"Are you out from Denver for a while?" Lana asked.

"Me and the family. I don't know for how long. I don't know when we should go back, or if."

She nodded, frowned. "A lot of the old crowd came back here. Jimmie, Carol, Suze. I don't know if they wanted to be home at a time like this, if it even still feels like home, or if they thought it'd be better here. It's *not* really, I don't think. But it's more open out here. Maybe they figure these things will be easier to dodge out in the open." She shook her head.

"I know. But they come up so quickly. Maybe they're not dangerous, but maybe they are."

"I was sorry to hear about your dad," she said. "He didn't run into one of these things, did he?"

"No, he started getting confused, I don't know, at least a year before the first one appeared. I don't see how there could be a connection." She didn't say anything about Jeff, so Will figured she didn't know. Will wasn't about to bring him up. "The doctor prescribed a couple of drugs—they don't seem to help much, but I still make sure he takes them. And for now at least, the pharmacy here still gets them. And the grocery store still gets his favorite chocolate candies. If he didn't get those, well, he'd aggravate us all, I reckon." Will forced a chuckle, and was embarrassed by the fakeness of it.

"Do you think we'll have shortages? My sister does. She says we'll probably see the last supply deliveries any day now. She says why would people continue to do their jobs with all this going on?"

So here they were talking about illnesses and medicines and disasters freely roaming the world threatening everything. Just like old people. Why hadn't they worried about those things when they were younger? Maybe when you were young you really didn't understand what time it was, or how late it could all get to be. "What else are they going to do?" he asked. "It's like the president said—no one knows how long this will last, what it means, or what the final outcome will be, so people need to go on with their lives." It sounded stupid saying it, but he imagined it was still true.

"But that broadcast was three weeks ago. How's your television reception? We have a dish, and we're getting nothing."

"Nothing much at our place either. What does Ray say about all this?" He hoped he had the name right—he hadn't been there when she'd married, only heard about it.

The girl, Julie, looked flushed, and turned her head away. Lana's face fell back into the shadows, and her voice came out shakily. "My Ray died about three months back. COPD. He said it got a lot worse with this new weather, or whatever you want to call it. I don't know, Will—it was already pretty bad."

And again Will felt shame, because along with his sadness for her came this vaguely-formed notion that there might be a new opportunity for him in this. What was wrong with him? He wasn't going to leave his wife and son, so why think about it? He apologized, but of course did not fully explain why, and continued home toward Tracy, his family, and his present.

His eighth grade teacher Mrs. Anderson used to emphasize in her social studies class that even kids from a small town school could become anything they wanted to be if only they applied themselves. "Dream big!" she'd say, "your dreams are the only thing that will limit you." In order to back up her thesis, throughout the school year she would sprinkle in inspirational stories about people from small towns who had "made a difference," who had made it "big."

Halfway into high school Will, and many of his friends, had concluded that this was all just so much propaganda, the purpose of which was—well—he wasn't sure, maybe to make Mrs. Anderson feel better about teaching in such a small town. But they heard similar messages from other teachers, parents, pretty much anyone who came to speak to their class. Like relatively recent graduates on their way to the army or the peace corps.

Big dreams were great, but they almost always seemed to shrink when you talked to guidance counselors, recruiters, or anyone else charged with evaluating your prospects realistically. There were some important, socially conscious things you could do with your life, certainly, but not *here*, and not for much monetary compensation. And these other careers, the ones Mrs. Anderson talked about—the thinkers and writers and scientists and actors—well, all you had to be was somebody else, somebody else entirely, and from some other place.

On the trip back to his parents' farm it was relatively easy for Will to imagine himself, and this land, as something else entirely. The road, the fields, were bleached, as white as he could imagine, and as far as he could see. The whiteness intensified at times to such transparency Will imagined he could almost see to where life both entered the plants and exited them, where time ate through the world and transformed it all into something else. He might have been traveling across Russia before the revolution in his wagon, his buggy, or in middle Europe as it began its entry into the ice age, in nineteenth-century Oklahoma in the dead of winter, the children starving, the wife suffering in their bed, a new baby on the way. And Will couldn't do much more than observe, and try to live, and keep his four wheels on the road, steady toward home.

The farmhouse looked as it had during that long-remembered blizzard the winter he was nine years old, when so many of the cows had died, and a stiffened pheasant stared at him from the front yard, its shining eyes frozen into jewels. A series of flashes drew his own eyes to that distant horizon line in the direction of Denver, and he considered it might be lightning, even though he knew better. Great blocks shifted there, weaving in and out of each other's way as if they had some sort of rudimentary intelligence. They appeared closer by the second, as if that city's buildings themselves were slowly advancing toward him across the eastern plains.

He pulled into the yard at the side of the house and jumped down onto the snow-laden ground, which cracked like layers of candy, allowing a white powdery residue to explode into the air with each of his steps. Of course this wasn't snow—it was nothing like snow. It was like the moments had been snatched from the air and allowed to die, left to litter the ground. He tried to step carefully, but still they fractured with very little force.

Inside the house there was the strong smell of cooking apples. A tree had been propped up in one corner. There were a few decorations on it, and his mother was sitting on the couch singing to herself and stringing popcorn into a garland.

Tracy pushed Jeff into the room and set the wheelchair brake. Their son's moaning stopped and he gazed at the tree. Will looked around for his father, found him in the corner by the front window, staring outside, motionless. Tracy came up to Will and stood there. She didn't smile, but for the first time in a long time she didn't look furious. "What's all this?" he asked.

"Christmas," she replied. "At least according to your mother."

"But it's not Christmas," he said, although truthfully he wasn't completely sure anymore.

"Maybe, maybe not. Is there going to be another Christmas this year, Will? I certainly don't know. Do you?"

He shrugged. "I guess it won't hurt anything. It sure seems to have helped Jeff."

"'Hold on to the moment.' You used to say that a lot, remember? Why did you stop saying it—was it because of me?"

He shrugged again. "You know I used to like it when you hummed in the bathroom? But the last few years it really annoyed me. That was something I shouldn't have held on to. I mean really, why would that bother me so much?"

"You used to turn the dumbest things into a celebration. Remember when it was Thomas Edison's birthday, and you turned on all the lights in the house?"

"That was before Jeff's—accident. He'd had a really bad day. I ordered pizza and made a pretty bad birthday cake. It cheered him up."

"You wore a lamp on your head, plugged in, and turned on. I thought you were going to electrocute yourself! I got so mad."

"You didn't want to be married to a child. I burned my ear pretty badly taking that contraption off."

"Your mother thought this would be a perfect thing, give us all a little something to look forward to. Is that where you got the idea to create all those special holidays? From her?"

"It was my dad," Will replied. "One day he bought my mother an alligator handbag. From that year on we celebrated 'Alligator Handbag Day.' There were special sandwiches. We wore tails made out of newspaper and did a little dance. Actually, my mother didn't always fully appreciate Alligator Handbag Day."

"I can believe that."

There were several moments of awkward silence, then Will said, "This doesn't mean you still love me, does it? I mean, this celebration, this stolen moment, doesn't change anything fundamentally, does it?"

"I don't think I blame you for Jeff anymore. I really don't."

"Things change, moments get away from you, the past pays a visit, and although there's no blame, still nothing is forgiven. It's hard to live here. It always has been," he said.

"Will—" she started to say, but his father drowned her out.

"Whooh whooh!" his father yelled by the window. "Whooh whooh!" The house shook with thunder.

A great striated wall moved past the glass. Will wondered if his healthy son was trapped inside there somewhere, if inside that wall he might find his wife's love again, or some other Will, some other life. He tried to say something to Tracy, but he couldn't even hear himself, so loud everything had suddenly become. He could feel time circling outside the house, circling again, raising its voice and ready to run them down.

ה

THE MAN WHO ENDED HISTORY: A DOCUMENTARY

₪

Ken Liu

Akemi Kirino, Chief Scientist, Feynman Laboratories:
[Dr. Kirino is in her early forties. She has the kind of beauty that doesn't require much makeup. If you look closely, you can see bits of white in her otherwise black hair.]

Every night, when you stand outside and gaze upon the stars, you are bathing in time as well as light.

For example, when you look at this star in the constellation Libra called Gliese 581, you are really seeing it as it was just over two decades ago because it's about twenty light years from us. And conversely, if someone around Gliese 581 had a powerful enough telescope pointed to around *here* right now, they'd be able to see Evan and me walking around Harvard Yard, back when we were graduate students.

[She points to Massachusetts on the globe on her desk, as the camera pans to zoom in on it. She pauses, thinking over her words. The camera pulls back, moving us further and further away from the globe, as though we were flying away from it.]

The best telescopes we have today can see as far back as about thirteen billion years ago. If you strap one of those to a rocket moving away from the Earth at a speed that's faster than light—a detail that I'll get to in a minute—and point the telescope back at the Earth, you'll see the history of humanity unfold before you in reverse. The view of everything that has happened on Earth leaves here in an ever-expanding sphere of light. And you only have to control how far away you travel in space to determine how far back you'll go in time.

[The camera keeps on pulling back, through the door of her office, down the hall, as the globe and Dr. Kirino become smaller and smaller in our

view. The long hallway we are backing down is dark, and in that sea of
darkness, the open door of the office becomes a rectangle of bright light
framing the globe and the woman.]

Somewhere about here you'll witness Prince Charles's sad face as
Hong Kong is finally returned to China. Somewhere about here you'll see
Japan's surrender aboard the *USS Missouri*. Somewhere about here you'll
see Hideyoshi's troops set foot on the soil of Korea for the first time. And
somewhere about here you'll see Lady Murasaki completing the first chapter
of the *Tale of Genji*. If you keep on going, you can go back to the beginning
of civilization and beyond.

But the past is consumed even as it is seen. The photons enter the lens,
and from there they strike an imaging surface, be it your retina or a sheet of
film or a digital sensor, and then they are gone, stopped dead in their paths.
If you look but don't pay attention and miss a moment, you cannot travel
further out to catch it again. That moment is erased from the universe,
forever.

[From the shadows next to the door to the office an arm reaches out to
slam the door shut. Darkness swallows Dr. Kirino, the globe, and the
bright rectangle of light. The screen stays black for a few seconds before
the opening credits roll.]

Remembrance Films HK Ltd.
in association with
Yurushi Studios
presents
a Heraclitus Twice Production
THE MAN WHO ENDED HISTORY
This film has been banned by the Ministry of Culture
of the People's Republic of China and is released
under strong protest from the government of Japan

Akemi Kirino:
[We are back in the warm glow of her office.]

Because we have not yet solved the problem of how to travel faster than
light, there is no real way for us to actually get a telescope out there to see
the past. But we've found a way to cheat.

Theorists long suspected that at each moment, the world around us is
literally exploding with newly created subatomic particles of a certain type,
now known as Bohm-Kirino particles. My modest contribution to physics

was to confirm their existence and to discover that these particles always come in pairs. One member of the pair shoots away from the Earth, riding the photon that gave it birth and traveling at the speed of light. The other remains behind, oscillating in the vicinity of its creation.

The pairs of Bohm-Kirino particles are under quantum entanglement. This means that they are bound together in such a way that no matter how far apart they are from each other physically, their properties are linked together as though they are but aspects of a single system. If you take a measurement on one member of the pair, thereby collapsing the wave function, you would immediately know the state of the other member of the pair, even if it is light years away.

Since the energy levels of Bohm-Kirino particles decay at a known rate, by tuning the sensitivity of the detection field, we can attempt to capture and measure Bohm-Kirino particles of a precise age created in a specific place.

When a measurement is taken on the local Bohm-Kirino particle in an entangled pair, it is equivalent to taking a measurement on that particle's entangled twin, which, along with its host photon, may be trillions of miles away, and thus, decades in the past. Through some complex but standard mathematics, the measurement allows us to calculate and infer the state of the host photon. But, like any measurement performed on entangled pairs, the measurement can be taken only once, and the information is then gone forever.

In other words, it is as though we have found a way to place a telescope as far away from the Earth, and as far back in time, as we like. If you want, you can look back on the day you were married, your first kiss, the moment you were born. But for each moment in the past, we get only one chance to look.

Archival Footage: September 18, 20__. Courtesy of
APAC Broadcasting Corporation

[The camera shows an idle factory on the outskirts of the city of Harbin, Heilongjiang Province, China. It looks just like any other factory in the industrial heartland of China in the grip of another downturn in the country's merciless boom-and-bust cycles: ramshackle, silent, dusty, the windows and doors shuttered and boarded up. Samantha Paine, the correspondent, wears a wool cap and scarf. Her cheeks are bright red with the cold, and her eyes are tired. As she speaks in her calm voice, the condensation from her breath curls and lingers before her face.]

Samantha: On this day, back in 1931, the first shots in the Second Sino-Japanese War were fired near Shenyang, here in Manchuria. For the Chinese, that was the beginning of World War Two, more than a decade before the United States would be involved.

We are in Pingfang District, on the outskirts of Harbin. Although the name "Pingfang" means nothing to most people in the West, some have called Pingfang the Asian Auschwitz. Here, Unit 731 of the Japanese Imperial Army performed gruesome experiments on thousands of Chinese and Allied prisoners throughout the war as part of Japan's effort to develop biological weapons and to conduct research into the limits of human endurance.

On these premises, Japanese army doctors directly killed thousands of Chinese and Allied prisoners through medical and weapons experiments, vivisections, amputations, and other systematic methods of torture. At the end of the War, the retreating Japanese army killed all remaining prisoners and burned the complex to the ground, leaving behind only the shell of the administrative building and some pits used to breed disease-carrying rats. There were no survivors.

Historians estimate that between two-hundred thousand and half-a-million Chinese persons, almost all civilians, were killed by the biological and chemical weapons researched and developed in this place and other satellite labs: anthrax, cholera, the bubonic plague. At the end of the War, General MacArthur, supreme commander of the Allied forces, granted all members of Unit 731 immunity from war crimes prosecution in order to get the data from their experiments and to keep the data away from the Soviet Union.

Today, except for a small museum nearby with few visitors, little evidence of those atrocities is visible. Over there, at the edge of an empty field, a pile of rubble stands where the incinerator for destroying the bodies of the victims used to be. This factory behind me is built on the foundation of a storage depot used by Unit 731 for germ-breeding supplies. Until the recent economic downturn, which shuttered its doors, the factory built moped engines for a Sino-Japanese joint venture in Harbin. And in a gruesome echo of the past, several pharmaceutical companies have quietly settled in around the site of Unit 731's former headquarters.

Perhaps the Chinese are content to leave behind this part of their past and move on. And if they do, the rest of the world will probably move on as well.

But not if Evan Wei has anything to say about it.

[Samantha speaks over a montage of images of Evan Wei lecturing in front of a classroom and posing before complex machinery with Dr. Kirino. In the photographs they look to be in their twenties.]

Dr. Evan Wei, a Chinese-American historian specializing in Classical Japan, is determined to make the world focus on the suffering of the victims of Unit 731. He and his wife, Dr. Akemi Kirino, a noted Japanese-American experimental physicist, have developed a controversial technique that they claim will allow people to travel back in time and experience history as it occurred. Today, he will publicly demonstrate his technique by traveling back to the year 1940, at the height of Unit 731's activities, and personally bear witness to the atrocities of Unit 731.

The Japanese government claims that China is engaged in a propaganda stunt, and it has filed a strongly worded protest with Beijing for allowing this demonstration. Citing principles of international law, Japan argues that China does not have the right to sponsor an expedition into World War Two-era Harbin because Harbin was then under the control of Manchukuo, a puppet regime of the Japanese Empire. China has rejected the Japanese claim, and responded by declaring Dr. Wei's demonstration an "excavation of national heritage" and now claims ownership rights over any visual or audio record of Dr. Wei's proposed journey to the past under Chinese antiquities-export laws.

Dr. Wei has insisted that he and his wife are conducting this experiment in their capacities as individual American citizens, with no connection to any government. They have asked the American Consul General in nearby Shenyang, as well as representatives of the United Nations, to intervene and protect their effort from any governmental interference. It's unclear how this legal mess will be resolved.

Meanwhile, numerous groups from China and overseas, some in support of Dr. Wei, some against, have gathered to hold protests. China has mobilized thousands of riot police to keep these demonstrators from approaching Pingfang.

Stay tuned, and we will bring you up-to-date reports on this historical occasion. This is Samantha Paine, for APAC.

Akemi Kirino:

To truly travel back in time, we still had to jump over one more hurdle.

The Bohm-Kirino particles allow us to reconstruct, in detail, all types of information about the moment of their creation: sight, sound, microwaves, ultrasound, the smell of antiseptic and blood, and the sting of cordite and gunpowder in the back of the nose.

But this is a staggering amount of information, even for a single second. We had no realistic way to store it, let alone process it in real time. The amount of data gathered for a few minutes would have overwhelmed all the storage servers at Harvard. We could open up a door to the past, but would see nothing in the tsunami of bits that flooded forth.

[Behind Dr. Kirino is a machine that looks like a large clinical MRI scanner. She steps to the side so that the camera can zoom slowly inside the tube of the scanner where the volunteer's body would go during the process. As the camera moves through the tube, continuing towards the light at the end of the tunnel, her voice continues off camera.]

Perhaps given enough time, we could have come up with a solution that would have allowed the data to be recorded. But Evan believed that we could not afford to wait. The surviving relatives of the victims were aging, dying, and the War was about to fade out of living memory. There was a duty, he felt, to offer the surviving relatives whatever answers we could get.

So I came up with the idea of using the human brain to process the information gathered by the Bohm-Kirino detectors. The brain's massively parallel processing capabilities, the bedrock of consciousness, proved quite effective at filtering and making sense of the torrent of data from the detectors. The brain could be given the raw electrical signals, throw 99.999 percent of it away, and turn the rest into sight, sound, smell, and make sense of it all and record them as memories.

This really shouldn't surprise us. After all, this is what our brains do, every second of our lives. The raw signals from our eyes, ears, skin, and tongue would overwhelm any supercomputer, but from second to second, our brain manages to construct the consciousness of our existence from all that noise.

"For our volunteer subjects, the process creates the illusion of experiencing the past, as though they were in that place, at that time," I wrote in *Nature*.

How I regret using the word "illusion" now. So much weight ended up being placed on my poor word choice. History is like that: the truly important decisions never seemed important at the time.

Yes, the brain takes the signals and makes a story out of them, but there's nothing illusory about it, whether in the past or now.

Archibald Ezary, Radhabinod Pal Professor of Law, Codirector of East Asian Studies, Harvard Law School:

[Ezary has a placid face that is belied by the intensity of his gaze. He enjoys giving lectures, not because he likes hearing himself talk, but because he thinks he will learn something new each time he tries to explain.]

The legal debate between China and Japan about Wei's work, almost twenty years ago, was not really new. Who should have control over the past is a question that has troubled all of us, in various forms, for many years. But the invention of the Kirino Process made this struggle to control the past a literal, rather than merely a metaphorical, issue.

A state has a temporal dimension as well as a spatial one. It grows and shrinks over time, subjugating new peoples and sometimes freeing their descendants. Japan today may be thought of as just the home islands, but back in 1942, at its height, the Japanese Empire ruled Korea, most of China, Taiwan, Sakhalin, the Philippines, Vietnam, Thailand, Laos, Burma, Malaysia, and large parts of Indonesia, as well as large swaths of the islands in the Pacific. The legacy of that time shapes Asia to this day.

One of the most vexing problems created by the violent and unstable process by which states expand and contract over time is this: as control over a territory shifts between sovereigns over time, which sovereign should have jurisdiction over that territory's past?

Before Evan Wei's demonstration, the most that the issue of jurisdiction over the past intruded on real life was an argument over whether Spain or America would have the right to the sovereign's share of treasure from sunken sixteenth-century Spanish galleons recovered in contemporary American waters, or whether Greece or England should keep the Elgin Marbles. But now the stakes are much higher.

So, is Harbin during the years between 1931 and 1945 Japanese territory, as the Japanese government contends? Or is it Chinese, as the People's Republic argues? Or perhaps we should treat the past as something held in trust for all of humanity by the United Nations?

The Chinese view would have had the support of most of the Western world—the Japanese position is akin to Germany arguing that attempts to travel to Auschwitz-Birkenau between 1939 and 1945 should be subject to its approval—but for the fact that it is the People's Republic of China, a Western pariah, which is now making the claim. And so you see how the present and the past will strangle each other to death.

Moreover, behind both the Japanese and the Chinese positions is the unquestioned assumption that if we can resolve whether *China* or *Japan* has sovereignty over World War Two-era Harbin, then either the People's Republic or the present Japanese government would be the right authority to exercise that sovereignty. But this is far from clear. Both sides have problems making the legal case.

First, Japan has always argued, when it comes to Chinese claims for compensation for wartime atrocities, that the present Japan, founded on the Constitution drafted by America, cannot be the responsible party. Japan believes that those claims are against its predecessor government, the Empire of Japan, and all such claims have been resolved by the Treaty of San Francisco and other bilateral treaties. But if that is so, for Japan now to assert sovereignty over that era in Manchuria, when it has previously disavowed all responsibility for it, is more than a little inconsistent.

But the People's Republic is not home free either. At the time Japanese forces took control of Manchuria in 1932, it was only nominally under the control of the Republic of China, the entity that we think of as the "official" China during the Second World War, and the People's Republic of China did not even exist. It is true that during the War, armed resistance in Manchuria to the Japanese occupation came almost entirely from the Han Chinese, Manchu, and Korean guerillas led by Chinese and Korean Communists. But these guerillas were not under the real direction of the Chinese Communist Party led by Mao Zedong, and so had little to do with the eventual founding of the People's Republic.

So why should we think that either the present government of Japan or China has any claim to Harbin during that era? Wouldn't the Republic of China, which now resides in Taipei and calls itself Taiwan, have a more legitimate claim? Or perhaps we should conjure up a "Provisional Historical Manchurian Authority" to assume jurisdiction over it?

Our doctrines concerning the succession of states, developed under the Westphalian framework, simply cannot deal with these questions raised by Dr. Wei's experiments.

If these debates have a clinical and evasive air to them, that is intentional. "Sovereignty," "jurisdiction," and similar words have always been mere conveniences to allow people to evade responsibility or to sever inconvenient bonds. "Independence" is declared, and suddenly the past is forgotten; a "revolution" occurs, and suddenly memories and blood debts are wiped clean; a treaty is signed, and suddenly the past is buried and gone. Real life does not work like that.

However you want to parse the robber's logic that we dignify under the name "international law," the fact remains that the people who call themselves Japanese today are connected to those who called themselves Japanese in Manchuria in 1937, and the people who call themselves Chinese today are connected to those who called themselves Chinese there and then. These are the messy realities, and we make do with what we are given.

All along, we have made international law work only by assuming that the past would remain silent. But Dr. Wei has given the past a voice, and made dead memories come alive. What role, if any, we wish to give the voices of the past in the present is up to us.

Akemi Kirino:

Evan always called me *Tóngyě Míngměi*, or just *Míngměi*, which are the Mandarin readings for the kanji that are used to write my name (桐野明美). Although this is the customary way to pronounce Japanese names in Chinese, he's the only Chinese I've ever permitted that liberty to.

Saying my name like that, he told me, allowed him to picture it in those old characters that are the common heritage of China and Japan, and thus keep in mind their meaning. The way he saw it, "the sound of a name doesn't tell you anything about the person, only the characters do."

My name was the first thing he loved about me.

"A paulownia tree alone in the field, bright and beautiful," he said to me, the first time we met at a Graduate School of Arts and Sciences mixer.

That was also how my grandfather explained my name to me, years earlier, when he taught me how to write the characters in my name as a little girl. A paulownia is a pretty, deciduous tree, and in old Japan it was the custom to plant one when a baby girl was born and make a dresser out of the wood for her trousseau when she got married. I remember the first time my grandfather showed me the paulownia that he had planted for me the day I was born, and I told him that I didn't think it looked very special.

"But a paulownia is the only tree on which a phoenix would land and rest," my grandfather then said, stroking my hair in that slow, gentle way that he had that I loved. I nodded, and I was glad that I had such a special tree for my name.

Until Evan spoke to me, I hadn't thought about that day with my grandfather in years.

"Have you found your phoenix yet?" Evan asked, and then he asked me out.

Evan wasn't shy, not like most Chinese men I knew. I felt at ease listening to him. And he seemed genuinely happy about his life, which was rare among the grad students and made it fun to be around him.

In a way it was natural that we would be drawn to each other. We had both come to America as young children, and knew something about the meaning of growing up as outsiders trying hard to become Americans. It made it easy for us to appreciate each other's foibles, the little corners of our personalities that remained defiantly fresh-off-the-boat.

He wasn't intimidated by the fact that I had a much better sense about numbers, statistics, the "hard" qualities in life. Some of my old boyfriends used to tell me that my focus on the quantifiable and the logic of mathematics made me seem cold and unfeminine. It didn't help that I knew my way around power tools better than most of them—a necessary skill for a lab physicist. Evan was the only man I knew who was perfectly happy to defer to me when I told him that I could do something requiring mechanical skills better than he could.

Memories of our courtship have grown hazy with time, and are now coated with the smooth, golden glow of sentiment—but they are all that I have left. If ever I am allowed to run my machine again, I would like to go back to those times.

I liked driving with him to bed-and-breakfasts up in New Hampshire in the fall to pick apples. I liked making simple dishes from a book of recipes and seeing that silly grin on his face. I liked waking up next to him in the mornings and feeling happy that I was a woman. I liked that he could argue passionately with me and hold his ground when he was right and back down gracefully when he was wrong. I liked that he always took my side whenever I was in an argument with others, and backed me up to the hilt, even when he thought I was wrong.

But the best part was when he talked to me about the history of Japan.

Actually, he gave me an interest in Japan that I never had. Growing up, whenever people found out that I was Japanese they assumed that I would be interested in anime, love karaoke, and giggle into my cupped hands, and the boys, in particular, thought I would act out their Oriental sex fantasies. It was tiring. As a teenager, I rebelled by refusing to do anything that seemed "Japanese," including speaking Japanese at home. Just imagine how my poor parents felt.

Evan told the history of Japan to me not as a recitation of dates or myths, but as an illustration of scientific principles embedded in humanity. He showed me that the history of Japan is not a story about emperors and generals, poets and monks. Rather, the history of Japan is a model demonstrating the way all human societies grow and adapt to the natural world as the environment, in turn, adapts to their presence.

As hunter-gatherers, the ancient Jōmon Japanese were the top predators in their environment; as self-sufficient agriculturalists, the Japanese of the Nara and Heian periods began to shape and cultivate the ecology of Japan into a human-centric symbiotic biota, a process that wasn't completed until the intensive agriculture and population growth that came with feudal Japan; finally, as industrialists and entrepreneurs, the people of Imperial Japan began to exploit not merely the living biota, but also the dead biota of the past: the drive for reliable sources of fossil fuels would dominate the history of modern Japan, as it has the rest of the modern world. We are all now exploiters of the dead.

Clearing away the superficial structure of the reigns of emperors and the dates of battles, there was the deeper rhythm of history's ebb and flow not as the deeds of great men, but as lives lived by ordinary men and women wading through the currents of the natural world around them: its geology, its seasons, its climate and ecology, the abundance and scarcity of the raw material for life. It was the kind of history that a physicist could love.

Japan was at once universal and unique. Evan made me aware of the connection between me and the people who have called themselves Japanese for millennia.

Yet, history was not merely deep patterns and the long now. There was also a time and a place where individuals could leave an extraordinary impact. Evan's specialty was the Heian Period, he told me, because that was when Japan first became *Japan*. A courtly elite of at most a few thousand people transformed continental influences into a uniquely native, Japanese aesthetic ideal that would reverberate throughout the centuries and define what it meant to be Japanese until the present day. Unique among the world's ancient cultures, the high culture of Heian Japan was made as much by women as by men. It was a golden age as lovely as it was implausible, unrepeatable. That was the kind of surprise that made Evan love history.

Inspired, I took a Japanese history class, and asked my father to teach me calligraphy. I took a new interest in advanced Japanese language classes, and I learned to write *tanka*, the clean, minimalist Japanese poems that follow strict, mathematical metrical requirements. When I was finally satisfied with my first attempt, I was so happy, and I'm certain that I did, for a moment, feel what Murasaki Shikibu felt when she completed her first *tanka*. More than a millennium in time and more than ten thousand miles in space separated us, but there, in that moment, we would surely have understood each other.

Evan made me proud to be Japanese, and so he made me love myself. That was how I knew I was really in love with him.

Li Jianjian, Manager, Tianjin Sony Store:

The War has been over for a long time, and at some point you have to move on. What is the point of digging up memories like this now? Japanese investment in China has been very important for jobs, and all the young people in China like Japanese culture. I don't like it that Japan does not want to apologize, but what can we do? If we dwell on it, then only we will be angry and sad.

Song Yuanwu, waitress:

I read about it in the newspapers. That Dr. Wei is not Chinese; he's an American. The Chinese all know about Unit 731, so it's not news to us.

I don't want to think about it much. Some stupid young people shout about how we should boycott Japanese goods but then they can't wait to buy the next issue of manga. Why should I listen to them? This just upsets people without accomplishing anything.

Name withheld, executive:

Truth be told, the people who were killed there in Harbin were mostly peasants, and they died like weeds during that time all over China. Bad things happen in wars, that's all.

What I'm going to say will make everyone hate me, but many people also died during the Three Years of Natural Disasters under the Chairman and then during the Cultural Revolution. The War is sad, but it is just one sadness among many for the Chinese. The bulk of China's sorrow lies unmourned. That Dr. Wei is a stupid troublemaker. You can't eat, drink, or wear memories.

Nie Liang and Fang Rui, college students:

Nie: I'm glad that Wei did his work. Japan has never faced up to its history. Every Chinese knows that these things happened, but Westerners don't, and they don't care. Maybe now that they know the truth they'll put pressure on Japan to apologize.

Fang: Be careful, Nie. When Westerners see this, they are going to call you a *fenqing* and a brainwashed nationalist. They like Japan in the West. China, not so much. The Westerners don't want to understand China. Maybe they just can't. We have nothing to say to these journalists. They won't believe us anyway.

Sun Maying, office worker:
I don't know who Wei is, and I don't care.

Akemi Kirino:
Evan and I wanted to go see a movie that night. The romantic comedy we wanted was sold out, and so we chose the movie with the next earliest start time. It was called *Philosophy of a Knife*. Neither of us had heard of it. We just wanted to spend some time together.

Our lives are ruled by these small, seemingly ordinary moments that turn out to have improbably large effects. Such randomness is much more common in human affairs than in nature, and there was no way that I, as a physicist, could have foreseen what happened next.

[*Scenes from Andrey Iskanov's* Philosophy of a Knife *are shown as Dr. Kirino speaks.*]

The movie was a graphical portrayal of the activities of Unit 731, with many of the experiments reenacted. "God created heaven, men created hell" was the tag line.

Neither of us could get up at the end of it. "I didn't know," Evan murmured to me. "I'm sorry. I didn't know."

He was not apologizing for taking me to the movie. Instead, he was consumed by guilt because he had not known about the horrors committed by Unit 731. He had never encountered it in his classes or in his research. Because his grandparents had taken refuge in Shanghai during the War, no one in his family was directly affected.

But due to their employment with the puppet government in Japanese-occupied Shanghai, his grandparents were later labeled collaborationists after the War, and their harsh treatment at the hands of the government of the People's Republic eventually caused his family to flee for the United States. And so the War shaped Evan's life, as it has shaped the lives of all Chinese, even if he was not aware of all of its ramifications.

For Evan, ignorance of history, a history that determined who he was in many ways, was a sin in itself.

"It's just a film," our friends told him. "Fiction."

But in that moment, history as he understood it ended for Evan. The distance he had once maintained, the abstractions of history at a grand scale, which had so delighted him before, lost meaning to him in the bloody scenes on the screen.

He began to dig into the truth behind the film, and it soon consumed all his waking moments. He became obsessed with the activities of Unit 731. It became his waking life and his nightmare. For him, his ignorance of those horrors was simultaneously a rebuke and a call to arms. He could not let the victims' suffering be forgotten. He would not allow their torturers to get away.

That was when I explained to him the possibilities presented by Bohm-Kirino particles.

Evan believed that time travel would make people care.

When Darfur was merely a name on a distant continent, it was possible to ignore the deaths and atrocities. But what if your neighbors came to you and told you of what they had seen in their travels to Darfur? What if the victims' relatives showed up at the door to recount their memories in that land? Could you still ignore it?

Evan believed that something similar would happen with time travel. If people could see and hear the past, then it would no longer be possible to remain apathetic.

Excerpts from the televised hearing before the Subcommittee on Asia, the Pacific, and the Global Environment of the Committee on Foreign Affairs, House of Representatives, 11_th Congress, courtesy of C-SPAN

Testimony of Lillian C. Chang-Wyeth, witness:

Mr. Chairman and Members of the Subcommittee, thank you for giving me the opportunity to testify here today. I would also like to thank Dr. Wei and Dr. Kirino, whose work has made my presence here today possible.

I was born on January 5, 1962, in Hong Kong. My father, Jaiyi "Jimmy" Chang, had come to Hong Kong from mainland China after World War Two. There, he became a successful merchant of men's shirts and married my mother. Each year, we celebrated my birthday one day early. When I asked my mother why we did this, she said that it had something to do with the War.

As a little girl, I didn't know much about my father's life before I was born. I knew that he had grown up in Japanese-occupied Manchuria, that his whole family was killed by the Japanese, and that he was rescued by Communist guerrillas. But he did not tell me any details.

Only once did Father talk to me directly about his life during the War. It was the summer before I went to college, in 1980. A traditionalist, he held a *jíjīlǐ* ceremony for me where I would pick my *biǎozì*, or courtesy name. That is the name young Chinese people traditionally chose for themselves when they came of age, and by which name they would be known by their peers. It wasn't something that most Chinese, even the Hong Kong Chinese, did any more.

We prayed together, bowing before the shrine to our ancestors, and I lit my joss sticks and placed them in the bronze incense brazier in the courtyard. For the first time in my life, instead of me pouring tea for him, my father poured tea for *me*. We lifted our cups and drank tea together, and my father told me how proud he was of me.

I put down the teacup and asked him which of my older female relatives he most admired so that I might choose a name that would honor her memory. That was when he showed me the only photograph he had of his family. I have brought it here today, and would like to enter it into the record.

This picture was taken in 1940, on the occasion of my father's tenth birthday. The family lived in Sanjiajiao, a village about twenty kilometers from Harbin, where they went to take this portrait in a studio. In this picture you can see my grandparents sitting together in the center. My father is standing next to my grandfather, and here, next to my grandmother, is my aunt, Changyi (暢怡). Her name means "smooth happiness." Until my father showed me this picture, I did not know that I had an aunt.

My aunt was not a pretty girl. You can see that she was born with a large, dark birthmark shaped like a bat on her face that disfigured her. Like most girls in her village, she never went to school and was illiterate. But she was very gentle and kind and clever, and she did all of the cooking and cleaning in the house starting at the age of eight. My grandparents worked in the fields all day, and as the big sister, Changyi was like a mother to my father. She bathed him, fed him, changed his swaddling clothes, played with him, and protected him from the other kids in the village. At the time this picture was taken, she was sixteen.

What happened to her? I asked my father.

She was taken, he said. The Japanese came to our village on January 5, 1941, because they wanted to make an example of it so that other villages would not dare to support the guerrillas. I was eleven at the time and

Changyi was seventeen. My parents told me to hide in the hole under the granary. After the soldiers bayoneted our parents, I saw them drag Changyi to a truck and drive her away.

Where was she taken?

They said they were taking her to a place called Pingfang, south of Harbin.

What kind of place was it?

Nobody knew. At the time the Japanese said the place was a lumber mill. But trains passing by there had to pull down their curtains, and the Japanese evicted all the villages nearby and patrolled the area heavily. The guerrillas who saved me thought it was probably a weapons depot or a headquarters building for important Japanese generals. I think maybe she was taken there to serve as a sex slave for the Japanese soldiers. I do not know if she survived.

And so I picked my *biǎozì* to be Changyi (長憶) to honor my aunt, who was like a mother to my father. My name sounds like hers but it is written with different characters, and instead of "smooth happiness," it means "long remembrance." We prayed that she had survived the War and was still alive in Manchuria.

The next year, in 1981, the Japanese author Morimura Seiichi published *The Devil's Gluttony*, which was the first Japanese publication ever to talk about the history of Unit 731. I read the Chinese translation of the book, and the name Pingfang suddenly took on a different meaning. For years, I had nightmares about what happened to my aunt.

My father died in 2002. Before his death, he asked that if I ever found out for sure what happened to my aunt, I should let him know when I made my annual visit to his grave. I promised him that I would.

This is why, a decade later, I volunteered to undertake the journey when Dr. Wei offered this opportunity. I wanted to know what happened to my aunt. I hoped against hope that she had survived and escaped, even though I knew there were no Unit 731 survivors.

Chung-Nian Shih, Director, Department of Archaeology, National Independent University of Taiwan:

I was one of the first to question Evan's decision to prioritize sending volunteers who are relatives of the victims of Unit 731 rather than professional historians or journalists. I understand that he wanted to bring peace to the victims' families, but it also meant large segments of history were consumed in private grief, and are now lost forever to the world. His technique, as you know, is destructive. Once he has sent an observer to a particular place at a particular time, the Bohm-Kirino particles are gone, and no one can ever go back there again.

There are moral arguments for and against his choice: is the suffering of the victims above all a private pain? Or should it primarily be seen as a part of our shared history?

It's one of the central paradoxes of archaeology that in order to excavate a site so as to study it, we must consume it and destroy it in that process. Within the profession we are always debating over whether it's better to excavate a site now or to preserve it *in situ* until less destructive techniques could be developed. But without such destructive excavations, how can new techniques be developed?

Perhaps Evan should also have waited until they developed a way to record the past without erasing it in the process. But by then it may have been too late for the families of the victims, who would benefit from those memories the most. Evan was forever struggling with the competing claims between the past and the present.

Lillian C. Chang-Wyeth:

I took my first trip five years ago, just as Dr. Wei first began to send people back.

I went to January 6, 1941, the day after my aunt was captured.

I arrived on a field surrounded by a complex of brick buildings. It was very cold. I don't know exactly how cold, but Harbin in January usually stayed far below zero degrees Fahrenheit. Dr. Wei had taught me how to move with my mind only, but it was still shocking to suddenly find yourself in a place with no physical presence while feeling everything, a ghost. I was still getting used to moving around when I heard a loud "whack, whack" sound behind me.

I turned around and saw a line of Chinese prisoners standing in the field. They were chained together by their legs and wore just a thin layer of rags. But what struck me was that their arms were left bare, and they held them out in the freezing wind.

A Japanese officer walked in front of them, striking their frozen arms with a short stick. "Whack, whack."

Interview with Shiro Yamagata, former member of Unit 731,
courtesy of Nippon Broadcasting Co.

[Yamagata and his wife sit on chairs behind a long folding table. He is in his nineties. His hands are folded in front of him on the table, as are his wife's. He keeps his face placid and does not engage in any histrionics. His voice is frail but clear underneath that of the translator's.]

We marched the prisoners outside with bare arms so that the arms would freeze solid quicker in the Manchurian air. It was very cold, and I did not like the times when it was my duty to march them out.

We sprayed the prisoners with water to create frostbite quicker. To make sure that the arms have been frozen solid, we would hit them with a short stick. If we heard a crisp whack, it meant that the arms were frozen all the way through and ready for the experiments. It sounded like whacking against a piece of wood.

I thought that was why we called the prisoners *maruta*, wood logs. *Hey, how many logs did you saw today?* We'd joke with each other. *Not many, just three small logs.*

We performed those experiments to study the effects of frostbite and extreme temperatures on the human body. They were valuable. We learned that the best way to treat frostbite is to immerse the limb in warm water, not rubbing it. It probably saved many Japanese soldiers' lives. We also observed the effects of gangrene and disease as the frozen limbs died on the prisoners.

I heard that there were experiments where we increased the pressure in an air-tight room until the person inside exploded, but I did not personally witness them.

I was one of a group of medical assistants who arrived in January 1941. In order to practice our surgery techniques, we performed amputations and other surgery on the prisoners. We used both healthy prisoners and prisoners from the frostbite experiments. When all the limbs had been amputated, the survivors were used to test biological weapons.

Once, two of my friends amputated a man's arms and reattached them to opposite sides of his body. I watched but did not participate. I did not think it was a useful experiment.

Lillian C. Chang-Wyeth:

I followed the line of prisoners into the compound. I walked around to see if I could find my aunt.

I was very lucky, and after only about half an hour, I found where the women prisoners were kept. But when I looked through all the cells, I did not see a woman that looked like my aunt. I then continued walking around aimlessly, looking into all the rooms. I saw many specimen jars with preserved body parts. I remember that in one of the rooms I saw a very tall jar in which one half of a person's body, cleaved vertically in half, was floating.

Eventually I came to an operating room filled with young Japanese doctors. I heard a woman scream, and I went in. One doctor was raping a Chinese woman on the operating table. There were several other Chinese women in the room, all of them naked and they were holding the woman on the table down so that the Japanese doctor could focus on the rape.

The other doctors looked on and spoke in a friendly manner with each other. One of them said something, and everybody laughed, including the doctor who was raping the woman on the table. I looked at the women who were holding her down and saw that one of them had a bat-shaped birthmark that covered half of her face. She was talking to the woman on the table, trying to comfort her.

What truly shocked me wasn't the fact that she was naked, or what was happening. It was the fact that she looked so young. Seventeen, she was a year younger than I was when I left for college. Except for the birthmark, she looked just like me from back then, and just like my daughter.

[She stops.]

Representative Kotler: Ms. Chang, would you like to take a break? I'm sure the Subcommittee would understand—

Lillian C. Chang-Wyeth: No, thank you. I'm sorry. Please let me continue.

After the first doctor was done, the woman on the table was brought away. The group of doctors laughed and joked amongst themselves. In a few minutes two soldiers returned with a naked Chinese man walking between them. The first doctor pointed to my aunt, and the other women pushed her onto the table without speaking. She did not resist.

The doctor then pointed to the Chinese man, and gestured towards my aunt. The man did not at first understand what was wanted of him. The doctor said something, and the two soldiers prodded the man with their bayonets, making him jump. My aunt looked up at him.

They want you to fuck me, she said.

Shiro Yamagata:

Sometimes we took turns raping the women and girls. Many of us had not ever been with a woman or seen a live woman's organs. It was a kind of sex education.

One of the problems the army faced was venereal disease. The military doctors examined the comfort women weekly and gave them shots, but the soldiers would rape the Russian and Chinese women and got infected all the time. We needed to understand better the development of syphilis, in particular, and to devise treatments.

In order to do so, we would inject some prisoners with syphilis and make the prisoners have sex with each other so that they could be infected the regular way. Of course we would not then touch these infected women. We could then study the effects of the disease on body organs. It was all research that had not been done before.

Lillian C. Chang-Wyeth:

The second time I went back was a year later, and this time I went back to June 8, 1941, about five months after my aunt's capture. I thought that if I picked a date much later my aunt might have already been killed. Dr. Wei was facing a lot of opposition, and he was concerned that taking too many trips to the era would destroy too much of the evidence. He explained that it would have to be my last trip.

I found my aunt in a cell by herself. She was very thin, and I saw that her palms were covered with a rash, and there were bumps around her neck from inflamed lymph nodes. I could also tell that she was pregnant. She must have been very sick because she was lying on the floor, her eyes open and making a light moan—"*aiya, aiya*"—the whole time I was with her.

I stayed with her all day, watching her. I kept on trying to comfort her, but of course she couldn't hear me or feel my touch. The words were for my benefit, not hers. I sang a song for her, a song that my father used to sing to me when I was little:

> 萬里長城萬里長, 長城外面是故鄉
> 高粱肥, 大豆香, 遍地黃金少災殃。

> *The Great Wall is ten thousand* li *long,*
> on the other side is my hometown
> Rich sorghum, sweet soybeans,
> happiness spreads like gold on the ground.

I was getting to know her and saying goodbye to her at the same time.

■　■　■

Shiro Yamagata:

To study the progress of syphilis and other venereal diseases, we would vivisect the women at various intervals after they were infected. It was important to understand the effects of the disease on living organs, and vivisection also provided valuable surgical practice. The vivisection was sometimes done with chloroform, sometimes not. We usually vivisected the subjects for the anthrax and cholera experiments without use of anesthesia since anesthesia might have affected the results, and it was felt that the same would be true with the women with syphilis.

I do not remember how many women I vivisected.

Some of the women were very brave, and would lie down on the table without being forced. I learned to say, "*bútòng, bútòng*" or "it won't hurt" in Chinese to calm them down. We would then tie them to the table.

Usually the first incision, from thorax to stomach, would cause the women to scream horribly. Some of them would keep on screaming for a long while during the vivisection. We used gags later because the screaming interfered with discussion during the vivisections. Generally the women stayed alive until we cut open the heart, and so we saved that for last.

I remember once vivisecting a woman who was pregnant. We did not use chloroform initially, but then she begged us, "Please kill me, but do not kill my child." We then used chloroform to put her under before finishing her.

None of us had seen a pregnant woman's insides before, and it was very informative. I thought about keeping the fetus for some experiment, but it was too weak and died soon after being removed. We tried to guess whether the fetus was from the seed of a Japanese doctor or one of the Chinese prisoners, and I think most of us agreed in the end that it was probably one of the prisoners due to the ugliness of the fetus.

I believed that the work we did on the women was very valuable, and gained us many insights.

I did not think that the work we did at Unit 731 was particularly strange. After 1941, I was assigned to northern China, first in Hebei Province and then in Shanxi Province. In army hospitals, we military doctors regularly scheduled surgery practice sessions with live Chinese subjects. The army would provide the subjects on the announced days. We practiced amputations, cutting out sections of intestines and suturing together the remaining sections, and removing various internal organs.

Often the practice surgeries were done without anesthesia to simulate battlefield conditions. Sometimes a doctor would shoot a prisoner in the stomach to simulate war wounds for us to practice on. After the surgeries, one of the officers would behead the Chinese subject or strangle him. Sometimes vivisections were also used as anatomy lessons for the younger trainees and to give them a thrill. It was important for the army to produce good surgeons quickly, so that we could help the soldiers.

"John," last name withheld, high school teacher, Perth, Australia:

You know old people are very lonely, so when they want attention, they'll say anything. They would confess to these ridiculous made-up stories about what they did. It's really sad. I'm sure I can find some old Australian soldier who'll confess to cutting up some abo woman if you put out an ad asking about it. The people who tell these stories just want attention, like those Korean prostitutes who claim to have been kidnapped by the Japanese Army during the War.

Patty Ashby, homemaker, Milwaukee, Wisconsin:

I think it's hard to judge someone if you weren't there. It was during the War, and bad things happen during wars. The Christian thing to do is to forget and forgive. Dragging up things like this is uncharitable. And it's wrong to mess with time like that. Nothing good can come of it.

Sharon, actress, New York, New York:

You know, the thing is that the Chinese have been very cruel to dogs, and they even eat dogs. They have also been very mean to the Tibetans. So it makes you think, was it karma?

Shiro Yamagata:

On August 15, 1945, we heard that the Emperor had surrendered to America. Like many other Japanese in China at that time, my unit decided that it was easier to surrender to the Chinese Nationalists. My unit was then reformed and drafted into a unit of the Nationalist Army under Chiang Kai-Shek, and I continued to work as an army doctor assisting the Nationalists against the Communists in the Chinese Civil War. As the Chinese had almost no qualified surgeons, my work was very much needed, and I was treated well.

The Nationalists were no match for the Communists, however, and in January, 1949, the Communists captured the army field hospital I was staffed in, and took me prisoner. For the first month, we were not allowed to leave our cells. I tried to make friends with the guards. The Communists soldiers were very young and thin, but they seemed to be in much better spirits than their Nationalist counterparts.

After a month, we, along with the guards, were given daily lessons on Marxism and Maoism.

The War was not my fault and I was not to be blamed, I was told. I was just a soldier, deceived by the Showa Emperor and Hideki Tojo into fighting a war of invasion and oppression against the Chinese. Through studying Marxism, I was told, I would come to understand that all poor men, the Chinese and Japanese alike, were brothers. We were expected to reflect on what we did to the Chinese people, and to write confessions about the crimes we committed during the War. Our punishment would be lessened, we were told, if our confessions showed sincere hearts. I wrote confessions, but they were always rejected for not being sincere enough.

Still, because I was a doctor, I was allowed to work at the provincial hospital to treat patients. I was the most senior surgeon at the hospital and had my own staff.

We heard rumors that a new war was about to start between the United States and China in Korea. How could China win against the United States, I thought. Even the mighty Japanese Army could not stand against America. Perhaps I will be captured by the Americans next. I suppose I was never very good at predicting the outcomes of wars.

Food became scarce after the Korean War began. The guards ate rice with scallions and wild weeds, while prisoners like me were given rice and fish.

Why is this? I asked.

You are prisoners, my guard, who was only sixteen, said. You are from Japan. Japan is a wealthy country, and you must be treated in a manner that matched as closely as possible the conditions in your home country.

I offered the guard my fish, and he refused.

You do not want to touch the food that had been touched by a Japanese Devil? I joked with him. I was also teaching him how to read, and he would sneak me cigarettes.

I was a very good surgeon, and I was proud of my work. Sometimes I felt that despite the War, I was doing China a great deal of good, and I helped many patients with my skills.

One day, a woman came to see me in the hospital. She had broken her leg, and because she lived far from the hospital, by the time her family brought her to me, gangrene had set in, and the leg had to be amputated.

She was on the table, and I was getting ready to administer anesthesia. I looked into her eyes, trying to calm her. "*Bútòng, bútòng.*"

Her eyes became very wide, and she screamed. She screamed and screamed, and scrambled off the table, dragging her dead leg with her until she was as far away from me as possible.

I recognized her then. She had been one of the Chinese girl prisoners that we had trained to help us as nurses at the army hospital during the War with China. She had helped me with some of the practice surgery sessions. I had slept with her a few times. I didn't know her name. She was just "Number Four" to me, and some of the younger doctors had joked about cutting her open if Japan lost and we had to retreat.

[Interviewer (off-camera): Mr. Yamagata, you cannot cry. You know that. We cannot show you being emotional on film. We have to stop if you cannot control yourself.]

I was filled with unspeakable grief. It was only then that I understood what kind of a life and career I had. Because I wanted to be a successful doctor, I did things that no human being should do. I wrote my confession then, and when my guard read my confession, he would not speak to me.

I served my sentence and was released and allowed to return to Japan in 1956.

I felt lost. Everyone was working so hard in Japan. But I didn't know what to do.

"You should not have confessed to anything," one of my friends, who was in the same unit with me, told me. "I didn't, and they released me years ago. I have a good job now. My son is going to be a doctor. Don't say anything about what happened during the War."

I moved here to Hokkaido to be a farmer, as far away from the heart of Japan as possible. For all these years I stayed silent to protect my friend. And I believed that I would die before him, and so take my secret to the grave.

But my friend is now dead, and so, even though I have not said anything about what I did all these years, I will not stop speaking now.

Lillian C. Chang-Wyeth:

I am speaking only for myself, and perhaps for my aunt. I am the last connection between her and the living world. And I am turning into an old woman myself.

I don't know much about politics, and don't care much for it. I have told you what I saw, and I will remember the way my aunt cried in that cell until the day I die.

You ask me what I want. I don't know how to answer that.

Some have said that I should demand that the surviving members of Unit 731 be brought to justice. But what does that mean? I am no longer a child. I do not want to see trials, parades, spectacles. The law does not give you real justice.

What I really want is for what I saw to never have happened. But no one can give me that. And so I resort to wanting to have my aunt's story remembered, to have the guilt of her killers and torturers laid bare to the gaze of the world, the way that they laid her bare to their needle and scalpel.

I do not know how to describe those acts other than as crimes against humanity. They were denials against the very idea of life itself.

The Japanese government has never acknowledged the actions of Unit 731, and it has never apologized for them. Over the years, more and more evidence of the atrocities committed during those years have come to life, but always the answer is the same: there is not enough evidence to know what happened.

Well, now there is. I have seen what happened with my own eyes. And I will speak about what happened, speak out against the denialists. I will tell my story as often as I can.

The men and women of Unit 731 committed those acts in the name of Japan and the Japanese people. I demand that the government of Japan acknowledge these crimes against humanity, that it apologize for them, and that it commit to preserving the memory of the victims and condemning the guilt of those criminals so long as the word *justice* still has meaning.

I am also sorry to say, Mr. Chairman and Members of the Subcommittee, that the government of the United States has also never acknowledged or apologized for its role in shielding these criminals from justice after the War, or in making use of the information bought at the expense of torture, rape, and death. I demand that the government of the United States acknowledge and apologize for these acts.

That is all.

Representative Hogart:

I would like to again remind members of the public that they must maintain order and decorum during this hearing or risk being forcibly removed from this room.

Ms. Chang-Wyeth, I am sorry for whatever it is you think you have experienced. I have no doubt that it has deeply affected you. I thank the other witnesses as well for sharing their stories.

Mr. Chairman, and Members of the Subcommittee, I must again note for the record my objection to this hearing and to the Resolution which has been proposed by my colleague, Representative Kotler.

The Second World War was an extraordinary time during which the ordinary rules of human conduct did not apply, and there is no doubt that terrible events occurred and terrible suffering resulted. But whatever happened—and we have no definitive proof of anything other than the results of some sensational high-energy physics that no one present, other than Dr. Kirino herself, understands—it would be a mistake for us to become slaves to history, and to subject the present to the control of the past.

The Japan of today is the most important ally of the United States in the Pacific, if not the world, while the People's Republic of China takes daily steps to challenge our interests in the region. Japan is vital in our efforts to contain and confront the Chinese threat.

It is ill-advised at best, and counterproductive at worst, for Representative Kotler to introduce his Resolution at this time. The Resolution will no doubt embarrass and dishearten our ally and give encouragement and comfort to our challengers at a time when we cannot afford to indulge in theatrical sentiments, premised upon stories told by emotional witnesses who may have been experiencing "illusions," and I am quoting the words of Dr. Kirino, the creator of the technology involved.

Again, I must call upon the Subcommittee to stop this destructive, useless process.

Representative Kotler:

Mr. Chairman, and Members of the Subcommittee, thank you for giving me the chance to respond to Representative Hogart.

It's easy to hide behind intransitive verbal formulations like "terrible events occurred" and "suffering resulted." And I am sorry to hear my honored colleague, a member of the United States Congress, engage in the same shameful tactics of denial and evasion employed by those who denied that the Holocaust was real.

Every successive Japanese government, with the encouragement and complicity of the successive administrations in this country, has refused to even acknowledge, let alone apologize for, the activities of Unit 731. In fact, for many years, the Unit's very existence was unacknowledged. These denials and refusals to face Japanese atrocities committed during the Second World War form a pattern of playing-down and denial of the war record, whether we are talking about the so-called "Comfort Women," the Nanjing Massacre, or the forced slave laborers of Korea and China. This pattern has harmed the relationship of Japan with its Asian neighbors.

The issue of Unit 731 presents its unique challenges. Here, the United States is not an uninterested third party. As an ally and close friend of Japan, it is the duty of the United States to point out where our friend has erred. But more than that, the United States played an active role in helping the perpetrators of the crimes of Unit 731 escape justice. General MacArthur granted the men of Unit 731 immunity to get their experimental data. We are in part responsible for the denials and the cover-ups because we valued the tainted fruits of those atrocities more than we valued our own integrity. We have sinned as well.

What I want to emphasize is that Representative Hogart has misunderstood the Resolution. What the witnesses and I are asking for, Mr. Chairman, is not some admission of guilt by the present government of Japan or its people. What we are asking for is a declaration from this body that it is the belief of the United States Congress that the victims of Unit 731 should be honored and remembered, and that the perpetrators of these heinous crimes be condemned. There is no Bill of Attainder here, no corruption of blood. We are not calling on Japan to pay compensation. All we are asking for is a commitment to truth, a commitment to remember.

Like memorials to the Holocaust, the value of such a declaration is simply a public affirmation of our common bond of humanity with the victims, and our unity in standing against the ideology of evil and barbarity of the Unit 731 butchers and the Japanese militarist society that permitted and ordered such evil.

Now, I want to make it clear that "Japan" is not a monolithic thing, and it is not just the Japanese government. Individual Japanese citizens have done heroic work in bringing these atrocities to light throughout the years, almost always against government resistance and against the public's wish to forget and move on. And I offer them my heartfelt thanks.

The truth cannot be brushed away, and the families of the victims and the people of China should not be told that justice is not possible, that because their present government is repugnant to the government of the United States, that a great injustice should be covered up and hidden from the judgment of the world. Is there any doubt that this *non-binding*

Resolution, or even much more stringent versions of it, would have passed without trouble if the victims were a people whose government has the favor of the United States? If we, for "strategic" reasons, sacrifice the truth in the name of gaining something of value for short-term advantage, then we will have simply repeated the errors of our forefathers at the end of the War.

It is not who we are. Dr. Wei has offered us a way to speak the truth about the past, and we must ask the government of Japan and our government to stand up and take up our collective responsibility to history.

Li Ruming, Director of the Department of History, Zhejiang University, The People's Republic of China:

When I was finishing my doctorate in Boston, Evan and Akemi often had my wife and me over to their place. They were very friendly and helpful, and made us feel the enthusiasm and warmth that America is rightly famous for. Unlike many Chinese-Americans I met, Evan did not give off a sense that he felt he was superior to the Chinese from the mainland. It was wonderful to have him and Akemi as life-long friends, and not have every interaction between us filtered through the lens of the politics between our two countries, as is so often the case between Chinese and American scholars.

Because I am his friend and I am also Chinese, it is difficult for me to speak about Evan's work with objectivity, but I will try my best.

When Evan first announced his intention to go to Harbin and try to travel to the past, the Chinese government was cautiously supportive. As none of it had been tried before, the full implications of Evan's destructive process for time travel were not yet clear. Due to destruction of evidence at the end of the War and continuing stonewalling by the Japanese government, we do not have access to large archives of documentary evidence and artifacts from Unit 731, and it was felt that Evan's work would help fill in the gap by providing first-hand accounts of what happened. The Chinese government granted Evan and Akemi visas under the assumption that their work would help promote Western understanding of China's historical disputes with Japan.

But they wanted to monitor his work. The War is deeply emotional for my compatriots, its unhealed wounds exacerbated by years of post-War disputes with Japan, and as such, it was not politically feasible for the government to not be involved. World War Two was not the distant past, involving ancient peoples, and China could not permit two foreigners to go traipsing through that recent history like adventurers through ancient tombs.

But from Evan's point of view—and I think he was justified in his belief—any support, monitoring, or affiliation with the Chinese government would have destroyed all credibility for his work in Western eyes.

He thus rejected all offers of Chinese involvement and even called for intervention by American diplomats. This angered many Chinese and alienated him from them. Later, when the Chinese government finally shut down his work after the storm of negative publicity, very few Chinese would speak up for him because they felt that he and Akemi had—perhaps even intentionally—done more damage to China's history and her people. The accusations were unfair, and I'm sorry to say that I do not feel that I did enough to defend his reputation.

Evan's focus throughout his project was both more universal and more atomistic than the people of China. On the one hand, he had an American devotion to the idea of the individual, and his commitment was first and foremost to the individual voice and memory of each victim. On the other hand, he was also trying to transcend nations, to make people all over the world empathize with these victims, condemn their torturers, and affirm the common humanity of us all.

But in that process, he was forced to distance his effort from the Chinese people in order to preserve the political credibility of his project in the West. He sacrificed their goodwill in a bid to make the West care. Evan tried to appease the West and Western prejudices against China. Was it cowardly? Should he have challenged them more? I do not know.

History is not merely a private matter. Even the family members of the victims understand that there is a communitarian aspect to history. The War of Resistance Against the Japanese Invasion is the founding story of modern China, much as the Holocaust is the founding story of Israel and the Revolution and the Civil War are the founding stories of America. Perhaps this is difficult to understand for a Westerner, but to many Chinese, Evan, because he feared and rejected their involvement, was *stealing* and erasing their history. He sacrificed the history of the Chinese people, without their consent, for a Western ideal. I understand why he did it, but I cannot agree that his choice was right.

As a Chinese, I do not share Evan's utter devotion to the idea of a personalized sense of history. Telling the individual stories of all the victims, as Evan sought to do, is not possible and in any event would not solve all problems.

Because of our limited capacity for empathy for mass suffering, I think there's a risk that his approach would result in sentimentality and only

selective memory. More than sixteen million civilians died in China from
the Japanese invasion. The great bulk of this suffering did not occur in death
factories like Pingfang or killing fields like Nanjing, which grab headlines
and shout for our attention; rather, it occurred in the countless quiet
villages, towns, remote outposts, where men and women were slaughtered
and raped and slaughtered again, their screams fading with the chill wind,
until even their names became blanks and forgotten. But they also deserve
to be remembered.

It is not possible that every atrocity would find a spokesperson as eloquent
as Anne Frank, and I do not believe that we should seek to reduce all of
history to a collection of such narratives.

But Evan always told me that an American would rather work on the
problem that he could solve rather than wring his hands over the vast realm
of problems that he could not.

It was not an easy choice that he made, and I would not have chosen the
same way. But Evan was always true to his American ideals.

*Bill Pacer, Professor of Modern Chinese Language and Culture, University of
Hawaii at Manoa:*

It has often been said that since everybody in China knew about Unit 731,
Dr. Wei had nothing useful to teach the Chinese, and was only an activist
campaigning against Japan. That's not quite right. One of the more tragic
aspects of the dispute between China and Japan over history is how much
their responses have mirrored each other. Wei's goal was to rescue history
from both.

In the early days of the People's Republic, between 1945 and 1956, the
Communists' overall ideological approach was to treat the Japanese invasion
as just another historical stage in mankind's unstoppable march towards
socialism. While Japanese militarism was condemned and the Resistance
celebrated, the Communists also sought to forgive the Japanese individually
if they showed contrition—a surprisingly Christian/Confucian approach for
an atheistic regime. In this atmosphere of revolutionary zeal, the Japanese
prisoners were treated, for the most part, humanely. They were given
Marxist classes and told to write confessions of their crimes. (These classes
became the basis for the Japanese public's belief that any man who would
confess to horrible crimes during the War must have been brainwashed by
the Communists.) Once they were deemed sufficiently reformed through
"re-education," they were released back to Japan. Memories of the War

were then suppressed in China as the country feverishly moved to build a Socialist utopia, with well-known disastrous consequences.

Yet, this generosity towards the Japanese was matched by Stalinist harsh treatment of landowners, capitalists, intellectuals, and the Chinese who collaborated with the Japanese. Hundreds of thousands of people were killed, often on little evidence and with no effort given to observe legal forms.

Later, during the 1990s, the government of the People's Republic began to invoke memories of the War in the context of patriotism to legitimize itself in the wake of the collapse of Communism. Ironically, this obvious ploy prevented large segments of the populace from being able to come to terms with the War—distrust of the government infected everything it touched.

And so the People's Republic's approach to historical memory created a series of connected problems. First, the leniency they showed the prisoners became the ground for denialists to later question the veracity of confessions by Japanese soldiers. Second, yoking patriotism to the memory of the War invited charges that any effort to remember was politically motivated. And lastly, individual victims of the atrocities became symbols, anonymized to serve the needs of the State.

However, it has rarely been acknowledged that behind Japan's post-War silence regarding wartime atrocities lay the same impulses that drove the Chinese responses. On the left, the peace movement attributed all suffering during the War to the concept of war itself, and advocated universal forgiveness and peace among all nations without a sense of blame. In the center, focus was placed on material development as a bandage to cover the wounds of the War. On the right, the question of wartime guilt became inextricably yoked to patriotism. In contrast to Germany, which could rely on Nazism—distinct from the nation itself—to absorb the blame, it was impossible to acknowledge the atrocities committed by the Japanese during the War without implicating a sense that Japan itself was under attack.

And so, across a narrow sea, China and Japan unwittingly converged on the same set of responses to the barbarities of World War Two: forgetting in the name of universal ideals like "peace" and "socialism"; welding memories of the War to patriotism; abstracting victims and perpetrators alike into symbols to serve the State. Seen in this light, the abstract, incomplete, fragmentary memories in China and the silence in Japan are flip sides of the same coin.

The core of Wei's belief is that without real memory, there can be no real reconciliation. Without real memory, the individual persons of each nation have not been able to empathize with and remember and experience the suffering of the victims. An individualized story that each of us can tell ourselves about what happened is required before we can move beyond the trap of history. That, all along, was what Wei's project was about.

"Cross-Talk," January 21, 20__, courtesy of FXNN

Amy Rowe: Thank you, Ambassador Yoshida and Dr. Wei, for agreeing to come on to Cross-Talk tonight. Our viewers want to have their questions answered, and I want to see some fireworks!

Ambassador Yoshida, let's start with you. Why won't Japan apologize?

Yoshida: Amy, Japan has apologized. This is the whole point. Japan has apologized many many times for World War Two. Every few years we have to go through this spectacle where it's said that Japan needs to apologize for its actions during World War Two. But Japan has done so, repeatedly. Let me read you a few quotes.

This is from a statement by Prime Minister Tomiichi Murayama, on August 31, 1994. "Japan's actions in a certain period of the past not only claimed numerous victims here in Japan but also left the peoples of neighboring Asia and elsewhere with scars that are painful even today. I am thus taking this opportunity to state my belief, based on my profound remorse for these acts of aggression, colonial rule, and the like caused such unbearable suffering and sorrow for so many people, that Japan's future path should be one of making every effort to build world peace in line with my no-war commitment. It is imperative for us Japanese to look squarely to our history with the peoples of neighboring Asia and elsewhere."

And again, from a statement by the Diet, on June 9, 1995: "On the occasion of the 50th anniversary of the end of World War II, this House offers its sincere condolences to those who fell in action and victims of wars and similar actions all over the world. Solemnly reflecting upon many instances of colonial rule and acts of aggression in the modern history of the world, and recognizing that Japan carried out those acts in the past, inflicting pain and suffering upon the peoples of other countries, especially in Asia, the Members of this House express a sense of deep remorse."

I can go on and read you dozens of other quotes like this. Japan *has* apologized, Amy.

Yet, every few years, the propaganda organs of certain regimes hostile to a free and prosperous Japan try to dredge up settled historical events to manufacture controversy. When is this going to end? And some men of otherwise good intellect have allowed themselves to become the tools of propaganda. I wish they would wake up and see how they are being used.

Rowe: Dr. Wei, I have to say, those do sound like apologies to me.

Wei: Amy, it is not my aim or goal to humiliate Japan. My commitment is to the victims and their memory, not theatre. What I'm asking for is for Japan to acknowledge the truth of what happened at Pingfang. I want to focus on specifics, and acknowledgment of specifics, not empty platitudes.

But since Ambassador Yoshida has decided to bring up the issue of apologies, let's look closer at them, shall we?

The statements quoted by the Ambassador are grand and abstract, and they refer to vague and unspecified sufferings. They are apologies only in the most watered-down sense. What the Ambassador is not telling you is the Japanese government's continuing refusal to admit many specific war crimes and to honor and remember the real victims.

Moreover, every time one of these statements quoted by the Ambassador is made, it is matched soon after by another statement from a prominent Japanese politician purporting to cast doubt upon what happened in World War Two. Year after year, we are treated to this show of the Japanese government as a Janus speaking with two faces.

Yoshida: It's not that unusual to have differences of opinion when it comes to matters of history, Dr. Wei. In a democracy it's what you would expect.

Wei: Actually, Ambassador, Unit 731 *has* been consistently handled by the Japanese government: for more than fifty years the official position was absolute silence regarding Unit 731, despite the steady accumulation of physical evidence, including human remains, from Unit 731's activities. Even the Unit's existence was not admitted until the 1990s, and the government consistently denied that it had researched or used biological weapons during the War.

It wasn't until 2005, in response to a lawsuit by some relatives of Unit 731's victims for compensation, that the Tokyo High Court finally acknowledged Japan's use of biological weapons during the War. This was the first time that an official voice of the Japanese government admitted to that fact. Amy, you'll notice that this was a decade after those lofty statements read by Ambassador Yoshida. The Court denied compensation.

Since then the Japanese government has consistently stated that there is insufficient evidence to confirm exactly what experiments were carried out by Unit 731 or the details of their conduct. Official denial and silence continue despite the dedicated efforts of some Japanese scholars to bring the truth to light.

But numerous former members of Unit 731 have come forward since the 1980s to testify and confess to the grisly acts they committed. And we have confirmed and expanded upon those accounts with new eyewitness accounts by volunteers who have traveled to Pingfang. Everyday, we are finding out more about Unit 731's crimes. We will tell the world all the victims' stories.

Yoshida: I am not sure that "telling stories" is what historians should be doing. If you want to make fiction, go ahead, but do not tell people that it is history. Extraordinary claims require extraordinary proof. And there is insufficient proof for the accusations currently being directed against Japan.

Wei: Ambassador Yoshida, is your position really that nothing happened at Pingfang? Are you saying that these reports by the American occupational authority from immediately after the War are lies? Are you saying that these contemporaneous diary entries by the officers of Unit 731 are lies? Are you really denying all of this?

There is a simple solution to all this. Will you take a trip to Pingfang in 1941? Will you believe your own eyes?

Yoshida: I'm—I am not—I'm making a distinction—It was a time of war, Dr. Wei, and perhaps it is possible that some unfortunate things happened. But "stories" are not evidence.

Wei: Will you take a trip, Ambassador?

Yoshida: I will not. I see no reason to subject myself to your process. I see no reason to undergo your "time travel" hallucinations.

Rowe: Now we are seeing some fireworks!

Wei: Ambassador Yoshida, let me make this clear. The deniers are committing a fresh crime against the victims of those atrocities: not only would they stand with the torturers and the killers, but they are also engaged in the practice of erasing and silencing the victims from history, to kill them afresh.

In the past, their task was easy. Unless the denials were actively resisted, eventually memories would dim with old age and death, and the voices of the past would fade away, and the denialists would win. The people of the present would then become exploiters of the dead, and that has always been the way history was written.

But we have now come to the end of history. What my wife and I have done is to take narrative away, and to give us all a chance to see the past with our own eyes. In place of memory, we now have incontrovertible evidence. Instead of exploiting the dead, we must look into the face of the dying. *I have seen these crimes with my own eyes.* You cannot deny that.

[Archival footage of Dr. Evan Wei delivering the keynote for the Fifth International War Crimes Studies Conference in San Francisco, on November 20, 20__. Courtesy of the Stanford University Archives.]

History is a narrative enterprise, and the telling of stories that are true, that affirm and explain our existence, is the fundamental task of the historian. But truth is delicate, and it has many enemies. Perhaps that is why, although we academics are supposedly in the business of pursuing the truth, the word "truth" is rarely uttered without hedges, adornments, and qualifications.

Every time we tell a story about a great atrocity, like the Holocaust or Pingfang, the forces of denial are always ready to pounce, to erase, to silence, to forget. History has always been difficult because of the delicacy of the truth, and denialists have always been able to resort to labeling the truth as fiction.

One has to be careful, whenever one tells a story about a great injustice. We are a species that loves narrative, but we have also been taught not to trust an individual speaker.

Yes, it is true that no nation, and no historian, can tell a story that completely encompasses every aspect of the truth. But it is not true that just because all narratives are constructed, that they are equally far from the truth. The Earth is neither a perfect sphere nor a flat disk, but the model of the sphere is much closer to the truth. Similarly, there are some narratives that are closer to the truth than others, and we must always try to tell a story that comes as close to the truth as is humanly possible.

The fact that we can never have complete, perfect knowledge does not absolve us of the moral duty to judge and to take a stand against evil.

Victor P. Lowenson, Professor of East Asian History, Director of the Institute of East Asian Studies, UC Berkeley:

I have been called a denialist, and I have been called worse. But I am not a Japanese right-winger who believes that Unit 731 is a myth. I do not say that nothing happened there. What I am saying is that, unfortunately, we do not have enough evidence to be able to describe with certainty all that happened there.

I have enormous respect for Wei, and he remains and will remain one of my best students. But in my view, he has abdicated the responsibility of the historian to ensure that the truth is not ensnared in doubt. He has crossed the line that divides a historian from an activist.

As I see it, the fight here isn't ideological, but methodological. What we are fighting over is what constitutes *proof.* Historians trained in Western and Asian traditions have always relied on the documentary record, but Dr. Wei is now raising the primacy of eyewitness accounts, and not even contemporaneous eyewitness accounts, mind you, but accounts by witnesses out of the stream of time.

There are many problems with his approach. We have a great deal of experience from psychology and the law to doubt the reliability of eyewitness accounts. We also have serious concerns with the single-use nature of the Kirino Process, which seems to destroy the very thing it is studying, and erases history even as it purports to allow it to be witnessed. You literally cannot ever go back to a moment of time that has already been experienced— and thus consumed—by another witness. When each eyewitness account is impossible to verify independently of *that* account, how can we rely on such a process to establish the truth of what happened?

I understand that from the perspective of supporters of Dr. Wei, the raw experience of actually seeing history unfold before your eyes makes it impossible to doubt the evidence indelibly etched in your mind. But that is simply not good enough for the rest of us. The Kirino Process requires a leap of faith: those who have witnessed the ineffable have no doubt of its existence, but that clarity is incapable of being replicated for anyone else. And so we are stuck here, in the present, trying to make sense of the past.

Dr. Wei has ended the process of rational historical inquiry and transformed it into a form of personal religion. What one witness has seen, no one else can ever see. This is madness.

Naoki, last name withheld, clerk:

I have seen the videos of the old soldiers who supposedly confessed to these horrible things. I do not believe them. They cry and act so emotional, as though they are insane. The Communists were great brainwashers, and it is undoubtedly a result of their plot.

I remember one of those old men describing the kindness of his Communist guards. *Kind* Communist guards! If that is not evidence of brainwashing, what is?

■   ■   ■

Kazue Sato, housewife:

The Chinese are great manufacturers of lies. They have produced fake food, fake Olympics, and fake statistics. Their history is also faked. This Wei is an American, but he is also Chinese, and so we cannot trust anything he does.

Hiroshi Abe, retired soldier:

The soldiers who "confessed" have brought great shame upon their country.

Interviewer:

Because of what they did?

Hiroshi Abe:

Because of what they said.

Ienaga Ito, Professor of Oriental History, Kyoto University:

We live in an age that prizes authenticity and personalized narratives, as embodied in the form of the memoir. Eyewitness accounts have an immediacy and reality that compels belief, and we think they can convey a truth greater than any fiction. Yet, perhaps paradoxically, we are also eager to seize upon any factual deviation and inconsistency in such narratives, and declare the entirety to be *mere* fiction. There's an all-or-nothing bleakness to this dynamic. But we should have conceded from the start that narrative is irreducibly subjective, though that does not mean that they do not also convey the truth.

Evan was a greater radical than most people realized. He sought to free the past from the present so that history could not be ignored, put out of our minds, or made to serve the needs of the present. The possibility of witnessing actual history and experiencing that past by all of us means that the past is not past, but alive at this very moment.

What Evan did was to transform historical investigation itself into a form of memoir writing. That kind of emotional experience is important in the way we think about history and make decisions. Culture is not merely a product of reason but also of real, visceral empathy. And I am afraid that it is primarily empathy that has been missing from the post-War Japanese responses to history.

Evan tried to introduce more empathy and emotion into historical inquiry. For this he was crucified by the academic establishment. But adding empathy and the irreducibly subjective dimension of the personal narrative to history does not detract from the truth. It enhances the truth. That we accept our own frailties and subjectivity does not free us to abdicate the moral responsibility to tell the truth, even if, and especially if, "truth" is not singular but a set of shared experiences and shared understandings that together make up our humanity.

Of course, drawing attention to the importance and primacy of eyewitness accounts unleashed a new danger. With a little money and the right equipment, anyone can eliminate the Bohm-Kirino particles from a desired era, in a specified place, and so erase those events from direct experience. Unwittingly, Evan had also invented the technology to end history forever, by denying us and future generations of that emotional experience of the past that he so cherished.

Akemi Kirino:

It was difficult during the years immediately after the Comprehensive Time Travel Moratorium was signed. Evan was denied tenure in a close vote, and that editorial in the *Wall Street Journal* by his old friend and teacher, Victor Lowenson, calling him a "tool of propaganda," deeply hurt him. Then, there were the death threats and harassing phone calls, every day.

But I think it was what they did to me that really got to him. At the height of the attacks from the denialists, the IT division of the Institute asked me if I would mind being de-listed from the public faculty directory. Whenever they listed me on the web site, the site would be hacked within hours, and the denialists would replace my bio page with pictures where these men, so brave and eloquent, displayed their courage and intellect by illustrating what they would do to me if they had me in their power. And you probably remember the news reports about that night when I walked home alone from work.

I don't really want to dwell on that time, if that's all right with you.

We moved away to Boise, where we tried to hide from the worst of it. We kept a low profile, got an unlisted number, and basically stayed out of sight. Evan went on medication for his depression. On the weekends we went hiking in the Sawtooth Mountains, and Evan took up charting abandoned mining sites and ghost towns from during the gold rush. That was a happy time for us, and I thought he was feeling better. The sojourn in Idaho reminded him that sometimes the world is a kind place, and all is not darkness and denial.

But he was feeling lost. He felt that he was hiding from the truth. I knew that he was feeling torn between his sense of duty to the past, and his sense of loyalty to the present, to me.

I could not bear to see him being torn apart, and so I asked if he wanted to return to the fight.

We flew back to Boston, and things had grown even worse. He had sought to end history as mere *history*, and to give the past living voices to speak to the present. But it did not work out the way he had intended. The past did come to life, but when faced with it, the present decided to recast history as religion.

The more Evan did, the more he felt he had to do. He would not come to bed, and fell asleep at his desk. He was writing, writing, constantly writing. He believed that he had to single-handedly refute all the lies, and take on all his enemies. It was never enough, never enough for him. I stood by, helpless.

"I have to speak for them, because they have no one else," he would tell me.

By then perhaps he was living more in the past than in the present. Even though he no longer had access to our machine, in his mind he relived those trips he took, over and over again. He believed that he had let the victims down.

A great responsibility had been thrust upon him, and he had failed them. He was trying to uncover to the world a great injustice, and yet in the process he seemed to have only stirred up the forces of denial, hate, and silence.

Excerpts from The Economist, *November 26, 20__*
[A woman's voice, flat, calm, reads out loud the article text as the camera swoops over the ocean, the beaches, and then the forests and hills of Manchuria. From the shadow of a small plane racing along the ground beneath us we can tell that the camera is shooting from the open door of the airplane. An arm, the hand clenched tight into a fist, moves into the foreground from off-frame. The fingers open. Dark ashes are scattered into the air beneath the airplane.]

We will soon come upon the ninetieth anniversary of the Mukden Incident, the start of the Japanese invasion of China. To this day, that war remains the alpha and omega of the relationship between the two countries.

[A series of photographs of the leaders of Unit 731 are shown. The reader's voice fades out and then fades back in.]

The men of Unit 731 then moved on to prominent careers in post-War Japan. Three of them founded the Japan Blood Bank (which later became the Green Cross, Japan's largest pharmaceutical company) and used their knowledge of methods for freezing and drying blood derived from human experiments during the War to produce dried-blood products for sale to the United States Army at great profit. General Shiro Ishii, the commander of Unit 731, may have spent some time after the War working in Maryland, researching biological weapons. Papers were published using data obtained from human subjects, including babies (sometimes the word "monkey" was substituted as a cover-up) -- and it is possible that medical papers published today still contain citations traceable to these results, making all of us the unwitting beneficiaries of these atrocities.

[The reading voice fades out as the sound of the airplane's engine cuts in. The camera shifts to images of clashing protestors waving Japanese flags and Chinese flags, some of the flags on fire . . . Then the voice fades in again.]

Many inside and outside Japan objected to the testimonies by the surviving members of Unit 731: the men are old, they point out, with failing memories; they may be seeking attention; they may be mentally ill; they may have been brainwashed by the Chinese Communists. Reliance on oral testimony alone is an unwise way to construct a solid historical case. To the Chinese this sounded like more of the same excuses issued by the deniers of the Nanjing Massacre and other Japanese atrocities.

Year after year, history grew as a wall between the two peoples.

[The camera switches to a montage of pictures of Evan Wei and Akemi Kirino throughout their lives. In the first pictures, they smile for the camera. In later pictures, Kirino's face is tired, withdrawn, impassive. Wei's face is defiant, angry, and then full of despair.]

Evan Wei, a young Chinese-American specialist on Heian Japan, and Akemi Kirino, a Japanese-American experimental physicist, did not seem like the kind of revolutionary figures who would bring the world to the brink of war. But history has a way of mocking our expectations.

If lack of evidence was the issue, they had a way to provide irrefutable evidence: you could watch history as it occurred, like a play.

The governments of the world went into a frenzy. While Wei sent relatives of the victims of Unit 731 into the past to bear witness to the horrors committed in the operating rooms and prison cells of Pingfang, China and Japan waged a bitter war in courts and in front of cameras, staking out their rival claims to the past. The United States was reluctantly drawn into the fight, and, citing national security reasons, finally shut down Wei's machine when he unveiled plans to investigate the truth of America's alleged use of biological weapons (possibly derived from Unit 731's research) during the Korean War.

Armenians, Jews, Tibetans, Native Americans, Indians, the Kikuyu, the descendants of slaves in the New World—victim groups around the world lined up and demanded use of the machine, some out of fear that their history might be erased by the groups in power, others wishing to use their history for present political gain. As well, the countries who initially advocated access to the machine hesitated when the implications became clear: did the French wish to relive the depravity of their own people under Vichy France? Did the Chinese want to reexperience the self-inflicted horrors of the Cultural Revolution? Did the British want to see the genocides that lay behind their Empire?

With remarkable alacrity, democracies and dictatorships around the world signed the Comprehensive Time Travel Moratorium while they wrangled over the minutiae of the rules for how to divide up jurisdiction of the past. Everyone, it seemed, preferred not to have to deal with the past just yet.

Wei wrote, "All written history shares one goal: to bring a coherent narrative to a set of historical facts. For far too long we have been mired in controversy over facts. Time travel will make truth as accessible as looking outside the window."

But Wei did not help his case by sending large numbers of Chinese relatives of Unit 731 victims, rather than professional historians, through his machine. (Though it is also fair to ask if things really would have turned out differently had he sent more professional historians. Perhaps accusations would still have been made that the visions were mere fabrications of the machine or historians partisan to his cause.) In any event, the relatives, being untrained observers, did not make great witnesses. They failed to correctly answer observational questions posed by skeptics ("Did the Japanese doctors wear uniforms with breast pockets?" "How many prisoners in total were in the compound at that time?") They did not understand the Japanese they heard on their trips. Their rhetoric had the unfortunate habit of echoing that of their distrusted government. Their accounts contained minor discrepancies between one retelling and the next. Moreover, as they broke down on camera, their emotional testimonies simply added to the skeptics' charge that Wei was more interested in emotional catharsis rather than historical inquiry.

The criticisms outraged Wei. A great atrocity had occurred in Pingfang, and it was being willfully forgotten by the world through a cover-up. Because China's government was despised, the world was countenancing Japan's denial. Debates over whether the doctors vivisected all or only some of the victims without use of anesthesia, whether most of the victims were political prisoners, innocent villagers caught on raids, or common criminals, whether the use of babies and infants in experiments was known to Ishii, and so forth, seemed to him beside the point. That the questioners would focus on inconsequential details of the uniform of the Japanese doctors as a way to discredit his witnesses did not seem to him to deserve a response.

As he continued the trips to the past, other historians who saw the promise of the technology objected. History, as it turned out, was a limited resource, and each of Wei's trips took out a chunk of the past that could never be replaced. He was riddling the past with holes like Swiss cheese. Like early archaeologists who destroyed entire sites as they sought a few precious artifacts, thereby consigning valuable information about the past to oblivion, Wei was destroying the very history that he was trying to save.

When Wei jumped onto the tracks in front of a Boston subway train last Friday, he was undoubtedly haunted by the past. Perhaps he was also despondent over the unintended boost his work had given to the forces of denial. Seeking to end controversy in history, he succeeded only in causing more of it. Seeking to give voice to the victims of a great injustice, he succeeded only in silencing some of them forever.

Akemi Kirino:

[Dr. Kirino speaks to us from in front of Evan Wei's grave. In the bright May sunlight of New England, the dark shadows beneath her eyes make her seem older, more frail.]

I've kept only one secret from Evan. Well, actually two.

The first is my grandfather. He died before Evan and I met. I never took Evan to visit his grave, which is in California. I just told him that it wasn't something I wanted to share with him, and I never told Evan his name.

The second is a trip I took to the past, the only one I've ever taken personally. We were in Pingfang at the time, and I went to July 9, 1941. I knew the layout of the place pretty well from the descriptions and the maps, and I avoided the prison cells and the laboratories. I went to the building that housed the command center.

I looked around until I found the office for the Director of Pathology Studies. The Director was inside. He was a very handsome man: tall, slim, and he held his back very straight. He was writing a letter. I knew he was 32, which was the same age as mine at that time.

I looked over his shoulder at the letter he was writing. He had beautiful calligraphy.

I have now finally settled into my work routine, and things are going well. Manchukuo is a very beautiful place. The sorghum fields spread out as far as the eye can see, like an ocean. The street vendors here make wonderful tofu from fresh soybeans, which smells delicious. Not quite as good as the Japanese tofu, but very good nonetheless.

You will like Harbin. Now that the Russians are gone, the streets of Harbin are a harmonious patchwork of the five races: the Chinese, Manchus, Mongolians, and Koreans bow as our beloved Japanese soldiers and colonists pass by, grateful for the liberation and wealth we have brought to this beautiful land. It has taken a decade to pacify this place and eliminate the Communist bandits, who are but an occasional and minor nuisance now. Most of the Chinese are very docile and safe.

But all that I really can think about these days when I am not working are you and Naoko. It is for her sake that you and I are apart. It is for her sake and the sake of her generation that we make our sacrifices. I am sad that I will miss her first birthday, but it gladdens my heart to see the Greater East Asia Co-Prosperity Sphere blossom in this remote but rich hinterland. Here, you truly feel that our Japan is the light of Asia, her salvation.

Take heart, my dear, and smile. All our sacrifices today will mean that one day, Naoko and her children will see Asia take its rightful place in the world, freed from the yoke of the European killers and robbers who now trample over her and desecrate her beauty. We will celebrate together when we finally chase the British out of Hong Kong and Singapore.

> *Red sea of sorghum*
> *Fragrant bowls of crushed soybeans*
> *I see only you*
> *And her, our treasure*
> *Now, if only you were here.*

This was not the first time I had read this letter. I had seen it once before, as a little girl. It was one of my mother's treasured possessions, and I remember asking her to explain all the faded characters to me.

"He was very proud of his literary learning," my mother had said. "He always closed his letters with a *tanka*."

By then Grandfather was well into his long slide into dementia. Often he would confuse me with my mother and call me by her name. He would also teach me how to make origami animals. His fingers were very dextrous— the legacy of being a good surgeon.

I watched my grandfather finish his letter and fold it. I followed him out of the office to his lab. He was getting ready for an experiment, his notebook and instruments laid out neatly along the workbench.

He called to one of the medical assistants. He asked the assistant to bring him something for the experiment. The assistants returned about ten minutes later, holding a bloody mess on a tray, like a dish of steaming tofu. It was a human brain, still warm from the body from which it was taken that I could see the heat rising from it.

"Very good," my grandfather nodded. "Very fresh. This will do."

Akemi Kirino:

There have been times when I wished Evan weren't Chinese, just as there have been times when I wished I weren't Japanese. But these are moments of passing weakness. I don't mean them. We are born into strong currents of history, and it is our lot to swim or sink, not to complain about our luck.

Ever since I became an American, people have told me that America is about leaving your past behind. I've never understood that. You can no more leave behind your past than you can leave behind your skin.

The compulsion to delve into the past, to speak for the dead, to recover their stories: that's part of who Evan was, and why I loved him. Just the same, my grandfather is part of who I am, and what he did, he did in the name of my mother and me and my children. I am responsible for his sins, in the same way that I take pride in inheriting the tradition of a great people, a people who, in my grandfather's time, committed great evil.

In an extraordinary time, he faced extraordinary choices, and maybe some would say this means that we cannot judge him. But how can we really judge anyone except in the most extraordinary of circumstances? It's easy to be civilized and display a patina of orderliness in calm times, but your true character only emerges in darkness and under great pressure: is it a diamond or merely a lump of the blackest coal?

Yet, my grandfather was not a monster. He was simply a man of ordinary moral courage whose capacity for great evil was revealed to his and my lasting shame. Labeling someone a monster implies that he is from another world, one which has nothing to do with us. It cuts off the bonds of affection and fear, assures us of our own superiority, but there's nothing learned, nothing gained. It's simple, but it's cowardly. I know now that only by empathizing with a man like my grandfather can we understand the depth of the suffering he caused. There are no monsters. The monster is us.

Why didn't I tell Evan about my grandfather? I don't know. I suppose I was a coward. I was afraid that he might feel that something in me would be tainted, a corruption of blood. Because I could not then find a way to empathize with my grandfather, I was afraid that Evan could not empathize with me. I kept my grandfather's story to myself, and so I locked away a part of myself from my husband. There were times when I thought I would go to the grave with my secret, and so erase forever my grandfather's story.

I regret it, now that Evan is dead. He deserved to know his wife whole, complete, and I should have trusted him rather than silenced my grandfather's story, which is also my story. Evan died believing that by unearthing more stories, he caused people to doubt their truth. But he was wrong. The truth is not delicate and it does not suffer from denial—the truth only dies when true stories are untold.

This urge to speak, to tell the story, I share with the aging and dying former members of Unit 731, with the descendants of the victims, with all the untold horrors of history. The silence of the victims of the past imposes a duty on the present to recover their voices, and we are most free when we willingly take up that duty.

[Dr. Kirino's voice comes to us off-camera, as the camera pans to the star-studded sky.]

It has been a decade since Evan's death, and the Comprehensive Time Travel Moratorium remains in place. We still do not know quite what to do with a past that is transparently accessible, a past that will not be silenced or forgotten. For now, we hesitate.

Evan died thinking that he had sacrificed the memory of the Unit 731 victims and permanently erased the traces that their truth left in our world, all for nought, but he was wrong. He was forgetting that even with the Bohm-Kirino particles gone, the actual photons forming the images of those moments of unbearable suffering and quiet heroism are still out there, traveling as a sphere of light into the void of space.

Look up at the stars, and we are bombarded by light generated on the day the last victim at Pingfang died, the day the last train arrived at Auschwitz, the day the last Cherokee walked out of Georgia. And we know that the inhabitants of those distant worlds, if they are watching, will see those moments, in time, as they stream from here to there at the speed of light. It is not possible to capture all of those photons, to erase all of those images. They are our permanent record, the testimony of our existence, the story that we tell the future. Every moment, as we walk on this earth, we are watched and judged by the eyes of the universe.

For far too long, historians, and all of us, have acted as exploiters of the dead. But the past is not dead. It is with us. Everywhere we walk, we are bombarded by fields of Bohm-Kirino particles that will let us see the past like looking through a window. The agony of the dead is with us, and we hear their screams and walk among their ghosts. We cannot avert our eyes or plug up our ears. We must bear witness and speak for those who cannot speak. We have only one chance to get it right.

ᛄ

THE CARPET BEDS OF SUTRO PARK
〄
Kage Baker

I had been watching her for years.

Her mother used to bring her, when she was a child. Thin irritable woman dragging her offspring by the hand. "Kristy *Ann*! For God's sake, come *on*!" The mother would stop to light a cigarette or chat with a neighbor encountered on the paths, and the little girl would sidle away to stare at the old well house, or pet the stone lions.

Later she came alone, a tall adolescent with a sketchpad under her arm. She'd spend hours wandering under the big cypress trees, or leaning on the battlements where the statues used to be, staring out to sea. Her sweater was thin. She'd shiver in the fog.

I remember when the statues used to be there. Spring and Winter and Prometheus and all the rest of them, and Sutro's house that rose behind them on the parapet. I sat here then and I could see his observatory tower lifting above the trees. Turning my head I could see the spire of the Flower Conservatory. All gone now. Doesn't matter. I recorded them. As I record everything. My memory goes back a long way . . .

I remember my parents fighting. He wanted to go off to the gold fields. She screamed at him to go, then. He left, swearing. I think she must have died not long after. I remember being a little older and playing among the deserted ships, where they sat abandoned on the waterfront by crews who had gone hunting for gold. Sometimes people fed me. A lady noticed that I was alone and invited me to come live with her.

She took me into her house and there were strange things in it, things that shouldn't have been there in 1851: boxes that spoke and flameless lamps. She told me she was from the future. Her job was saving things from Time. She said she was immortal, and asked me if I'd like to be immortal too. I said I guessed I would.

I was taken to a hospital and they did a lot of surgery on me to make me like them. Had it worked, I'd have been an immortal genius.

The immortal part worked but the Cognitive Enhancement Procedure was a disaster. I woke up and couldn't talk to anyone, was frightened to death of people talking to me, because I could see all possible outcomes to any conversation and couldn't process any of them and it was too much, too much. I had to avoid looking into their eyes. I focused on anything else to calm myself: books, music, pictures.

My new guardians were very disappointed. They put me through years of therapy, without results. They spoke over my head.

What the fuck do we do with him now? He can't function as an operative. Should we put him in storage?

No; the Company spent too much money on him.

Gentlemen, please; Ezra's intelligent, he can hear you, you know, he understands—

You could always send him out as a camera. Let him wander around recording the city. There'll be a lot of demand for historic images after 2125.

He could do that! My therapist sounded eager. *Give him a structured schedule, exact routes to take, a case officer willing to work with his limitations—*

So I was put to work. I crossed and recrossed the city with open eyes, watching everything. I was a bee collecting the pollen of my time, bringing it back to be stored away as future honey. The sounds and images went straight from my sensory receptors to a receiver at Company HQ. I had a room in the basement at the Company HQ, to which I came back every night. I had Gleason, my case officer. I had my routes. I had my rules.

I must never allow myself to look like a street vagrant. I must wash myself and wear clean clothing daily. I must never draw attention to myself in any way.

If approached by a mortal, I was to Avoid.

If I could not avoid, Evaluate: was the mortal a policeman?

If so I was to Present him with my card. In the early days the card said I was a deaf mute, and any questions should be directed to my keeper, Dr. Gleason, residing on Kearney Street. In later years the card said I was a mentally disabled person under the care of the Gleason Sanatorium on Chestnut Street.

The one I carry now says I have an autiform disorder and directs the concerned reader to the Gleason Outpatient Clinic on Geary.

For the first sixty years I used to get sent out with an Augmented Equine Companion. I liked that. Norton was a big bay gelding, Edwin was a dapple gray and Andy was a palomino. They weren't immortal—the Company never made animals immortal—but they had human intelligence, and nobody ever bothered me when I was perched up on an impressive-looking steed. I liked animals; they were aware of details and pattern changes in the same way I was. They took care of remembering my routes. They could transmit cues to me.

We're approaching three females. Tip your hat.

Don't dismount here. We're going up to get footage of Nob Hill.

Hold on. I'm going to kick this dog.

Ezra, the fog's coming in. We won't be able to see Fort Point from here today. I'll take you back to HQ.

I was riding Edwin the first time I saw Sutro Park. That was in 1885, when it had just been opened to the public. He took me up over the hills through the sand dunes, far out of the city, toward Cliff House. The park had been built on the bluff high above.

I recorded it all, brand new: the many statues and flower urns gleaming white, the green lawns carefully tended, the neat paths and gracious Palm Avenue straight and well-kept. There was a beautiful decorative gate then, arching above the main entrance where the stone lions sit. The Conservatory, with its inlaid tile floor, housed exotic plants. The fountains jetted. The little millionaire Sutro ambled through, looking like the Monopoly man in his high silk hat, nodding to visitors and pointing out especially nice sights with his walking stick.

He was proudest of the carpet beds, the elaborate living tapestries of flowers along Palm Avenue. It took a boarding-house full of gardeners to manicure them, keeping the patterns perfect. Parterres like brocade, swag and wreath designs, a lyre, floral Grecian urns. Clipped boxwood edging, blue-green aloes and silver sempervivum; red and pink petunias, marigolds, pansies, alyssum in violet and white, blue lobelia. The colors sang out so bright they almost hurt my eyes.

They were an unnatural miracle, as lovely as the far more unnatural and miraculous phenomenon responsible for them: that a rich man should open his private garden to the public.

The mortals didn't appreciate it. They never do.

The years passed. The little millionaire built other gifts for San Francisco, his immense public baths and towering Cliff House. The little millionaire died and faded from memory, though not mine.

The Great Earthquake barely affected Sutro Park, isolated as it was
beyond the sand dunes; a few statues toppled from their plinths, but the
flowers still sang at the sky for a while. Sutro's Cliff House went up in smoke.
After automobiles came, horses vanished from the streets. I had to walk
everywhere now by myself.

So I watched Kristy Ann and I don't think she ever saw me once, over the
years, though I was always on that same bench. But I watched the little girl
discovering the remnant of the Conservatory's tiled floor, watched her get
down on her hands and knees and dig furtively, hoping to uncover more of
the lost city before her mother could call her away.

I watched the older Kristy Ann bringing her boyfriends there, the tall
one with red hair and then the black one with dreadlocks. There were furtive
kisses in amongst the trees and, at least once, furtive sex. There were long
afternoons while they grew bored watching her paint the cypress trees. At
last she came alone, and there were no more boys after that.

She walked there every afternoon, after work I suppose. She must
have lived nearby. Weekends she came with her paints and did endless
impressions of the view from the empty battlements, or the statue of Diana
that had survived, back among the trees. Once or twice I wandered past
her to look at her canvases. I wouldn't have said she had talent, but she had
passion.

I didn't like the twentieth century, but it finally went away. Everything went
into my eyes: the Pan Pacific Exhibition, Dashiell Hammett lurching out of
John's Grill, the building of the Golden Gate Bridge. Soldiers and sailors.
Sutro's Baths destroyed. Mortals in bright rags, their bare feet dirty, carrying
guitars. Workmen digging a pit to lay the foundations of the Transamerica
Building and finding the old buried waterfront, the abandoned ships of my
mortal childhood still down there in the mud. The Embarcadero Freeway
rising, and falling; the Marina District burning, and coming back with
fresh white paint.

My costume changed to fit the times. Now and again I caught a glimpse
of myself, impartial observer, in a shop window reflection. I was hard to
recognize, though I saw the same blank and eternally smooth face every
time under the sideburns, or the mustache, or the glasses.

The new world was loud and hard. It didn't matter. I had all the literature
and music of past ages to give me human contact, if secondhand through

Dickens or Austen. And I had kept copies of the times I'd liked, out of what I sent into the Company storage banks. I could close my eyes at night and replay the old city as I'd known it, in holo.

Everything time had taken away was still there, in my city. Sutro was still there, in his silk hat. I could walk the paths of his park beside him, as I'd never done in his time, and imagine a conversation, though of course I'd never spoken to him or anyone. I didn't want to tell him about his house being torn down, or his park being "reduced" as the San Francisco Park Department put it, for easier maintenance, the Conservatory gone, the statues almost all gone, the carpet beds mown over.

Kristy Ann in her twenties became grim and intense, a thin girl who dressed carelessly. Sometimes she brought books of photographs to the park with her and stalked along the paths, holding up the old images to compare them with the bare modern reality. One day she came with a crowd of young mortals from her college class, and talked knowledgeably about the park. The term *urban archaeology* was used a number of times.

Now, when she painted the park, she worked with the old photographs beside her, imposing the light and colors of the present day on representations of the past. I knew what she was doing. I'd done it myself, hadn't I?

Kristy Ann in her thirties grew thinner, seldom smiled. She took to patrolling the park for trash, muttering savagely to herself as she picked up empty pop cans or discarded snack wrappers.

She came once to the park with two other women and a news crew from KQED. They were filmed in front of the statue of Diana, talking about a Park Preservation Society they'd founded. There was talk of budget cuts. A petition. One of the cameramen made a joke about the statue and I could see the rage flaring in Kristy Ann's eyes. She began to rant about the importance of restoring Sutro Park, replacing the statues, replanting the parterres.

Her two companions exchanged glances and tactfully cut her off, changing the focus of the interview to the increasing deterioration of Golden Gate Park and the need for native, drought-resistant plantings.

A year later a big smiling man with a microphone did a segment of his California history series there in the park, and Kristy Ann was on hand to be interviewed as "a local historian." She took his arm and pulled him to the bare slopes where the carpet beds had bloomed. She showed him her photocopies of the old photographs, which were growing tattered nowadays.

She talked and talked and talked about how the beds must be restored.

The big man was too polite to interrupt her, but I could see the cameraman and assistant director rolling their eyes. Finally the assistant director led her away by the arm and gave her a handful of twenty-dollar bills.

A couple of months after that she stopped coming to the park. Kristy Ann was gone, for most of a year. I wondered if she'd gone mad or gone to jail or one of those other places mortals go.

The Company had less and less for me to film, as the years rolled on. Evidently archivists weren't as interested in twenty-first century San Francisco. I was sent out for newsworthy events, but more and more of my time was my own. Gleason structured it for me, or I couldn't have managed.

I had a list: Shower, Breakfast, Walk, Park Time, Lunch at Park, Park Time, Walk, Dinner, Shower, Bed. I needed patterns. Gleason said I was like a train, where other people were like automobiles: they went anywhere, I had iron wheels and had to stay on my iron track. But a train carries more than an automobile. I carried the freight of Time. I carried the fiery colors of Sutro's design, the patterns of his flowerbeds.

I had a route worked out, from HQ to Sutro Park, and I carried my lunch in a paper bag, the same meal every day: wheat bread and butter sandwich, apple, bottle of water. I didn't want anything else. I was safe on my track. I was happy.

I sat in the park and watched the fog drifting through the cypress trees. I knew, after so many years, how to be invisible: never bothered anyone, never did anything to make a mortal notice I was there. There weren't many mortals, anyway. People only cut through Sutro Park on their way from 48th Avenue to Point Lobos Road. They didn't promenade there anymore.

When Kristy Ann wandered back into the park, she was rail-thin and all her hair was gone. She wore shapeless, stained sweat clothes and a stocking cap pulled down over her bare skull. She found a bench, quite near mine, that got the sunlight most of the day except when the fog rolled in, and she stayed there. All day, every day. Most days she had a cup of coffee with her, and always a laptop.

I found I could tune into her broadband connection, as she worked. She spent most of her day posting on various forums for San Francisco historical societies. I followed the forum discussions with interest.

At first she'd be welcomed into the groups, and complimented on her erudition. Gradually her humorlessness, her obsession came to the fore.

Flame wars erupted when forum members wanted to discuss something other than the restoration of Sutro Park. She was always asked to leave, in the end, when she didn't storm out of her own accord. Once or twice she re-registered under a different name, but almost immediately was recognized. The forum exchanges degenerated into mutual name-calling.

After that Kristy Ann spent her days blogging, on a site decorated with gifs of her old photographs and scans of her lovingly colored recreations of the park. Her entries were mostly bitter reflections on her failed efforts to restore the carpet beds. They became less and less coherent. A couple of months later, she disappeared again. I assumed her cancer had metastasized.

Ezra? Gleason was uncomfortable about something. *Ezra, we need to talk. The Company has been going over its profit and loss statements. They're spending more on your upkeep than they're making from your recordings. It's been suggested that we re-train you. Or relocate you. This may be difficult, Ezra . . .*

I don't think anyone but me would have recognized Kristy Ann, when she came creeping back. She moved like an old woman. She seemed to have shrunken away. There was no sign of the laptop; I don't think she was strong enough to carry it, now. She had a purse with her meds in it. She had a water bottle.

She found her bench in the sunlight and sat there, looking around her with bewildered eyes, all their anger gone.

Her electromagnetic field, the drifting halo of electricity that all mortals generate around their bodies, had begun to fluctuate around Kristy Ann. It happens, when mortals begin to die.

I wondered if I could do it.

I did; I got to my feet and walked toward her, cautious, keeping my eyes on the ground. I came to her bench and sat down beside her. My heart was pounding. I risked a glance sideways. She was looking at me with utter apathy. She wouldn't have cared if I'd grabbed her purse, slapped her, or pulled off her clothes. Her eyes tracked off to my left.

I turned and followed her stare. She was looking at an old stone basin on its pedestal, the last of Sutro's fountains, its sculpted waterworks long since gone.

I edged closer. I reached into her electromagnetic field. I touched her hand—she was cold as ice—and tuned into the electrical patterns of her brain, as I had tuned into her broadband signal. I downloaded her.

I didn't hurt her. She saw the fountain restored, wirework shooting up to outline its second tier, its dolphins, its cherubs. Then it was solid and real. Clear water jetted upward into a lost sky. The green lawn spread out, flawless.

White statues rose from the earth: the Dancing Girls. The Dreaming Satyr. Venus de Milo. Antinous. The Boy with Bird. Hebe. The Griffin. All the Gilded Age's conception of what was artistic, copied and brought out to the western edge of the world to refine and educate its uncultured masses.

Sutro's house lifted into its place again; the man himself rose up through the path and stood, in his black silk hat. Brass glinted on the bandstand. Music began to play. Before us the Conservatory took shape, for a moment a skeletal frame and then a paned bubble of glass flashing in the sun. Orchids and aspidistras steamed its windows from inside. And below it—

The colors exploded into being like fireworks, red and blue and gold, variegated tropical greens, purples, the carpet beds in all their precise glory. Managed Nature, in the nineteenth century's confident belief that unruly Nature *should* be managed to pleasing aesthetic effect. The intricate floral designs glowed, surreal grace notes, defying entropy and chaos.

She was struggling to stand, gasping, staring at it. The tether broke and she was pulled into the image. I gave her back her hair, with a straw hat for the sun. I gave her a long flounced skirt that swept the gravel, a suitable blouse and jacket. I gave her buttoned boots and a parasol. I gave her the body of young Kristy Ann, who had wandered alone with her sketchbook. Now she was part of the picture, not the dead thing cooling on the bench beside me.

She walked forward, her eyes fixed on the carpet beds, her lips parted. Color came into her face.

The fog came in, grayed the twenty-first century world. I heard crunching footsteps. A pair of women were coming up the path from the Point Lobos Road entrance. I got to my feet. I approached them, head turned aside, and managed to point at what was sitting on the park bench. One of the women said something horrified in Russian, the other put her hands to her white face and screamed.

They drew back from me. I pulled out my card and thrust it at them. Finally, suspicious, one of them took it and spelled out its message. I stared at my shoes while she put two and two together, and then I heard her pulling out her cell phone and calling the police.

I wasn't arrested. Once the police were able to look at the body and see its emaciation, the hospital band on its wrist, once they read the labels on the pill bottles in the purse, they knew. They called the morgue and then they called Gleason. He came and talked to them a while. Then he took me back to HQ.

They don't send me out much, anymore. I sleep a lot, in the place where the Company keeps me. I don't mind; at least I don't have to deal with strangers, and after all I have my memory.

I ride there on Edwin and the weather is always fine, the fog far out on the edge of the blue sea. The green park is always full of people, the poor of San Francisco out for a day of fresh air, sunlight, and as much beauty as a rich man's money can provide for them. Pipefitters and laundresses sit together on the benches. Children run and scream happily. Courting couples sit on little iron folding chairs and listen to the band play favorites by Sir Arthur Sullivan. The intricate patterns blaze.

She will always be there, sometimes chatting with Mr. Sutro. Sometimes bustling from one carpet bed to the next with a watering can or gardening tools. I tip my hat and say the only words I can say, have ever said: "Good morning, Christiane."

She smiles and nods. Perhaps she recognizes me, in a vague kind of way. But I never dismount to attempt conversation, and in any case she is too busy, weeding, watering, clipping to maintain the place she loves.

₪

MATING HABITS OF THE LATE CRETACEOUS
₪
Dale Bailey

They'd come to the Cretaceous to save their marriage.

"Why not the Paleogene?" said Peter, who had resolutely refused to look at any of the material Gwyneth had sent him. "Or the Little Ice Age for that matter? Some place without carnivores."

"There are only two resorts," Gwyneth said, waving a brochure at him. "Jurassic and Cretaceous. People want to see dinosaurs."

She wanted to see dinosaurs.

"And I'm afraid travel to inhabited eras is no longer permitted, Mr. Braunmiller," the agent put in. "Ever since the Eckels Incident. So the Little Ice Age is out."

"Besides," Gwyneth said. "I wouldn't mind a few carnivores."

Peter sighed.

Cool air misted down from unseen vents. The agent's desk, a curved wedge of gleaming mahogany, floated in emptiness. Surround screens immersed them in sensory-enhanced three-dimensional renderings from the available eras. One moment the hot siroccos of some time-vanished desert stung their skin. The next, the damp, shrieking hothouse of a Jurassic jungle sprang sweat from their brows.

"Why not a sim?" Peter asked.

"I've had enough of simulations, Peter," Gwyneth said, thinking of the expense. Over Peter's protests, she had mortgaged the house they'd bought three years ago, cashed in retirement and savings accounts, taken on loans they couldn't afford.

All for this.

"You're certain, then?" the agent asked.

Peter opened his mouth and closed it again.

Twilight waters washed the barren shingles of some ancient inland sea.

"We're certain," Gwyneth said.

Tablets materialized in front of them.

"Just a few releases to sign," the agent said. "Warranties, indemnities against personal injury—"

"I thought the yoke—" Peter said, and a fresh draft of whispering air blew down upon them.

"The lawyers insist," the agent said, smiling.

An hour later, forms signed in triplicate, notarized, and filed away, the agent ushered them into an airlock. When they stripped, Gwyneth could feel Peter's gaze upon her; she didn't so much as glance at him, though he was lean and fit, as well muscled at thirty-five as he had been at their wedding seven years before. Stinging jets of anti-bacterial spray enveloped them. Industrial-strength compressors blasted them dry. They dressed in tailored, featherweight safari gear, and cycled through another airlock, their luggage hovering behind them. The adjoining chamber was bereft of luxury—no surround screens or polished mahogany, no calming mists of murmuring air. Their boots rang on polished concrete. Fluorescent globes floated high in the latticed spaces above them, leaching color from their faces. White-clad technicians looked up from their tablets as the airlock dilated. Behind them crackled the time machine, more impressive than Gwyneth had thought it would be, a miracle of sizzling yellow-green energy, the raw stuff of creation itself, harnessed by human ingenuity and bound screaming into colossal spider arms of curving steel and iron.

The technicians took charge of them. The hiss of hypodermic injections followed, then diaphanous bands of black that melted closed around their wrists like wax. The technician touched Gwyneth's; far down in its polished depths a series of lights—orange and red and green—flashed once and was gone.

Her yoke.

The other technician, finishing up with Peter, smiled. "Your guide will meet you on the other side," he said. "Ready to go?"

The time machine spat fire, throwing off scorching arcs of green and yellow.

They stepped into the light.

And were gone.

A sheet of green flame blinded them. Time blurred—a day, a week, a year, then more, the centuries peeling away like leaves, so that Gwyneth, who was barely thirty-four, felt young and alive as she had not felt in this last year. The time machine stank of history, of the sun beating down upon the tiered pyramids of new-built Aztec temples; of wheat flourishing for the first time under the hands of men; and further yet, of a dark age where shrewd monkeys huddled in terror around their lightning-struck fires. But Eckels had closed all that to them, and just as well, Gwyneth supposed, for he had bestowed upon them in its lieu the immense panorama of geologic time. And how she longed to step out of her life into a world fresh made, where great Triceratops lifted his three-pronged head and the sky-flung demon of the age, titanic Quetzalcoatlus, still spread his leathery wings; where the greatest of the thunder lizards, the tyrant king of all that he surveyed, Tyrannosaurus Rex, yet bestrode the terrified earth. Where, most of all, none of it had happened yet, and she could pretend that maybe it never would.

Then there was an enormous jolt, and Gwyneth cried aloud in terror or delight. Peter reached for her hand, and a lean, leathery man whose smile never reached his eyes stood before them.

They were there.

It was a resort, all right—a rugged dream carved out of the primeval wilderness. Below and to the west, a long savannah sloped away to a distant glimmer of sea. Above and to the east a jagged mountain range knifed through the earth's crust, so that morning came late there and afternoons lingered into a blue twilight that seemed to stretch out forever. To the south and to the north, encircling arms of forest fell in ranks toward the distant plain. And in the heart of it all, like a precious stone set in swirls of green and brown, gleamed Cretacia, a maze of sandy paths and hidden glades where clear fountains tumbled and stone benches grew black with lichen. Private cabanas perched on tiers cut into the wooded ridges, and jeweled swimming pools glinted among the trees. Below the whitewashed sprawl of the hotel itself wound a quaint commercial district. Restaurants staffed by murmuring servers crowded up against narrow shops that sold books— actual books—and bath salts and summer dresses at such exorbitant rates that Gwyneth laughed in disbelief.

Yet her heart quickened in delight when the tall man with fine crinkles around his eyes—Wilson, Robert Wilson, he'd introduced himself— thumbed open their door for the first time and she saw the sheer decadence of the place: a bower of eggshell white and blue with a bed veiled in gauzy shadow, a vase of tropical flowers, and a south-facing floor-to-ceiling window (no sim screen, but glass, thick, reinforced glass) that gave upon a forested ravine, where something small and dappled scurried through the shadows, and if you stood on tip-toe and craned your neck, you could catch a glimpse of diamonds glittering upon the sea.

"I'll leave you to unpack," Wilson said, and turning from the window Gwyneth saw him—really saw him—for the first time: a hard, sun-baked man with sandy hair and an unhandsome face like a promontory of granite. His khakis were worn and stained, his boots scuffed. For a moment she was ashamed of their own gear, so new that it rustled when they walked.

"The concierge can take care of all your needs here on the grounds," Wilson said. "If you want to go outside—when you want to go outside—I'll be your guide."

Turning from the window, Peter extended his hand. Gwyneth saw to her horror the folded fifty inside it.

Wilson stiffened. "No thank you, sir. That's very kind of you."

The door closed softly behind him.

"Peter," Gywneth said. "You've insulted him now. He's a wilderness guide, not a bellhop."

"Just as well, I suppose. God knows we can't afford to spend another dime." Then:

"Well, how was I to know?"

"Perhaps if you'd bothered to read some of the material I sent you—"

"This was your idea, not mine, Gwyneth."

"But it's *our* vacation," she snapped. "And you ought to remember why and start acting like it."

She crossed her arms and turned back to the windows.

It was still and peaceful out there.

A moment passed. They waited to see if what had been so long unsaid would break through the stillness. She knew that it would sometime soon, or that it had better. The wound had festered. It needed to be lanced and drained.

Peter came up and stood behind her, so close she could feel his breath, warm upon the back of her neck. "I'm sorry." His hand came up to her lower back.

Did she flinch? And did he feel it?

She wanted this to work, yet her body betrayed her.

"I'm sorry," he said.

When he leaned in to kiss her, she turned her face away.

■   ■   ■

They breakfasted on a long shaded terrace overlooking a pool. Fans stirred the air overhead. Just outside the compound, bright tiny dinosaurs strutted, pecking at the earth like chickens. Far below, beyond a stunning vista of tree-studded cliffs, huge sauropods feasted on towering groves of conifer. Something else had spooked a dinosaur herd. A cloud of dust obscured them, but their cries—a mournful lowing like the faraway lament of a foghorn—rose up to the terrace. Gwyneth wondered what had set them running.

"The coffee is fine," Peter said, the meal done.

A server took their plates. He came back and used a long blade to scrape the linen cloth of crumbs.

Gwyneth took her coffee black; to please Peter she took a sip. "It is fine," she said. Insipid banalities—that was all they could find to say. They'd forgotten the language of their own marriage, so they skated along the surface, stripping away any hint of ugliness as efficiently as the hotel staff spirited away a stained pillow. Last night, in a darkness rich with the strange music of the Cretaceous woods, he had reached out to touch her, and her body had gone rigid of its own accord. They had lain like that, so stiff and silent and distant that they might have been on separate continents, lying wakeful under foreign skies. Now, when he reached out to rest a hand upon her own where it lay brown against the white tablecloth, her fingers twitched and were still.

She felt tears well up, and choked them back, determined not to cry.

She said, "Peter—"

Then Robert Wilson was leaning over them, his own hand closing about the back rail of her chair and brushing her shoulder blade. He smelled of earth and dusty leather and the dry plain below. Gwyneth looked up through a sheen of unshed tears. When he returned her smile, his eyes remained as watchful and cold as marbles under the bony ridge of his brow. They were the color of agates, washed out and narrow from squinting across the blazing savannah. Something quickened inside her. She leaned forward and he wasn't touching her shoulder anymore.

"Something spooked down there," she said.

"Hydrosaurs," he said. "Bloody cows startle easily enough. Could have been anything. A pack of raptors, maybe, but mostly they lie up under the trees until dusk."

"But the big ones—" Peter said.

"The Alamosaurs. Go right on munching at the treetops, don't they? Not much spooks an Alamosaur. A T-Rex maybe. Too big to worry about the raptors, and tails like whips. It's an ecosystem, right? Like the African veldt. An elephant doesn't worry much about a lion, does he?"

"Will we see a T-Rex?" Gwyneth asked.

"You'll hear them cough at night if one's around," he said. "Last night was silent as a grave. Snorkeling today. Plesiosaurs, maybe a Kronosaur— T-Rex of the sea—if we're lucky."

"Sounds dangerous," Gwyneth said.

"Feels dangerous," Wilson said. "Safe as houses, though. Your yoke will see a Kronosaur turning aggressive before we even know it's there," he added, and for the first time Gwyneth noticed that his wrist was bare.

"You're not yoked."

He laughed. "I'm too ornery too eat."

"Let's take a pass," Peter said. "I think we'll spend the day settling in."

"Your call. You'll have plenty of time."

Wilson nodded and strode away into the shadows.

They sat in silence for a moment, listening to the subdued babble of conversation around them.

"I think I'd like to be consulted about any future decisions, if you don't mind," she said quietly.

"Gwyneth—"

"It's *my* vacation, right?"

"He's talking about swimming with dinosaurs, for Christ's sake."

"Well, what did you think we were here to do, Peter?"

"To—"

"To what?"

"To try and fix things." He shook his head. "To try and fix things, that's all."

"Well, we're not going to fix them sitting on the terrace drinking coffee, are we? We might as well get our money's worth." She set her cup down and stood. "I think I'll go change into something more appropriate for settling in."

Gwyneth was halfway across the room, weaving her way between the tables, when someone reached out and touched her elbow. A woman— blonde and handsome, with a strong jaw line and narrow lips—smiled up at her. Her companion looked up from his breakfast.

"I'm Angela," she said. "And this mannerless brute"—

—said brute swiped his face with a linen napkin—

—"is Frank—"

"Stafford," the brute said, clambering to his feet. "Frank Stafford. But just Frank'll do." He took Gwyneth's fingertips, and bowed slightly, lifting his eyebrows. Crockery rattled.

"Careful, Frank—" the woman—Angela—cried.

But by this time Peter had appeared at Gwyneth's shoulder, and the brute—he really was something of a brute, Gwyneth thought, barrel chested and broad shouldered as an ox—was reaching past her to shake Peter's hand.

"Just Frank," Peter said—Stafford acknowledged this tepid witticism with a deep belly laugh—"Peter Braunmiller."

"Here, have a sit." Stafford shoved a chair in their direction, and when they were seated over fresh cups of coffee, he said, "That guy, Wilson, he's your guide, too? What a piece of work, huh?"

"Fearless as a bandersnatch," Angela said. "We did a trail with him the other day, and got within twenty feet of this awful thing called an anklysaur—"

"Armored bastard. Club on its tail the size of a fucking Volkswagen. He started to swing that thing when he saw us, and I swear to God I felt the wind on my face, we were that close." Stafford laughed. "Felt my yoke give a good tug, I swear I did."

"Anyway," Angela said. "We overheard—really we weren't eavesdropping —that you weren't going on the excursion today, and since we aren't either—"

"Can't swim a lick," Stafford said. "Afraid of the water my whole life. Sink like a stone, and if I didn't a dinosaur'd eat me for sure."

"—we were hoping you might play tennis. Please say you do or we'll just sit on the terrace and drink Bloody Marys all morning."

"Terrible for the health, Bloody Marys."

"I suppose we could play tennis," Peter said, and then—was he mocking her? Gwyneth wondered—"You up for tennis, Gwen?"

And Gwyneth, thinking of the Kronosaur—the T-Rex of the seas— forced a smile. "Tennis it is," she said.

Gwyneth and Peter lost in straight sets.

The Staffords were formidable opponents. Peter, a finesse player who relied on superior endurance, couldn't handle Stafford's powerful serves. Angela's shots had a wicked backspin that Gwyneth never quite mastered.

"Luck, that's all," Stafford assured them, clapping Peter on the back, but as they headed back to the room to clean up, Peter whispered, "All the same to you, Gwen, I think I'd rather have gone snorkeling with the Karnosaurs."

"Kronosaurs," she said.

"Right. Except Frank Stafford is the damned carnivore," he said. "Seriously. I think my yoke must be malfunctioning. I was getting the life beat out of me, and it didn't so much as twitch."

Against her will, Gwyneth laughed. Peter flung an arm across her shoulder, and for a moment the effortless camaraderie of their first years together—that playful, irreverent sense of humor, the easy way their bodies seemed to fit together—came back to her. For a moment she even thought of Peter's hand upon her in the night, of how it might have been if she had turned to face him—

And then, of its own accord, her mind swerved away.

They showered and met the Staffords for lunch, where they learned that their tennis partner had been a subcontractor on the Museum of Post-Modern Art in D.C., among other things.

"Just a little piece of it," Stafford said, holding up pinched fingers. "The duct work. Keep people cool in all that heat."

"That's a lot of duct work," Peter said.

"You bet it is," Stafford said, and Gwyneth suddenly had a sense of just how much she and Peter had sacrificed for this trip—of how much she had forced him to sacrifice. Stafford could buy and sell them a hundred times over, and she had nearly impoverished them.

"Angela's idea, this trip," Stafford was saying. "I told her I'd already found my niche. A lot of money in duct bills." He dropped them a wink. "My little evolution joke," he said.

"His only joke," Angela said drily. And then: "What do you do, Peter?"

"I'm an assets manager."

"Gambling," Stafford said, thrusting his plate away. "Pushing money around, that's all that is. End of the day, I like to put my hands on something solid. Like to say, I did that."

Peter flinched, but if Stafford noticed, he didn't let on.

Afterward, the men strolled off in search of cigars, though Gwyneth had never known Peter to smoke a cigar in her life. The two women found themselves in a secluded bar overlooking the cliffs.

"Sorry about that last bit," Angela said over gin and tonics.

"Peter's too sensitive."

Gwyneth sipped her drink. She was beginning to feel the alcohol. The world had taken on a lush beauty. The edges of everything had sharpened. Each discrete bead of condensation glistened on her glass; every needle of the nearby conifers stood articulate against the azure sky. The full heat of the day had come on, and the plain below stretched empty toward the blue horizon. Gwyneth supposed the raptors must be lying up under the trees, and that made her think of Robert Wilson. She wondered if he had found his Kronosaurs, and if he was back from the sea yet.

"It's very quiet in the Cretaceous," Angela said. "There's something missing, I can't figure out what."

Gwyneth listened.

But for them, the bar was empty. The barman stood polishing glasses. The stillness was pervasive. "Birds," she said suddenly. "There were no birds"— and then, laughing, corrected herself. "There *are* no birds. Or hardly any. They haven't evolved yet. Birds are dinosaurs. Or dinosaurs are birds. Or will be. I remember reading that somewhere."

"You're very amusing, Gwyneth Braunmiller."

The barman came and freshened their drinks. When he was gone, Angela said, "What do you do?"

"I'm a technical writer. I mostly write instruction manuals," Gwyneth said. "Or rewrite them, anyway." She laughed. "You've probably read some of my stuff."

Angela absorbed this in silence.

"Do you have children?"

Gwyneth laughed ruefully.

"I'm awfully nosy," Angela said. "You needn't answer."

"No, I don't mind. It's just—" She broke off.

"You haven't reached an agreement on that issue."

"No, I guess we haven't."

The truth was they'd never really talked about it much. Neither of them felt strongly either way, she supposed. The problems were deeper than that, harder to pin down—the way minor disagreements had of settling into arguments and arguments into something worse, a cool distance, like planets orbiting different stars. And then, not wanting to be rude, she said, "What do you do, Angela?"

"I sit on charity boards. I spend Frank's money. You'd be surprised how taxing it can be—no pun intended." She raised her eyebrows and smiled.

"Children?"

"None. Frank has a grown son from a previous marriage. Musn't threaten the heir to the empire."

The alcohol made Gwyneth incautious. "And what brings you here?"

"Our twentieth anniversary."

She sipped her drink.

"I still remember the wedding. Predictions for longevity were dire." Angela laughed and touched Gwyneth's hand. "What a pleasure to have proven them wrong."

"To love," Gwyneth said, lifting her glass.

They were quiet then, listening to the birdless afternoon.

The next day they went hiking—fifteen of them, Wilson's entire excursion group. Despite the novelty of the towering conifers and angiosperms, a bleak melancholy fell over Gwyneth. The medication prescribed by her psychiatrist—"just to get you through this rough patch," she'd said—hadn't helped, nor had the trouble with Peter, the—what, exactly? The silence where there had been voices, the blind staring into the dark, their bodies separate and apart. And underneath that, turning its immense body in the fretful depths of sleep that finally claimed them, that unspoken sense of despair that eluded words. Malaise? Ennui? She didn't know. Day after day after day it had worsened, for months, for a year and more, until one listless afternoon, Gwyneth happened across a documentary on Time Safaris, Ltd. Not since college paleontology had she seen live footage of dinosaurs. A desire to see them for herself, to plant her feet on the soil of another age, had seized her. And something else, as well: the conviction that two weeks away from the world—*really* away from the world—might fix the broken things between them.

"Jesus, Gwyneth, do you want to break us?" Peter had asked when he'd seen the cost.

She didn't quite have the nerve to respond as she had wanted to: *We're already broken.*

Her foot slipped on an outcropping of stone, and she would have fallen but for Angela's steadying hand at her elbow. Gwyneth swiped perspiration from her eyes with the back of one hand.

"Drinks, darling. The moment we return," Angela whispered—quiet being a condition imposed upon them at the beginning of the excursion—and Gwyneth laughed, and said, "By all means, yes," feeling closer to this virtual stranger than her own husband of almost a decade.

That morning the two women had gravitated toward one another like old friends. They tramped side-by-side, midway in the group strung out along the trail like pearls. Their husbands forged along behind Wilson, who took the rocky path without effort, a canteen at his belt and a rifle slung across one shoulder. Late afternoon and the Cretaceous alive with sound, the hooting complaint of the striped, knee-high theropods that scattered into the underbrush before them, the steady hush of insects, the arboreal rustle of mammals the size of squirrels—"Our forbears," Wilson had said. "The meek shall inherit the earth."

From on high the alien shriek of some sky-borne pteranodon drifted down.

They stopped in a clearing of tall, flowering grass to search the thing out.

It was Stafford who spotted it, his arm out-stretched. They gathered around him to stare at the creature circling high above them in a sky of sun-shot blue.

"Quetzalcoatlus?" someone asked.

"Nothing so large, I should think." Wilson unclipped his binoculars. "Looks to have a wingspan of maybe fifteen feet, about half that of Queztalcoatlus. Could be a juvenile, I suppose, but it's hard to tell at this distance. Anyone want to see?"

The binoculars made the rounds. When her turn came, Gwyneth lifted them to her eyes, but she could never hold the image in frame long enough to get anything more than a glimpse of the creature, a fleeting impression of beak and bony crest, the vast leathery wings taut as a wind-blown kite.

They moved on then, deeper into the woods. The familiar smell of pine needles and dry loam enveloped her, the scent of unfamiliar flowers. Stafford had acquired the aura of a minor hero. Wilson had clapped him on the shoulder. "Sharp eyes," he'd said, and the big man seemed to have expanded still more under the praise. Despite his size, he moved through the woods with a confidence Peter lacked, sure-footed, a creature of the physical world, his bearish frame poised over his center of gravity.

The terrain grew more forgiving, dropping away into a broad vale. The pace slowed, as Wilson paused to point out the flowering angiosperms and broad-leaved deciduous trees that had only recently—geologically speaking—evolved to compete with the pervasive conifers. They paused for water. Wilson moved among them, spare and purposeful, no gesture wasted.

"Okay, then?" he said to Gwyneth.

"I'm fine."

He nodded, and moved on.

They got moving again fifteen minutes later.

Not long after that the woods thinned. Another glade opened ahead of them. Moted beams of sunlight slanted through the treetops, firing the bracken with a yellow-green glow. The boles of trees climbed the heavens in dark silhouette, dwarfing Wilson where he stood black against the green effulgence, the back of his hand upraised in universal semaphore. He waved the straggling line to either side. Something snorted, blew out breath in a long waning note. It called out—a kind of groan, long and deep-pitched, like a rusty nail being wrenched from an ancient board. Then it took a step. Weeds thrashed. Gwyneth slipped with Peter through the ferny undergrowth to the right.

The trees fell away and the glade unveiled itself.

Gwyneth gasped for the beauty of it, the shining clearing and the creatures that grazed there: majestic, ponderous beasts—three horned, twenty-five or thirty feet long, ten feet at the shoulder—cropping peacefully at the waist-high grass. Triceratops, Gwyneth thought, gazing in wonder at the massive bony frill that curved up behind their heads, flushed bright with pink and red. The breeze combing the grass smelled of the creatures in the glade, a scent of old leather and manure and fresh-mown grass.

She caught snatches of Wilson murmuring—

" . . . a bull, two cows—the smaller ones—and a yearling. See it?"

He broke off as the largest of the dinosaurs—the bull—swung its elongated head in their direction. It regarded them with a single beady eye. In three quarter profile, the beast was more impressive still, battle scarred and ancient, the horns above its eyes razor-sharp spears of bone, jutting out three feet or more. It lumbered toward them, a single step, then two and three—

"Steady, now," Wilson whispered. "Steady—"

—chuffed, and paused, as if assessing the danger they posed; a moment later, it lowered its beaked snout and began to tear at the weeds once again. This close Gwyneth could see parasites—insects maybe—crawling across its mottled green and brown hide. She was about to ask about them, when her eye caught a rustle in the tall grass—

The underbrush erupted, shrieking.

For a moment, Gwyneth didn't see them, they were so well camouflaged. Then she did, three, four—was it five, or more?—green- and yellow-striped raptors the size of men or larger, hurtling across the clearing from half a dozen woody blinds, so fast that the eye could barely track them. Three of them corralled the yearling and herded it toward the trees. More than half the pack—there were seven of them, she saw—no, eight—wheeled away to face the charge of the bull Triceratops. Just as it lowered its head to impale them, they gave ground, hurling themselves at the monster's unprotected haunches, their razor-clawed feet digging for purchase in its hide. The animal's belly split, spilling a bulge of glistening viscera—

Peter clutched at her, trying to drag her deeper under the trees. The bull Triceratops wheeled around, lunging at its tormentors. Its tail whipped the air, flinging a raptor screeching into the undergrowth, and somewhere at the edge of the clearing the yearling screamed and screamed and screamed, until, abruptly, it fell silent. Dear God, she could see the raptors tearing it limb from limb. Grass thrashed. Geysers of blood erupted. Her heart pounding, Gwyneth wrenched free of Peter's hand. She stepped into the clearing, she didn't know why. The yearling's companions, the bleeding bull among them, broke for the trees. As the remaining raptors swung around to their kill, they saw her—

—they *saw* her—

—and for a heartbeat—she felt a single nightmarish pulse at her temple— the moment hung in equipoise. Fathomless silence enveloped her. Then, shrieking, the nearest raptor hurtled toward her, its taloned feet clawing the earth. Gwyneth felt the tug of the yoke, like gravity seizing her as she careened through the loop of a roller coaster—

Then Robert Wilson stepped up beside her, leveling the rifle. The thing was almost upon them—the scene going watery around her as the yoke began to draw her home—when he pulled the trigger. There was a sound of thunder. The raptor's skull dissolved into a spray of blood and bone. Its body spun convulsing to the ground. The next moment her vision cleared.

The glade was silent and empty.

"Quickly, now," Wilson said, touching her shoulder. "They'll be back soon."

He spun her around and they retreated under the trees. The rest of the group awaited them there. She saw Peter, his long face pale with fury, and she reached out an entreating hand to him.

"Peter—" she said.

But he turned away.

Then Angela was there, catching an arm around her waist and cooing, "It's okay now, it's all over." And then, half-supporting her as they trudged homeward through the suddenly menacing woods: "We'll get a drink into you first thing," she whispered. "A drink is what it wants."

A drink, thought Gwyneth, with a mounting hilarity she did not recognize as her own. A drink would be just the thing.

Yes, a drink.

Maybe two, Gwyneth thought—definitely two, as it turned out, and she sensed a third one coming on. Fire pits threw up sparks and music swirled in the night air. She leaned against the railing, lifted her face to the breeze, sipped her martini. The gin smelled of pine trees, of the vast conifer forest, unsullied by human hands, that sprawled across the continent.

The scent triggered a flash of memory: the raptor hurling itself across the clearing at her, Wilson leveling the gun—

And here he was, speak of the devil.

Elbows on the railing, he leaned beside her. The party was in full swing now. Dancers twirled under muted lights. Wisps of conversation drifted through the air. She spied Peter, talking to Stafford by the buffet, and glanced away.

Wilson set her empty glass on the tray of a passing server and handed her a fresh martini. "Cheers," he said.

They touched glasses. She held the gin in her mouth, savoring it.

They turned their backs to the party. For a long time, they leaned on their elbows, staring out into the dark. Before them ran the long blue savannah.

"Something else, isn't it?" he said.

She gazed up at the sky, bereft of the old constellations. Or was it new? She laughed, and a small voice inside her said, *You must be careful. He'll think you're drunk.* Which she was. Why it should matter, she could not say.

"The stars look strange."

"The skies change in sixty-five million years. Or seventy."

"You don't know, then?"

"No one knows."

"But Eckels—"

"The recent past they're pretty good at. The further back you go—" He shrugged. "Slippage."

"And why is that, Mr. Wilson?"

"You're talking to the wrong man, Mrs.—"

"Gwyneth."

"—Braunmiller. You'd need a physicist to answer that."

"Yet you were waiting the moment we arrived."

"Once they have a focal point to lock in on—once some brave soul plants a flag, so to speak—then you're fine."

"But you don't know when that focal point is?"

"Never will. Rough calculations can pin it down some—we're toward the end of the era, we know that. But dinosaurs don't keep calendars, I'm afraid."

She could feel the alcohol buzzing through her veins. Her face was not unpleasantly numb.

"Dance?" he said.

"If you insist."

Leaving their drinks on a nearby table, they stepped on to the dance floor.

"I haven't thanked you for saving my life today."

"I didn't save your life."

"Didn't you?"

"Your yoke would have saved you if it came to that. You could feel it, couldn't you?"

"Like gravity moving through me. A roller coaster. That's what I thought."

Her mind replayed that snippet of memory once again—the raptor lunging at her, Wilson lifting the gun—

"Why did you wait so long to shoot?"

"Wouldn't do to miss, would it? We're not all yoked."

"You've been yoked before, Mr. Wilson?"

"Yes."

"And had to use it."

"Oh sure."

"What happened?"

"Female tyrannosaur cornered me in a ravine. They're the bad ones. The females."

He raised his eyebrows. She wasn't sure if he was joking.

"What's it feel like?"

"The yoke?"

"Yes."

"Like being turned inside out."

"So why aren't you wearing one now?"

"Because it feels like being turned inside out."

"Seriously."

"It would hardly do if your guide disappeared, would it? If I'd been yoked today, we both might have gone home. Who'd have led your intrepid hikers back to the hotel?"

She glimpsed Peter, watching them from the buffet, and had a momentary image of him trying to find his way back through the woods alone—Peter, who lived almost entirely in a world of complex financial transactions, a world where meaning was not innate, but created by the universal assent of billions. What had Stafford called it the other day? Pushing money around. He'd said something else, too: *I like to put my hands on something solid. Like to say, I did that.*

Yet—

"You risk your life for that?"

"There's money, of course. And more."

"More?"

"It doesn't bear talking to death."

She fell silent. They revolved to the music.

Wilson said: "What the devil possessed you to do that, anyway?"

The sound of the yearling screaming echoed in her memory.

"I don't know," she said. She said, "I can't stand to see things in pain."

"This is no good for you, then."

"I'm not sure what's good for me, anymore."

"Who is?"

"You seem to be pretty certain."

"I've stripped my life to certain basics, that's all."

"There's no Mrs. Wilson?"

"Not for many years now."

"Are you lonely?"

"You're very curious, aren't you? Let's collect our drinks."

They stood at the railing again. Gwyneth sipped her martini. She was being careful now.

"I thought perhaps some great heartache in your past—"

"Nothing so romantic, I'm afraid. She wasn't willing to live with the risks I take. I wasn't willing to live without them."

"Why not?"

"Do you know Wallace Stevens? Death is the mother of beauty?"

"Poetry, too?"

"You know it then."

"I've read it, I think. In college once."

"You should read it again."

She laughed. "What would I find there, Robert Wilson. Truth or beauty?"

"A bit of both, maybe."

"You must feel great disdain for your charges."

He shrugged.

"You must feel great disdain for me."

"If I felt disdain, I wouldn't be talking to you, would I?"

"What do you feel?"

"Are you flirting with me, Mrs. Braunmiller?"

"I'm curious, that's all."

"What you did was very brave. Also very stupid. I admire the courage."

"And the stupidity?"

Wilson didn't answer. He lifted his glass and finished his whiskey. He held it in his mouth for a long moment. He set the glass on the railing. "Laphroaig," he said. "Nectar of the gods."

"Mr. Wilson—"

He squared up to face her. "I don't admire stupidity in anyone, Mrs. Braunmiller. But I admire courage very much. Courage compensates for many failings." Then, after a moment: "It was the yearling, was it?"

"I suppose."

"It won't do to anthropomorphize them. You're likely to get me killed that way."

When she didn't answer, he said, "What have you come here for? Nobody comes here without a reason."

"To see the dinosaurs, what else?"

But he wouldn't take that as an answer. She could see it in the set of his shoulders, in the observing blue eyes that held hers to account.

"I'm not sure," she said.

"No one ever is," he said.

The party settled into the languid rhythm that dying parties acquire. The band swung into something soft and jazzy. There was no more dancing. The guests who lingered clustered around the fire pits and talked quietly, occasional bursts of laughter lifting into the air like larks.

Gwyneth stood at the edge of the terrace with a glass of wine, watching as someone threw a log onto a dying fire. A shower of sparks swirled up to print themselves against the swollen moon that had lately cleared the mountains. She felt a surge of gladness, a kind of nostalgia in reverse, that at least that had not changed. The old familiar moon still gazed down upon her from the alien wash of stars.

A hand touched her elbow.

She turned, half expecting to see Wilson—she wasn't sure where he had gone, or when—and found herself staring into Peter's face instead.

"It's late," he said.

She didn't know the time.

They leaned their elbows on the railing and stared into the night.

"I waited up."

"I thought you might." Her wine caught a spark of firelight and held it. "I didn't mean to worry you."

"You didn't worry me."

She saw the lie in the set of his jaw, the muscle twitching there.

"I just wondered where you were."

"I've been right here."

"I know." That twitch of muscle. "I just wondered, that's all."

They were silent for a time.

"We didn't dance," he said.

"You didn't ask."

Gwyneth turned to look at him. In the moonlight, Peter's face looked older, gaunt, his eyes deeply shadowed. How strange he had become to her.

What had happened to them?

Peter laughed quietly. "No, I suppose I didn't."

Then: "Was he scolding you?"

"Mr. Wilson?"

She hadn't thought so at the time, but—

"Not scolding exactly," she said. "Reminding me, maybe."

"Reminding you?"

"That he wasn't yoked. That he was putting himself at risk in ways the rest of us are not."

And now, for the second time that evening: "What possessed you, Gwen?"

"Something came over me. I don't know."

The whole thing—the entire trip from the moment she'd seen that footage on her screen back home—had been something she'd had to do, a mute imperative that she could not resist. *Why did you come here?* Wilson had asked her.

I don't know.

Something came over me, she thought.

"You could have gotten the man killed."

Wind rustled the conifer needles. The cries of unknown creatures rose up to her. Gwyneth thought about the thousand battles for survival unfolding in the darkness below, marveling that someday millions of years hence, that eternal struggle would give rise to men, and that not long after that as the earth measured its days, men too would reach their apogee and subside into the muck.

Sighing, Peter said, "Come on, it's late, Gwen."

And this time, with a wistful glance back at the glowing fire pits and the looming globe of the enormous moon, she consented. As they climbed the plush stairs to their room, Peter put his hand to the small of her back and drew her to him. Their lips brushed in a cool, dry kiss. Gwyneth turned away. A veil of dark hair fell between them. When Gwyneth hooked it over her ear, she could not bear to look him in the face.

"Gwen—"

"Not here," she whispered.

Yet later still, in the moon-splashed room, as they lay together in their gauzy eggshell bower, Gwyneth drew away once more. Peter turned his back to her. She watched the rigid line of his shoulders. When at last he spoke, Peter's voice was tense with fury.

"The hell with it then."

"Peter," she said. "I'm sorry. I'm sorry," she said.

But it wasn't enough.

Gwyneth turned away, tears welling in her eyes. They lay still then, back to back, like slow continents adrift. After a time, Peter's breathing deepened into sleep, but Gwyneth lay awake for hours, staring out the moonlit square of window into the shadowy forest beyond. As she hovered at the edge of sleep, there came a faraway cough in the darkness. She tossed restlessly.

Something ponderous moved in her dreams.

She woke at seven to find Peter staring across the bed at her.

"What?" she said.

"Nothing."

But his voice was cool and he didn't seem to be in any hurry to get up. He lounged in a nest of sheets and watched her dress, scratching his chest and tossing out an occasional desultory comment like a bomb. And when he finally joined her for breakfast, he sprawled unshaven in his chair, ordered pancakes, and leveled his gaze over the table at her. "So what's on the agenda for today, Gwen?"

She sipped her coffee. "Yet to be seen."

"A Stegosaurus? A Brontosaurus? A fucking woolly mammoth?"

"Not tennis, you can be sure of that."

"Tennis might do us good. At least we'd be spending some time together."

She threw her napkin to the table. "Jesus, Peter! Why can't you be reasona—"

"Why can't you, Gwen? Why can't you—"

Robert Wilson pulled out a chair and sat between them.

"You've got your eras confused, Mr. Braunmiller."

Gwen slumped in embarrassment. How much had he overhead?

When Wilson spoke again, he leaned forward. "Today it's the biggest game of all, my friends. The one animal everyone comes here to see, the one most of them never do—"

"A T-Rex," Gwen breathed, embarrassment forgotten.

"Did you hear it in the night?"

"I thought I dreamed it."

"It was no dream. I woke at five. It was far away, but moving closer."

Peter kicked out the fourth chair and propped up his feet.

"And how would you know this?"

"I'm a professional, Mr. Braunmiller. I'm very good at what I do. I forget what it is you do exactly—"

"I'm a financial analyst."

"That's right. And I'm betting you would spot a trend in the markets long before I would, wouldn't you?" He didn't wait for Peter to answer. "Look, I've been hunting these animals for the last twenty-five years, and I've only seen fourteen of them—one of them nearly killed me, I was telling Mrs. Braunmiller about it last night. These creatures are the apex predators of their era. They're rare as hell and they can pick up the scent of blood thirty miles away or more."

"The triceratops," Gwyneth said.

"You're a natural, Mrs. Braunmiller." He propped his elbows on the table. "The way I figure it, this bastard got upwind of that wounded triceratops, and has been following the scent down out of the mountains all night. We'll be hard-pressed to catch up to it—but if we do—" He shook his head. "Six-and-a half-tons of pure carnivorous aggression. Forty-two feet, nose to tail. Thirteen feet at the hip. Olfactory bulbs the size of grapefruit. A fucking monster is what I'm saying—and I apologize for the language, but there's really no other way I can say it. You'll never forget it."

He put his hands flat on the table and pushed himself to his feet.

"West gate in fifteen minutes. See you there."

"Along with all the other excursion groups, I'd imagine," Peter said.

"You underestimate my expertise, Mr. Braunmiller," Wilson said without rancor. "And overestimate that of my colleagues. Besides, we know something they don't: we'll be tracking the bloody triceratops."

He didn't wait for a response.

Peter's pancakes arrived. He buttered them in silence.

Gwyneth finished her coffee and stood. "I'll go to the room and get our things together."

"You needn't bother with mine."

She turned in disbelief.

"What did you say?"

He cut a bite of pancake, taking his time about it. When he was done, he said, "I said, you needn't bother about mine."

"You have to be kidding me."

"No."

"Don't sulk, Peter. It's not attractive."

"You don't seem to find me attractive, anyway."

People at surrounding tables had begun to sneak glances at them.

Gwyneth sat down, pushing her plate away. She leaned forward.

"Look," she said quietly. "The only way we're going to solve anything is if we spend time together."

"But we're not, are we?"

He speared another deliberate forkful of pancake.

"We're spending time with a dozen other people—not to mention your friend Wilson—chasing down giant lizards—"

"Jesus, Peter, did you read anything I sent you? They're not lizards. They're—"

"Warm blooded. I know. That's not the point. The point is that you care more about that than you do about trying to fix things. They've been dead sixty-five million years or more. And staring in awe at them isn't working on our marriage. Isn't that what we spent all this money to do? Isn't that what we both wanted?"

"Yes, but—"

"But what? We could have had gone to the Caymans for a twentieth of the expense and actually spent some time together—"

"We've been to the Caymans. We've been to Paris, for God's sake. None of it helped, Peter. None of it—"

And then he said something that stopped her cold in her tracks. "The problem isn't in Paris, Gwen. The problem isn't in the goddamn Cretaceous. The problem is in us."

"Then come with me and help me fix it, Peter. Please."

"Help *me*," he said. "For God's sake, help me."

She stared at him for a long moment, and then, like Wilson, she put her hands flat against the table and pushed herself to her feet.

"I'm going to get my things," she said.

Peter was right: when the west gate swung open, a mass of excursion groups was sorting themselves out. Most of them chose the more difficult route, clambering up the steep ridge in fifteen minute intervals. Wilson's alone struck out in the direction of the clearing where the raptors had taken down the yearling.

Later, two memories from the journey stuck in Gwyneth's mind:

Robert Wilson's cool competence.

And the beast.

The rest was but hazy recollection. The march triple time through the looming woodland. The sweat that poured down her face till it stung her eyes. The tiny theropods that scattered before them. Even the charnel house stench of the clearing itself.

The yearling's carcass lay on its side in a bed of thrashed and flattened grass, the great ribcage nearly stripped of flesh. Its horns lanced from a face that had been gashed and half devoured. Scavengers had descended upon what remained: opalescent maggots the size of a man's thumb, chittering insects that were larger still, a clutch of knee-high dinosaurs, ruddy and yellow, that screeched at them in fury, feathered ruffs billowing out to either side of their narrow-beaked maws.

Wilson ignored them.

"Photos, anyone?" he asked, and several of the men shuffled forward.

Great white hunters, Gwyneth thought, as if they'd personally felled the thing. She and Angela and Frank Stafford stood to the side, sipping cool spring water from canteens, and watched.

"Peter not well?" Stafford asked.

"No," Gwyneth said, and she felt Angela give her a knowing look.

Then they were on the move again, following the path trampled by the fleeing triceratops. Waist-high grass swayed to either side. On the far side of the clearing, the forest enveloped them once again: colonnades of towering conifers and angiosperms, damp soil underfoot. Late morning now, cool shadows under the trees, motes adrift in green air.

Gwyneth watched Wilson, lanky and tall, his neck dusky from wind and sun, slip among the trees like he'd been born of the landscape himself. Deep into the forest, the trail split.

Wilson paused, studying the sign.

"The cows went left, working their way down toward the plain," he said, pointing. "The bull climbed the ridge-line, looking for a place to hole up."

"Why?" someone asked.

"Who knows? Instinct, maybe. To protect the cows. He knows the carnivores will be coming for him."

Something coughed in the distance.

Gwyneth shivered.

"We're close now," Wilson said.

He set a faster pace after that. Winded, they trudged after him, still climbing. Wilson moved with unswerving grace, almost invisible as he cut through shadows and the golden blades of sunlight that knifed through the forest canopy.

Perspiration slid down the channel of Gwyneth's spine.

They followed some spoor that Wilson alone could see, continuing to climb—hard climbing, too, upon occasion, clutching-at-tree-branch climbing, scree sliding loose underfoot. A thin, bearded man slipped and fell, bloodying his forearm. They paused while Wilson disinfected the cut—it must have been three inches long—and applied a pressure bandage with deft, sure hands. "That'll hold it for now," he said, gripping the man's shoulder, and Gwyneth couldn't help noticing the grace of those long fingers, the blunt crescents of his nails. "You'll want to get it looked at back at the hotel," he was saying. "A couple of stitches might be in order."

They found the wounded triceratops forty minutes' hike beyond that. The ridge towered above them here, a rocky cliff face that stood sharp against the azure sky. A thick stand of conifers screened a wide ravine. Maybe a hundred-and-fifty yards from side to side, the chasm narrowed as it deepened. The triceratops lay inside, far back in an angle of stone.

"Can we get closer?" someone asked.

"I wouldn't advise it," Wilson said.

The binoculars made the rounds. Gwyneth studied the triceratops. The great bellows of its lungs heaved irregularly. Dirt caked the exposed wound. Insects buzzed around the glistening bulge of viscera. She could smell the thing from here, a stench of rot and shit and death. It moaned when it saw them, that long rusty sound, like a nail being wrenched from ancient wood. Wilson drew them into a blind of towering angiosperms, admonishing them to silence.

"Soon now," he said, and they hunkered down to wait.

The fronds of the angiosperms waved above them in the midday heat. Then, like God himself flipping a switch, the air went abruptly still. Gwyneth lifted her head, listening. It was more than the lack of birds. The tiny mammals in the treetops had fallen silent; the insects that moments ago had whickered in the air around them disappeared. The forest held its breath. Something big—something dangerous—was on the move. She could sense it: a charged stillness in the air, a tension in the blood.

Something snorted beyond the trees that screened the mouth of the ravine.

Gwyneth could see it in her mind, lifting its vast head to taste of the unmoving air.

Her heart quickened.

Twenty-five years, and Wilson had seen fourteen of them. Fourteen of them. And fucking Peter back at the hotel.

A callused hand touched her elbow.

"This is a time for courage, Mrs. Braunmiller. Not stupidity."

Indeed not, she thought. She could feel his breath tickle erect the fine hairs at the nape of her neck, and for a moment she was aware of nothing else, not the desperate gasping of the felled triceratops, not the expedition group arrayed in the greenery around her, not even the vast creature that shifted its weight beyond the curtain of trees—

Wilson touched her elbow again.

"There you go," he breathed, and then she saw the thing: monstrous, the beast of the apocalypse itself, like some foregone doom from the age of Revelation. It did not emerge from the trees, it simply appeared among them, ghost-like and huge and utterly silent, bigger even than the creature that had run in her dreams, invisible one moment, visible the next, like a long lens pulling focus.

And silent. So silent.

Someone moaned in terror—this wasn't what they'd bargained for, not at all—and the monster swung its vast head toward the grove of angiosperms. Another moan—Wilson hissed, *"Shut up, you fool!"*—and the tyrannosaur moved, shedding the camouflage of the trees like water, one step, then two, its great taloned feet tearing at the dark soil, its tiny, ridiculous arms— evolution's prank—folded at its breast. One slow step, then another, and a third. And did the earth shake beneath its feet? Surely not, yet Gwyneth felt it all the same, felt the earth rumble as the monster lunged toward them, gathering speed, fast, oh fast, and sweet Jesus who could have imagined the thing, death rampant and alive and more beautiful than she could have dreamed; she marveled at its sunshot hide, golden streaked and green, its bullet head weaving hollow-cheeked upon its cobra neck, its nostrils flaring, its eyes ravening and aflame.

It closed fast, forty yards, thirty, twenty-five. Someone broke and ran, she didn't see who, and then the monster—this impossible beast from an era out of time—at last gave vent to the fury that burned in its furnace heart. It roared, its jaws unhinging to reveal a shark's hoard of yellow teeth the size of railroad spikes. A gust of carrion stench blasted over Gwyneth. Her yoke seized her and she found herself careening once again toward the gravity well of the future, trying to hang on for a moment longer just to stare in wonder at the thing—

Her stomach twisted—

And then a rusty-hinge screech of agony reminded the tyrannosaur that other prey—bigger prey, and easy—was to be had. It wheeled to face the triceratops, its tail lashing, and loped the length of the ravine, its feet hammering tracks six inches into the soil. The triceratops somehow staggered to its feet, the bloody rent in its side disgorged fresh loops of tangled viscera.

And then the beast was upon it.

The triceratops lowered its head to meet the titan. Tearing at the soil with legs sheathed in swelling ropes of muscle, the tyrannosaur wheeled around the swinging horns. The wounded triceratops was too slow. One of the T-Rex's taloned feet ripped open its hindquarters. The next moment— Gwyneth looking on, choked with terror and some other strong emotion, she couldn't quite say what—the tyrannosaur closed its massive jaws just behind the triceratops's frill.

The killing blow.

The triceratops went down, feet spasming as the tyrannosaur tore lose a giant chunk of flesh and swallowed. It lifted its monstrous head to the sky and bellowed in triumph.

After that it was awful.

The party that night—there were parties every night—hummed with excitement.

Three of the excursion groups had caught sight of the T-Rex, but only one of them, Wilson's, had seen the kill. *You lucky bastard,* his colleagues said, shaking their heads, but Gwyneth knew that it was more than luck, that it was skill and knowledge; she recalled the swift precision of his lean hands applying the pressure bandage, she recalled his words in her ear: *This is the time for courage, not stupidity.*

She was done with stupidity, Gwyneth thought. She felt that she had opened a new angle of vision upon the world; she understood now that pain was sometimes necessary, that it ruined some things to speak of them too much, that truth could equal beauty. Her fellow guests seemed faintly diminished, their conversation—

—*snapped its neck like a pretzel stick*—

—*magnificent creature*—

—empty of any genuine comprehension of what they had seen.

Maybe the change—if there was a change—showed in her face, for as they sat down to dinner Angela said, "You look flushed, darling. Maybe this afternoon was too much for you."

"Looks like you got a fever is what it looks like," Frank opined, ordering the duckbill steak. ("Appropriate, eh?" he joked.)

Appropriate enough, Gwyneth supposed.

The truth was, she *didn't* feel quite herself. Frank had been right: fever was the word for it. Fever—ever since she had seen that monster for herself, and felt the blast of its carrion breath. She had read about it, she had seen it on video, but not until this afternoon had she really known such things existed in the world. Fever. The fever called living, she thought, another fragment of old poetry rattling around inside her head like a piece of angry candy.

She only wished Peter had been with her.

"Where is Peter, anyway?" Frank said, as if he'd sensed the run of her thoughts.

"I think he *is* coming down with something," she said. "Maybe we both are."

"Up to the room with you, the minute you're finished eating," Angela said.

Frank grunted.

But it wasn't up to the room that Angela dragged her when Frank had finished his steak and wandered off to hold court at the party. It was to the little bar overlooking the plain, where a fire-pit burned and a pair of lovers whispered in the shadows.

"Something warm," she told the bartender, and afterwards, cupping Irish coffee as they stood by the fire pit, "Peter's not sick and you know it."

"How do you know?"

"I've been married twice, love. He's sulking. Sulking this morning and sulking at dinner, making it worse for himself every moment because he can't stay in that room forever, and he knows it. Stupid male pride. Whatever in the world has gone wrong with you two?"

"I don't know," Gwyneth said.

Down below, in the darkness beyond the tree-studded escarpment, something roared on the savannah. She wondered what it was—something big, no doubt—but nothing she could shape inside her head. And that was how it was with Peter, too, wasn't it? Something big had happened to them somewhere along the way, but she couldn't put her finger on when, or what.

She couldn't find the shape of it inside her head.

"I don't know."

She swiped at tears with one hand.

"You must think I'm an idiot."

"I think you're confused. It's okay to be confused."

"But there's nothing wrong. There shouldn't *be* anything wrong. He's a good man, he's kind and he's gentle and he's handsome—anyone could see that he's a good man."

Angela wrapped an arm around Gwyneth's shoulder and pulled her close.

"I know. I—"

"He said—" Gwyneth sobbed discreetly.

The lovers had departed.

The barman found something pressing to do at the far end of the bar.

"He said that what was wrong with us wasn't in the Caymans or in Paris or in the Cretaceous. He said it was inside us."

"He's probably right about that."

"I thought that I could save us by coming here. I really did. I risked everything on it, everything we had." She sniffed and met the other woman's gaze. "Somehow I thought that I could save us. I don't know how."

"Do you love him, Gwyneth?"

"I don't know. We just drifted away from each other," she said, and that image came to her once again: continental drift: landmasses on the move, so slow you didn't even notice it until an ocean lay between you.

It would have been easier if one of them had cheated.

"Shhhh," Angela said.

Gradually, the sobs subsided.

The barman brought them another coffee. The night had turned cool, and the moon had just started to slide over the massif to their back, laying down a patchwork of shadows on the ridge below them. Once again, Gwyneth felt that new knowledge take shape inside her: that some things could not be spoken, that truth could equal beauty, that pain was sometimes necessary, and real.

"Why on earth did you ever come here?" Angela said.

They caught up with Frank at the party, but soon after, he and Angela departed—another shot at Kronosaurs had been promised for the morning, and Angela had shamed him into going along this time. "We didn't come here to play tennis," she said. "Besides you'll be wearing a lifesuit. It's not like you can drown."

Afterwards, Gwyneth floated ghost-like through the party, waiting for Peter. She had resolved to kiss him on the stairs when he came, but he did not come, and at last it was late. The moon had risen high into the alien sky. The fires had dwindled to coals. Even the hard-core drinkers were pouring themselves one by one into their rooms.

Somehow—afterward Gwyneth could never quite figure out precisely how it happened, how the decision came to her or if it had been a decision at all and not some foreordained conclusion—she found herself at the concierge's desk. Inquiries were made. The concierge responded without lifting an eyebrow. Apparently such inquiries were not uncommon.

The corridor was in the basement of the hotel.

She knocked on the door.

Robert Wilson opened it.

"Are you sure?" he said.

"I'm sure."

His hands were callused. They felt real against her flesh.

Later—it must have been three or after—Gwyneth slipped through the door of her room. Peter stirred in the depths of the eggshell bower.

"What time is it, Gwen?" he said in the darkness, as though he didn't know, as though his voice wasn't wide awake, and waiting.

"It's late, Peter."

He was silent for a long time. Gwyneth stood by the door until her eyes adjusted. She made her way across the shadowy room. She stood by the window, staring out into the Cretaceous night. It had grown darker, but the moon in its long descent still frosted the leaves outside the window. If she squinted, she could see—or imagined that she could see—something moving out there near the forest floor. A low-slung night grazer, maybe, or maybe just the wind-drift fronds of some ground-hugging fern.

"The party must have gone late."

"I guess it did."

"The T-Rex and everything. People must have been excited."

"It's all anyone could talk about."

"I'm sorry I was ill. I wish I could have been there."

She said nothing.

"What was it like?"

"The party or the T-Rex?"

He laughed in the gloom.

She had no words for it, no way to begin.

"There was something spiritual to it," she said. "I don't know how to explain."

Now his laughter had a bitter edge.

"Spiritual? Seeing one giant animal tear another one to pieces?"

"It's not that—"

But it was. The blood sport of the thing had excited her.

"—or not that alone, anyway. It was the thing's purity of purpose, I think. So devoid of confusion or . . . or ambiguity. Just pure appetite. Every sinew of its body had evolved to serve it."

She said, "It doesn't make any sense. I know it doesn't make any sense."

In the silence that followed, she felt once again the distance between them: continental drift, something so big she couldn't quite shape it in her mind.

"You weren't ill," she said.

"No."

"You could have come." Then: "What are we going to do?"

He was silent for a long time.

"Was it worth it, Gwyneth?"

She stared into the moon-silvered dark.

Peter turned on the bedside lamp.

Her face hovered in the glass, hollowed out and half transparent, ghost-like.

"Turn it off. Turn it off, Peter."

He did, and the Cretaceous dark rose up to envelop her.

"Another shot at Kronosaurs, tomorrow," he said, and she felt a doorway open between them.

Some things you could not speak of. Some wounds healed in silence.

"We should get some sleep," he said.

Gwyneth stood in the threshold. Her body was wide awake. She felt like she might never sleep again. Peter swept back the veils of the eggshell bower and stood, tall in the darkness, and came to her. He put a hand to the small of her back and leaned over, brushing her ear with his lips.

"Come to bed, Gwen," he said.

But she only stood there, his hand at her back, his breath at her ear. The night deepened. Even the moon was gone. Something huge and bright streaked across the sky. It erupted on the horizon, red and orange, a god-light towering into vacuum far above. Shockwaves followed, flattening the trees on the distant ridges in a broad expanding circle, as though a great fist had slammed down upon the planet, rocking them so that they had to clutch at one another to stay on their feet. The thick glass spider-webbed in its frame. Somewhere in the depths of the hotel, something crashed. Someone screamed. Then the fire, burning from horizon to horizon as it ate the dark. Some things could not be saved, Gwyneth thought. Some wounds did not heal. Then the yoke took her. It was just as Wilson had said: it was like being turned inside out.

₪

BLUE INK
₪
Yoon Ha Lee

It's harder than you thought, walking from the battle at the end of time and down a street that reeks of entropy and fire and spilled lives. Your eyes aren't dry. Neither is the alien sky. Your shoulders ache and your stomach hurts. *Blue woman, blue woman,* the chant runs through your head as you limp toward a portal's bright mouth. You're leaving, but you intend to return. You have allies yet.

Blue stands for many things at the end of time: for the forgotten, blazing blue stars of aeons past; the antithesis of redshift; the color of uncut veins beneath your skin.

This story is written in blue ink, although you do not know that yet.

Blue is more than a fortunate accident. Jenny Chang usually writes in black ink or pencil. She's been snowed in at her mom's house since yesterday and is dawdling over physics homework. Now she's out of lead. The only working pen in the house is blue.

"We'll go shopping the instant the roads are clear," her mom says.

Jenny mumbles something about how she hates homework over winter break. Actually, she isn't displeased. There's something neatly alien about all those equations copied out in blue ink, problems and their page numbers. It's as if blue equations come from a different universe than the ones printed in the textbook.

While her mom sprawls on the couch watching TV, Jenny pads upstairs to the guestroom and curls up in bed next to the window. Fingers of frost cover the glass. With her index finger, Jenny writes a list of numbers: pi, H_0 for Hubble's constant, her dad's cellphone number, her school's zip code. Then she wipes the window clear of mist, and shivers. Everything outside is almost blue-rimmed in the twilight.

Jenny resumes her homework, biting her nails between copying out answers to two significant figures and doodling spaceships in the margins.

There's a draft from the window, but that's all right. Winter's child that she is—February 16, to be exact—Jenny thinks better with a breath of cold.

Except, for a moment, the draft is hot like a foretaste of hell. Jenny stops still. All the frost has melted and is running in rivulets down the glass. And there's a face at the window.

The sensible thing to do would be to scream. But the face is familiar, the way equations in blue are familiar. It could be Jenny's own, five ragged years in the future. The woman's eyes are dark and bleak, asking for help without expecting it.

"Hold on," Jenny says. She goes to the closet to grab her coat. From downstairs, she hears her mom laughing at some TV witticism.

Then Jenny opens the window, and the world falls out. This doesn't surprise her as much as it should. The wind shrieks and the cold hits her like a fist. It's too bad she didn't put on her scarf and gloves while she was at it.

The woman offers a hand. She isn't wearing gloves. Nor is she shivering. Maybe extremes of temperature don't mean the same thing in blue universes. Maybe it's normal to have blue-tinted lips, there. Jenny doesn't even wear make-up.

The woman's touch warms Jenny, as though they've stepped into a bubble of purloined heat. Above them, stars shine in constellations that Jenny recognizes from the ceiling of her father's house, the ones Mom and Dad helped her put up when she was in third grade. Constellations with names like Fire Truck and Ladybug Come Home, constellations that you won't find in any astronomer's catalogue.

Jenny looks at her double and raises an eyebrow, because any words she could think of would emerge frozen, like the world around them. She wonders where that hell-wind came from and if it has a name.

"The end of the world is coming," the blue woman says. Each syllable is crisp and certain.

I don't believe in the end of the world, Jenny wants to say, except she's read her physics textbook. She's read the sidebar about things like the sun swelling into a red giant and the universe's heat-death. She looks up again, and maybe she's imagining it, but these stars are all the wrong colors, and they're either too bright or not bright enough. Instead, Jenny asks, "Are my mom and dad going to be okay?"

"As okay as anyone else," the blue woman says.

"What can I do?" She can no more doubt the blue woman than she can doubt the shape of the sun.

This earns her a moment's smile. "There's a fight," the blue woman says, "and everyone fell. Everyone fell." She says it the second time as though things might change, as though there's a magic charm for reversing the course of events. "I'm the only one left, because I can walk through possibilities. Now there's you."

They set off together. A touch at her elbow tells Jenny to turn left. There's a bright flash at the corner of her eyes. Between one blink and the next, they're standing in a devastated city, crisscrossed by skewed bridges made of something brighter than steel, more brilliant than glass.

"Where are we?" Jenny asks.

"We're at humanity's last outpost," the blue woman says. "Tell me what you see."

"Rats with red eyes and metal hands," Jenny says just as one pauses to stare at her. It stands up on its hind feet and makes a circle-sign at her with one of its hands, as if it's telling her things will be all right. Then it scurries into the darkness. "Buildings that go so high up I can't see their tops, and bridges between them. Flying cars." They come in every color, these faraway cars, every color but blue. Jenny begins to stammer under the weight of detail: "Skeletons wrapped in silver wires"—out of the corner of her eye, she thinks she sees one twitch, and decides she'd rather not know—"and glowing red clocks on the walls that say it's midnight even though there's light in the sky, and silhouettes far away, like people except their joints are all wrong."

And the smells, too, mostly smoke and ozone, as though everything has been burned away by fire and lightning, leaving behind the ghost-essence of a city, nothing solid.

"What you see isn't actually there," the blue woman says. She taps Jenny's shoulder again.

They resume walking. The only reason Jenny doesn't halt dead in her tracks is that she's afraid that the street will crumble into pebbles, the pebbles into dust, and leave her falling through eternity the moment she stops.

The blue woman smiles a little. "Not like that. Things are very different at the end of time. Your mind is seeing a translation of everything into more familiar terms."

"What are we doing here?" Jenny asks. "I—I don't know how to fight. If it's that kind of battle." She draws mini-comics in the margins of her notes sometimes, when the teachers think she's paying attention. Sometimes, in the comics, she wields two mismatched swords, and sometimes a gun;

sometimes she has taloned wings, and sometimes she rides in a starship sized perfectly for one. She fights storm-dragons and equations turned into sideways alien creatures. (If pressed, she will admit the influence of *Calvin and Hobbes*.) But unless she's supposed to brain someone with the flute she didn't think to bring (she plays in the school band), she's not going to be any use in a fight, at least not the kind of fight that happens at the end of time. Jenny's mom made her take a self-defense class two years ago, before the divorce, and mostly what Jenny remembers is the floppy-haired instructor saying, *If someone pulls a gun on you and asks for your wallet, give him your wallet. You are not an action hero.*

The blue woman says, "I know. I wanted a veteran of the final battles"— she says it without disapproval—"but they all died, too."

This time Jenny does stop. "You brought them here to die."

The woman lifts her chin. "I wouldn't have done that. I showed them the final battle, the very last one, and they chose to fight. We're going there now, so you can decide."

Jenny read the stories where you travel back in time and shoot someone's grandfather or step on some protozoan, and the act unravels the present stitch by stitch until all that's left is a skein of history gone wrong. "Is that such a good idea?" she asks.

"They won't see us. We won't be able to affect anything."

"I don't even have a weapon," Jenny says, thinking of the girl in the mini-comics with her two swords, her gun. Jenny is tolerably good at arm-wrestling her girl friends at high school, but she doesn't think that's going to help.

The woman says, "That can be changed."

Not *fixed*, as though Jenny were something wrong, but *changed*. The word choice is what makes her decide to keep going. "Let's go to the battle," Jenny says.

The light in the sky changes as they walk, as though all of winter were compressed into a single day of silver and gray and scudding darkness. Once or twice, Jenny could almost swear that she sees a flying car change shape, growing wings like that of a delta kite and swooping out of sight. There's soot in the air, subtle and unpleasant, and Jenny wishes for sunglasses, even though it's not all that bright, any sort of protection. Lightning runs along the streets like a living thing, writing jagged blue-white equations. It keeps its distance, however.

"It's just curious," the blue woman says when Jenny asks about it. She doesn't elaborate.

The first sign of the battle, although Jenny doesn't realize it for a while, is the rain. "Is the rain real?" Jenny says, wondering what future oddity would translate into inclement weather.

"Everything's an expression of some reality."

That probably means *no*. Especially since the rain is touching everything in the world except them.

The second sign is all the corpses, and this she does recognize. The stench hits her first. It's not the smell of meat, or formaldehyde from 9th grade biology (she knows a fresh corpse shouldn't smell like formaldehyde, but that's the association her brain makes), but asphalt and rust and fire. She would have expected to hear something first, like the deafening chatter of guns. Maybe fights in the future are silent.

Then she sees the fallen. Bone-deep, she knows which are *ours* and which are *theirs*. *Ours* are the rats with the clever metal hands, their fingers twisted beyond salvage; the sleek bicycles (bicycles!) with broken spokes, reflectors flashing crazily in the lightning; the men and women in coats the color of winter rain, red washing away from their wounds. The blue woman's breath hitches as though she's seeing this for the first time, as though each body belongs to an old friend. Jenny can't take in all the raw death. The rats grieve her the most, maybe because one of them greeted her in this place of unrelenting strangeness.

Theirs are all manner of things, including steel serpents, their scales etched with letters from an alphabet of despair; stilt-legged robots with guns for arms; more men and women, in uniforms of all stripes, for at the evening of the world there will be people fighting for entropy as well as against it. Some of them are still standing, and written in their faces—even the ones who don't *have* faces—is their triumph.

Jenny looks at the blue woman. The blue woman continues walking, so Jenny keeps pace with her. They stop before one of the fallen, a dark-skinned man. Jenny swallows and eyes one of the serpents, which is swaying next to her, but it takes no notice of her.

"He was so determined that we should fight, whatever the cost," the blue woman says. "And now he's gone."

There's a gun not far from the fallen man's hand. Jenny reaches for it, then hesitates, waiting for permission. The blue woman doesn't say yes, doesn't say no, so Jenny touches it anyway. The metal is utterly cold. Jenny pulls her fingers away with a bitten-off yelp.

"It's empty," the blue woman says. "Everything's empty."

"I'm sorry," Jenny says. She doesn't know this man, but it's not about her.

The blue woman watches as Jenny straightens, leaving the gun on the ground.

"If I say no," Jenny says slowly, "is there anyone else?"

The blue woman's eyes close for a moment. "No. You're the last. I would have spared you the choice if I could have."

"How many of me were there?"

"I lost count after a thousand or so," the blue woman says. "Most of them were more like me. Some of them were more like you."

A thousand Jenny Changs, a thousand blue women. More. Gone, one by one, like a scatterfall of rain. "Did all of them say yes?" Jenny asks.

The blue woman shakes her head.

"And none of the ones who said yes survived."

"None of them."

"If that's the case," Jenny says, "what makes you special?"

"I'm living on borrowed possibilities," she says. "When the battle ends, I'll be gone too, no matter which way it ends."

Jenny looks around her, then squeezes her eyes shut, thinking. *Two significant figures,* she thinks inanely. "Who started the fight?" She's appalled that she sounds like her mom.

"There's always an armageddon around the corner," the blue woman says. "This happens to be the one that *he* found."

The dark-skinned man. Who was he, that he could persuade people to take a last stand like this? Maybe it's not so difficult when a last stand is the only thing left. That solution displeases her, though.

Her heart is hammering. "I won't do it," Jenny says. "Take me home."

The blue woman's eyes narrow. "You are the last," she says quietly. "I thought you would understand."

Everything hinges on one thing: is the blue woman different enough from Jenny that Jenny can lie to her, and be believed?

"I'm sorry," Jenny says.

"Very well," the blue woman says.

Jenny strains to keep her eyes open at the crucial moment. When the blue woman reaches for her hand, Jenny sees the portal, a shimmer of blue light. She grabs the blue woman and shoves her through. The last thing Jenny hears from the blue woman is a muffled protest.

Whatever protection the blue woman's touch afforded her is gone. The rain drenches her shirt and runs in cold rivulets through her hair, into her eyes, down her back. Jenny reaches again for the fallen man's gun. It's cold, but she has a moment's warmth in her yet.

She might not be able to save the world, but she can at least save herself.

It's the end of the school day and you're waiting for Jenny's mother to pick you up. A man walks up to you. He wears a coat as gray as rain, and his eyes are pale against dark skin. "You have to come with me," he says, awkward and serious at once. You recognize him, of course. You remember when he first recruited you, in another timeline. You remember what he looked like fallen in the battle at the end of time, with a gun knocked out of his hand.

"I can't," you say, kindly, because it will take him time to understand that you're not the blue woman anymore, that you won't do the things the blue woman did.

"What?" he says. "Please. It's urgent." He knows better than to grab your arm. "There's a battle—"

Once upon a time, you listened to his plea. Part of you is tempted to listen this time around, to abandon the life that Jenny left you and take up his banner. But you know how that story ends.

"I'm not in your story anymore," you explain to him. "You're in mine."

The man doesn't look like he belongs in a world of parking tickets and potted begonias and pencil sharpeners. But he can learn, the way you have.

₪

TWO SHOTS FROM FLY'S PHOTO GALLERY

(Inspired by *Somewhere in Time* by Richard Matheson)

₪

John Shirley

I tell myself I had no way of knowing Becky would kill herself that night. It was *morning,* really, when she did it. At about 3:30 in the morning, July 16th, 1975, Rebecca Clanton, the young woman I had married not so long before, threw herself off the roof of her sister's twelve-story high-rise apartment building. She'd come to see her sister Sandra on a visit—to stay overnight, supposedly just to spend time. But Sandra said that Becky hardly spoke that night—just smoked, and nodded, now and then, as Sandra talked about whatever came into her mind, whatever offered to fill the silence. Then Sandra went to bed. And in the dead hours of the morning, Becky got up from the sofa bed, went to the kitchen, wrote out a brief suicide note, and took the elevator to the roof. Had probably come there to do just that, leave a note where someone who mattered would find it. It was just too lonely to kill herself alone at home, somehow. With me out of town . . .

She threw herself off the roof in a way that carried her right down into the empty swimming pool, which was being repaired, out behind the building. Figured Sandra wouldn't have the shock of finding her there—maybe she thought the repairmen would find her first, and they did.

I didn't see her body there, in person, but Sandra told me about it. And somehow I still see it in my mind's eye, as if looking down from the roof. I picture Becky's splayed, broken, blood-laced body centered in the blue rectangle of the pool as if in a picture frame.

Me, I was out of town when she died. I was in Albuquerque, for a conference on Billy the Kid. I write westerns—well, I've published only one novel, but a good many nonfiction books about the Old West. *Henry McCarty AKA William Bonney AKA Billy The Kid* was one of mine, from the University of New Mexico Press; *The Murder of Morgan Earp* was another.

My day job was teaching American history at a minor college, but I spent so much time on research trips to ghost towns and pioneer cemeteries covered with weeds, I was always on the verge of losing the job.

I took Becky on a research trip to a particular cemetery in Cobalt Dust, Arizona. She affected to be interested, but when she saw the skeletons, pulled partly out of the yellow dirt by the tree roots muscled into the forgotten old cemetery, she got a faraway look in her eyes, and went back to the motel. And that night she said, "I have to wonder why you want to spend so much of your time with the dead."

They weren't dead to me, I told her. It was like I traveled in time, when I did the research. Like I had one foot in the Old West.

She shook her head then, and muttered something about arrested adolescence and macho fixations and wouldn't say anymore.

The night she died I was in an Albuquerque bar arguing about whether or not Billy the Kid would really have gotten that amnesty from governor Lew Wallace if he'd been more cooperative. I remember realizing it was almost midnight, and I had promised to call Becky at her sister's that night. So I called, piling a double handful of quarters in the pay phone, and her sister answered, her every syllable iced with passive aggressive reproach:

"She's gone to bed. Naturally."

"I see. Are you sure she's asleep, Sandra? I got caught up in an academic discussion . . . "

Just then the noise level in the bar peaked. Someone giggled and someone else dropped a glass and everyone applauded as it broke.

"Yes, I can hear the academic discussion going on," Sandra said. "Becky's gone to bed. I'm not going to get her up. She's been feeling down and she needs her rest. Goodbye." And she hung up.

She's been feeling down . . .

She'd talked about suicide more than once. Becky was a pale woman with curly black hair, full lips, a face that showed the angularity, a hint of the Native American planes of many from the Southwest—she'd grown up in Arizona. She had a wistful smile, an air of nonchalant resignation. She wore long dark old-fashioned dresses, and black-spangled old lady's feathered hats she found in second-hand stores.

I first found Becky in Bisbee, where her mother owned a souvenir shop for tourists hunting remnants of the Old West. She sat behind the counter, using the same resigned expression for attending to a customer as just staring out the dusty, fly-blown window. A small record player set up behind the cash register was playing "Oh! Sweet Nothin'" by the Velvet Underground, not very loud. It was only later that I learned the name of the song.

"Afternoon," I said. "You're Miss Rebecca Clanton?"

She nodded. "You're that guy from the university?"

"College. North San Diego College of the Humanities."

"I got your postcard. Researching a book on the Clanton gang, you said?" She shook her head apologetically. "I don't know anything about my ancestors. I meant to write you back about that. Sorry you made the trip to glorious Bisbee, if you came to talk to me."

She gave out with that wistful smile. Immediately, I wanted to take her in my arms and comfort her. And kiss those large soft lips.

"Lots of times, people know more about their family than they realize. Or they remember that an aunt has some old letters or . . . Could I take you to dinner and just see if anything comes to mind?"

She looked at me doubtfully. "What's your name?" she asked.

"It's Bill Washoe."

" 'Lonesome Cowboy Bill.' " She smiled. Sort of smiled. It was only later, too, that I found out that "Lonesome Cowboy Bill" was a song from the same Velvet Underground album. "Okay, Lonesome. Let's go, as soon as I ring this lady up . . . "

I was right, there was Clanton history to be gleaned from Becky. Turned out that her great-grandmother had been shacked up with Billy Clanton—the same Billy Clanton, cowboy and sometime rustler, who'd been shot to death, along with Frank and Tom McClaury, by the Earps and Doc Holliday in a small vacant lot near the OK Corral on October 26, 1881. Ike Clanton's younger brother, Old Man Clanton's youngest kid, Billy had fallen for a mixed-race dance hall girl named Isabella Chavez, a girl whom some called "Issy" or "Easy"; she was said to be a quarter French, a quarter black, a quarter Indian, a quarter Chinese—but no one knew for sure. Billy had gotten Issy knocked up, and had promised he'd marry her, but hadn't made good on it, and it was said that just before the gunfight Ike had been trying to talk him out of the marriage. Then they'd gotten on the wrong side of the Earp brothers, in Tombstone, and Billy'd been shot down. Isabella had her child, and had given the boy, William Jose, Billy Clanton's surname; the local registrar, some said in exchange for a sexual favor, had stretched a point and made the name official, though she'd never been married to Billy Clanton. That much I'd known. Consulting County records, I also learned that William Jose Clanton, the semiofficial Billy Clanton Jr., had married one Dolores Plainville, who'd borne a boy, James Isaac Clanton, who'd married Rebecca's mother Louella. Rebecca revealed that William Clanton the Second had deserted Dolores early on, and "Jimmy Ike," as Becky's dad had been called, had deserted Becky and her Mom when she was three.

"We don't have any papers going all the way back to Billy," said Becky, over a steak salad, which was the only kind of salad they had in that Bisbee restaurant. *The Happy Widow,* the restaurant was called. She picked at the lettuce around the beef, leaving the meat alone on her plate when she'd done. "So a lot of these gunfighter history guys, they don't take my family name too seriously. Mom tried to get them interested, so we could sell some stuff. She got an old pistol and said it was Billy's. She actually bought it in a pawn shop."

"You think your mom would talk to me?"

"If you can get her out of the bars long enough. And offer her money. But she'll just make stuff up. I'm pretty sure the Clanton thing is real, though. I look at a picture of him, of Billy Clanton, and he looks like us. And . . . he was shot down. That's almost like saying he was in my family. We're all shot down one way or another. Not always by guns. He was shot down young. My granddad ran off to avoid the draft—and maybe to get away from the family—and he was killed when they tried to arrest him. And my dad, we haven't heard from him since he left, but I heard he's in prison over in Texas. They just run off and get shot or put in jail somewhere."

"Do they? You've had some bad luck with your family. Maybe you should . . . make another one."

I felt my face redden, when I said that. A blurted stupid clumsy thing to say. It just came out. But understand: I'm not a good-looking guy, I'm shaped like a salt shaker, I'm short, I've got a bald spot, a nose like a tuber. Not a lot of experience. And I had been thinking about going to bed with her since I saw her sitting behind the counter, gazing sadly out the dirty window . . .

She gave her almost-smile, then, and looked at me with something close to real interest. Finally she said, "My sister's the one who's done the best— she got out of Bisbee. She's in San Diego, she teaches school."

"San Diego!"

"I know—that's where you're from. Well, she got divorced. But she's dating a guy. And she likes teaching, I guess. Do you like rock music?"

I pretended to be a lot more interested in rock music than I was and expressed a liking for Janis Joplin.

"There's a concert up in Phoenix I'd like to go to this weekend," she said, with a somewhat theatrical wistfulness. "The Cactus Ridge Festival, but I can't really afford to get there and back."

"In fact," I lied, without hesitation, "I'm planning to go to that same concert . . . So, uh, if . . . "

I remember walking in the desert dusk, hand in hand with Becky.

It was yet another cemetery. This one she didn't mind—it was Boot Hill, in Tombstone, Arizona, carefully preserved: the town lived on entirely through tourism.

At this hour the wooden tombstones were darkening to silhouettes, seemed like something grown from the sandy dun earth like the cacti, the small twisted desert trees. We saw Les Moore's grave: *no Les, no more.* We had to look close, in the fading light, to see the grave marker of Billy Clanton.

Murdered in the Streets of Tombstone.

I'd brought her to get a Kodak of her with the marker of her ancestor, for inclusion in my book. And because I thought it was my best shot for getting her into bed. She'd been pretty warm during the concert, and afterward, she squeezed my hand before rushing into the house. The trip to Arizona meant two rooms in the motel, but the rest of the time we were together, and now, gazing down at Billy's grave, she let me take her hand and keep holding it.

She seemed almost happy. With its constant references to her ancestor— her martyred ancestor, in the view of anti-Earp historians—Tombstone made her feel important. When I introduced her as Billy's great-granddaughter, much was made of her. She was interviewed and photographed for the local paper.

"It's funny," she said, gazing down at the grave. A prickly pear cactus, beginning to bud, was sprouting from the spot corresponding to Billy Clanton's heart. "I feel almost happy—because I'm part of a famous tragedy . . . "

"Some say it was a tragedy, some say it was Earp and Holliday heroics . . . "

"I can't go with heroics. And if Billy'd lived he might've married Isabella, and then . . . maybe things would've been better in my family."

That planted the seed of what was to come. It started me thinking about her psychotherapeutically. It occurred to me that if I helped her, made her feel better about herself, she'd feel more attachment to me.

As if reading my thoughts, Becky turned to me, as the cemetery caretaker shouted at us that they were closing for the night; she turned her face to me—tilting it down, because she was a little taller. She leaned closer, and she let me kiss her.

Then she put her arms around me, and whispered in my ear, "You give me hope."

That night in bed she gave me hope, too.

Nine days later, Becky's mother was dead. Out on a drunk, the old woman had stumbled into the street, and had been run over by a Ford pickup truck with beer kegs in the back.

Becky hadn't been close to her mother, but the death seemed to backhand her emotionally; it sent her reeling. "She wasn't much good, but she loved me the best she knew how," Becky said at the funeral. Becky and I were the only ones attending that cut-rate event. "She was all I had. Every Sunday morning, hangover or not, she made me breakfast . . . "

I told her, "I'll make breakfast for you on Sunday." And that seemed to help. We got closer, then, Becky and I. We went to more concerts, we went on trips—I fought with the college administration to get the time. She came out to visit San Diego . . . and when I popped the question, she said yes. She only thought about it for an hour or two.

We got married in San Diego. And at the wedding, which we held at the Hotel del Coronado, one of the guests was my Uncle Roger who brought his "partner"—a rather taciturn man, a doctor named Crosswell. While we were waiting for the bride to come out, we started talking about the Coronado, a landmark built in 1888, and about old hotels, and I said how visiting old places, for me, could feel like time travel, and the doctor stared at me—and asked, rather suspiciously, what had prompted the remark.

Roger looked at him and said, "He doesn't know about Collier. Almost no one does. Forget it."

But when my uncle wandered off to get a drink, I pressed Crosswell, my journalistic instinct piqued, and he muttered something rather grumpily about having a transcription of certain tape recordings by a Richard Collier who'd stayed at this hotel, and allegations of Collier's experiments in time travel. References to Collier's obsession with one Elise McKenna.

Then out came Becky in her wedding dress, really smiling for once, and drove away all thoughts of my being anywhere, anytime, but right there.

We were happy for as long as Becky was capable of being happy, which was a week or so, and then we were happy sporadically for a time . . . and then only

I was happy. And after a while, when I realized I was alone in that gladness, neither of us were.

It all came down to the implicit tragedy of Becky's life—of life itself, in Becky's view. If we went on a walk, Becky was sure to notice a dead bird in the gutter; if we went to the beach she saw the trash on the sand and a bird pecking out the eyes of a dead fish, and didn't seem to notice anything else; if we went to Disneyland she pointed out the wasteland of parking lot and the high prices and the long lines; she speculated on the exhaustion and resentment of the people dressed as Goofy and Mickey. At home, she listened to a great deal of Tim Buckley and the Velvet Underground and she re-read *The Bell Jar*. Reading *The Bell Jar* more than once should be in some clinical psychology book as a warning sign.

"Don't you see?" she'd say to me. "I'm doomed. It's in my blood to be doomed. Some people are born losers—it's built into their chromosomes. You've hitched your wagon to a falling star . . . "

She started sleeping twelve, fourteen hours a day, and not getting out of bed when she did wake up. The house fell into a piled-up disorder like a sculpture representing her depression. She started talking about suicide. Suicidal depression had been a black tsunami poised over her just before we'd met—and then my intercession had let her run from it, for a time. But it couldn't be outrun, she insisted. The giant black wave was falling on her at last. Perhaps, she suggested, we could die together . . .

I went to see my Uncle Roger, but really it was to talk to Crosswell. "You're a physician, Doctor Crosswell—do you know somebody good for this kind of illness?"

He recommended a Dr. Hale Vennetty. I went to see him, for a consultation about my wife. He was a tall pale dour psychiatrist with a phlegmatic, fatalistic air, and he was convinced that once a person was "imprinted" by their childhood, that imprint was their destiny and there was little to be done, though electroshock could be tried. He was interested in Becky's case, since it had an affinity with his pet theory, evolved mostly to account for cyclic ghetto miseries: parental abandonment led to a tendency to abandon one's own children, as if the abandoner were re-enacting the despair of their own childhood. It was a vicious circle that spiraled through the generations, abandonment leading to abandonment. "Why," he chuckled, "the only way to change it, really, once the imprint has happened, would be to travel back in time and persuade someone who started the cycle of abandonment not to do it . . . "

I couldn't believe it was hopeless. I went to two more doctors, one of whom suggested an experimental new drug, something called an "antidepressant." I was planning to persuade Becky to sign on for the experimental therapy program . . .

I'd talk to her about it, I decided, right after I got back from Albuquerque.

Then she was dead. I was alone.

I would grieve, and find someone else. Someone healthier.

But I drank a great deal of beer, and over ate, and put on forty pounds, becoming even less attractive. Worse, I was dogged by self-loathing that other people infallibly sensed. Self-loathing is not an attractive quality. But I couldn't shake it. I just kept thinking I could have saved her, after all. If I had stayed with her . . . Hadn't gone on that trip. I'd known she was at risk for suicide but I went anyway. Because she was becoming a burden to me—I wanted to get away from her.

I tried blaming it on her sister Sandra. *If only she'd let me talk to Becky that night, I might've cheered her up . . .*

But it didn't take. I blamed myself. I spent much of 1975 and most of 1976 blaming myself . . .

By degrees, I became fixated on Vennetty's theory, his cycle of abandonment. Then I remembered Crosswell's story about Collier. The recordings. The tale of time travel . . .

Crosswell wouldn't talk about it. But I had a key to my Uncle's house because I fed their four cats when they were out of town. I let myself in one day and searched the file box in the den Crosswell used for an office. It took me all of five minutes to find the manila envelope, at the back of the lowest drawer, with the transcription of the tapes. I took it home and read it with a mixture of dread, disbelief, and growing excitement.

The description of the method used for time travel had an eerie verisimilitude for me. On rare occasions, as I'd hinted to Crosswell, I'd experienced something of the sort myself. In the little ghost towns I'd visited, I had felt, sometimes, for perhaps just a second, that the veil of the ages had drawn back, and I'd glimpsed the town in its teeming heyday; had smelled the reeking mules and the reeking prospectors, had blinked in the rising dust . . . before it had faded away. I had almost . . . *almost* traveled in time.

Collier's process was the same method, crystallized by fanatical dedication. It was a psychological, then a psychic, process. You surrounded yourself with artifacts of the era you wanted to travel to. You dressed for the era. You visualized the era. You fixed the date and time in your mind. You repeated, over and over again, the time, the place, the destination you wanted to travel to. You visualized, you visualized, you visualized. And since the quantum uncertainty hidden at the heart of the universe is penetrable by mind itself, a persistent man might just project himself into the past through sheer force of will . . .

Was it really possible? Was it possible I could project myself a year into the past, and stop Becky's death?

The apartment Becky had died in had grim associations for Sandra and she'd recently given it up. I rented it, splurging my tiny savings to do it, and sat on a chair in the bedroom, staring at a newspaper from the day before Becky had died—it'd taken some doing to get hold of it. Then I tried for hours to travel back to that night . . .

Now and then, there was a flicker. I almost went. The room would shift— Sandra's old furniture would start to appear. Once I thought I glimpsed Becky. But the trouble was, 1975 was too much like 1976. It wasn't different enough, somehow, for the mind to find its bearings. I kept slipping back to my own time.

But I had confirmed that time travel was possible. I had gone into the past—if only for a moment. And there was one other possibility for saving Becky. Suppose . . .

Suppose I took seriously what Dr. Vennetty had suggested facetiously. Suppose I traveled back to the time of the Old West's Billy Clanton—and stopped him from being there, in Tombstone, that October day in 1881. He was reputed to be a pretty good-natured kid, overall. With any luck, if he weren't shot down in the OK Corral fight, he'd marry Isabella, and he'd stay with her, and raise that child, and the cycle of abandonment would be broken, and that child's children would not be marked with despair, would not be imprinted, and Rebecca Clanton would not be seeded with depression—and suicide.

I freely confess, I wasn't quite in my right mind in those days. I felt haunted by Becky—as if some black shimmering from her despair had settled over me, an invisible cloak I always wore. It drew itself over my eyes, and made me see things in extremes. Forgetting about Becky, letting her go, was not an option. I had to save her—or die myself.

So I went to Tombstone, Arizona, in October 1976—went there in period costume. It isn't strange to dress in the manner of the 1880s there. No one even stared at my frock coat, the watch and chain on my weskit, the silk top hat. I rented a room in a bed-and-breakfast, a tourist-outfitted building that had existed in 1881, and retreated to a room already furnished with the right antiques. My pockets were heavy with silver dollars wrapped in outdated paper money. I'd sold my car to get enough money to buy the antique funds from a numismatist. I even had a small pistol, circa 1879, hidden in my coat.

I decided I should try to go right to the morning of the day the gunfight happened, so that there were fewer variables to deal with—and because, since I was a historian of the Old West, that day was already firmly fixed in my mind. I had visited it many times in my imagination, reading and re-reading accounts of the gunfight and the events leading up to it. I had the edge, a jump on visiting Tombstone, Arizona, October 26, 1881.

I set up my own tape recorder, and recorded the words over and over again . . . "October 26, 1881 . . . it is nine in the morning, the morning of the OK Corral gunfight, in Tombstone, Arizona . . . October 26, 1881 . . . it is nine in the morning . . . " And in the background was music, not too loud, a tape loop of tunes recorded by contemporary folk musicians but on acoustic instruments, only songs that were extant in 1881. "Camptown Races" . . . "The Man on the Flying Trapeze" . . .

It took three days, scarcely resting, with only a few breaks to eat dried food and drink bottled water, the occasional short nap, for the process to really begin. On my few visits to the men's room, down the hall, I encountered tourists, people who stared at me suspiciously. They'd heard the mantra-like drone from my room, the interminable music . . .

October 26, 1881 . . . it is nine in the morning, the morning of the OK Corral gunfight, in Tombstone, Arizona. Picturing this room, that day. The street outside, what it must have been like. Envisioning faces familiar to Tombstone in those days—faces I knew from old tintypes and photographs— that would be nearby. Wyatt Earp, Doc Holliday, Big Nose Kate Elder, Mayor Clum, George Parsons, Fred Dodge. Seeing them in my mind's eye. *October 26, 1881 . . . it is nine in the morning . . .*

And then what Collier had called "the absorption" began. Suddenly I was drawn inward, caught up in a drifting sensation—I understood now exactly what Collier meant—and a mounting disorientation. The room around me seemed distant, detached. The sound of my droning voice, those songs, became thick, distorted, as if I were going deaf. Then I ceased to hear them—and heard instead a shouting from the street, the clatter of horse's hooves. The tinkle of a cheap piano.

The sounds of Tombstone, October 1881.

The officiating lady of the whorehouse was a stout woman with flaming red hair contrasting vividly with her blowsy blue dress; she was leaning back in a rocking chair on the front porch, her pale thick-ankled left leg cocked over her right knee, smoking a pipe. She didn't seem particularly surprised to see me, a stranger, walk out of her house, though she hadn't marked my entrance.

"Now did that Marissa bring herself a man up there without consulting me?" she asked, almost rhetorically, as she frowned at her pipe, knocking its dottle clear on the railing. "The wicked vixen owes me a dollar and no mistake . . . "

"Here is your dollar, ma'am, and good day to you," I said, my voice trembling as I laid the worn silver dollar the porch railing beside her.

She chuckled and went back to singing wordlessly to herself. I stepped out into the October morning, into the smell of sage and horse dung and leather . . .

Believe, I told myself, feeling dreamlike as I stepped off Fifth Street and onto Allen, in the Tombstone, Arizona, of October 1881. *Believe!*

I turned left, passing the Golden Eagle Brewery, striding by several shops including a hostelry, Campbell and Hatch Billiards, the Cosmopolitan Hotel, the Eagle Meat Market, Hafford's Saloon . . . *Believe in this. This is no dream.* These creaking wagons pulled by oxen and horses; that stagecoach arriving; these weary ladies of the night blinking in the morning light as they stumped blearily to their beds in their high-button shoes; this shopkeeper, with the flaring muttonchops and the red gaiters, opening up his emporium; the smell of alkali dust and new-cut lumber and the smell of horses and the raw rich scent of privies, many privies, blowing in on the sharp desert wind . . . *It's no dream!*

But it was the dream of every Old West historian. To actually visit Dodge City or Virginia City or Tombstone—back then. And this day of days, the day of the most storied gunfight of the Old West! I could get the truth about the gunfight—no one would ever believe me, of course, but *I'd* know. I'd know who started the fight, and if indeed the Clantons and McClaurys had not even drawn their weapons, as the anti-Earp Tombstone *Nugget* had claimed, or if it was, as the pro-Earp Tombstone *Epitaph* had insisted, a straight-up fight with Frank McClaury and Billy Clanton drawing first . . .

Too bad I didn't bring a camera back with me, a Polaroid, say, or—

The streets of Tombstone rippled; I seemed to glimpse a Cadillac glimmering into visibility, asphalt appearing under my feet . . .

No! Don't think of things like that! *Focus.* Be here. There's only here and now—October 26, 1881!

I saw an apothecary's shop then, across the street. *Focus on that.* An old-fashioned apothecary's shop. *You have a plan. You must go there and make a purchase . . .*

I went into the shop, and found the apothecary's assistant—a sallow, sleepy-eyed, greasy-haired woman in a long black dress—and I instantly suspected her of being a laudanum addict. No matter. I made my enquiry and, wordlessly, she sold me what I needed to carry out my plan.

I stepped out to the wooden sidewalk, shivering in the chill wind, and looked fiercely around, trying to fixate on something that would keep me in this time. I focused on a man walking unsteadily along, across the dusty street, a man in a sombrero. He was a plump-faced white man with an oiled mustache and a small pointed beard; the silver and black sombrero didn't seem to go with his stained frock coat, his tall black boots. Then I knew the man for who he was. It was Ike Clanton, full up with liquor.

I understood the dark, intent look on his face, too. There was fear and anger, perfectly mixed, in that expression, the whole framed by the sullen stupidity of alcohol. I knew what was behind that look . . . and how it would lead to the "Gunfight at the OK Corral."

Earlier that year, the stage had been robbed, and Bob Paul had been killed. The Earps had learned that the robbers were local ne'er-do-wells surnamed Leonard, Head, and Crane. But the stage robbers had made good their getaway. Wyatt Earp knew that Ike Clanton and the McClaury brothers were close acquaintances of the stage robbers—"acquaintances" at the very least. He'd approached cowboys Ike Clanton and Frank McClaury secretly and said that if they'd ask around, and then tell him how to find the stage robbers, he'd see that Ike and the McClaurys would get the reward money on the quiet, with Earp taking credit for the arrest, and in consequence getting himself elected to the lucrative job of town sheriff. Ike and Frank agreed and traded some information—but before it could be acted on, local ranchers Isaac Haslett and his brother Bill, in need of the reward money, had bushwhacked Leonard and Head, only to be killed, presumably by a vengeful Crane, soon after—Crane vanished and the whole deal between the Earps and the cowboys fell apart.

Still, Ike was afraid that the leader of the cowboy gang, Curly Bill Brocius, would find out Ike had played along with Wyatt Earp. Rumors seemed to suggest as much. Ike felt he had to bluster and damn the Earps, and call it all a lie, in order to keep his standing in the gang. Earp pal, former dentist and fulltime gambler John Henry "Doc" Holliday, knew Curley Bill, and Crane too, and Ike was afraid Doc had told them. So it was necessary to call Doc Holliday a dirty liar, all around, which didn't please Holliday. Meanwhile the Earps accused the other Clantons of rustling, and Tom McClaury and his brother of stealing government mules. Though it was hard to convict them with corrupt Sheriff Behan covering up for them, rancor grew on both sides.

Holliday by now had breezed into town from Tucson, at the request of the Earps, Big Nose Kate in tow. Sometime after midnight, Wyatt Earp ran into Ike Clanton at the Eagle Brewery, where Wyatt ran a faro game. Ike had hinted that Holliday was betraying him to the gang, and telling lies about him, and he was going to have to fight him. "I am not fixed just right," Ike had said then, meaning he hadn't been carrying his weapons. "But in the morning I'll have a man-for-man with you and Holliday."

Trying to defuse the situation, Wyatt had replied he'd fight no one "because there's no money in it." Ike was known for his bluster, after all. There was no need to take his threats seriously.

But Ike Clanton kept on blustering, confronting Holliday in a restaurant around midnight—and only the intercession of Deputy Marshal Morgan Earp prevented Doc from shooting Clanton down. "You son of a bitch," Doc told him, "you ain't heeled." Meaning armed. "Go heel yourself."

Ike kept drinking, guzzling hooch all night long. Weirdly, he played poker with Virgil Earp with something approaching civility, till around 7:00 a.m. But when Virgil got up to go home, Ike gave him a message for Holliday: "The damned son of a bitch has got to fight."

An hour later Ike told the bartender at the Oriental that if the Earps and Holliday showed on the street, "the ball would open" and they would have to fight. Having stayed up all night drinking . . . Ike judiciously went on drinking. Going from bar to bar, uttering threats, stoking the fires with his cronies where he could.

And it was still morning when I found him. Staring at Ike Clanton, in the drunk and belligerent flesh, fixed me firmly in October 26, 1881. Ike glowered at me and swaggered unsteadily off down the wooden sidewalk.

I followed him, hoping he'd bring me to his brother Billy. A block down, Ike slipped into the Grand Hotel, where he kept a room—to catch a little fitful sleep, perhaps. Not knowing where else to go, and knowing that Ike would eventually meet up with his brother Billy—for they were both there at the OK Corral gunfight—I went into a café next door to Dexter Livery and Feed, across from the hotel, to keep an eye out for Ike's emergence.

I ate a hearty breakfast, the food remarkable for its rich taste in some way I could not identify. I over-tipped the owner so there'd be no complaint if I was there for some time, telling the man with the handlebar mustache I might have to wait for some hours, watching the street, as a friend was coming on a mule all the way from San Simon. Looking over the silver dollars, he winked and said I was to make myself comfortable.

I tried to remember where Billy Clanton had first been seen, after he'd ridden into town that day—but I was overwhelmed by all that had happened, all that I was seeing, and the information would not come into my recollection. So I sat at the window, drinking coffee—as if I'd never tasted coffee before!—and watched the street, the dour shopkeepers and ladies in their stately dresses, silver miners on a day off, cowboys riding through from outlying ranches; I sat there glorying in it all, fascinated with the town's quality of newness, of enterprising energy.

About half an hour before noon, his eyes red, his face pale, Ike emerged from the Grand Hotel, swaying, now carrying a Winchester rifle, a pistol on his hip. He wandered down the street, seeming to have no definite destination, and I followed—and was unsurprised when he went into a saloon. I stepped over a sleeping drunk, the man's urine soaking the sawdust coating the floor for just such eventualities, and posted myself at the bar, the other end from Ike, hoping to see Billy Clanton arrive. Perhaps I should ask around town for him, head him off before he found Ike. But if I missed him—

Meanwhile Ike was muttering threats to anyone who'd listen and knocking back whiskey.

Around noon I looked at my goose-egg watch and knew that about now Marshal Virgil Earp was being awakened by Deputy Marshal Andy Bronk, after all too little sleep. "There is likely to be Hell, Virgil," Bronk would tell him. Virgil, his head pounding, would go out to see about all these threats made against himself and his brothers.

Minutes later Virgil found Ike outside the very saloon I was in—I watched the encounter through the window. A cold wind was blowing, searching through the half-open door, when Virgil stepped up behind Ike and grabbed the Winchester. Ike snatched at his pistol and Virgil neatly "buffaloed" him, cracking his own six-shooter over Ike's head, knocking him down. (My historian's heart was pounding—that was Virgil Earp himself, a big man in a dark suit with a bushy ginger mustache, and the slender man with the black mustache joining him was his younger brother Morgan!)

"I heard you were hunting for me, Ike," Virgil said, staring down at the fallen Ike.

"I was," Ike said, holding his head. "And if I'd seen you a second sooner you'd now be dead."

"You're under arrest for carrying firearms within city limits."

I knew what would happen then. Ike would be dragged by Virgil and Morgan Earp into Judge Wallace's court. There'd be an altercation there, with Wyatt Earp arriving and calling Ike a "damned dirty cow thief," and adding, "You have been threatening our lives and I know it."

"Fight is my racket, and all I want is four feet of ground," Clanton would respond.

The judge would merely fine Ike, and his weapons would be sent over to his hotel room. As the Earps left the court, they'd encounter Tom McClaury outside, who'd come to check on Ike. Earp would demand to know if McClaury was heeled, and McClaury would say that he'd fight Earp anywhere, if he wanted it. Still furious from the encounter with Ike, Wyatt would pistol-whip Tom McClaury for his impertinence, knocking him to the ground. And so the fury on both sides would build.

Billy Claiborne would find Frank McClaury and Billy Clanton at the bar of the Grand Hotel and tell them that Wyatt had pistol-whipped Tom—

That was it! That's where Billy would be, having come in with Frank McClaury. *The Grand Hotel.* From there, trying to avoid trouble with the Earps—who after all were local lawmen—Frank McClaury would take Billy to the OK Corral to get their horses. At the OK Corral they'd encounter Tom McClaury, his head bandaged, with the same idea, and then Ike, who'd unknowingly doom them with his drunken nattering about the Earps, keeping them in the vacant lot next to Fly's Photo Gallery and the OK Corral a few minutes too long.

And local men, having heard talk of a gunfight all night and day, would see the Clantons and McLaurys gathered near the OK Corral, talking earnestly, Frank and Billy with hands on their guns, and suppose them making ready to fight the Earps. And those helpful townsmen would warn the Earps and Holliday that the outlaws were massing for a fight—when in fact they were probably going to leave town—and the Earps and Holliday, assuming Ike's threats were real, would come marching down the street to "make a fight."

And a few minutes later, in a gunfight lasting about thirty seconds, three men would be shot dead by the Earps and Holliday: Frank McClaury, Tom McLaury, Billy Clanton. In Billy's case, it took him a while longer than the others to die.

That's how it would happen, inexorably—unless I could get Billy Clanton out of the line of fire.

I made my way to the Grand Hotel, getting there before Billy and Frank arrived. I ordered a sarsparilla—no one looked askance at that, for it was still early—and watched the doorway.

Could I really bring myself to do it? Rather than witnessing this cornerstone of gunfighter history, I'd be interfering with it—perhaps stopping it. Sending up perturbations in the flow of time. Affecting history, perhaps, in bigger ways than I intended—for all I knew, Billy Clanton, if he lived, might get it into his head to assassinate a president, some day.

Unlikely. These were minor players on the stage of history. No great large-scale change would come about.

But the urge to witness the gunfight was strong. Perhaps I could witness it as it had been known to happen—and then come back again, and change it next time. Perhaps . . .

But here was Billy Clanton, walking through the door, coming into the room with me. I knew him instantly—and I saw echoes of my Becky in his face. I could not let him be shot down. I could not forget my mission to save Becky. He was a living reminder of my purpose.

Both men were dressed in suits for a visit to town, Frank's a bit too small for him, Billy's a tad too large. Billy was but nineteen years old—a fresh-faced boy, smiling, glad to be in town.

The smile would fade when Claiborne came in, with news of Wyatt Earp's pistol-whipping of Tom. I had to intercept Billy quickly—tell him that I was a friend of his brother Ike, and Ike was out in the alley with urgent news, wanting to see him alone. I'd take him out there and bring out the ether I'd bought at the apothecary's, and I'd grab him from behind, dose him before he knew what was up, drag him somewhere and keep him safe there. Maybe the gunfight would go on without him, maybe not, but he would be safe.

I strode over to him—Frank a dark, bearded man; Billy a hulking, fresh-faced youth taking off his Stetson, wiping dust from his eyes. "Blowin' out there, mister. Say, do I know you?"

"Why, no, sir. My name is Wells. I have lately become a business partner with your older brother, Mr. Isaac Clanton—and he waits without. He has information he would impart to you, and only to you."

"Ike and me have no secrets, mister," McClaury rumbled.

"Well, sir, he was hoping you would watch the front door . . . For the Earps are coming."

"Are they now? And I'm to watch for them? So be it. But keep your hand on your Colt, Billy, you don't know this man."

Billy shrugged and gestured for me to lead the way. My heart hammering, one hand going into my pocket for the bottle of ether, I led the way out the back, into the dirt alleyway. Billy came out alone with me. And stared at the man waiting there—we both stared at him. I was more shocked by the man's presence than Billy was.

It was myself. Dressed just as I was. The only difference was, this version of me, of Bill Washoe, had not shaved in a day or two, and his hair looked lank.

"What the blue blazes have we got here?" Billy said wonderingly. "Your twin! And I never saw two men more alike. And where's my own brother? What's afoot?" His hand went to his gun.

"Ike will meet you at the OK Corral," said the other, unshaven Bill Washoe. "There's been a change my twin here didn't know about. You'll talk with Ike there. It's an emergency—you boys are in danger!"

Billy backed away from us, not wanting to turn his back till he had to—then he hustled through the door. "Frank!" he shouted, as he went in. "We got to go to the OK Corral!"

I was too busy staring at myself, this other version of myself, too busy trying to cope, to interfere with Billy. Finally I managed, "What . . . uh . . . ?"

"I'm you," I said, stating the obvious with an apologetic shrug. "From a little bit in your future—your future a little later than the Bill Washoe of 1976 that you were, when you came here. I tried to get here earlier in the day but somehow—I was drawn here, and now. Probably by you. There's some kind of psychic magnetism between us—and you reached some kind of peak intensity here when you interfered with Billy. This is the point where you started changing events."

Bill Washoe of 1976! The wooden walls of the buildings around us wavered, and began to seem distant. The sounds from the street became murky, distorted . . .

"Don't!" I said. "I am here—*here* in October 26th, 1881!" I looked down the alley to the side street and saw a buggy going by with a lady in a bustle sitting up very straight in it, buggy whip in hand. *1881.* Renewed by my focus on that distinct feature of the time, the alley reified, became more definite.

The later me made a suggestion. "There's a secret Collier didn't know, for staying in the past—pain." He . . . the other *I* . . . raised his hand and I saw he had a badge in it, an antique U.S. Marshal's badge from this era—he'd held it so tightly it had bloodied his hand. He squeezed it there again so that fresh blood dripped. "Once you're in the past, pain fixes you there, if you sustain it." He tossed me a similar badge. I caught it. "Squeeze it till it hurts, cuts your hand. That'll keep you as I tell you what I must."

I squeezed it till the pain came and he went on: "Billy stayed with Isabella, because of what I did—what you want to do—and her son stayed with his wife and so on. And Becky's father stayed with the family. That much you accomplished. Some behavior is imprinted—but some is inherited. Like the tendency to cruelty. And it can be carried on both by imprinting and genes. Billy abused Isabella and the boy abused his wife and child and . . . and Becky's father carried it even farther."

Blood was dripping from my hand . . . 1881 stayed firmly in place, stuck on the thorn of my pain . . . and my growing fear.

"*He raped Becky.*" The two of me said it, together. As I realized and he simply explained. He spoke on, alone: "When I . . . when *you* . . . got back from Tombstone, it was hard to find Becky. I established that she hadn't committed suicide—but where was she? We were no longer married. But she was out there, alive somewhere—I found her in Phoenix, found her by harassing her sister till she told me what had happened to her. Sandra got away from the family before the father returned from jail—and it seems Becky's dad made her his little sex slave. Eventually she ran away, only to become a junkie. To pay for the heroin she fell into prostitution. She was stoned out—so she wasn't careful. She got serum hepatitis, and syphilis. Got very sick—very, very sick—and when I left the future to come back here again, she was dying . . . dying very slowly. It was too late to treat the syphilis and she was . . . Oh, God, *she would have been far, far better off dead.*" The other Bill Washoe swallowed and went on. "I came back to stop you from saving Billy. If you'd left it alone, she would have had some happiness. And it would have ended quickly, at least, in that empty swimming pool . . ."

I stared. "I don't care," I said at last. A terrible momentum was on me. My sense of purpose had a life of its own. "I can go back to our time—I can perfect time travel and I can go back to save her from her father and . . . and . . ."

"No, no you can't. I've tried. You can't travel in time endlessly—you go mad if you do. Maybe I have gone mad. I'm not even sure I'm talking to you now. You seem real enough . . . I mean—*I* seem real enough . . . "

I shook my head emphatically. "I'm not going to lose my focus. I'm going after Billy and I'm going to save him. Stop him from the OK Corral fight. Then I'll do something about her father—I'll save her from that life too. I'm going after Billy now—don't try to stop me." I started for the OK Corral.

"No!" The other, later Bill Washoe stepped in front of me. He was reaching for his pistol . . .

I drew mine first. I outdrew myself. I think I—he—had been drinking . . .

And I shot him down. Shooting myself down felt kind of good, really.

The other Bill Washoe lay there in a pool of blood . . . I was aware of the portly, aproned bartender coming to the door behind me, staring.

The dying man looked up at me and said, hoarsely, "You slowed Billy down already . . . you, trying to stop him . . . from before . . . time has an inertia . . . it's . . . psychic, what we do. Our minds will . . . and you will . . . you must . . . "

He didn't finish saying it. His eyes went glassy and his let out a final breath—and died. But I soon knew what he was trying to say. Because in a few moments I felt a long, icy shiver pass through me, as his consciousness left him . . . and merged with mine.

We were the same person. The same soul. The spirit has its own thermodynamics, its own "law of conservation of matter"—so our souls merged. *And I knew what he knew.* What he'd been through, since he'd gone back to our time, poured into me, when our souls combined. His memories became mine.

And the most aching of his memories asserted itself: *Rebecca Clanton lying in the hospital bed, covered in sores, foaming at the mouth, her face the color of rancid butter, her wrists raw in the restraints, as a droning doctor explained that it was too late for her, too late.*

It would be a slow, horrible death. A murder, really—by her father. By extension. And maybe, by me. Maybe I'd murdered her with my interference.

I saw the other Bill Washoe had been right. I knew what had to be done. I had slowed Billy Clanton down, interfered with the original pattern. Things would be a little different. He would be a little later getting to the OK Corral, and even more on his guard now. Maybe he wouldn't die in the gunfight . . .

I ignored the shouting bartender, and I ran to the OK Corral.

The OK Corral was actually a long strip of land between Allen and

Fremont Streets. I ran through the corral, past horses and water troughs, and climbed the fence, coming to the narrow strip alley behind Camillus Fly's Photo Gallery, a small building that stood behind Camillus Fly's Boarding House. I still had my gun in my hand—and I saw the two parties lined up in the eighteen-foot-wide lot, with Tom McClaury to one side, standing behind a horse, his hand on a Winchester in its saddle scabbard; Doc Holliday, a small ash-blond man with a black mustache, bringing a shotgun from under his gray cloak; beside him were Virgil, Morgan—and there was Wyatt, with a droopy sandy mustache: a tall, almost skinny man in a long black coat, wide-brimmed black hat. He was just pulling a pistol from his coat as Billy Clanton—not standing where I thought he'd be, historically, but now half hidden behind a post—drew his pistol and fired, at the same time as Earp. But Earp fired at Frank McClaury, hitting him in the stomach—McClaury already had his gun out, while Ike Clanton shrieked that this must stop, and he tried to grab Wyatt Earp's gun hand, saying he was not armed himself, and Earp shouted, "The fight has commenced! Go to fighting or get away!" and shoved him so that Ike turned and stumbled into Fly's Boarding House, as the wounded McClaury shot Virgil in the leg, knocking him down, and Doc fired at Tom McClaury with the shotgun before Tom could get that Winchester free, hitting him twice, then dropping the shotgun to pull a silvery pistol which he fired at Billy—

But the bullets hit the post, and Billy wasn't hit yet—my interference had been just enough. He was going to get away! He was turned sideways—and he was aiming carefully at Wyatt Earp . . .

Firing from the corner of Fly's Photo Gallery, out of sight of the Earps and everyone else, I shot Billy Clanton, twice.

I shot the son of a bitch down myself. Saw him spin and fall.

Then I drew back under cover and let go of the bloody badge, and as the pain ebbed, I thought about 1976. I thought about disco, and hollow-eyed Vietnam vets . . .

The last of the shooting died away. Billy was lying on the ground screaming in pain . . . his voice becoming distant, distorted . . . the wall beside me wavered . . . and then became solid again. And it stayed that way.

I looked around, and realized that I was going to stay in this time. Pain and time and my interference and thus intertwining with this time, perhaps, had fixed me here.

There was shouting from the lot beside Fly's Boarding House. Someone was saying, "Was there shots, too, from back there?"

I turned and stumbled away, around the corner, through the Corral, between buildings, almost blindly . . . till I found myself approaching a group of men behind the bar where I'd shot . . .

Where I'd shot myself dead.

I expected to find them marveling at the bartender's story—how a man had shot his twin and the twin had vanished. For surely the body would not remain in this time.

But there it was—six men turned to stare at me, and the portly bartender pointed. "Why, it's the killer himself! Look at his face and the man dead before you! He is the spitting image! He has killed his own twin brother!"

"They even wear the same clothing!"

Guns were pointed at me then and, numbly, I dropped my own.

Now I sit in the territorial jail awaiting execution. The gallows has long been built—I watched from my jail cell window as they used it for a couple of renegade Apaches just last week. I have asked for this sheaf of paper and this pen so that I may write this account, to seal in an envelope and give to the exasperated man appointed as my lawyer. I wish I had the clip from the *Nugget* to include—but it exists in my own time. Old West historians routinely read the pioneer newspapers, and I remember once, in my time, reading in the *Nugget,* with some bemusement, about the man who killed his own twin, in Tombstone, and how the man would say only, "Is it a murder for a man to kill himself? I cannot explain, gentlemen, you would not understand." I said the same yesterday, and never remembered the article till I spoke those words. The story about twin murdering twin had been buried in all the excitement about the "OK Corral fight," scarcely noted. I'd assumed the article a fabrication, not uncommon in frontier newspapers, in the effort to amuse the public. Especially when it was revealed that neither man had identity papers and the surviving man would not reveal his name. Surely it was a story someone had made up.

I chuckled then—and I laugh sadly, now, thinking about it.

I will ask my lawyer to send this to a certain library archive in San Diego, which exists even in this time, the envelope addressed to "Doctor Crosswell"—who does not yet exist—in the hopes it may find its way to him someday. Someone should know what I shared, and didn't share, with Richard Collier. Not just time travel—but love lost.

Perhaps there's an afterlife. Perhaps I'll meet Becky there, her burden lifted at last.

The only thing certain, though, is that at dawn they will hang me for murdering myself.

I might've made up a story about my psychotic twin, and shooting him in self-defense, to save my life—a gun was found on him, after all. But I didn't have the heart for it. You see, Bill Washoe was an arrogant man, who did too little for the woman he loved when she was alive; who did all the wrong things once she was gone. So I was glad to shoot Bill Washoe dead. And it will be a good thing when he has been marched to the gallows and hung.

For he deserved it.

₪

THE MISTS OF TIME
₪
Tom Purdom

The cry from the lookout perked up every officer, rating, and common seaman on deck. The two-masted brig they were intercepting was being followed by sharks—a sure sign it was a slaver. Slave ships fouled the ocean with a trail of bodies as they worked their way across the Atlantic.

John Harrington was standing in front of the rear deckhouse when the midshipman's yell floated down from the mast. His three officers were loitering around him with their eyes fixed on the sails three miles off their port bow—a mass of wind-filled cloth that had aroused, once again, the hope that their weeks of tedious, eventless cruising were coming to an end.

The ship rolling under their own feet, HMS *Sparrow*, was a sixty-foot schooner—one of the smallest warships carried on the rolls of Her Majesty's navy. There was no raised quarterdeck her commander could pace in majestic isolation. The officers merely stood in front of the deckhouse and looked down a deck crowded with two boats, spare spars, and the sweating bodies of crewmen who were constantly working the big triangular sails into new positions in response to the shipmaster's efforts to draw the last increment of movement from the insipid push of the African coastal breezes. A single six-pound gun, mounted on a turntable, dominated the bow.

Sub-lieutenant Bonfors opened his telescope and pointed it at the other ship. He was a broad, well-padded young man and he beamed at the image in his lenses with the smile of a gourmand who was contemplating a particularly interesting table.

"*Blackbirds*, gentlemen. She's low in the water, too. I believe a good packer can squeeze five hundred prime blackbirds into a hull that long—twenty-five hundred good English pounds if they're all still breathing and pulsing."

It was the paradox of time travel. You were there and you weren't there, the laws of physics prohibited it and it was the laws of physics that got you there.

You were the cat that was neither dead nor alive, the photon that could be in two places at once, the wave function that hadn't collapsed. You slipped through a world in which you could see but not be seen, exist and not exist. Sometimes there was a flickering moment when you really were there—a moment, oddly enough, when they could see you and you couldn't see them. It was the paradox of time travel—a paradox built upon the contradictions and inconsistencies that lie at the heart of the sloppy, fundamentally unsolvable mystery human beings call the physical universe.

For Emory FitzGordon the paradox meant that he was crammed into an invisible, transparent space/time bubble, strapped into a two-chair rig shoulder to shoulder with a bony, hyperactive young woman, thirty feet above the tepid water twenty miles off the coast of Africa, six years after the young Princess Victoria had become Queen of England, Wales, Scotland, Ireland, and all the heathen lands Her government ruled beyond the seas. The hyperactive young woman, in addition, was an up-and-coming video auteur who possessed all the personality quirks traditionally associated with the arts.

"Four-minute check completed," the hal running the bubble said. "Conditions on all four co-ordinates register satisfactory and stable. You have full clearance for two hours, provisional clearance for five hours."

Giva Lombardo's hands had already started bustling across the screenbank attached to her chair. The cameras attached to the rig had started recording as soon as the bubble had completed the space/time relocation. Giva was obviously rearranging the angles and magnifications chosen by the hal's programming.

"It didn't take them long to start talking about that twenty-five hundred pounds, did it?" Giva murmured.

John Harrington glanced at the other two officers. A hint of mischief flickered across his face. He tried to maintain a captainly gravity when he was on deck but he was, after all, only twenty-three.

"So how does that break down, Mr. Bonfors?"

"For the slaves alone," the stout sub-lieutenant said, "*conservatively*, it's two hundred and sixty pounds for you, eighty-nine for your hard working first lieutenant, seventy-two for our two esteemed colleagues here, sixteen for the young gentleman in the lookout, and two-and-a-half pounds for every hand in the crew. The value of the ship itself might increase every share by another fifth, depending on the judgment of our lords at the Admiralty."

The sailing master, Mr. Whitjoy, rolled his eyes at the sky. The gunnery officer, Sub-lieutenant Terry, shook his head.

"I see there's one branch of mathematics you seem to have thoroughly mastered, Mr. Bonfors," Terry said.

"I may not have your knowledge of the calculus and other arcane matters, Mr. Terry," Bonfors said, "but I know that the quantity of roast beef and claret a man can consume is directly related to the mass of his purse."

Harrington raised his head. His eyes ranged over the rigging as if he was inspecting every knot. It would take them two hours—perhaps two and a half—to close with the slave ship. *Sparrow* was small and lightly armed but he could at least be thankful she was faster than her opposition. Most of the ships the Admiralty assigned to the West African antislavery squadron were two-masted brigs that wallowed through the water like sick whales.

How would they behave when the shooting started? Should he be glad they were still bantering? This would be the first time any of them had actually faced an armed enemy. Mr. Whitjoy was a forty-year-old veteran of the struggle against the Corsican tyrant but his seagoing service had been limited to blockade duty in the last three years of the Napoleonic wars. For the rest of them—including their captain and all the hands—"active service" had been a placid round of uneventful cruises punctuated by interludes in the seamier quarters of foreign ports.

"We'll keep flying the Portuguese flag until we come into range," Harrington said. "We still have a bit of ship handling ahead of us. We may sail a touch faster than an overloaded slaver but let's not forget they have four guns on each side. Let's make sure we're positioned straight across their bow when we bring them to, Mr. Whitjoy."

Giva had leaped on the prize money issue during their first planning session. She hadn't known the British sailors received special financial bonuses when she had applied for the job. She had circled around the topic, once she became aware of it, as if she had been tethered to it with a leash.

The scholar assigned to oversee the project, Dr. Peter LeGrundy, was a specialist in the cultural and social history of the Victorian British Empire. Peter claimed he normally avoided the details of Victorian military history—a subject his colleagues associated with excessive popular appeal—but in this case he had obviously had to master the relevant complexities. The ships assigned to the West African antislavery patrol had received five pounds for every slave they liberated, as a substitute for the prize money they would have received if they had been fighting in a conventional nation-state war. Prize money had been a traditional wartime incentive. The wages the Crown paid its seaborne warriors had not, after all, been princely. The arbitrary five-pound figure had actually been a rather modest compensation, in Peter's opinion, compared to the sums the *Sparrow's* crew would have received in wartime, from a cargo the government could actually sell.

Peter had explained all that to Giva—several times. And received the same reaction each time.

"There were five hundred captives on that ship," Giva said. "Twenty-five hundred pounds would be what—two or three million today? Audiences aren't totally stupid, Peter. I think most of them will manage to see that the great antislavery crusade could be a very profitable little business."

John Harrington had been reading about the Napoleonic Wars ever since his youngest uncle had given him a biography of Lord Nelson for his ninth birthday. None of the books he had read had captured the stately tempo of naval warfare. He knew the British had spent three hours advancing toward the Franco-Spanish fleet at Trafalgar but most authors covered that phase of the battle in a handful of paragraphs and hurried straight to the thunder that followed. Lieutenant Bonfors and Lieutenant Terry both made two trips to their quarters while *Sparrow* plodded across the gentle African waves toward their quarry. They were probably visiting their chamber pots, Harrington presumed. Mr. Whitjoy, on the other hand, directed the handling of the ship with his usual stolid competence. Harrington thought he caught Whitjoy praying at one point, but the master could have been frowning at a patch of deck that needed a touch of the holystone.

Harrington had stifled his own urge to visit the chamber pot. He had caught two of the hands smiling the second time Bonfors had trudged off the deck.

It had been Midshipmen Montgomery who had spotted the sharks. The other midshipman, Davey Clarke, had replaced Montgomery in the lookout. Montgomery could have gone below but he was circling the deck instead. He stopped at the gun every few minutes and gave it a thorough inspection. Montgomery would be assisting Mr. Terry when the time came to open fire.

Giva had started defending her artistic integrity at the very beginning of her pre-hiring interview. "I get the final edit," Giva had advised the oversight committee. "I won't work under any other conditions. If it's got my name on it, it represents my take on the subject."

Giva had been in Moscow, working on a historical drama. Emory had been staring at seven head-and-shoulder images on his living room imaging stage and Giva had been the only participant in the montage who had chosen a setting that accented her status. All the other participants had selected neutral backdrops. Giva had arranged herself so the committee could see, just beyond her shoulder, two actors who were dressed in flat, twenty-first century brain-link hats.

"There's one thing I absolutely have to say, Mr. FitzGordon," Giva said. "I appreciate your generosity. I will try to repay you by turning out the best possible product I can. But please don't think you can expect to have any influence on the way I do it. I'm not interested in creating public relations fog jobs for wealthy families."

Emory had listened to Giva's tirade with the thin, polite smile a tolerant parent might bestow on a child. "I wouldn't expect you to produce a fog job," Emory responded. "I believe the facts in this case will speak for themselves. I can't deny that I specified this particular incident when I offered the agency this grant partly because my ancestor was involved in it. I wouldn't have known the Royal Navy had engaged in an antislavery campaign if it hadn't been part of our family chronicles. But I also feel this episode is a typical example of the courage and devotion of a group of men who deserve to be remembered and honored. The crews of the West African antislavery patrol saved a hundred thousand human beings from slavery. They deserve a memorial that has been created by an honest, first-class artist."

The committee had already let Emory know Giva Lombardo was the candidate they wanted to hire. Giva had friends in the Agency for Chronautical Studies, it seemed.

She also had ability and the kind of name recognition that would attract an audience. Emory had been impressed with both the docs that had catapulted Giva out of the would-be class. The first doc had been a one-hour essay on women who bought sexually enhancing personality modifications. The second had been a rhapsodic portrait of a cruise on a fully automated sailing ship. The cruise doc was essentially an advertisement funded by the cruise company but it had aroused the enthusiasm of the super-aesthete audience.

Emory's family had been dealing with artists for a hundred and fifty years. His great-grandfather's encounter with the architect who designed his primary residence was a standard item in popular accounts of the history of architecture. It had become a family legend encrusted with advice and observations. *All interactions between artists and the rich hinge on one basic fact*, Emory's great-grandfather had said. *You need the creatives. The creatives need your money.*

Harrington placed his hands behind his back. The approach was coming to an end. Mr. Whitjoy had placed *Sparrow* on a course that would cross the slaver's bow in just four or five minutes.

He took a deep breath and forced the tension out of his neck muscles. He was the captain of a ship of war. He must offer his crew a voice that sounded confident and unperturbed.

"Let's show them our true colors, Mr. Whitjoy. You may advise them of our request as soon as we start to raise our ensign, Mr. Terry."

Lieutenant Bonfors led the boarding party. The slaver hove to in response to Lieutenant Terry's shot across its bow and Lieutenant Bonfors settled his bulk in the stern of a longboat and assumed a rigid, upright dignity that reminded Emory of the recordings of his great-grandfather he had viewed when he had been a child. Harrison FitzGordon had been an ideal role model, in the opinion of Emory's father. He was courteous to everyone he encountered, according to the family catechism, but he never forgot his position in society. He always behaved like someone who assumed the people around him would treat him with deference—just as Lieutenant Bonfors obviously took it for granted that others would row and he would be rowed.

Bonfors maintained the same air of haughty indifference when he hauled himself aboard the slaver and ran his eyes down its guns. Two or three crewmen were lounging near the rear of each gun. Most of them had flintlock pistols stuck in their belts.

A tall man in a loose blue coat hurried across the deck. He held out his hand and Bonfors put his own hands behind his back.

"I am Sub-lieutenant Barry Richard Bonfors of Her Majesty's Ship *Sparrow*. I am here to inspect your ship and your papers in accordance with the treaties currently in effect between my government and the government of the nation whose flag is flying from your masthead."

"I am William Zachary," the officer in the blue coat said, "and I am the commander of this ship. If you will do me the honor of stepping into my cabin, I will be happy to present you with our papers."

"I would prefer to start with an inspection of your hold."

"I'm afraid that won't be possible, sub-lieutenant. I assure you our papers will give you all the information you need."

"The treaties in effect between our countries require the inspection of your entire ship, sir. I would be neglecting my duties if I failed to visit your hold."

Captain Zachary gestured at the guns. "I have two twelve-pound guns and two eighteen-pounders on each side of my ship, sub-lieutenant. You have, as far as I can tell, one six-pounder. I have almost fifty hands. What do you have? Twenty-five? And some of them boys? I'm certain a visit to my cabin and an inspection of my papers will provide you with a satisfactory report to your superiors. As you will see from our papers, our hold is stuffed with jute and bananas."

Zachary was speaking with an accent that sounded, to Emory's ear, a lot like some of the varieties of English emitted by the crew on the *Sparrow*. Giva's microphone arrangement had picked up some of the cries coming from the slaver's crew as Bonfors had made his progress across the waters and Emory had heard several examples of the best-known English nouns and verbs. The ship was flying a Brazilian flag, Emory assumed, because it offered the crew legal advantages they would have missed if they had sailed under their true colors. British citizens who engaged in the slave trade could be hanged as pirates.

The legal complexities of the antislavery crusade had been one of the subjects that had amused Emory when he had been a boy. The officers of the West African Squadron had operated under legal restrictions that were so complicated the Admiralty had issued them an instruction manual they could carry in their uniforms. The Royal Navy could stop the ships of some nations and not others and it could do some things on one country's ships and other things on others.

Emory had been five when he had first heard about John Harrington's exploits off the African coast. Normally the FitzGordon adults just mentioned it now and then. You were reminded you had an ancestor who had liberated slaves when your elders felt you were spending too much time thinking about some of the other things your ancestors had done, such as their contributions to the coal mining and timber cutting industries. In Emory's case, it had become a schoolboy enthusiasm. He had scoured the databanks for information on Lieutenant John Harrington and the great fifty-year struggle in which Harrington had participated. Almost no one outside of his family had heard about the Royal Navy's antislavery campaign, but the historians who had studied it had all concluded it was one of the great epics of the sea. Young officers in small ships had fought the slavers for over half a century. They had engaged in hotly contested ship-to-ship actions. They had ventured up the rivers that communicated with the interior and attacked fortified slaveholding pens. Thousands of British seamen had died from the diseases that infested the African coast. The African slave markets north of the equator had been shut down. One hundred thousand men, women, and children had been rescued from the horrors of the slave ships.

The campaign had been promoted by a British politician, Lord Palmerston, who had tried to negotiate a general international treaty outlawing the slave trade. Palmerston had failed to achieve his goal and British diplomats had been forced to negotiate special agreements country by country. The officers on the spot were supposed to keep all the agreements straight and remember they could be fined, or sued, if they looked in the wrong cupboard or detained the wrong ship.

In this case, the situation was relatively straightforward. The ship was flying the flag of Brazil and the *Sparrow* therefore had the right to examine its papers and search its hull. If the searchers found any evidence the ship was engaging in the slave trade—such as the presence of several hundred chained Africans—the *Sparrow* could seize the slaver and bring the ship, its crew, and all its contents before the courts the navy had established in Freetown, Sierra Leone.

"Look at that," Emory said. "Look at the way he's handling himself."

Bonfors had turned his back on Captain Zachary. He was walking toward the ladder on the side of the ship with the same unhurried serenity he had exhibited when he came aboard.

Did Bonfor's back itch? Was he counting the number of steps that stretched between his present position and the minimal safety he would enjoy when he reached the boat? For Emory it was a thrilling moment—a display of the values and attitudes that had shaped his own conduct since he had been a child. Most of the officers on the *Sparrow* shared a common heritage. Their family lines had been molded, generation after generation, by the demands of the position they occupied in their society.

"You are now provisionally cleared for six hours total," the hal said. "All coordinates register satisfactory and stable."

■　■　■

The slaver was turning. Harrington noted the hands in the rigging making minor adjustments to the sails and realized the slaver's bow was shifting to the right—so it could bring its four starboard guns to bear on *Sparrow.*

Mr. Whitjoy had seen the movement, too. His voice was already bellowing orders. He had been told to hold *Sparrow* lined up across the slaver's bows. He didn't need further instructions.

Conflicting courses churned across Harrington's brain. Bonfors had reboarded his boat and he was still crossing the gap between the ships. The slave ship couldn't hit the boat with the side guns but it had a small chaser on the bow—a four-pounder that could shatter the boat with a single lucky shot. The wind favored the slaver, too. The two ships had hove to with the wind behind the slaver, hitting its sails at a twenty-degree angle . . .

He hurried down the narrow deck toward the bow. Terry and Montgomery both looked at him expectantly. The swivel gun was loaded with chain shot. The slow match smoldered in a bucket.

"Let's give our good friend Mr. Bonfors time to get aboard," Harrington said.

"Aren't you afraid they'll fire on the boat with their chaser?" Montgomery said. "Sir."

Terry started to say something and Harrington stopped him with his hand. Montgomery should have kept his thoughts to himself but this wasn't the time to rebuke him.

"It's obvious Mr. Bonfors didn't finish the inspection," Harrington said. "But we won't be certain they refused to let him go below until he makes his report. We don't want to give the lawyers any unnecessary grounds for complaint."

He glanced around the men standing near the gun. "Besides, everybody says these slavers tend to be poor shots. They're businessmen. They go to sea to make money."

He paused for what he hoped would be an effect. "We go to sea to make *war.*"

Montgomery straightened. Harrington thought he saw a light flash in the eyes of one of the seamen in the gun crew. He turned away from the gun and made his way toward the stern with his hands behind his back, in exactly the same pose his second commanding officer, Captain Ferris, would have assumed. A good commander had to be an actor. Good actors never ruined an exit line with too much talk.

■   ■   ■

Emory had started campaigning for Giva's removal a week after he had audited the first planning meeting. Giva had nagged at the prize money issue for a tiresome fifteen minutes at the end of the fourth meeting and Emory had maintained his link to Peter LeGrundy after she had exited. Giva had still been in Russia at that state of their association. Emory was staying at his New York residence, where he was sampling the opening premieres of the entertainment season. Peter had based himself in London, so he could take a first hand look at the Royal Navy archives.

"Are you really sure we can't do anything about her supporters in the chronautical bureaucracy?" Emory said. "It seems to me there should be some *small* possibility we can overcome their personal predilections and convince them she has a bias that is obviously incompatible with scholarship. A ten minute conversation with her would probably be sufficient."

"She's peppery, Emory. She feels she has to assert herself. She's young and she's an artist."

"And what's she going to be like when she's actually recording? We'll only have one opportunity, Peter—the only opportunity anybody will ever have. Whatever she records, that's it."

Under the rules laid down by the chrono bureaucrats, the *Sparrow*'s encounter with the slaver was surrounded by a restricted zone that encompassed hundreds of square miles of ocean and twenty hours of time. No one knew what would happen if a bubble entered a space/time volume occupied by another bubble—and the bureaucrats had decided they would avoid the smallest risk they would ever find out. The academics and fundraisers who had written the preamble to the agency's charter had decreed that its chrononauts would "dispel the mists of time with disciplined onsite observations," and the careerists and political appointees who ran the agency had decreed each site would receive only one dispelling. Once their bubble left the restricted zone, no one else would ever return to it.

"She's what they want," Peter said. "I've counted the votes. There's only one way you can get her out of that bubble—withdraw your grant and cancel the project."

"And let the media have a fiesta reporting on the rich idler who tried to bribe a committee of dedicated scholars."

Peter was being cautious, in Emory's opinion. He could have changed the committee's mind if he had made a determined effort. Giva had flaunted her biases as if she thought they were a fashion statement. But Peter also knew he would make some permanent enemies among the losing minority if he pressed his case.

Peter was a freelance scholar who lived from grant to grant. He had never managed to land a permanent academic position. He was balancing two forces that could have a potent impact on his future: a rich individual who could be a fertile source of grants and a committee composed of scholars who could help him capture a permanent job.

Emory could, of course, offer Peter some inducements that might overcome his respect for Giva's supporters. But that was a course that had its own risks. You never knew when an academic might decide his scholarly integrity had to be asserted. In the end, Emory had adopted a more straightforward approach and applied for a seat in the bubble under the agency's Chrono Tourist program. The extra passenger would cost the agency nothing and the fee would increase his grant by thirty percent. Giva would still control the cameras on the bubble but he could make his own amateurish record with his personal recording implant. He would have evidence he could use to support any claim that she had distorted the truth.

Harrington could have leaned over the side of the ship and called for a report while Bonfors was still en route but he was certain Captain Ferris would never have done that. Neither would Nelson. Instead, he stood by the deckhouse and remained at his post while Bonfors climbed over the side, saluted the stern, and marched across the deck.

"He threatened me," Bonfors said. "He pointed at his guns and told me I could learn all I needed to know from his account books."

"He refused to let you visit the hold?"

"He told me I could learn all I needed from his books. He told me he had eight guns and fifty hands and we only had one gun and twenty-five."

Harrington frowned. Would a court interpret that as a threat? Could a lawyer claim Bonfors had deliberately misinterpreted the slave captain's words?

"It was a clear refusal," Bonfors said. "He gave me no indication he was going to let me inspect the hold."

Harrington turned toward the gun. He sucked in a good lungful and enjoyed a small pulse of satisfaction when he heard his voice ring down the ship.

"You may fire at your discretion, Mr. Terry."

Montgomery broke into a smile. Terry said something to his crew and the lead gunner drew the slow match from its bucket.

Terry folded his arms over his chest and judged the rise and fall of the two ships. Chain shot consisted of two balls, connected by a length of chain. It could spin through the enemy rigging and wreak havoc on any rope or wood that intersected its trajectory.

Terry moved his arm. The lead gunner laid the end of the match across the touchhole.

It was the first time in his life Harrington had stood on a ship that was firing on other human beings. It was the moment he had been preparing for since he had been a twelve-year-old novice at the Naval School at Portsmouth but the crash of the gun still caught him by surprise.

Montgomery was standing on tiptoe staring at the other ship. Terry was already snapping out orders. The sponger was pulling his tool out of its water bucket. Drill and training were doing their job. On the entire ship, there might have been six men who could feel the full weight of the moment, undistracted by the demands of their posts—and one of them was that supreme idler, the commanding officer.

The slaver's foremast quivered. A rip spread across a topsail. Bonfors pulled his telescope out of his coat and ran it across the slaver's upper rigging.

"I can see two lines dangling from the foretopsail," Bonfors said.

Harrington was playing his own telescope across the slaver's deck. Four men had gathered around the bowchaser. The two ships were positioned so its ball would hit the *Sparrow* toward the rear midships—a little forward of the exact spot where he was standing

He had assumed they should start by destroying the slaver's sails. Then, when there was no danger their quarry could slip away, they could pick it off at their leisure, from positions that kept them safe from its broadsides. Should he change that plan merely because he was staring at the muzzle of the enemy gun? Wouldn't it make more sense to fire at the gun? Even though it was a small, hard-to-hit target?

It was a tempting thought. The slavers might even strike their colors if the shot missed the stern gun and broke a few bodies as it hurtled down the deck.

It was a thought generated by fear.

"Well started, Mr. Terry. Continue as you are."

The slaver's gun flashed. There was a short pause—just time enough to feel himself stiffen—and then, almost simultaneously, his brain picked up the crash of the gun and the thud of the ball striking the side of *Sparrow*'s hull.

The ball had hit the ship about where he had guessed it would. If it had been aimed a few degrees higher, it would have crossed the deck three steps to his right.

The *Sparrow*'s gun fired its second shot moments after the slaver's ball hit the hull. The sponger shoved his tool down the gun barrel, the crew fell into their drill, and the *Sparrow* hurled a third ball across the gap while the slaver's crew was still loading their second shot.

"The slaver's got a crew working on the rear boat," Giva said.

Emory had been watching the two gun crews and looking for signs they were actually creating some damage. The third shot from the *Sparrow*'s gun had drawn an excited, arms-raised leap from the midshipman posted with the gun crew. The upper third of the slaver's forward mast had bounced away from the lower section, and sagged against the rigging.

Harrington's report to the Admiralty said the slaver had brought out a boat and used it to pull the ship around, to bring its broadside into play. Harrington hadn't said when they had lowered the boat. Emory had assumed they had done it after the battle had raged for a while.

"It looks like they're going to lower it on the other side of their ship," Emory said. "Is that going to cause any problems?"

"The rotation program can correct for most of the deficiencies. We can always have a talking head explain some of the tactics—some professor who's goofy about old weapons. We could even have you do it, Emory. You probably know more about the antislavery patrol than Peter and all the rest of the committee combined. That could be a real tingler—the hero's descendant talking about the ancestor he hero-worshipped as a boy. After he had actually seen him in action."

Harrington was making another calculation. The slaver's boat was pulling the slaver's bow into the wind. There was no way Mr. Whitjoy could stay with the bow as it turned and avoid a broadside. Should he pull out of range, circle around, and place *Sparrow* across the enemy's stern? Or should he hold his current position, take the broadside, and inflict more damage on their sails?

The blow to the slaver's mast had weakened its sailing capabilities but it wasn't decisive. He wanted them dead in the water—totally at his mercy.

The slaver's bow gun was already pointing away from *Sparrow*. There would be a period—who knew how long?—when *Sparrow* could fire on the slaver and the slaver couldn't fire back.

"Hold position, Mr. Whitjoy. Keep up the good work, Mr. Terry."

Harrington was holding his pocket watch in his hand. The swivel gun roared again and he noted that Terry's crew was firing a shot every minute and twenty seconds.

He put his hands behind his back and watched the enemy ship creep around. It was all a matter of luck. The balls from the slaver's broadside would fly high or low—or pass over the deck at the height of a young commander's belly. They would intersect the place where you were standing or pass a few feet to your right or left. The odds were on your side.

And there was nothing you could do about it.

Bonfors glanced back. He saw what Harrington was doing and resumed his telescopic observations of the enemy ship.

Terry's crew fired three more times while the slaver made its turn. The second shot cut the broken topmast free from its support lines and sent it sliding through the rigging to the deck. The third shot slammed into the main mast with an impact that would have made every captive in the hold howl with joy if they could have seen the result—and understood what it meant. The top of the mast lurched to the right. The whole structure, complete with spars and furled sails, toppled toward the deck and sprawled over the slaver's side.

Harrington felt himself yield to an uncontrollable rush of emotion. "*Take her about, Mr. Whitjoy! Take us out of range.*"

Whitjoy barked orders. Hands raced to their stations. The big triangular main sail swung across *Sparrow*'s deck. The hand at the wheel adjusted the angle of the rudder and Harrington's ship began to turn away from the wind.

Some of the crew on the other ship had left their guns and rushed to the fallen sail. With luck, one or two of their compatriots would be lying under the wreckage.

If there was one virtue the Navy taught you, it was patience. You stood your watches, no matter how you felt. You endured storms that went on and on, for days at a time, without any sign they were coming to an end. You waited out calms. And now you locked yourself in your post and watched the elephantine motions of the ships, as *Sparrow* turned away from the wind, and the muzzles of the enemy guns slowly came to bear on the deck you were standing on . . .

The flash of the first gun caught him by surprise. He would have waited at least another minute before he fired if he had been commanding the other ship. A huge noise whined past *Sparrow*'s stern. The second gun lit up a few seconds later, and he realized they were firing one gun at a time.

This time the invisible Thing passed over his head, about fifty feet up. Mr. Terry fired the swivel gun and he heard Montgomery's treble shout a word of encouragement at the ball.

The slaver hurled its third shot. A tremendous bang shook the entire length of *Sparrow*'s hull. He looked up and down the deck, trying to find some sign of damage, and saw Montgomery covering his face with both hands.

A gunner grabbed Montgomery's shoulders. Terry stepped in front of the boy and seized his wrists. The rest of the gun crew gathered around.

"Mr. Bonfors—please see what the trouble is. See if you can get the gun back in action."

Bonfors shot him one of the most hostile looks he had ever received from another human being. It only lasted a moment but Harrington knew exactly what his second in command was thinking. The captain had seen an unpleasant duty and passed it to the appropriate subordinate. They both knew it was the right thing to do—the only thing a captain *could* do—but that didn't alter the basic fact that the coldhearted brute had calmly handed you a job that both of you would have given almost anything to avoid.

A crewman was standing by the railing near the bow. He pointed at the railing and Harrington understood what had happened. The big bang had been a glancing blow from a cannon ball. Wooden splinters had flown off the rail at the speed of musket balls. One of the splinters had apparently hit Montgomery in the face.

"It looks like we now know who Montgomery is," Emory said.

Giva was looking at a rerun on her display. "I got it all. The camera had him centered the whole time. I lost him when they all crowded around him. But I got the moment he was hit."

Lieutenant Bonfors had reached the gun and started easing the crew away from Montgomery with a mixture of jovial comments and firm pushes. "Let's keep our minds on our work, gentlemen. Take Mr. Montgomery to the captain's cabin, Hawksbill. I believe we've got time for one more shot before we pull away from our opponent, Mr. Terry."

■ ■ ■

Their planning sessions had contained one moment of pure harmony. They had all agreed Giva would have two cameras continuously tracking both midshipmen. They knew one of the boys was going to be hit but they didn't know which one. They knew the boy was referred to as Mr. Montgomery in Harrington's report but they didn't know what he looked like or when it would happen. They only knew *Mr. Montgomery and Mr. Clarke acquitted themselves with courage and competence. I regret to report that Mr. Montgomery has lost the sight of his left eye. He is bearing his misfortune with commendable cheerfulness.*

Sparrow put a solid half-mile between its stern and the slaver before it turned into a long, slow curve that ended with it bearing down on the slaver's stern. The men in the slaver's boat tried to turn with it, but Mister Whitjoy outmaneuvered them. The duel between sail power and oar power came to an abrupt end as soon as *Sparrow* drew within firing range. Harrington ordered Terry to fire on the boat, the second shot raised a fountain of water near the boat's bow, and every slaver in the boat crew lunged at the ladder that hung from the side of their ship.

Bonfors chuckled as he watched them scramble onto the deck. "They don't seem to have much tolerance for being shot at, do they?"

Harrington was eyeing the relative positions of the two ships. In another five minutes *Sparrow* would be lying directly behind the slaver's stern, poised to hurl ball after ball down the entire length of the other ship.

"You may fire at the deck as you see fit, Mr. Terry. We'll give them three rounds. And pause to see if they strike."

"They're opening the hatch," Emory said.

Captain Zachary and four of his men were crouching around the hatch in the center of the slave ship. They had drawn their pistols and they were all holding themselves close to the deck, in anticipation of the metal horror that could fly across their ship at any moment.

The four crewmen dropped through the hatch. Captain Zachary slithered backward and crouched on one knee, with his pistol clutched in both hands.

Harrington threw out his arm as soon as he saw the first black figures stumble into the sunlight. "Hold your fire, Mr. Terry."

The slavers had arranged themselves so he could enjoy an unobstructed view of the slaves. The Africans were linked together with chains but the captain and his crew were still training guns on them. Two of the slaves slumped to the deck as they came out of the hold. Their companions picked them up and dragged them away from the hatch.

"I'd say a third of them appear to be women," Bonfors said.

Harrington raised his telescope and verified Bonfors' estimate. One of the women was holding a child.

He lowered his telescope and pushed it closed. "Organize a boarding party, Mr. Bonfors. I will lead it. You will take command of the ship."

"My God," Emory said. "He didn't waste a second."

They had known what Harrington was going to do. It was in his report. But nothing in the written record had prepared Emory for the speed of his decision.

I ascertained that we could no longer punish their crew with our gun, Harrington had written, *and I therefore determined to take their ship by assault, with one of our boats. The presence of the unfortunate innocents meant that our adversaries could repair their masts before our very eyes and perhaps slip away in the night. There was, in addition, the danger they would adopt the infamous course others have taken in such a situation and avoid prosecution by consigning their cargo to the sea.*

Terry volunteered at once. Davey Clarke wanted to go, but Harrington decreed they couldn't risk another midshipman.

"We'd have a fine time keeping the ship afloat with both of our young gentlemen laid up, Davey."

The hands obviously needed encouragement. Four men stepped forward. The expressions on the rest of them convinced Harrington he had to give Bonfors some support.

"A double share for every man who volunteers," Harrington called out. "Taken from the captain's portion."

A ball from the slaver's stern gun ploughed into the water forty feet from *Sparrow*'s port side. Bonfors' arm shot toward the splash while it was still hanging over the waves. "It's the easiest money you'll ever earn, lads. You've seen how these fellows shoot."

In the end, fifteen men shuffled up to the line. That would leave ten on the *Sparrow*—enough to get the ship back to port if worse came to worse.

Giva smiled. "He just doubled their profit, didn't he? He didn't mention that in his report."

■ ■ ■

Harrington placed himself in the front of the boat. Terry sat in the back, where the ranking officer would normally sit.

Their positions wouldn't matter that much during the approach. The slavers would be firing down from the deck. They would all be equally exposed. When they initiated the assault, however, he had to be in front. The whole enterprise might fail if he went down—but it was certain to fail if the men felt their captain was huddling in the rear. The assault had been his idea, after all.

They had boarded the boat on *Sparrow*'s starboard side, with *Sparrow*'s hull between them and the enemy guns. For the first few seconds after Terry gave the order, they traveled along the hull. Then they cleared the bow.

And there it was. There was nothing between him and the stern gun of the enemy ship but a hundred yards of sunlight and water.

Terry was supposed to steer them toward the rear of the slaver's starboard side. They had agreed he would aim them at a point that would accomplish two objectives. He would keep the boat outside the angle the slaver's broadside could cover and he would minimize the time they would spend inside the stern gun's field of fire. Terry was the best man to hold the tiller. No one on *Sparrow* had a better understanding of the strengths and limitations of nautical artillery.

They had overcome their boat's initial resistance as they had slid down *Sparrow*'s hull. Terry called out his first firm "*Stroke!*" and the bow shot toward its destination. Terry gave the rowers two cycles of *stroke* and *lift* at a moderate pace. Then he upped the pace and kept increasing it with every cycle.

Every push of the oars carried them out of the danger presented by the stern gun. But it also carried them toward the armed men who were crowding around the rail.

Harrington's hands tightened on the weapons he was holding—a pistol in his right hand, a cutlass in his left. He was keeping his fingers on the butt of the pistol, well away from the trigger and the possibility he would fire the gun by accident and leave himself one bullet short and looking like a fool. Two more pistols were tucked into his belt, right and left. The men behind him were all equipped with two pistols, two loaded muskets wrapped in oilcloth, and a cutlass laid across their feet.

The stern gun flashed. The impulse to squeeze himself into a package the size of his hat seemed irresistible but he focused his eyes on the side of the slaver and discovered he could hold himself fixed in place until he heard the bang of the gun reaching him from a distance that seemed as remote as the moons of Jupiter.

"*Stroke* . . . lift . . . *stroke* . . . lift."

Was there anything more beautiful than the crash of a gun that had just fired in your direction? The noise had made its way across the water and you were still alive. You could be certain four pounds of iron had sailed harmlessly past you, instead of slamming into your bones or knocking holes in your boat and mutilating your shipmates.

"That should be the last we'll hear from that thing," a voice muttered behind him.

"I should hope so," a brasher voice said. "Unless these darkiewhippers have picked up some pointers from Mr. Terry in the last half hour."

The second voice belonged to a hand named Bobby Dawkins—a veteran in his fourth decade who was noted for his monkeyish agility and the stream of good-natured comments he bestowed on everything that happened around him. Dawkins had been the first man to volunteer after Harrington had augmented the cash reward.

Armed men were lining up along the rail of the slave ship. More men were falling in behind them.

Emory ran his eyes down the rail picking out faces that looked particularly vicious or threatening. He had begun his recording as a weapon in his contest with Giva but he was beginning to think along other lines. He wanted a personal record of this—the kind of record a tourist would make. It wouldn't be as sharp as Giva's work but it would be *his*—a personal view of his ancestor's courage.

The slavers started firing their muskets when the boat was still fifty yards from its destination. Harrington had been hoping they would waste a few of their shots but he still felt himself flinch when he saw the first flash. Everybody else in the boat had something to do. The hands had to row. Terry had to steer. He had to sit here and be a target.

He knew he should give his men a few words of encouragement but he couldn't think of a single phrase. His mind had become a blank sheet. Was he afraid? Was this what people meant when they said someone was *paralyzed*?

The slavers shoved two African women up to the rail. The men in the center of the firing line stepped aside and more slaves took their place.

"The swine," Dawkins said. "Bloody. Cowardly. *Bastards*."

Black faces stared at the oncoming boat. Harrington peered at their stupefied expressions and realized they didn't have the slightest idea they were being used as shields. They had been pushed in chains along trails that might be hundreds of miles long. They had been packed into a hold as if they were kegs of rum. They were surrounded by men who didn't speak their language. By now they must be living in a fog.

"Make sure you aim before you shoot. Make these animals feel every ball you fire."

He was bellowing with rage. He would have stood up in the boat if he hadn't been restrained by years of training. He knew he was giving his men a stupid order. He knew there was no way they could shoot with that kind of accuracy. It didn't matter. The slavers had provoked emotions that were as uncontrollable as a hurricane.

More slaves were shoved to the railing. Muskets banged. Slavers were actually resting their guns on the shoulders of the slaves they were using for cover.

"We're inside their guns," Terry yelled. "I'll take us forward."

Harrington pointed at a spot just aft of the forward gun. "Take us there. Between one and two. First party—stow your oars. Shoulder your muskets. Wait for my order."

They had worked this out before they had boarded the boat. Half the men would guide the boat during the final approach. The other half would pick up their muskets and prepare to fight.

Giva had stopped making comments. Her face had acquired the taut, focused lines of a musician or athlete who was working at the limits of her capacity. She was scanning the drama taking place outside the bubble while she simultaneously tracked the images on six screens and adjusted angles and subjects with quick, decisive motions of her hands.

Emory had noted the change in her attitude and turned his attention to his own record. What difference did it make how she felt? The people who saw the finished product would see brave men hurling themselves into danger. Would anybody really care why they did it?

Musket balls cracked in the air around the boat. Metal hammered on the hull. Four members of the slaver crew were running toward the spot where Harrington planned to board. The rest of them were staying near the middle and firing over their human shields.

"Hold her against the side," Harrington yelled. "Throw up the grappling hooks."

The four hands who had been given the job threw their grappling hooks at the rail. The man beside Harrington tugged at the rope, to make sure it was firm, and Harrington fired his first pistol at the ship and handed the gun to one of the rowers. He grabbed the rope and walked himself up the side of the hull, past the gun that jutted out of the port on his left. His cutlass dangled from a loop around his wrist.

He knew he would be most vulnerable when he went over the rail. His hands would be occupied. He would be exposed to gunfire and hand to hand attacks. He seized the rail with both hands as soon as he came in reach and pulled himself over before he could hesitate.

Four men were crouching on the roof of the rear deckhouse. A gun flamed. Harrington jerked his left pistol out of his belt and fired back. He charged at the deckhouse with his cutlass raised.

The slavers fired their guns and scampered off the deckhouse. Harrington turned toward the bow, toward the men who were using the slaves as shields. His boarding party was crowding over the rails. He had half a dozen men scattered beside him. Most of them were firing their muskets at the slavers and their flesh and blood bulwarks.

"*Use your cutlasses! Make these bastards bleed!*"

He ran across the deck with his cutlass held high. He could hear himself screaming like a wild man. He had tried to think about the best way to attack while they had been crossing the water. Now he had stopped thinking. They couldn't stand on the deck and let the animals shoot at them.

The Africans' eyes widened. They twisted away from the lunatics rushing toward them and started pushing against the bodies behind them. The slavers had overlooked an important fact—they were hiding behind a wall that was composed of conscious, intelligent creatures.

The African directly in front of Harrington was a woman. She couldn't turn her back on him because of her chains but she had managed to make a half turn. The man looming behind her was so tall she didn't reach his shoulder. The man was pointing a pistol at Harrington and the woman was clawing at his face with one hand.

The pistol sounded like a cannon when it fired. Harrington covered the deck in front of him in two huge leaps—the longest leaps he had ever taken—and brought his cutlass down on the slaver with both hands.

Steel sliced through cloth and bit into the slaver's collarbone. The man's mouth gaped open. He fell back and Harrington shouldered the female slave aside and hoisted his legs over the chain dangling between her and the captive on her right.

Emory was clamping his jaw on the kind of bellow overwrought fans emitted at sports events. Giva had shifted the bubble to a location twenty-five meters from the side of the slave ship. He could see and hear every detail of Harrington's headlong rush.

Half a dozen men had joined Harrington's assault. More had fallen in behind as they had come over the side. Most of the men in the first rank were running at a crouch, about a step behind their captain. One sailor was holding his hand in front of his face, as if he thought he could stop a bullet with his palm. Emory had been watching combat scenes ever since he was a boy but no actor had ever captured the look on these men's faces—the intense, white-faced concentration of men who knew they were facing real bullets.

A slaver backed away from the pummeling fists of a tall, ribby slave and fired at the oncoming sailors. For a moment Emory thought the shot had gone wild. Then he glanced toward the rear of the assault. A sailor who had just pulled himself over the side was sagging against the rail.

Giva had expanded her display to eight monitors. Her hands were flying across her screens as if she was conducting the action taking place on the ship.

The slavers in front of Harrington were all falling back. Most of them seemed to be climbing the rigging or ducking behind boats and deck gear. On his right, his men had stopped their rush and started working their muskets with a ragged, hasty imitation of the procedure he had drilled into them when he had decided it would be a useful skill if they ever actually boarded a ship. They would never load and fire like three-shots-to-the-minute redcoats but they were doing well enough for a combat against a gang who normally fought unarmed primitives.

The slaver captain—Captain Zachary?—was standing on the front deckhouse, just behind the rail. He stared at Harrington across the heads of the slavers who were scattered between them and Harrington realized he was pulling a rod out of the pistol he was holding in his left hand.

It was one of those moments when everything around you seems to stand still. Harrington's cutlass dropped out of his hand. He reached for the pistol stuck in his belt. He pulled it out and cocked it—methodically, with no haste—with the heel of his left hand.

On the deckhouse, Zachary had poured a dab of powder into the firing pan without taking his eyes off Harrington. He cocked the gun with his thumb and clutched it in a solid two-handed grip as he raised it to the firing position.

"*Look at that!*" Emory said. "Are you getting that, Giva? They're facing each other like a pair of duelists."

If this had been a movie, Emory realized, the director would have captured the confrontation between Harrington and Zachary from at least three angles—one long shot to establish that they were facing each other, plus a close-up for each combatant. How did you work it when you were shooting the real thing and you couldn't re-enact it several times with the camera placed in different positions? He turned his head and peered at Giva's screens.

Giva's hands were hopping across her screens. She had centered the gunfight in a wideview, high angle shot in the second screen in her top row.

Zachary's hands flew apart. The tiny figure on Giva's screen sagged. The life-size figure standing on the real ship clutched at his stomach with both palms.

The captain of the slaver received a mortal bullet wound during the fray, Harrington had written. *His removal from the melee soon took the fight out of our adversaries.* There had been no mention that Harrington himself had fired the decisive shot.

"Is that all you got?" Emory said. "That one long shot?"

He had searched her screens twice, looking for a close-up of the duel. Half of Giva's screens seemed to be focused on the slaves.

Giva jabbed at her number three screen. Emory glanced at the scene on the ship and saw the African woman Harrington had shoved aside stiffening as if she was having a fit. The image on the screen zoomed to a close-up and the camera glimpsed a single glassy eye before the woman's head slumped forward.

Giva pulled the camera back and framed the body sprawling on the deck. The woman's only garment had been a piece of blue cloth she had wrapped around her breasts and hips. The big wound just above her left breast was clearly visible.

■ ■ ■

"You got him, sir! Right in the bastard's stomach!"

Bobby Dawkins was moving into a position on Harrington's right. He had a raised cutlass in his right hand and he was waving a pistol with his left.

More men took their places beside Dawkins. Nobody was actually stepping *between* Harrington and the enemy but they were all making some effort to indicate they were willing to advance with their captain.

Harrington's hands had automatically stuffed the empty pistol into his belt. He dropped into an awkward crouch and picked up his cutlass. Most of the slavers in front of him were looking back at the deckhouse.

"You just lost the most dramatic event of the whole assault—something we'd never have guessed from the printed record."

"I can zoom in on the scene when I'm editing," Giva muttered. "I'm a pro, Emory. Let me work."

"So why do you need the close-up you just got? Why do you have so many cameras focused on the slaves? Couldn't you edit that later, too?"

Four hands were standing beside Harrington. Three more hands were standing a pair of steps behind them. Three of them had muskets pressed into their shoulders. The other four were cursing and grunting as they worked their way through various sections of the reloading drill.

"Hold your fire!" Harrington snapped. "Train your piece on a target but hold your fire."

He heard the jumpy excitement in his voice and knew it would never do. Use the voice you use when the wind is whipping across the deck, he told himself. Pretend you're thundering at the mast and Davey Clarke has the lookout.

His right arm was raising his sword above his head. "Your captain has fallen! *Yield. Lay down your arms.* Lay down your arms or I'll order my men to keep firing."

"Is that your idea of *scholarship*, Giva—another weepy epic about suffering victims?"

John Harrington knew he would be talking about this moment for the rest of his life. He knew he had managed to sound like a captain was supposed to sound—like a man who had absolute control of the situation, and assumed everyone who heard him would obey his orders. Now he had to see if they really would submit. He had to stand here, fully exposed to a stray shot, and give them time to respond.

Captain Zachary was slumping against the railing of the deckhouse with his hands clutching his stomach. The two slavers who were standing directly in front of him had turned toward Harrington when they had heard his roar. Their eyes settled on the muskets leveled at their chests.

Zachary raised his head. He muttered something Harrington couldn't understand. One of the slavers immediately dropped to one knee. He placed his pistol on the deck.

"The captain says to surrender," the sailor yelled. "He says get it over with."

Harrington lowered his sword. He pushed himself across the deck—it was one of the hardest things he had ever done—and picked up the musket.

"You have my sincerest thanks, Captain Zachary. You have saved us all much discomfort."

"This is *my* project, Emory. I was given complete control of the cameras and the final product. Do you have any idea what you and the whole chrono bureaucracy would look like if I handed in my resignation because you tried to bully me while I was doing my job?"

"I'm not trying to bully you. You're the one with the power in this situation. No one has to draw me a power flowchart. I'm got my own record of the dueling incident. Anybody who looks at my recording—or yours for that matter—can see you've ignored a dramatic, critical event and focused on a peripheral incident."

"Don't you think those *blackbirds* deserve a little attention, too? Do you think they're having a fun time caught between two groups of money hungry berserkers?"

Dawkins was picking up the slavers' weapons as they collected near the starboard rail. Five other hands were aiming their muskets over the slavers' heads. Harrington had positioned the musket men six paces from their potential targets—close enough they couldn't miss, far enough none of their prisoners could convince themselves they could engage in a rush before the muskets could fire.

The regulations said the slavers had to be transported to *Sparrow*. The prize crew he assigned to the slaver would have enough trouble looking after the Africans. How many prisoners could he put in each boatload as they made the transfer, given the number of men he could spare for guard duty? He could put the prisoners in irons, of course. But that might be too provocative. They had been operating in a milieu in which chains were associated with slavery and racial inferiority.

He turned to Terry, who had taken up a position behind the musket men. "Keep an eye on things, Mr. Terry. I think it's time I ventured into the hold."

The world around the space/time bubble turned black—the deepest blackness Emory had ever experienced. They had known it could happen at any time—they had even been exposed to simulations during their pre-location training—but the reality still made him freeze. There was nothing outside the bubble. *Nothing.*

The world snapped back. A male slave near the front of the ship was staring their way with his mouth gaping. He gestured with a frantic right hand and the elderly man beside him squinted in their direction.

Harrington had known the hold would stink. Every officer who had ever served in the West African squadron agreed on that. He had picked up the stench when the boat had approached the ship's side but he had been too preoccupied to react to it. Now his stomach turned as soon as he settled his feet on the ladder.

In theory, the slavers were supposed to wash their cargo down, to fight disease and keep it alive until they could take their profit. In practice, nothing could eliminate the stink of hundreds of bodies pressed into their storage shelves like bales of cotton.

The noise was just as bad as the odor. Every captive in the hold seemed to be jabbering and screaming. The slaves in a cargo could come from every section of the continent. They were brought to the coast from the places where they had been captured—or bought from some native chief who had taken them prisoner during a tribal war—and assembled in big compounds before they were sold to the European slave traders. It would be a miracle if fifty of them spoke the same language.

He paused at the bottom of the ladder and stared at the patch of blue sky over the hatch. He was the commander of a British warship. Certain things were required.

He unhooked the lamp that hung beside the ladder and peered into the din. White eyes stared at him out of the darkness. A glance at the captives he saw told him Captain Zachary had adapted one of the standard plans. Each slave had been placed with his back between the legs of the slave behind him.

He had been listening to descriptions of slave holds since he had been a midshipman. He had assumed he had been prepared. The slaves had been arranged on three shelves, just as he had expected. They would spend most of the voyage staring at a ceiling a few inches above their faces. The passage that ran down the center of the hold was only a little wider than his shoulders.

"We have encountered a space/time instability," the hal said. "I must remind you an abort is strongly recommended."

"We have to stay," Emory said. "We haven't captured the liberation of the slaves. There's no finale."

The mission rules were clear. Two flickers and the hal would automatically abort. One, and they could stay if they thought it was worth the risk.

No one knew if those rules were necessary. The bureaucrats had established them and their electronic representative would enforce them. Time travel was a paradox and an impossibility. Intelligent people approached it with all the caution they would confer on a bomb with an unknown detonating mechanism.

Giva kept her eyes focused on her screens. If she voted with him, they would stay. If they split their vote, the hal would implement the "strong recommendation" it had received from its masters.

The slave who had pointed at them seemed to have been the only person who had seen the instability. There was no indication anyone else had noticed the apparition that had flickered beside the hull.

"I think we should stay," Giva said. "For now."

"The decision will be mandatorily reconsidered once every half hour. A termination may be initiated at any time."

Harrington made himself walk the entire length of the passage. He absorbed the odor. He let the clamor bang on his skull. He peered into the shelves on both sides every third step. He couldn't make his men come down here if he wasn't willing to do it himself.

On the deck, he had yielded to a flicker of sympathy for Zachary. Stomach wounds could inflict a painful slow death on their victims. Now he hoped Zachary took a whole month to die. And stayed fully conscious up to the last moment.

He marched back to the ladder with his eyes fixed straight ahead. He had lost his temper in the boat when he had seen Zachary's cutthroats using their captives as human shields. It had been an understandable lapse but it couldn't happen twice in the same day. His ship and his crew depended on his judgment.

Terry glanced at him when he assumed his place on the deck. Most of the slaver's crew had joined the cluster of prisoners. Some of them even looked moderately cheerful. They all knew the court at Freetown would set them free within a month at the most. An occasional incarceration was one of the inconveniences of their trade.

"There should be at least four hundred," Harrington said. "Two thousand pounds minimum. And the value of the ship."

Emory made a mental calculation as he watched the first boatload of prisoners crawl toward the *Sparrow*. At the rate the boat was moving, given the time it had taken to load it, they were going to sit here for at least two more hours.

Giva was devoting half her screens to the crew and half to the Africans but he knew he would look like a fool if he objected. The crew were stolidly holding their guns on their prisoners. The Africans were talking among themselves. The two Africans who were chained on either side of the fallen woman had dropped to their knees beside her.

The moment when the slaves would be brought into the sunlight was the moment Emory considered the emotional climax of the whole episode. He had been so enthusiastic when he described it during their planning sessions that Peter LeGrundy had told him he sounded like he had already seen it.

I ordered the liberated captives brought to the deck as circumstances allowed, Harrington had written. *They did not fully comprehend their change in status, and I could not explain it. Our small craft does not contain a translator among its complement. But the sight of so many souls rescued from such a terrible destiny stimulated the deepest feelings of satisfaction in every heart capable of such sentiments.*

"You think we could press this lad, captain? We could use some of that muscle."

Harrington turned his head. He had decided he should let the men standing guard take a few minutes rest, one at a time. Dawkins had wandered over the deck to the Africans and stopped in front of a particularly muscular specimen.

"I wouldn't get too close if I were you," Harrington said. "We still haven't given him any reason to think we're his friends."

Dawkins raised his hands in mock fright. He scurried back two steps and Harrington let himself yield to a smile.

"We'd get a sight more than five pounds for you if we took you to Brazil," Dawkins said to the African. "A blackbird like you would fetch three hundred clean if he scowled at white people like that for the rest of his jet-black life."

Giva was smiling again. She hadn't said anything about the way the British sailors used the word *blackbird* but Emory was certain she was noting every use she recorded. Emory had first encountered the word when he had started collecting memoirs and letters penned by men who had served in the antislavery patrol. Slave trading had been called "blackbirding" and British sailors had apparently started applying the term to the people they were supposed to rescue. Peter LeGrundy claimed the British thought up insulting names for every kind of foreigner they met.

"They called Africans blackbirds and other derogatory terms," Peter had said, "in the same way they attached contemptuous epithets to most of the inhabitants of our planet. Frenchmen were called frogs, for example, apparently because there was some belief they were especially fond of eating frogs. People from Asian countries were called wogs—an ironic acronym for Worthy Oriental Gentlemen."

Harrington watched the next-to-last boatload pull away from the slaver. The mob of prisoners had been reduced to a group of seven. Three of the prisoners were crouching beside their captain and offering him sips of water and occasional words of encouragement.

"Mr. Terry—will you please take a party below and bring about fifty of the unfortunates on deck? Concentrate on women and children. We don't have the strength to handle too many restless young bucks."

"Your ancestor doesn't seem to have much confidence in his ability to handle the animals," Giva said. "What do they call the African women? Does?"

"If you will do a little research before you edit your creation," Emory said, "I believe you'll discover *British* young men were called young bucks, too. It was just a term for young men with young attitudes. They would have called *you* a restless young buck if you'd been born male, Giva."

■   ■   ■

Harrington hadn't tried black women yet. His sexual experience had been limited to encounters with the kind of females who lifted their skirts for sailors in the Italian and South American ports he had visited on his first cruises. Bonfors claimed black women were more ardent than white women but Bonfors liked to talk. It had been Harrington's experience that most of his shipmates believed *all* foreign women were more ardent than their English counterparts.

Some of the women Terry's men were ushering on deck looked like they were younger than his sisters. Several were carrying infants. Most of them were wearing loose bits of cloth that exposed their legs and arms and other areas civilized women usually covered.

Harrington had read William Pitt's great speech on the abolition of the slave trade when he had been a boy, and he had read it again when his uncle had advised him the Admiralty had agreed to give him this command. There had been a time, Pitt had argued, when the inhabitants of ancient Britain had been just as savage and uncivilized as the inhabitants of modern Africa, "a time when even human sacrifices were offered on this island."

In those days, Pitt had suggested, some Roman senator could have pointed to *British barbarians* and predicted "*There* is a people that will never rise to civilization—there is a people destined never to be free—a people without the understanding necessary for the attainment of useful arts, depressed by the hand of nature below the level of the human species, and created to form a supply of slaves for the rest of the world."

The women in front of him might be barbarians. But they had, as Pitt had said, the potential to rise to the same levels the inhabitants of Britain had achieved. They had the right to live in freedom, so they might have the same opportunity to develop.

A woman sprawled on the deck as she emerged from the hatch. Two of the hands were pulling the captives through the opening. Two were probably pushing them from below.

One of the sailors on the deck bent over the fallen woman. His hand closed over her left breast.

"Now there's a proper young thing," the sailor said.

The sailor who was working with him broke out in a smile. "I can't say I'd have any objection to spending a few days on *this* prize crew."

The officer who was supposed to be supervising the operation—the gunnery officer, Mr. Terry—was standing just a step away. John Harrington had been watching the slaves stumble into the sunlight but now he turned toward the bow and eyed the seven prisoners lounging in front of the forward deckhouse.

The next African out of the hatch was a scrawny boy who looked like he might be somewhere around seven or eight, in Emory's unpracticed judgment. The woman who followed him—his mother?—received a long stroke on the side of her hip as she balanced herself against the roll of the ship.

"The African males don't seem to be the only restless young bucks," Giva said. "These boys have been locked up in that little ship for several weeks now, as I remember it."

"It has been one-half hour since your last mandatory stay/go decision," the hal said. "Do you wish to stay or go, Mr. FitzGordon?"

"Stay."

"Do you wish to stay or go, Ms. Lombardo?"

"Stay, of course. We're getting some interesting insights into the attractions of African cruises."

Harrington ran his eyes over the rigging of the slaver. He should pick the most morally fastidious hands for the prize crew. But who could that be? Could any of them resist the opportunity after all these months at sea?

He could proclaim strict rules, of course. And order Terry to enforce them. But did he really want to subject his crew to the lash and the chain merely because they had succumbed to the most natural of urges? They were good men. They had just faced bullets and cannon balls to save five hundred human souls from the worst evil the modern world inflicted on its inhabitants.

And what if some of the women were willing? What if some of them offered themselves for money?

He could tell Terry to keep carnal activity to a minimum. But wouldn't that be the same as giving him permission to let the men indulge? He was the captain. Anything he said would have implications.

"Mr. Terry. Will you come over here, please?"

Harrington was murmuring but the microphones could still pick up the conversation.

"I'm placing you in command of the prize, Mr. Terry. I am entrusting its cargo to your good sense and decency."

"I understand," Terry said.

"These people may be savages but they are still our responsibility."

■ ■ ■

Emory nodded. Harrington was staring at the two men working the hatch as he talked. The frown on his face underlined every word he was uttering. "That should take care of that matter," Emory said.

Giva turned away from her screens. "You really think that little speech will have an effect, Emory?"

"Is there any reason to think it won't? He won't be riding with the prize crew. But that lieutenant knows what he's supposed to do."

"It was a standard piece of bureaucratic vagueness! It was exactly the kind of thing slot-fillers always say when they want to put a fence around their precious little careers."

"It was just as precise as it needed to be, Giva. Harrington and his officers all come from the same background. That lieutenant knows exactly what he's supposed to do. He doesn't need a lot of detail."

"When was the last time you held a job? I've been dealing with *managers* all my life. They always say things like that. The only thing you know when they're done is that you're going to be the one who gets butchered if anything goes wrong."

Harrington stood by the railing as the last group of prisoners took their places in the boat. A babble of conversation rang over the deck. The African captives they had brought out of the hold had mingled with the captives who had been used as shields and they were all chattering away like guests at a lawn party.

It was an exhilarating sight. He had never felt so completely satisfied with the world. Five hours ago the people standing on the deck had been crowded into the hell below decks, with their future lives reduced to weeks of torment in the hold, followed by years of brutal servitude when they finally made land. Now they merely had to endure a three or four day voyage to the British colony in Freetown. Half of them would probably become farmers in the land around Freetown. Some would join British regiments. Many would go to the West Indies as laborers—but they would be indentured laborers, not slaves, free to take up their own lives when they had worked off their passage. A few would even acquire an education in the schools the missionaries had established in Freetown and begin their own personal rise toward civilization.

He had raised the flag above the slaver with his own hands. Several of the Africans had pointed at it and launched into excited comments when it was only a third of the way up the mast. He could still see some of them pointing and obviously explaining its significance to the newcomers. Some of them had even pointed at *him*. Most liberated slaves came from the interior. The captives who came from the coast would know about the antislavery patrol. They would understand the significance of the flag and the blue coat.

"We're all loaded and ready, sir."

Harrington turned away from the deck. The last prisoner had settled into his seat in the boat.

He nodded at Terry and Terry nodded back. The hands had managed to slip in a few more pawings under the guise of being helpful, but Terry seemed to have the overall situation under control.

"She's your ship, Mr. Terry. I'll send you the final word on your prize crew as soon as I've conferred with Mr. Bonfors."

"It looks to me like it's about time we hopped for home," Giva said.

"Now? He's only brought one load of slaves on deck."

"You don't really think he's going to decorate the deck with more Africans, do you? Look at my screens. I'm getting two usable images of your ancestor returning to his ship. It's a high-feel closure. All we need is a sunset."

"There's five hundred people in that hold. Don't you think he's going to give the rest of them a chance to breathe?"

"He exaggerated his report. Use your head, Emory. Would you go through all the hassle involved in controlling five hundred confused people when you knew they were only four or five days away from Freetown?"

"You are deliberately avoiding the most important scene in the entire drama. We'll never know what happened next if we go now."

"You're clinging to a fantasy. We're done. It's time to go. Hal—I request relocation to home base."

"I have a request for relocation to home base. Please confirm."

"I do not confirm. I insist that we—"

"Request confirmed, Hal. Request confirmed."

Time stopped. The universe blinked. A technology founded on the best contemporary scientific theories did something the best contemporary scientific theories said it couldn't do.

The rig dropped onto the padded stage in Transit Room One. The bubble had disappeared. Faces were peering at them through the windows that surrounded the room.

Giva jabbed her finger at the time strip mounted on the wall. They had been gone seven minutes and thirty-eight seconds local time.

"We were pushing it," Giva said. "We were pushing it more than either of us realized."

The average elapsed local time was three minutes—a fact they had both committed to memory the moment they had heard it during their first orientation lecture. The bump when they hit the stage had seemed harder than the bumps they had experienced during training, too. The engineers always set the return coordinates for a position two meters above the stage—a precaution that placed the surface of the stage just outside the margin of error and assured the passengers they wouldn't relocate *below* it. They had come home extra late and extra high. Giva would have some objective support for her decision to return.

The narrow armored hatch under the time strip swung open. An engineer hopped through it with a medic right behind her.

"Is everything all right?"

"I can't feel anything malfunctioning," Giva said. "We had a flicker about two hours before we told Hal to shoot us home."

Emory ripped off his seat belt. He jumped to his feet and the medic immediately dropped into his soothe-the-patient mode. "You really should sit down, Mr. FitzGordon. You shouldn't stand up until we've checked you out."

The soft, controlled tones only added more points to the spurs driving Emory's rage. Giva was sprawling in her chair, legs stretched in front of her, obviously doing her best to create the picture of the relaxed daredevil who had courageously held off until the last minute. And now the medic was treating him like he was some kind of disoriented patient . . .

He swung toward the medic and the man froze when he saw the hostility on Emory's face. He was a solid, broad shouldered type with a face that probably looked pleasant and experienced when he was helping chrononauts disembark. Now he slipped into a stance that looked like a slightly disguised on guard.

"You're back, Mr. FitzGordon. Everything's okay. We'll have you checked out and ready for debriefing before you know it."

Peter LeGrundy crouched through the hatch. He flashed his standard-issue smile at the two figures on the rig and Emory realized he had to get himself under control.

"So how did it go?" Peter said. "Did you have a nice trip?"

Emory forced his muscles to relax. He lowered his head and settled into the chair as if he was recovering from a momentary lapse—the kind of thing any normal human could feel when he had just violated the laws of physics and traveled through three centuries of time. He gave the medic a quick thumbs up and the medic nodded.

He had his own record of the event. He had Giva's comments. Above all, he had Peter LeGrundy. And Peter LeGrundy's ambitions. He could cover every grant Peter could need for the rest of Peter's scholarly career if he had to. The battle wasn't over. Not yet.

You need the creatives. The creatives need your money.

I ordered the liberated captives brought to the deck as circumstances allowed. They did not fully comprehend their change in status, and I could not explain it. Our small craft does not contain a translator among its complement. But the sight of so many souls rescued from such a terrible destiny stimulated the deepest feelings of satisfaction in every heart capable of such sentiments.

Two well-placed candles illuminated the paper on John Harrington's writing desk without casting distracting shadows. The creak of *Sparrow's* structure created a background that offered him a steady flow of information about the state of his command.

He lowered his pen. He had been struggling with his report for almost two hours. The emotions he had ignored during the battle had flooded over him as soon as he had closed the door of his cabin. The pistol that had roared in his face had exploded half a dozen times.

He shook his head and forced out a sentence advising the Admiralty he had placed Mr. Terry in command of the prize. He had already commended Terry's gunnery and his role in the assault. He had given Bonfors due mention. Dawkins and several other hands had been noted by name. The dead and the wounded had been properly honored.

It had been a small battle by the standards of the war against Napoleon. A skirmish really. Against an inept adversary. But the bullets had been real. Men had died. *He* could have died. He had boarded an enemy ship under fire. He had led a headlong assault at an enemy line. He had exchanged shots with the captain of the enemy.

The emotions he was feeling now would fade. One hard, unshakeable truth would remain. He had faced enemy fire and done his duty.

He had met the test. He had become the kind of man he had read about when he was a boy.

₪

THE KING OF WHERE-I-GO
₪
Howard Waldrop

When I was eight, in 1954, my sister caught polio.

It wasn't my fault, although it took twenty years before I talked myself out of believing it was. See, we had this fight . . .

We were at my paternal grandparents' house in Alabama, where we were always taken in the summer, either being driven from Texas to there on Memorial Day and picked up on the Fourth of July, or taken the Fourth and retrieved Labor Day weekend, just before school started again in Texas.

This was the first of the two times when we spent the whole summer in Alabama. Our parents were taking a break from us for three entire months. We essentially ran wild all that time. This was a whole new experience. Ten years later, when it happened the second time, we would return to find our parents separated—me and my sister living with my mother in a garage apartment that backed up on the railroad tracks and my father living in what was a former motel that had been turned into day-laborer apartments a half-mile away.

Our father worked as an assembler in a radio factory that would go out of business in the early 1960s, when the Japanese started making them better, smaller, and cheaper. Our mother worked in the Ben Franklin 5¢-10¢-25¢ store downtown. Our father had to carpool every day into a Dallas suburb, so he would come and get the car one day a week. We would be going to junior high by then, and it was two blocks away.

But that was in the future. *This* was the summer of 1954.

Every two weeks we would get in our aunt's purple Kaiser and she would drive us the forty-five miles to our maternal grandparents' farm in the next county, and we would spend the next two weeks there. Then they'd come and get us after two weeks and bring us back. Like the movie title says, two weeks in another town.

We were back for the second time at the paternal grandparents' place. It was after the Fourth of July because there were burned patches on my grandfather's lower field where they'd had to go beat out the fires started by errant Roman candles and skyrockets.

There was a concrete walk up to the porch of our grandparents' house that divided the lawn in two. The house was three miles out of town; some time in the 1980s the city limits would move past the place when a highway bypass was built to rejoin the highway that went through town and the town made a landgrab.

On the left side of the lawn we'd set up a croquet game (the croquet set would cost a small fortune now, I realize, though neither my grandparents or aunt was what people called well-off).

My sister and I were playing. My grandfather had gone off to his job somewhere in the county. My grandmother was lying down, with what was probably a migraine, or maybe the start of the cancer that would kill her in a few years. (For those not raised in the South: in older homes the bedroom was also the front parlor—there was a stove, chairs for entertaining, and the beds in the main room of the house.) The bed my grandmother lay on was next to the front window.

My sister Ethel did something wrong in the game. Usually I would have been out fishing from before sunup until after dark with a few breaks during the day when I'd have to come back to the house. Breakfast was always made by my grandfather—who had a field holler that carried a mile, which he would let out from the back porch when breakfast was ready, and I'd come reluctantly back from the Big Pond. My grandfather used a third of a pound of coffee a day, and he percolated it for at least fifteen minutes—you could stand a spoon up in it. Then lunch, which in the South is called dinner, when my aunt would come out from her job in town and eat with me and my sister, my grandmother, and any cousins, uncles, or kin who dropped by (always arranged ahead of time, I'm sure), then supper, the evening meal, after my grandfather got home. Usually I went fishing after that, too, until it got too dark to see and the water moccasins came out.

But this morning we were playing croquet and it was still cool so I must have come back from fishing for some reason and been snookered into playing croquet.

"Hey! You can't do that!" I yelled at my sister.

"Do what?" she yelled back.

"Whatever you just did!" I said.

"I didn't do anything!" she yelled.

"You children please be quiet," yelled my grandmother from her bed by the window.

"You cheated!" I yelled at my sister.

"I did not!" she hollered back.

One thing led to another and my sister hit me between the eyes with the green-striped croquet mallet about as hard as a six-year-old can hit. I went down in a heap near a wicket. I sat up, grabbed the blue croquet ball, and threw it as hard as I could into my sister's right kneecap. She went down screaming.

My grandmother was now standing outside the screen door on the porch (which rich people called a verandah) in her housecoat.

"I asked you children to be quiet, please," she said.

"*You* shut up!" said my sister, holding her knee and crying.

My forehead had swelled up to the size of an apple.

My grandmother moved like the wind then, like Roger Bannister who had just broken the four-minute mile. Suddenly there was a willow switch in her hand and she had my sister's right arm and she was tanning her hide with the switch.

So here was my sister, screaming in two kinds of pain and regretting the invention of language and my grandmother was saying with every movement of her arm, "Don't-you- ever-tell-me-to-shut-up-young-lady!"

She left her in a screaming pile and went back into the house and lay down to start dying some more.

I was well-pleased, with the casual cruelty of childhood, that I would *never*-ever-in-my-wildest-dreams *ever* tell my grandmother to shut up.

I got up, picked up my rod and tackle box, and went back over the hill to the Big Pond, which is what I would rather have been doing than playing croquet anyway.

That night my sister got what we thought was a cold, in the middle of July.

Next day, she was in the hospital with polio.

My aunt Noni had had a best friend who got poliomyelitis when they were nine, just after WWI, about the time Franklin Delano Roosevelt had gotten his. (Roosevelt had been president longer than anybody, through the

Depression the grownups were always talking about, and WWII, which was the exciting part of the history books you never *got to* in school. He'd died at the end of the war, more than a year before I was born. Then the president had been Truman, and now it was Ike.) My aunt knew what to do and had Ethel in the hospital quick. It probably saved my sister's life, and at least saved her from an iron lung, if it were going to be that kind of polio.

You can't imagine how much those pictures in newsreels scared us all— rows of kids, only their heads sticking out of what looked like long tubular industrial washing machines. Polio attacked many things; it could make it so you couldn't *breathe* on your own—the iron lung was alternately a hypo- and hyperbaric chamber—it did the work of your diaphragm. This still being in vacuum-tube radio times, miniaturization hadn't set in, so the things weighed a ton. They made noises like breathing, too, which made them even creepier.

If you were in one, there was a little mirror over your head (you were lying down) where you could look at yourself; you couldn't look anywhere else.

Normally that summer we would have gone, every three days or so, with our aunt back to town after dinner and gone to the swimming pool in town. But it was closed because of the polio scare, and so was the theater. (They didn't want young people congregating in one place so the disease could quickly spread.) So what you ended up with was a town full of bored school kids and teenagers out of school for the summer with nothing to do. Not what a Baptist town really cares for.

Of course you could swim in a lake or something. But the nearest lake was miles out of town. If you couldn't hitch a ride or find someone to drive you there, you were S.O.L. You could go to the drive-ins for movies. The nearest one was at the edge of the next county—again you needed someone with wheels, although once there you could sit on top of the car and watch the movie, leaving the car itself to the grownups or older teenage brothers and sisters. (They'd even taken away the seats in front of the snack bar where once you could sit like in a regular theater, only with a cloud of mosquitoes eating you all up—again because of polio.)

Me, I had fishing and I didn't care. Let the town wimps stew in their own juices.

But that was all before my sister made polio up close and personal in the family and brought back memories to my aunt.

But Aunt Noni became a ball of fire.

I couldn't go into the hospital to see my sister, of course—even though I had been right there when she started getting sick. Kids could absolutely not come down to the polio ward. This was just a small county hospital with about forty beds, but it also had a polio ward with two iron lungs ready to go, such was the fear in those days.

My aunt took me to the hospital one day, anyway. She had had a big picture-frame mirror with her, from her house.

"She's propped up on pillows and can't move much," my aunt said. "But I think we can get her to see you."

"Stay out here in the parking lot and watch *that* window," she said. She pointed to one of the half-windows in the basement. I stayed out there until I saw my aunt waving in the window. I waved back.

Then my aunt came out and asked, "Did you see her?"

"I saw you."

"She saw you," she said. "It made her happy." Yeah, I thought, the guy who kneecapped her with the croquet ball.

"I don't know *why*," I said.

Then Aunt Noni gave me some of my weekly allowance that my parents mailed to her in installments.

I took off to the drugstore like a bullet. I bought a cherry-lime-chocolate coke at the fountain, and a *Monster of Frankenstein*, a *Plastic Man*, and an *Uncle Scrooge* comic book. That took care of forty of my fifty cents. A whole dime, and nowhere to spend it. If it would have been open, and this had been a Saturday, when we usually got our allowance, I would have used the dime to go to the movies and seen eight cartoons, a Three Stooges short, a newsreel, a chapter of a serial, some previews, and a double feature: some SF flick and a Guy Madison movie if I was lucky, a couple of Westerns if I wasn't.

But it was a weekday, and I went back to the office where my aunt Noni was the Jill-of-all-trades plus secretary for a one-man business for forty-seven years (it turned out). It was upstairs next to the bank. Her boss, Mr. Jacks, lived in the biggest new house in town (until, much later, the new doctor in town built a house out on the highway modeled on Elvis' Graceland). Mr. Jacks' house, as fate would have it, was situated on a lot touching my aunt's, only set one house over and facing the other street back.

He wasn't in; he usually wasn't in the office when I was there. Aunt Noni was typing like a bunny, a real blur from the wrists down. She was the only one in the family who'd been to college. (Much later I would futz around in one for five years without graduating.) She could read, write, and speak

Latin, like I later could. She read books. She had the librarian at the Carnegie Library in town send off to Montgomery for books on polio; they'd arrived while I was having the Coca-Cola comic book orgy and she'd gone to get them when the librarian had called her. There was a pile on the third chair in the office.

I was sitting in the second one.

"I want to know," she said as she typed without looking at her shorthand pad or the typewriter, "enough so that I'll know if someone is steering me wrong on something. I don't want to know enough to become pedantic—"

"Huh?" I asked.

She nodded toward the big dictionary on the stand by the door.

I dutifully got up and went to it.

"P-?"

"P-E-D-A," said my aunt, still typing.

I looked it up. "Hmmm," I said. "Okay." Then I sat back down.

"They're talking like she won't walk again without braces or crutches. That's what they told my friend Frances in nineteen and twenty-one," she said. "You see her motorboatin' all around town now. She only limps a little when she gets really tired and worn out."

Frances worked down at the dress shop. She looked fine except her right leg was a little thinner than her left.

"My aim is to have your sister walking again by herself by next summer."

"Will it happen?"

"If I have anything to do with it, it will," said Aunt Noni.

I never felt so glum about the future as I did sitting there in my aunt's sunny office that July afternoon. What if she were wrong? What if my sister Ethel never walked again? What would her life be like? Who the hell would I play croquet with, in Alabama in the summer, if not her, when I wasn't fishing?

Of course, a year later, the Salk vaccine was developed and tried out and started the end of polio. And a couple of years after that came the Sabin oral vaccine, which they gave to you on sugar cubes and which tasted like your grandfather's old hunting socks smelled, which really ended the disease.

We didn't know any of that then. And the future didn't help my sister *any* right then.

My parents had of course taken off work and driven from Texas at the end of the first week; there were many family conferences to which the *me* part of the family was not privy. My parents went to see her and stayed at the hospital.

What was decided was that my sister was to remain in Alabama with my grandparents for the next year and that I was to return to my dead hometown in Texas with my parents and somegoddamnhow survive the rest of the summer there.

My sister Ethel would be enrolled in school in Alabama, provided she was strong enough to do the schoolwork. So I fished the Big Pond and the Little Pond one last time, till it was too dark to see and the bass lost interest in anything in the tackle box, and I went over the low hill to my grandparents' house, robbed of a summer.

Next morning we got the car packed, ready to return to Texas, a fourteen-hour drive in a Flathead 6 1952 Ford. Then we stopped by the hospital. Aunt Noni was already there, her purple Kaiser parked by the front door. My parents went in; after a while Aunt Noni waved at the window, then I saw a blur in the mirror and a shape and I waved and waved and jumped up and down with an enthusiasm I did not feel. Then I got in the car and we went back to Texas

Somehow, I did live through that summer.

One of the things that got me through it was the letters my aunt took down from my sister and typed up. The first couple were about the hospital, till they let her go, and then about what she could see from the back room of my grandparents' house.

We'd usually only gone to Alabama for the summer, and sometimes rushed trips at Christmas, where we were in the car fourteen hours (those days the Interstate Highway System was just a gleam in Ike's eye—so he could fight a two-front war and not be caught short moving stuff from one coast to the other like they had in the Korean War when he was running Columbia University in NYC). We stayed at our grandparents' places Christmas Eve and on Christmas morning and then drove fourteen hours back home just in time for my parents to go to work the day after Christmas.

So I'd never seen Alabama in the fall or the spring. My sister described the slow change from summer to fall there after school started (in Texas it was summer till early October, and you had the leaves finish falling off the trees the third week of December and new buds coming out the second week of January.) She wrote of the geese she heard going over on the Mississippi flyway.

She complained about the schoolwork; in letters back to her I complained about *school itself*: the same dorks were the same dorks, the same jerks the same jerks, the same bullies still bullies. And that was third grade. Then, you always think it's going to change the next year, until you realize: these jerks are going to be the same ones I'm stuck with the rest of their lives. (As "Scoop" Jackson the senator would later say—it's hard to turn fifty-five and realize the world is being run by people you used to beat up in the fourth grade.)

Third grade was the biggest grind of my life. My sister was finding Alabama second grade tough too; there was no Alamo, no Texas-under-six-flags. In Alabama there was stealing land from the Choctaws and Cherokees, there was the cotton gin and slavery, there was the War for Southern Independence, and then there was the boll weevil. That was about it. No Deaf Smith, no Ben Milam, no line drawn in the dirt with the sword, no last battle of the Civil War fought by two detachments who didn't *know* the war was over six weeks after Appomattox; no Spindletop, no oil boom, no great comic-book textbook called *Texas History Movies* which told you everything in a casually racist way but which you remembered better than any textbook the rest of your life.

I told her what I was doing (reading comics, watching TV) and what I caught in the city park pond or the creek coming out of it. It was the fifties in Texas. There was a drought; the town well had gone dry, and they were digging a lake west of town which, at the current seven inches of rain a year, would take twenty-two years to fill up, by which time we'd all be dead.

I told her about the movies I'd seen once the town's lone theater had opened back up. (There were three drive-ins: one in the next town west, with a great neon cowboy round-up scene on the back of the screen, facing the highway—one guy strummed a green neon guitar, a red neon fire burned at the chuck wagon, a *vaquero* twirled a pink neon lasso; one at the west edge of our town; and one near the next town to the east.)

Anyway, I got and wrote at least one letter a week to and from my sister, my aunt wrote separate letters to me and my parents, they called each other at least once a week.

Somehow, Christmas dragged its ass toward the school year; my parents decided we'd go to Alabama during the break and see my sister and try to have a happy holiday.

My sister was thinner and her eyes were shinier. She looked pretty much the same except her left leg was skinny. She was propped up in bed. Everybody made a big fuss over her all the time. There was a pile of Christmas presents for her out under the tree in the screened-in hall that would choke a mastodon.

I was finally in her room with no one else there.

"Bored, huh?" I asked.

"There's too many people playing the damned fool around here for me to get bored," she said.

"I mean, outside of Christmas?"

"Well, yeah. The physical therapist lady comes twice a day usually and we go through that rigmarole."

"I hope people got you lots of books," I said.

"I've read so many books I can't see straight, Bubba."

"Have you read *All About Dinosaurs*?" I asked.

"No."

"I've got my copy with me. You can read it but I gotta have it back before we leave. I stood in a Sears and Roebuck store in Fort Worth for six hours once while they shipped one over from the Dallas warehouse. The last truck came in and the book wasn't there. They were out and didn't know it. I'd saved up my allowance for *four weeks*! Without movies or comic books! I told anybody who would *listen* about it. A week later one came in the mail. Aunt Noni heard the story and ordered it for me."

"Bless her heart."

"I'm real sorry all this happened, Sis," I said, before I knew I was saying it. "I wish we hadn't fought the day before you got sick."

"What? What fight?"

"The croquet game. You hit me."

"You hit me!" she said.

"No. You backsassed Mamaw. She hit you."

"Yes she did," said my sister Ethel.

"Anyway, I'm sorry."

"It wasn't your fault," she said.

I really was going to talk to her more but some damnfool uncle came in wearing his hat upside down to make her laugh.

My sister grew up and walked again, and except for a slight limp and a sometime windmilling foot (like my aunt's friend Frances when she was very tired), she got around pretty well, even though she lost most of a year of her life in that bed in Alabama.

I remember walking with her the first day of school when she had come back to Texas and was starting third grade.

"Doing okay?" I asked. We lived three whole blocks from school then, but I wanted her to take it slow and not get too tired.

"Yeah. Sure," she said.

I remember the day they handed out the permission forms for the Salk polio vaccine, which was a big shot with a square needle in the meat of your arm. My sister laughed and laughed. "Oh, bitter irony!" she said "Oh, ashes and dust!"

"Yeah," I said, "well . . . "

"Have Mom and Pop sign yours *twice*," she said. "At least it'll do you some good."

"Once again, Sis, I'm sorry."

"Tell *that* to the school nurse," she said.

At some point, when we were in our late teens, we were having one of those long philosophical discussions brothers and sisters have when neither has a date and you're too damned tired from the school week to get up off your butt and go out and do something on your own and the public library closed early. Besides, your folks are yelling at each other in their bedroom.

The Time Machine was one of my favorite movies (they all are). I had the movie tie-in paperback with the photo of Rod Taylor on the back, the Dell Movie Classic comic book with art by Alex Toth, and the Classics Illustrated edition with art by Lou Cameron—it had been my favorite for years before the movie had come out in 1960.

"What would I do," I repeated Ethel's question, "if I could travel in time? Like go see dinosaurs, or go visit the spaceport they're going to build just outside this popsicle burg?

"Most people would do just what I'd do: first I'd go to the coin shop, buy ten early 1930s Mercury dimes, then go back to 1938 and buy ten copies of *Action Comics #1* with Superman's first story, and then I'd go write mash notes to Eve Arden."

I'd just finished watching reruns of *Our Miss Brooks* on TV.

"No," she said. "I mean, *really*?"

"No," I said. "I mean, really."

"Wouldn't you try to stop Oswald?" she asked. "Go strangle Hitler in his cradle?"

"You didn't ask 'What would you do if you could travel in time to make the world a better place?' You asked 'What would you do if you could travel in time?'"

"Be that way," she said.

"I *am* that way."

And then she went off to work at some Rhine-like lab in North Carolina. That's not what she set out to do—what she set out to do was be a carhop, get out of the house and our live local version of *The Bickersons*. (Bickering=*Pow! Sock! Crash!*)

She first worked as a carhop in town, from the time she was fourteen, and then she got the real glamour job over in Dallas at the biggest drive-in cafe there, twenty-five carhops, half of them on skates (not *her*). She moved in with two other carhops there. A few months later, King and Bobby Kennedy got killed and half the US burned down.

Something happened at the cafe—I never found out *exactly* what. But a week later she called home and said this research lab was flying her to North Carolina for a few days (she'd never flown before). And then she left.

I started getting letters from her. By then our parents had gotten a divorce; I was living in the house with my father (who would die in a few months of heart failure—and a broken heart). My mom had run off with the guy she'd been sneaking around with the last couple of years and we weren't talking much. I was in college and seeing the girl I would eventually marry, have a kid with, and divorce.

My sister told me *they* were really interested in her, that other institutes were trying to get her to come over to them and that she wasn't the only polio survivor there. My first thought was—what's going on? Is this like Himmler's interest in twins and gypsies, or was this just statistically average? This was the late sixties; lots of people our age had polio before 1955, so maybe that was it?

Her letters were a nice break in the college routine—classes, theater, part-time thirty-six-hour-a-week job. Of course I got an ulcer before I turned twenty-two. (Later it didn't keep me from being drafted; it had gotten better after I quit working thirty hours a week in theater plus the job plus only sleeping between three and six a.m. seven days a week.)

"The people here are nice," she said. "The tests are fun, except for the concentration. I get headaches like Mamaw used to get, every other day." She sent me a set of the cards—Rhine cards. Circle, triangle, star, square, plus sign, wavy horizontal lines. They had her across the table from a guy who turned the cards, fifty of them, randomly shuffled. She was supposed to intuit (or receive telepathically) which cards he'd turned over. She marked the symbol she thought it was. There was a big high partition across the middle of the table—she could barely see the top of the guy's head. Sometimes she was the one turning the cards and tried to send messages to him. There were other, more esoteric ones—the tests were supposed to be scientific *and* repeatable.

From one of her letters:

I don't mind the work here, and if they prove something by it, more's the better. What I do mind is that all the magazines I read here think that if there is something to extrasensory perception, then there also has to be mental contact with UFOs (what UFOs?) and the Atlanteans (what Atlantis?) and mental death rays and contact with the spirit-world (what spirit-world?).

I don't understand that; proving extrasensory perception only proves that exists, and they haven't even proved that yet. Next week they're moving me over to the PK unit—PsychoKinesis. Moving stuff at a distance without, as Morbius said, "instrumentality." That's more like what happened at the drive-in anyway. They wanted to test me for this stuff first. Evidently I'm not very good at this. Or, I'm the same as everybody else, except the ones they catch cheating, by what they call reading the other person—physical stuff like in poker, where somebody always lifts an eyebrow when the star comes up—stuff like that.

Will write to you when I get a handle on this PK stuff.

Your sis,

Ethel

"You would have thought I set off an atom bomb here," her next letter began. She then described what happened and the shady-looking new people who showed up to watch her tests.

Later, they showed her some film smuggled out of the USSR of ladies shaped like potatoes doing hand-*schtick* and making candles move toward them.

My sister told them her brother could do the same thing with two-pound-test nylon fishing line.

"If I want *that* candle *there* to move over here, I'll do it without using my hands," she'd said.

And then, the candle *didn't* move.

"They told me then my abilities may lie in some other area; that the cafe incident was an anomaly, or perhaps someone else, a cook or another carhop had the ability; it had just happened to her because she was the one with the trays and dishes.

"Perhaps," she had told them, "you were wrong about me entirely and are wasting your motel and cafeteria money and should send me back to Texas Real Soon. Or maybe I have the ability to move something *besides* candles, something no one else ever had. Or maybe we are just all pulling our puds." Or words to that effect.

A couple of days later she called me on the phone. The operator told her to deposit $1.15. I heard the *ching* and chime of coins in the pay phone.

"Franklin," said Ethel.

She *never* called me by my right name; I was Bubba to everyone in the family.

"Yes, Sis, what is it?"

"I think we had a little breakthrough here. We won't know till tomorrow. I want you to know I love you."

"What the hell you talkin' about?"

"I'll let you know," she said.

Then she hung up.

The next day was my usual Wednesday, which meant I wouldn't get any sleep. I'd gotten to bed the night before at 2:00 a.m. I was in class by 7:00 a.m. and had three classes and lab scattered across the day. At 6:00 p.m. I drove to the regional newspaper plant that printed all the suburban dailies. I was a linotype operator at minimum wage. The real newspaper that owned all the suburban ones was a union shop and the guys there made $3.25 an hour in 1968 dollars. I worked a twelve-hour shift (or a little less if we got all the type set early) three nights a week, Monday-Wednesday-Friday. That way, not only did you work for $1.25 an hour, they didn't owe you for overtime unless you pulled more than a sixteen-hour shift one night—and nobody ever did.

Linotypes were mechanical marvels—so much so that Mergenthaler, who finally perfected it, went slap-dab crazy before he died. It's like being in a room of mechanical monsters who spit out hot pieces of lead (and sometimes hot lead itself all over you—before they do that, they make a distinctive noise and you've got a second and a half to get ten feet away; it's called a backspill).

Once all linotype was set by hand, by the operators. By the time I came along, they had typists set copy on a tape machine. What came out there was perforated tape, brought into the linotype room in big, curling strands. The operator—me—put the front end of the tape into a reader-box built onto the keyboard, and the linotype clicked away like magic. The keys depressed, lines of type-mold keys fell into place from a big magazine above the keyboard; they were lifted up and moved over to the molder against the pot of hot lead; the line was cast, an arm came down, lifted the letter matrices up, another rod pushed them over onto an endless spiraled rod, and they fell back into the typecase when the side of the matrix equaled the space on the typecase, and the process started all over. If the tape code was wrong and a line went too long, you got either type matrices flying everywhere as the line was lifted to the molder, or it went over and you got a backspill and hot lead flew across the room.

Then you had to turn off the reader, take off the galley where the slugs of hot type came off to cool, open up the front of the machine, clean all the lead off with a wire brush, put it back together, and start the tape reader back up. When the whole galley was set and cool, you pulled a proof on a small rotary press and sent it back to the typists, where corrections would come back on shorter and shorter pieces of paper tape. You kept setting and inserting the corrections and throwing away the bad slugs until the galley was okayed; then you pulled a copy of the galley and sent it up to the composing room where they laid out the page of corrected galley, shot a page on a plate camera, and made a steel plate from that; that was put on the web press and the paper was run off and sent out to newsboys all over three counties.

It was a noisy, nasty twelve-hour hell with the possibility of being hit in the face with molten lead or asphyxiating when, in your copious free time, you took old dead galleys and incorrect slugs back to the lead smelter to melt down and then ladled out molten lead into pig-iron molds which, when cooled down, you took and hung by the hole in one end to the chain above the pot on each linotype—besides doing everything else it did, the machine lowered the lead pigs into the pots by a ratchet gear each time it set a line. No wonder Mergenthaler went mad.

I did all that twelve hours a night three nights a week for five years, besides college. There were five linotypes in the place, including one that Mergenthaler himself must have made around 1880, and usually three of them were down at a time with backspills or other problems.

Besides that, there were the practical jokers. Your first day on the job you were always sent for the type-stretcher, all over the printing plant. "Hell, I don't know *who* had that last!" they'd say. "Check the composing room." Then some night the phone would ring in the linotype room; you'd go to answer it and get an earful of printers' ink, about the consistency of axle grease. Someone had slathered a big gob on the earpiece and called you from somewhere else in the plant. *Nyuk nyuk nyuk.*

If you'd really pissed someone off (it never happened to me), they'd wait for a hot day and go out and fill all four of your hubcaps with fresh shrimp. It would take two or three days before they'd really stink; you'd check everywhere in the car but the hubcaps; finally something brown would start running from them and you'd figure it out. *Nyuk nyuk nyuk.*

That night I started to feel jumpy. Usually I was philosophical: *Why, this is hell, nor am I out of it.* Nothing was going on but the usual hot, repetitious drudgery. Something felt wrong. My head didn't exactly hurt, but I knew it was *there.* Things took on a distancing effect—I would recognize that from dope, later on. But there was no goofer dust in my life then. Then I noticed everybody else was moving and talking faster than normal. I looked at the clock with the big sweep second-hand outside the linotype room. It had slowed to a crawl.

I grabbed onto the bed of the cold iron proof-press and held on to it. Later, when I turned fifty or so, I was in a couple of earthquakes on the West Coast, but they were nothing compared to what I was feeling at that moment.

One of the tape compositor ladies, a blur, stopped in front of me and chirped out, "Do you feel all right, Frank?"

"Justa headache I'll be okay," I twittered back.

I looked at the clock again.

The sweep-hand stopped. I looked back into the linotype room.

People moved around like John Paul Stapp on the *Sonic Wind* rocket sled.

I looked at the clock again. The second hand moved backward.

And then the world blurred all out of focus and part of me left the clanging clattering linotypes behind.

I looked around the part of town I could see. (What was I doing downtown? Wasn't I at work?) The place looked like it did around 1962. The carpet shop was still in business—it had failed a few months before JFK was shot. Hamburgers were still four for a dollar on the menus outside the cafes. The theater was showing *The Horror Chamber of Dr. Faustus* and *The Manster,* which was a 1962 double feature. Hosey the usher was leaving in his '58 Chevy; he quit working at the theater in 1964, I knew. I had a feeling that if I walked one block north and four blocks west I could look in the window of a house and see myself reading a book or doing homework. I sure didn't want to do that.

Then the plant manager was in front of me. "Hey! You've got a backspill on number-five, that crappy old bastard, and number-three's quit reading tape."

"Sorry," I said. "I just got a splitting headache for a minute. Got any aspirin?" I asked, taking the galley off #5.

"Go ask one of the women who's having her period," he said. "I just took all the aspirin in the place. The publisher's *all over* my ass this week. Why, I don't know. I robbed the first-aid kit: don't go there."

"That would have been my next stop," I said. I brushed a cooled line of lead off the keyboard and from the seat and up the back of the caster chair in front of the linotype. I closed the machine back up and started it up and went over and pounded on the reader box of #3. It chattered away.

For a while I was too busy to think about what had happened.

"Feeling a little weird?" asked my sister, this time on a regular phone.

"What the hell happened?"

"Talk to this man," she said.

She put on some professor whose name I didn't catch.

He asked me some questions. I told him the answers. He said he was sending a questionnaire. My sister came back on.

"*I* think *they* think I gave you a bad dream two thousand miles away," she said. "That would be a big-cheese deal to them."

"What do *you* think?" I asked. "I saw Hosey."

"Either way, you would have done *that*," she said.

"What do you mean, either way? Why are you involving me? *Is this fun?*"

"Because," she said, "you're my brother and I love you."

"Yeah, well . . . " I said. "Why don't you mess with someone you *don't* like? Who's that guy who left you in Grand Prairie to walk home at five a.m.?"

"I killed him with a mental lightning bolt yesterday," she said. Then, "Just kidding.

"Well, I'm glad you're just kidding, because I just *shit my pants*. I don't want to ever feel like I did last night, again, ever. It was creepy."

"Of course it was creepy," she said. "We're working at the frontiers of science here."

"Are you on the frontiers of science there," I asked, "or . . . "

She finished the sentence with me: " . . . are we just pulling our puds?" She laughed. "I don't have a clue. They're trying to figure out how to do this scientifically. They may have to fly you in."

"No, thanks!" I said. "I've got a life to live. I'm actually dating a real-live girl. I'm also working myself to death. I don't have time for hot dates with Ouija boards, or whatever you're doing there. Include me out."

She laughed again. "We'll see."

"No you won't! Don't do this to me. I'm . . . "

There was a dial tone.

So the second time I knew what was happening. I was at home. I felt the distancing effect, the speeding up of everything around except the kitchen clock. It was the kind where parts of numbers flipped down, an analog readout. It slowed to a crawl. The thin metal strips the numbers were painted on took a real long time before they flipped down.

A bird rocketed through the yard. The neighbor's dog was a beige blur. I could barely move. My stomach churned like when I was on the Mad Octopus at the Texas State Fair. The clock hung between 10:29 and 10:50 a.m. Then it was 10:29. 10:28. 10:27. Then the readout turned into a high whining flutter.

This time everything was bigger. Don't ask *me* why. I was at my favorite drugstore, the one next to the theater. The drugstore was at the corner of Division and Center Street. I glanced at a newspaper. June 17, 1956. If memory serves, I would have been over in Alabama at the time, so I wouldn't be running into myself. I reached in my pocket and looked at my change. Half of it hadn't been minted yet. (How was *that* possible?) The guy at the register ignored me—he'd seen me a million times, and I wasn't one of the kids he had to give the Hairy Eyeball to. When I came in, I came to buy.

I looked at the funny book rack. Everything except the Dell Comics had the Comics Code Seal on them, which meant they'd go to Nice Heaven. No zombies, no monsters, no blood, no Blackhawks fighting the Commies, who used stuff that melts tanks, people—everything but wood. No vampires "saaaaking your blaaad." Dullsville. I picked up a *Mad* magazine, which was no longer a comic book, so it wouldn't be under the Comics Code, but had turned into a 25¢—*What, me cheap?*—magazine. It had a Kelly Freas cover of Alfred E. Neuman.

I fished out a 1952 quarter and put it down by the register. There wasn't any sales tax in Texas yet. Fifty years later, we would be paying more than New York City.

I looked at the theater marquee when I stepped outside. *The Bottom of the Bottle* and *Bandido*—one with Joseph Cotten and Richard Egan, the other with Glenn Ford and Gilbert Roland. I'd seen them later, bored by the first except for a storm scene, and liked the second because there were lots of explosions and Browning .50 caliber machine guns. Nothing for me there.

I walked down toward Main Street.

There was a swooping sensation and a flutter of light and I was back home.

The analog readout on the clock clicked to 10:50 a.m.

I went to the coin shop. I went to my doctor's office. I went to a couple of other places. I actually had to lie a couple of times, and I used one friendship badly, only *they* didn't know, but I did.

Then I found the second letter my sister had sent me from North Carolina and got the phone number of the lab. I called it the next morning. It took awhile, but they finally got Ethel to the phone.

"Feeling okay?" she asked.

"Hell no," I said. "I'm not having *any* fun. At least let me have *fun*. Two days from now give me a hallucination about Alabama. In the summer. I want to at least see if the fishing is as good as I remember it."

"So it is written," she said, imitating Yul Brynner in *The Ten Commandments*, "so it shall be done."

I knew it really didn't matter, but I kept my old Fiberglass spinning rod, with its Johnson Century spinning reel, and my old My Buddy tackle box as near me as I could the next two days. Inside the tackle box with all the other crap were three new double-hook rigged rubber eels, cheap as piss in 1969, but they cost $1.00 each in 1950s money when they'd first come out.

This time I was almost ready for it and didn't panic when the thing came on. I rode it out like the log flume ride out at Six Flags Over Texas, and when the clock outside the college classroom started jumping backward, I didn't even get woozy. I closed my eyes and made the jump myself.

I was at the Big Pond and had made a cast. A two-pound bass had taken the rubber eel. The Big Pond was even bigger than I remembered (although I knew it was only four acres). I got the bass in and put it on a stringer with its eleven big clamps and swivels between each clamp on the chain. I put the bass out about two feet in the water and put the clamp on the end of the stringer around a willow root.

Then I cast again, and the biggest bass I had ever had took it. There was a swirl in the water the size of a #5 washtub and I set the hook.

I had him on for maybe thirty seconds. He jumped in the shallow water as I reeled. He must have weighed ten pounds. When he came down there was a splash like a cow had fallen into the pond.

Then the rubber eel came sailing lazily out of the middle of the commotion, and the line went slack in a backflowing arc. It (probably *she*) had thrown the hook.

There was a big V-wake heading for deeper water when the bass realized it was free.

I was pissed off at myself. I picked up the stringer with the two-pound bass (which now didn't look as large as it had five minutes ago) and my tackle box and started off over the hill back toward my grandparents' house.

I walked through the back gate, with its plowshare counterweight on the chain that kept it closed. I took the fish off the stringer and eased it into the seventy-five gallon rain barrel, where it started to swim along with a catfish my uncle had caught at the Little Pond yesterday. In the summer, there was usually a fish fry every Friday. We got serious about fishing on Thursdays. By Friday there would be fifteen or twenty fish in the barrel, from small bluegills to a few crappie to a bunch of bass and catfish. On Fridays my uncle would get off early, start cleaning fish, heating up a cast-iron pot full of lard over a charcoal fire and making up batter for the fish and hush puppies. Then, after my grandfather came in, ten or eleven of us would eat until we fell over.

Later the cooled fish grease would be used to make dogbread for my grandfather's hounds. You didn't waste much in Alabama in those days.

I washed my hands off at the outside faucet and went through the long hall from the back door, being quiet, as the only sound in the house was of SuZan, the black lady who cooked for my grandmother, starting to make lunch. I looked into the front room and saw my grandmother sleeping on the main bed.

I went out onto the verandah. I'd taken stuff out of the tackle box in the back hall, when I'd leaned my fishing rod up against a bureau, where I kept it ready to go all summer.

I was eating from a box of Domino® sugar cubes when I came out. My sister was in one of the Adirondack-type wooden chairs, reading a *Katy*

Keene comic book; the kind where the girl readers sent in drawings of dresses and sunsuits they'd designed for Katy. The artist redrew them when they chose yours for a story, and they ran *your* name and address printed beside it so other Katy Keene fans could write you. (Few people know it, but that's how the Internet started.)

She must have been five or six—before she got sick. She was like a sparkle of light in a dark world.

"Back already?" she asked. "Quitter."

"I lost the biggest fish of my life," I said. "I tried to horse it in. I should have let it horse me but kept control, as the great A. J. McClane says in *Field and Stream*," I said. "I am truly disappointed in my fishing abilities for the first time in a long time."

"Papaw'll whip your ass if he finds out you lost that big fish he's been trying to catch," she said. "He would have gone in after it, if he ever had it on."

He *would have*, too.

"Yeah, he's a cane-pole fisherman, the best there ever was, but it was too shallow there for him to get his minnow in there with a pole. It was by that old stump in the shallow end." Then I held up the sugar-cube box.

"Look what I found," I said.

"Where'd you get those?"

"In the old chiffarobe."

"SuZan'll beat your butt if she finds you filchin' sugar from her kitchen."

"Probably some of Aunt Noni's for her tea. She probably bought it during the Coolidge administration and forgot about it." Aunt Noni was the only person I knew in Alabama who drank only one cup of coffee in the morning, and then drank only tea, iced or hot, the rest of the day.

"Gimme some," said Ethel.

"What's the magic word?"

"Please *and* thank you."

I moved the box so she took the ones I wanted her to. She made a face. "God, that stuff is old," she said.

"I *told* you they was," I said.

"Gimme more. Please," she said. "Those are better." Then: "I've read this *Katy Keene* about to death. Wanna play croquet till you get up your nerve to go back and try to catch that fish before Papaw gets home?"

"Sure," I said. "But that fish will have a sore jaw till tomorrow. He'll be real careful what he bites the rest of the day. I won't be able to tempt him again until tomorrow."

We started playing croquet. I had quite the little run there, making it to the middle wicket from the first tap. Then my sister came out of the starting double wicket and I could tell she was intent on hitting my ball, then getting to send me off down the hill. We had a rule that if you were knocked out of bounds, you could put the ball back in a mallet-head length from where it went out. But if you hit it hard enough, the ball went out of bounds, over the gravel parking area, down the long driveway, all the way down the hill and out onto Alabama Highway 12. You had to haul your ass all the way down the dirt drive, dodge the traffic, retrieve the ball from your cousin's front yard, and climb all the way back up to the croquet grounds to put your ball back into play.

My sister tapped my ball at the end of a long shot. She placed her ball against it, and put her foot on top of her croquet ball. She lined up her shot. She took a practice tap to make sure she had the right murderous swing.

"Hey!" I said. "My ball moved! That counts as your shot!"

"Does not!" she yelled.

"Yes it does!" I yelled.

"Take your next shot! *That* counted!" I added.

"It did not!" she screamed.

"You children be quiet!" my grandmother yelled from her bed of pain.

About that time was when Ethel hit me between the eyes with the green-striped croquet mallet; I kneecapped her with the blue croquet ball, and, with a smile on my swelling face as I heard the screen door open and close, I went away from there.

This time I felt like I had been beaten with more than a mallet wielded by a six-year-old. I felt like I'd been stoned by a crowd and left for dead. I was dehydrated. My right foot hurt like a bastard, and mucus was dripping from my nose. I'm pretty sure the crowds in the hall as classes let out noticed—they gave me a wide berth, like I was a big ugly rock in the path of migrating salmon.

I got home as quickly as I could, cutting History of the Totalitarian State 405, which was usually one of my favorites.

I called the lab long distance. Nobody knew about my sister. Maybe it was her day off. I called the Motel 6. Nobody was registered by her name. The manager said, "Thank you for calling Motel 6." Then he hung up.

Maybe she'd come back to Dallas. I called her number there.

"Hello," said somebody nice.

"Is Ethel there?"

"Ethel?"

"Yeah, Ethel."

"Oh. That must have been Joanie's *old* roommate."

I'd met Joanie once. "Put Joanie on, please?" I asked.

She was in, and took the phone.

"Joanie? Hi. This is Franklin—Bubba—Ethel's brother."

"Yeah?"

"I can't get ahold of her in North Carolina."

"Why would you be calling her *there*, honey?"

"'Cause that's where she was the last two weeks."

"I don't know about *that*. But she moved out of *here* four months ago. I got a number for her, but she's never there. The phone just rings and rings. If you happen to catch her, tell her she still owes me four dollars and thirty-one cents on that last electric bill. I'm workin' mostly days now, and I ain't waitin' around two hours to see her. She can leave it with Steve; he'll see I get it."

"Steve. Work. Four dollars," I mumbled.

She gave me the number. The prefix meant south Oak Cliff, a suburb that had been eaten by Dallas.

I dialed it.

"Ethel?"

"Who is this? What the hell you want? I just worked a double shift."

"It's Bubba," I said.

"Brother? I haven't heard from you in a month of Sundays."

"No wonder. You're in North Carolina, you come back *without* telling me, you didn't tell me you'd moved out from Joanie's . . . "

"What the hell you mean, North Carolina? I been pullin' double shifts for three solid weeks—I ain't had a day off since September twenty-sixth. I ain't never been to North Carolina in my life."

"Okay. First, Joanie says you owe her four dollars and thirty-one cents on the electric bill . . . "

"Four thirty-one," she said, like she was writing it down. "I'll be so glad when I pay her so she'll *shut up*."

"Okay. Let's start over. How's your leg?"

"*Which* leg?"

"Your *left* leg. The *polio* leg. Just the one that's given you trouble for fifteen years. That's which leg."

"Polio. Polio? The only person I know with polio is Noni's friend Frances, in Alabama."

"Does the year 1954 ring a bell?" I asked.

"Yeah. That was the first time we spent the *whole* summer in Alabama. Mom and Dad sure fooled us the second time, didn't they? Hi. Welcome back from vacation, kids. Welcome to your new broken homes."

"They should have divorced *long* before they did. They would have made themselves and a lot of people happier."

"No," she said. "They just never should have left backwoods Alabama and come to the Big City. *All* those glittering objects. *All* that excitement."

"Are we talking about the same town *here*?" I asked.

"Towns are as big as your capacity for wonder, as Fitzgerald said," said Ethel.

"Okay. Back to weird. Are you sure you never had polio when you were a kid? That you haven't *been* in North Carolina the last month at some weird science place? That you weren't causing me to hallucinate being a time-traveler?"

"Franklin," she said. "I have never seen it, but I *do* believe you are drunk. Why don't you hang up now and call me back when you are sober. I still love you, but I will not tolerate a drunken brother calling me while I am trying to sleep.

"Good-bye now—"

"Wait! Wait! I want to know, are my travels through? Can I get back to my real life now?"

"How would I know?" asked Ethel. "I'm not the King of Where-You-Go."

"Maybe. Maybe not."

"Go sober up now. Next time call me at work. Nights."

She hung up.

And then I thought: what would it be like to watch everyone slow down; the clock start whirling clockwise around the dial till it turned gray like it was full of dishwater, and then suddenly be out at the spaceport they're going to build out at the edge of town and watch the Mars rocket take off every Tuesday?

And: I would never know the thrill of standing, with a satchel full of comics under my arm, waiting at the end of Eve Arden's driveway for her to get home from the studio . . .

〢

BESPOKE
₪
Genevieve Valentine

Disease Control had sprayed while Petra was asleep, and her boots kicked up little puffs of pigment as she crunched across the butterfly wings to the shop.

Chronomode (*Fine Bespoke Clothing of the Past*, the sign read underneath) was the most exclusive Vagabonder boutique in the northern hemisphere. The floors were real dateverified oak, the velvet curtains shipped from Paris in a Chinese junk during the six weeks in '58 when one of the Vagabonder boys slept with a Wright brother and planes hadn't been invented.

Simone was already behind the counter arranging buttons by era of origin. Petra hadn't figured out until her fourth year working there that Simone didn't live upstairs, and Petra still wasn't convinced.

As Petra crossed the floor, an oak beam creaked.

Simone looked up and sighed. "Petra, wipe your feet on the mat. That's what it's for."

Petra glanced over her shoulder; behind her was a line of her footprints, mottled purple and blue and gold.

The first client of the day was the heiress to the O'Rourke fortune. Chronomode had a history with the family; the first one was the boy, James, who'd slept with Orville Wright and ruined Simone's drape delivery *par avion*. The O'Rourkes had generously paid for shipment by junk, and one of the plugs they sent back with James was able to fix things so that the historic flight was only two weeks late. Some stamps became very collectible, and the O'Rourkes became loyal clients of Simone's.

They gave a Vagabonding to each of their children as twenty-first-birthday presents. Of course, you had to be twenty-five before you were allowed to Bore back in time, but somehow exceptions were always made for O'Rourkes, who had to fit a lot of living into notoriously short life spans.

Simone escorted Fantasy O'Rourke personally to the center of the shop, a low dais with a three-frame mirror. The curtains in the windows were already closed by request; the O'Rourkes liked to maintain an alluring air of secrecy they could pass off as discretion.

"Ms. O'Rourke, it's a pleasure to have you with us," said Simone. Her hands, clasped behind her back, just skimmed the hem of her black jacket.

Never cut a jacket too long, Simone told Petra her first day. It's the first sign of an amateur.

"Of course," said Ms. O'Rourke. "I haven't decided on a destination, you know. I thought maybe Victorian England."

From behind the counter, Petra rolled her eyes. Everyone wanted Victorian England.

Simone said, "Excellent choice, Ms. O'Rourke."

"On the other hand, I saw a historian the other day in the listings who specializes in eighteenth-century Japan. He was delicious." She smiled. "A little temporary surgery, a trip to Kyoto's geisha district. What would I look like then?"

"A vision," said Simone through closed teeth.

Petra had apprenticed at a tailor downtown, and stayed there for three years afterward. She couldn't manage better, and had no hopes.

Simone came in two days after a calf-length black pencil skirt had gone out (some pleats under the knee needed mending).

Her gloves were black wool embroidered with black silk thread. Petra couldn't see anything but the gloves around the vast and smoky sewing machine that filled the tiny closet where she worked, but she knew at once it was the woman who belonged to the trim black skirt.

"You should be working in my shop," said Simone. "I offer superior conditions."

Petra looked over the top of the rattling machine. "You think?"

"You can leave the attitude here," said Simone, and went to the front of the shop to wait.

Simone showed Petra her back office (nothing but space and light and chrome), the image library, the labeled bolts of cloth—1300, 1570, China, Flanders, Rome.

"What's the shop name?" Petra asked finally.

"Chronomode," Simone said, and waited for Petra's exclamation of awe. When none came, she frowned. "I have a job for you," she continued, and walked to the table, tapping the wood with one finger. "See what's left to do. I want it by morning, so there's time to fix any mistakes."

The lithograph was a late nineteenth-century evening gown, nothing but pleats, and Petra pulled the fabrics from the library with shaking hands.

Simone came in the next day, tore out the hem of the petticoat, and sewed it again by hand before she handed it over to the client.

Later Petra ventured, "So you're unhappy with the quality of my work."

Simone looked up from a Byzantine dalmatic she was sewing with a bone needle. "Happiness is not the issue," she said, as though Petra was a simpleton. "Perfection is."

That was the year the mice disappeared.

Martin Spatz, the actor, had gone Vagabonding in 8000 BC and killed a wild dog that was about to attack him. (It was a blatant violation of the rules— you had to be prepared to die in the past, that was the first thing you signed on the contract. He went to jail over it. They trimmed two years off because he used a stick, and not the pistol he'd brought with him.)

No one could find a direct connection between the dog and the mice, but people speculated. People were still speculating, even though the mice were long dead.

Everything went, sooner or later; the small animals tended to last longer than the large ones, but eventually all that was left were some particularly hardy plants, and the butterflies. By the next year the butterflies were swarming enough to block out the summer sun, and Disease Control began to intervene.

The slow, steady disappearance of plants and animals was the only lasting problem from all the Vagabonding. Plugs were more loyal to their mission than the people who employed them, and if someone had to die in the line of work they were usually happy to do it. If they died, glory; if they lived, money.

Petra measured a plug once (German Renaissance, which seemed a pointless place to visit, but Petra didn't make the rules). He didn't say a word for the first hour. Then he said, "The cuffs go two inches past the wrist, not one and a half."

The client came back the next year with a yen for Colonial America. He brought two different plugs with him.

Petra asked, "What happened to the others?"

"They did their jobs," the client said, turned to Simone. "Now, Miss Carew, I was thinking I'd like to be a British commander. What do you think of that?"

"I would recommend civilian life," Simone said. "You'll find the Bore committee a little strict as regards impersonating the military."

When Petra was very young she'd taken her mother's sewing machine apart and put it back together. After that it didn't squeak, and Petra and her long thin fingers were sent to the tailor's place downtown for apprenticeship.

"At least you don't have any bad habits to undo," Simone had said the first week, dropping *The Dressmaker's Encyclopaedia 1890* on Petra's worktable. "Though it would behoove you to be a little ashamed of your ignorance. Why—" Simone looked away and blew air through her teeth. "Why do this if you don't respect it?"

"Don't ask me—I liked engines," Petra said, opening the book with a thump.

Ms. O'Rourke decided at last on an era (eighteenth-century Kyoto, so the historian must have been really good looking after all), and Simone insisted on several planning sessions before the staff was even brought in for dressing.

"It makes the ordering process smoother," she said.

"Oh, it's nothing, I'm easy to please," said Ms. O'Rourke.

Simone looked at Petra. Petra feigned interest in buttons.

Petra was assigned to the counter, and while Simone kept Ms. O'Rourke in the main room with the curtains discreetly drawn, Petra spent a week rewinding ribbons on their spools and looking at the portfolios of Italian armor-makers. Simone was considering buying a set to be able to gauge the best wadding for the vests beneath.

Petra looked at the joints, imagined the pivots as the arm moved back and forth. She wondered if the French hadn't had a better sense of how the body moved; some of the Italian stuff just looked like an excuse for filigree.

When the gentleman came up to the counter he had to clear his throat before she noticed him.

She put on a smile. "Good morning, sir. How can we help you?"

He turned and presented his back to her—three arrows stuck out from the left shoulder blade, four from the right.

"Looked sideways during the Crusades," he said proudly. "Not recommended, but I sort of like them. It's a souvenir. I'd like to keep them. Doctors said it was fine, nothing important was pierced."

Petra blinked. "I see. What can we do for you?"

"Well, I'd really like to have some shirts altered," he said, and when he laughed the tips of the arrows quivered like wings.

"You'd never catch me vagabonding back in time," Petra said that night.

Simone seemed surprised by the attempt at conversation (after five years she was still surprised). "It's lucky you'll never have the money, then."

Petra clipped a thread off the buttonhole she was finishing.

"I don't understand it," Simone said more quietly, as though she were alone.

Petra didn't know what she meant.

Simone turned the page on her costume book, paused to look at one of the hair ornaments.

"We'll need to find the ivory one," Simone said. "It's the most beautiful."

"Will Ms. O'Rourke notice?"

"I give my clients the best," Simone said, which wasn't really an answer.

"I've finished the alterations," Petra said finally, and held up one of the shirts, sliced open at the shoulder blades to give the arrows room, with buttons down the sides for ease of dressing.

Petra was surprised the first time she saw a Bore team in the shop—the Vagabond, the Historian, the translator, two plugs, and a "Consultant" whose job was ostensibly to provide a life story for the client, but who spent three hours insisting that Roman women could have worn corsets if the Empire had sailed far enough.

The Historian was either too stupid or too smart to argue, and Petra's protest had been cut short by Simone stepping forward to suggest they discuss jewelry for the Historian and plausible wardrobe for the plugs.

"Why, they're noble too, of course," the client had said, adjusting his high collar. "What else could they be?"

Plugs were always working-class, even Petra knew that—in case you had to stay behind and fix things for a noble who'd mangled the past, you didn't want to run the risk of a rival faction calling for your head, which they tended strongly to do.

Petra tallied the cost of the wardrobe for a Roman household: a million in material and labor, another half a million in jewelry. With salaries for the entourage and the fees for machine management and operation, his vacation would cost him ten million.

Ten million to go back in time in lovely clothes, and not be allowed to change a thing. Petra took dutiful notes and marked in the margin, *A Waste*.

She looked up from the paper when Simone said, "No."

The client had frowned, not used to the word. "But I'm absolutely sure it was possible—"

"It may be possible, depending on your source," Simone said, with a look at the Historian, "but it is not *right*."

"Well, no offense, Miss Carew, but I'm paying you to dress me, not to give me your opinion on what's right."

"Apologies, sir," said Simone, smiling. "You won't be paying me at all. Petra, please show the gentlemen out."

They made the papers; Mr. Bei couldn't keep from talking about his experience in the Crusades.

"I was going to plan another trip right away," he was quoted as saying, "but I don't know how to top this! I think I'll be staying here. The Institute has already asked me to come and speak about the importance of knowing your escape plan in an emergency, and believe me, I know it."

Under his photo was the tiny caption: *Clothes by Chronomode.*

"Mr. Bei doesn't mention his plugs," Petra said, feeling a little sick. "Guess he wasn't the only one that got riddled with arrows."

"It's what the job requires. If you have the aptitude, it's excellent work."

"It can't be worth it."

"Nothing is worth what we give it," said Simone. She dropped her copy of the paper on Petra's desk. "You need to practice your running stitch at home. The curve on that back seam looks like a six-year-old made it."

Tibi cornered Petra at the Threaders' Guild meeting. Tibi worked at Mansion, which outfitted Vagabonders with a lot more pomp and circumstance than Simone did.

Tibi had a dead butterfly pinned to her dress, and when she hugged Petra it left a dusting of pale green on Petra's shoulder.

"Petra! Lord, I was JUST thinking about you! I passed Chronomode the other day and thought, Poor Petra, it's *such* a prison in there. Holding up?" Tibi turned to a tall young tailor beside her. "Michael, darling, Petra works for Carew over at Chronomode."

The tailor raised his eyebrows. "There's a nightmare. How long have you hung in there, a week?"

Five years and counting. "Sure," Petra said.

"No, for *ages*," Tibi corrected. "I don't know how she makes it, I really don't, it's just so *horrible*." Tibi wrapped one arm around the tailor and cast a pitying glance at Petra. "I was there for a week, I made the Guild send me somewhere else a week later, it was just inhuman. What is it *like*, working there for *so* long without anyone getting you out of there?"

"Oh, who knows," said Petra. "What's it like getting investigated for sending people back to medieval France with machine-sewn clothes?"

Tibi frowned. "The company settled that."

Petra smiled at Tibi, then at the tailor. "I'm Petra."

"Michael," he said, and frowned at her hand when they shook.

"Those are just calluses from the needles," Petra said. "Don't mind them."

"Ms. O'Rourke's kimono is ready for you to look at," Petra said, bringing the mannequin to Simone's desk.

"No need," said Simone, her eyes on her computer screen, "you don't have enough imagination to invent mistakes."

Petra hoped that was praise, but suspected otherwise.

A moment later Simone slammed a hand on her desk. "Dammit, look at this. The hair ornament I need is a reproduction. Because naturally a reproduction is indistinguishable from an original. The people of 1743 Kyoto will never notice. Are they hiring antiques dealers out of primary school these days?"

Simone pushed away from the desk in disgust and left through the door to the shop, heels clicking.

Petra smoothed the front of the kimono. It was heavy gray silk, painted with cherry blossoms and chrysanthemums. Near the hem, Petra had added butterflies.

The light in the shop was still on; Petra saw it just as she was leaving.

Careless, she thought as she crossed the workshop. Simone would have killed me.

She had one hand on the door when the sound of a footstep stopped her. Were they being robbed? She thought about the Danish Bronze Age brooches hidden behind the counter in their velvet wrappers.

Petra grabbed a fabric weight in her fist and opened the door a crack.

Simone stood before the fitting mirror, holding a length of bright yellow silk against her shoulders. It washed her out (she'd never let a client with her complexion touch the stuff), but her reflection was smiling.

She hung it from her collarbones like a Roman; draped it across her shoulder like the pallav of a sari; bustled it around her waist. The bright gold slid through her fingers as if she was dancing with it.

Simone gathered the fabric against her in two hands, closed her eyes at the feel of it against her face.

Petra closed the door and went out the back way, eyes fixed on the wings at her feet.

When she came around the front of the shop the light was still on in the window, and Simone stood like a doll wrapped in a wide yellow ribbon, imagining a past she'd never see.

Petra turned for home.

Disease Control hadn't made the rounds yet, and the darkness was a swarm of wings, purple and blue and gold.

₪

FIRST FLIGHT
₪
Mary Robinette Kowal

Eleanor Louise Jackson stood inside the plain steel box of the time machine. It was about the size of an outhouse, but without a bench or windows. She clutched her cane with one hand and her handbag with the other. It felt like the scan was taking far too long, but she was fairly certain that was her nerves talking.

Her corset made her ribs creak with every breath. She'd expected to hate wearing the thing but there was a certain comfort from having something to support her back and give her a shape more like a woman than a sack of potatoes.

A gust of air puffed around her and the steel box was gone. She stood in a patch of tall grass under an October morning sky. The caravan of scientists, technicians, and reporters had vanished from the field where they'd set up camp. Louise inhaled with wonder that the time machine had worked. Assuming that this was 1905, of course—the year of her birth and the bottom limit to her time traveling range. Even with all the preparation for this trip, it baffled her sense of the order of things to be standing there.

The air tasted sweet and so pure that she could make out individual fragrances; the hard edge of oak mixed with the raw green of fresh mowed grass. Louise had thought her sense of smell had gotten worse because she'd gotten old.

She drew herself together and pulled the watch out from the chain around her neck to check the time, as if it would reflect the local time instead of the time she'd left: 8:30 on the dot, which looked about right judging by the light. Now, she had six hours before they spun the machine back down and she got returned to her present. If the Board of Directors had thought she could do everything faster, they would have sent her back for less time because it was expensive to keep the machine spun up, but even with all the physical therapy, Louise was still well over a hundred.

With that in mind, she headed for the road. She'd been walking the route from the box to Huffman Prairie for the last week, so they could get the timing on it. But this looked nothing like her present. There had been a housing development across the street from where she'd left and now there was a farm with a single tall white house sitting smack in the middle of the corn fields.

If she thought too much about it, she wasn't sure she'd have the nerve to keep going. Down the road, a wagon drawn by a bay horse came towards her. Besides the fellow driving it, the back of the wagon was crammed full of pigs that were squealing loud enough to be heard from here. It made her think of her husband, dead these long years or two years old, depending on how you counted it. She shook her head to get rid of that thought.

Louise patted her wig, though the makeup fellow had done a lovely job fixing it to her head. She'd had short hair since the 1940s and it felt strange to have that much weight on top of her head again. The white hair wound around her head in the style she remembered her own grandmother wearing. She checked to make sure her broad hat was settled and that the brooch masking the "hat-cam" was still pointing forward.

She hadn't got far when the wagon pulled up alongside her.

"Pardon ma'am." The boy driving it couldn't be more than thirteen with red hair like a snarl of yarn. He had a heavy array of freckles and his two front teeth stuck out past his lip. He had a nice smile for all that. "Seeing as how we're going the same way, might I offer you a ride?"

He had a book in his lap, like he'd been reading as he was driving. The stink of the pigs billowed around them with the wind. One of the sows gave a particularly loud squeal and Louise glanced back involuntarily.

The boy looked over his shoulder. "My charges are garrulous this morning." He patted the book in his lap and leaned toward her. "I'm pretending they're Odysseus's men and that helps some."

Louise couldn't help but chuckle at the boy's elevated language. "My husband was a hog farmer. He always said a pig talked more sense than a politician."

"Politicians or sailors. If you don't mind sharing a ride with them I'll be happy to offer it."

"Well now, that's kind of you. I'm on my way to Huffman Prairie."

He slid over on the bench and stuck his hand out to offer her a boost up. "I'm Homer Van Loon."

Well, that accounted for his taste in reading and vocabulary. Boys his age were more like to read the penny dreadfuls than anything else but anyone whose parents saddled him with a name like Homer was bound to be a bit odd.

"Pleased to make your acquaintance. I'm Louise Jackson." She passed him her cane and gripped his other hand. Holding that and the weathered wooden side of the wagon, she hauled herself aboard. Grunting in the sort of way that would have made her mama scold her, Louise dropped onto the wooden bench. Three months of physical therapy to get ready for this and climbing into a wagon almost wore her out.

"You walk all the way out here from town?" Homer picked up the reins and sat next to her.

"Lands, no." Louise settled her bag in her lap and told the lie the team of historians had prepared for her, in case someone asked. "I took the interurban rail out and then thought I'd walk the rest for a constitutional. The way was a bit longer than I thought, so I'm grateful to you." The Lord would forgive her for the lie, given the circumstance.

"Are you headed out to the Wright Brothers'?"

"I am. I never thought I'd see such a thing."

"That's for a certai—" His voice cut off.

Louise slammed hard against pavement. The wagon was gone. Power lines hung over her head and the acrid smell of asphalt stung her nose.

And smoke.

Shouting, half a dozen people ran toward her. Louise rolled over to her knees and looked around for her cane. It had landed on the road to her side and she grabbed it to lever herself back to her feet.

Mr. Barnes was near the front of the people running toward her. The poor thing looked as if his heart would give out with worry, though Louise wasn't sure if he was worried about her or his invention.

The young fellow who did her wig got to her first, helped her to her feet. It seemed as if everyone was chorusing questions about if she was all right. Louise nodded and kept repeating that she was fine until Mr. Barnes arrived, red-faced and blowing like a racehorse.

Louise drew herself up as tall as she could. "What happened?"

"We blew a transformer." Mr. Barnes gestured at one of the telephone poles, which had smoke billowing up from it. "Are you all right?" Up close, it was clear he was worried about her and Louise chided herself for doubting him. He hadn't been a thing but kind to her since the Time Travel Society recruited her.

"I'm fine. More worried about the boy I was talking to than anything else."

That stopped all the conversation flat. The program director, Dr. Connelly, pushed her way through the crowd, face pale. "Someone saw you vanish? You're sure?"

"I was sitting in his wagon." Louise settled her hat on her head. "Maybe, if you send me back a few seconds after I vanished, we can pretend that I fell out of the wagon."

"Out of the question." Dr. Connelly set her mouth into a hard line. With her dark hair drawn tight in a bun, she looked like a school marm with an unruly child.

"He'll think he's gone crazy."

"And having you reappear will make things better?"

"At least I can explain what's happening so he's not left wondering for the rest of his life."

"Explain what? That you are a time traveler?"

Louise gripped her cane and took a step closer to Dr. Connelly. When she was young, she would have been able to look down at the woman and still felt like she ought to, even though their eyes were on level. "That's exactly what I'll tell him. He's a twelve year-old boy reading Homer on his free time. I don't think he'll have a bit of a problem believing me."

A muscle pulsed in Dr. Connelly's jaw and she finally said, "There's no point in arguing out here in the heat. We'll take it to the rest of board and let them decide."

That was as clear a "no" as if she'd actually said the word. Louise leaned forward on her cane. "I look forward to speaking with them." She cut Dr. Connelly off before she could open her mouth. "As I'm the only one who's met the boy, I trust you'll want me to tell the Board about him." People shouldn't make the mistake of thinking that being old meant she was sweet.

Louise sat in her costume in a conference room with Dr. Connelly, Mr. Barnes, and two other members of the board, both white men who looked old but couldn't be much past retirement age. The conference room had flat panel screens set up with the other board members on them. They had been debating the issues for the past half hour largely going into details of why it was too dangerous to try to make her reappear on the wagon on account of it being a moving vehicle.

Louise cleared her throat. "Pardon me, but may I ask a question?"

"Of course." Mr. Barnes swiveled his chair to face her. The boy didn't seem that much older than Homer Van Loon for all that he'd invented the time machine.

"I hear you talking a lot about the program and I understand that's important and all, but I'm not hearing anyone talk about what's best for Homer Van Loon."

Dr. Connelly swiveled her chair to face Louise. "I appreciate your concern for the boy, but I don't think you have an understanding of the historical context of the issue."

Her disdain lay barely under the surface of civility. Louise had seen this sort of new money back when she'd been working in the department store and she always had been required to smile at them. No need now.

"Young lady," Louise snapped at Dr. Connelly like one of her own children. "I've lived through two world wars, the Great Depression, the Collapse. I lived through race riots, saw us put men on the moon, the Spanish Flu, AIDS, the *Titanic*, Suffrage, and the Internet. I've raised five children and buried two, got twenty-three grandchildren, eleven great-grandchildren, and five great-great grandchildren with more on the way. And you have the nerve to say I don't understand history?"

The room was silent except for the whir of the computer fans.

Dr. Connelly said, "I apologize if we've made you feel slighted, Louise. We'll take your concerns under advisement as we continue our deliberations."

If she hadn't been a good Christian woman, she would have cracked the woman on the head with her cane for the amount of condescension in her voice.

"How many people do you have that are my age?" She knew the answer to the question before she asked it. She might not use the Internet but she had grandchildren who were only to happy to do searches for her. A person couldn't travel back before she was born and Louise was born in 1905. There weren't that many people of her age, let alone able-bodied ones.

"Six." Dr. Connelly looked flatly unimpressed with Louise's longevity.

Mr. Barnes either didn't know where she was headed or agreed with her. "But you're the only that's a native English speaker."

Louise nodded her head in appreciation. "So it seems to me that you might want to do more than keep my concerns 'under consideration.'"

A man on one of the screens spoke. "Are you blackmailing us, Mrs. Jackson?"

"No sir, I'm not. I'm trying to get you to pay attention." She straightened in her chair now that they were all looking at her. "You saw the video of me meeting him. Homer Van Loon is a boy out of time himself. He's reading the *Odyssey*, which if you know anything about farm boys from 1905 ought to tell you everything you need to know right there. Not only will he believe me, he'll understand why it needs to be kept secret—as if anyone would believe him anyhow. And if you think on it, having someone local to the time might be handy. He's twelve now. When you send someone back to Black Friday, which you will I expect, he'll be in his thirties. You think a man like that wouldn't be helpful?"

Mr. Barnes shook his head. "But we researched him today. His life was entirely unremarkable. If he knew you were a time traveler, wouldn't that show up?"

Louise took a breath to calm herself. "If he's told to keep it a secret, and does, do you think his history would look any different?"

One of the board members in the room, a lean man with wire-rim glasses spoke for the first time since they started. "You've convinced me."

"Gerald!" Dr. Connelly swiveled to glare. "Conversations with a pig farmer are not what our investors have paid for."

And that was the real point that they had been dancing around in her presence. "I can do both."

They stared at her again but she only looked at Mr. Barnes. "Can't I? There's no reason I can't go back to the same time twice, is there?"

He shook his head, slowly smiling. Oh, but he was completely on her side, wasn't he. Louise beamed at him.

"Well, then, why don't you send me back for twenty minutes to talk to Homer to see how he took it. Twenty minutes. That's all and then I'll come back to the present and tell you how the conversation went. If Homer believes me, then I can hop back to the same spot and he can give me a ride to Huffman Prairie. I'll get there about the same time as I would have walking. If it doesn't then you can send me to the B point and we'll have tried."

Slowly, in the screens heads began to nod. Dr. Connelly scowled and threw her hands up. "That's two set-ups. Do you people know how much that costs? Just the transformer delay is cutting into our return. I can't conscience this. We're contracted to deliver footage of the Wright Flyer III and you, madam, are contracted to do that for us." She pointed at Mr. Barnes. "If she can go to the same time twice, then send her to the same place she went today but after she met the boy. We'd built in extra time for the walk, right?"

Louise prayed that the Good Lord would grant her patience and give her strength to forgive this woman. And then Louise added a prayer that He would forgive her for being devious. "That should be fine."

Mr. Barnes shook his head. "He'll still be there unless we send you too late to get to the field."

Never in her life had Louise wished for someone to lie, but she was beside herself wanting Mr. Barnes to be quiet. She was hoping that Homer had stuck around, in fact, she was counting on it so she could explain things to him.

Dr. Connelly rolled her eyes. "Not you too. You haven't even met the boy."

"No, but on the video he reminds me a lot of myself and, well, I'd still be there." Mr. Barnes shrugged. "Can you imagine being twelve and seeing someone vanish?"

"Anyone with sense would high-tail it out of there so whatever got her wouldn't get them, too." Dr. Connelly rolled her shoulders with blatant aggravation. "All right. Let's say he's more like you and still there. Send her back earlier so she can clear the site before the boy comes along. How much extra time will you need."

The teeth Louise had left all hurt to answer civilly. "It doesn't take me but thirty minutes to get down the road to Huffman Prairie."

Dr. Connelly narrowed her eyes. "I trust that you won't try to wait and contact the boy instead of performing your contractual obligations.

Louise sucked in her dentures and set her jaw before answering. "I said I'd get you photos of that Wright Flyer and I plan to do so."

"That's not the same. I'll need your word, Louise."

"*Dr.* Connelly. You have my word that I will not wait for Homer. But I want you to understand that I think this is a terrible thing."

"Noted." She turned her attention to Mr. Barnes. "Given the trial runs, what's the shortest amount of time she'll need to be out of sight?"

"There's a bend in the road that she should reach in about ten minutes."

"Let's set her down fifteen minutes early then." She surveyed the board. "Unless there are objections?

Nobody but Louise seemed to care and she kept her mouth shut before she could say something not very Christian.

When the steel booth vanished this time, the field looked exactly as it had before, save that the sun hadn't risen quite as high in the sky. The dust kicked up around her shoes as she walked and it smelled of the mud pies she used to make as a child. She passed the knotted fence about where Homer had picked her up and kept on to where she thought they been when she vanished. The trees came down almost to the edge of the road and made a place to hide. Oh, but wasn't she tempted to turn off and rest, waiting for Homer to turn up. There was even a natural bench where a tree had fallen.

But even if she hadn't given her word, they'd know if she waited because of that hat-cam. There was nothing to do but to get the photos fast enough so she could come back and talk to Homer before the plane flew. That wasn't supposed to happen until eleven o'clock, which should give her plenty of time.

She got to the bend in the road and looked back to see if Homer's wagon was in sight but didn't see a sign of him yet. Louise headed on to Huffman Prairie and felt every year of her life as she walked. Dust coated her shoes and the hem of her dress by the time she reached the field. A trickle of sweat crept between her scalp and the wig, driving her crazy with its slow progress across her skin.

The hangar in the middle of the field was in worse shape than it was in her present. Some historical society had built a replica of the rough structure but it bore little resemblance to the original. She dug into her handbag and pulled out a pair of opera glasses. Thumbing the switch, she turned on the high-definition digital camera embedded inside the case and began filming the barn and surrounding field. Sun cut across the field, weaving in and out of the tall grass like a child playing hide and seek. Across the way, a group of men in suits and ties were carrying the Wright Flyer III to the single rail track next to the hangar. The catapult tower stood in front of them, waiting to hurl the flyer down the rail and into the air.

Louise lowered the opera glasses. Well now, she hadn't expected them to start moving it so early, so maybe Dr. Connelly had a point after all.

She'd seen photos of the plane, of course, but until this moment the reality of time travel hadn't hit her. She recognized the Wright Brothers like they were her own family. The fellow down at the end with the handlebar mustache, that was Orville. And over there, with the bright blue eyes, was Wilbur, covering his bald head with a bowler, even while he was working.

And then there was the plane. It was like a child's model made large. A wood and cloth construction that was equal parts grace and lumbering ox. Looking at it, it was hard to believe that it would roll down the track, much less fly for half an hour. Louise raised the opera glasses to her eyes and filmed the men settle the plane on the track. They milled around then, while Orville Wright did something with the one wheel trolley underneath.

She checked her watch. 8:45, which was about when she'd vanished on the first trip. There was two hours yet before the flight was going to happen. She'd need to hurry and snap the photo of that gear they wanted and then hurry down the road to meet Homer. There ought to be more than enough time to get down the road to Homer and be back for the flight.

The board had their mission and she had hers. Tucking the opera glasses back into her bag, Louise made her way across the field. She wanted to run, but the uneven ground would cause her to stumble if she stepped out of walking pace.

Wilbur looked up as she approached. From his face, she must make quite a picture. An old lady, in a fine plum walking suit, out by herself in a field full of men and machinery. Louise nodded her head. "Morning. I hope I'm not disturbing you."

"No ma'am." Wilbur pulled a rag out of his pocket and hastily wiped his grease stained fingers off. "Can I help you with anything?"

That was one of the handy things about being old, people were always wanting to help out. No telling if the people at the Time Travel Institute had thought of that or not. "I wanted to see what you gentlemen were doing out here. I've been reading about your efforts and they're inspiring, I'll tell you." Louise moved around the wing of the plane toward the rudders, where the missing part was. Or not missing. Since the plane was whole and perfect. She turned so her hat-cam was pointing straight at him, recording for posterity. "Please don't mind me. I'm just the nosy type."

"Um. Well. We're getting ready for a trial flight, so if you don't mind . . . "

"Oh, I'll stand over on the side when you take off." She lifted the glasses again and aimed them at the part, moving around to get it from a different angle.

He laughed. "I appreciate that ma'am. It'll be another ten minutes or so."

Louise gasped. The records showed that they took off at eleven and that was two hours from now.

"Something wrong ma'am?" His face was flushed and so alive that it was hard for Louise to credit that he'd been dead for close to seventy years where she came from.

"No, no. I didn't realize how soon it was. Somehow I got it in my mind that you were going to fly later today." This time travel was a marvel. Standing here as they fiddled with whatever it was on the airplane, it made her pity poor Mr. Barnes who couldn't travel back more than thirty years. What had there been to see in his lifetime that was like this?

It made her wish she was a few years older so she could see their first flight. Louise worked her way around the plane, determined to film every inch of it. Did they know that it would break records today? "How long do you think you'll fly today?"

He grinned and rubbed the back of his neck. "It's good of you to think it'll get off the ground, ma'am."

Orville gave the wrench a twist on the gizmo. "The gentlemen are taking wagers so my brother doesn't feel as if he can make predictions. It wouldn't be 'sporting.'" He lowered the tool and gestured at her with it. "How long do you think we'll stay aloft?"

"Well now, I'm not a betting person, so I couldn't say." If truth be told, she knew exactly how long it would take. Eighteen minutes and forty-two seconds. In two days, they would do the flight everyone talked about, where the machine stayed aloft for thirty minutes. But this flight, today, marks the first time it will stay aloft for more than a few minutes. There were no records of it because no one knew that it would be a historic moment.

"Go on. We won't write your name down," one of the men said.

"No, thank you sir. It'd be betting in my heart, because I'd still be hoping I was right." Louise smiled at him but he shifted uncomfortably and tugged on his collar. Well, if it made him think better of his ways, that was all to the good, even if it wasn't why she'd traveled through time to get here.

After a few moments of uncomfortable silence, they got back to work and more or less ignored Louise, which suited her fine. She took pains to look at every inch of the flyer so no one at the Time Travel Institute could say she had neglected her duty when she went off after Homer.

Orville said, "Is there anything you're looking for in particular?"

"Oh! No. Thank you. I'm fascinated."

He grunted and lifted his head. "Wilbur! Would you get me the oilcan?" Orville jiggled a gizmo on the front of the plane. "I don't like the way the elevator is responding."

Nodding, Wilbur trotted over to the hangar while Orville continued to tweak the Flyer. "Wilbur's a trusting sort." He beckoned Louise closer. "The thing is, I don't think we've ever had someone display so much interest in one of our flyers before, except industrial spies, of course." He smiled at her, but his eyes were hard and narrow.

It hadn't even occurred to her, what it must look like for her to be staring at the plane with opera glasses. "I'd so wished I'd seen your first flight that I'm determined not to miss a thing about this one." She put on her best sweet little old lady face and pointed at the rudder. "What does this do?"

Leaning in close to her, Orville kept his smile fixed. "It helps the flyer fly."

Behind her, Louise heard the squeal of pigs. She lost all interest in Orville and turned as Homer came thundering up to the field, driving the wagon faster than was wise. He pulled the horse up in a cloud of dust. Standing, he pointed at her. "I thought so!"

"Excuse me, gentlemen." Louise set her back to them and started walking across the field to meet Homer.

He half ran at her but stopped before he got near enough to touch. "Are you a witch?"

Back at the plane, one of the men muttered. "Well she's old enough to be."

Louise half-turned her head to him. "I'm old but there isn't a thing wrong with my hearing." She faced Homer again. "And I'm not a witch."

"How do you explain disappearing and then turning up here?"

She shook her head. "Walk with me, young man, and I'll explain."

He crossed his arms. "Not a chance. I want witnesses to whatever you're going to say. There's no way that I'm going to let you take me off and enchant me."

The snickers again from behind her. Louise sighed. "You want these gentlemen to think you've read too many penny dreadfuls? Have you ever heard of witches outside of a storybook? Ever read about one in the papers? No. Because there's no such thing."

"That might be so, but I saw you disappear with my own two eyes and I ain't taking any chances."

"You took a chance coming here, didn't you? If I'm what you say I am. What's to stop me from vanishing right now and taking you with me if it were something I could do? So when I ask you to walk with me, I'd take it kindly if you would."

"What have you got to say that you're afraid to say in front of these folks?"

"Not a thing. I'm more worried about them thinking you're any more touched than they already do." She gestured toward the hangar. "I'm going to walk over there and you can come with me or not, as you like. I'll keep at arm's distance though so you aren't thinking I'll grab you and haul you Lord knows where." Without waiting for Homer to respond, she set out, stabbing the ground with her cane as she went. She figured that curiosity had brought him here and curiosity would make him follow her. Sure enough, she hadn't got more than ten steps before she heard him coming along after.

She waited until she was fairly sure she was out of earshot of the men at the flyer and then waited a mite more before she started talking. "You ever read H. G. Wells?"

"Of course I have."

"Well, that'll make things a little easier." She stopped abruptly and turned to face him. Homer was almost on her heels and half-stumbled back to keep out of arm's reach. Louise snorted. "Do you remember the book *The Time Machine*?"

Homer blinked and then guffawed. "You aren't trying to tell me you're from the future."

"Being a witch is more believable?"

"Well . . . no offense, ma'am." He dug his toe into the ground. "But a time traveler wouldn't be old."

"I wouldn't have thought so either but it turns out that time travel only works within the span of a person's lifetime. They picked me because I was born this year."

His face screwed up with concentration. "Let's say that's so. Give me a good reason for you to vanish then."

"The machine broke and I can only stay here for so long as it's turned on. It took a full day for them to fix it while I was back in my own time." She shook her head. "I told them to set me down near you so I could explain, but they thought you wouldn't understand. I'm very sorry about that."

"Prove it. Bring me tomorrow's paper or something." Those arms were crossed across his chest again as if he were preparing for war. At least Louise knew he'd survive the Great War, because the records they'd found about him showed Homer dying in the seventies.

"I can't nip back and forth in time on a whim. It's an expensive machine that's sent me here and the operator is back in my own time." Louise pursed her lips, thinking. Dr. Connelly wouldn't approve, but the only obviously modern thing she had with her was the opera glass camera. Pulling it out of her handbag, Louise rewound the footage a little, so he could watch it. "Here. This is a moving picture camera, disguised as opera glasses. I was filming the plane."

Homer started to reach for them and then stopped. "What if this is just a story and that's ensorcelled?"

"Young man. I don't know why you're so set on me being a witch instead of a time traveler. Why on earth would I pretend to be something so unbelievable if I were trying to hide being a witch? It doesn't make a spot of sense. If I were going to make up a story, it'd be a cleverer one than that—

unless I'm telling the truth. Now you tell me why I'd pretend to be time-traveler instead of letting you think I'm a witch?"

"There are laws against witchcraft. You could be burned at the stake."

She didn't say anything to that, just sighed and looked over the rim of her glasses at him. Living as long as she had gave her plenty of time to perfect the withering glare of scorn. She'd decimated sons and grandsons with it and this boy melted as easily as the others. His face colored right out to the tips of his ears, which burned bright enough to serve as a landing beacon for the Flyer. He rocked back on his heels and raised his shoulders as if he were trying to protect his neck from the butcher's knife.

Swallowing, Homer said, "I guess that's not too likely."

"No. It's not. Now are you going to look at this or not?"

He took the opera glasses from her and held them up to his eyes. Immediately he yanked them away, eyes wide with shock. Spinning on his heel, he stared at the airplane. Homer brought the glasses up to his eyes and even with his back to her, Louise could see his hands shaking. "What is this?"

"It's a camera."

"I mean, why are you taking all these pictures of the flyer?" He lowered the glasses, turning to face her.

"Because, today is the first day that they really fly. Wilbur will go up for eighteen minutes and not come down until he drains the gas tank. It's a historic moment but they weren't expecting it, so there's no photographer here. Day after tomorrow, Orville will fly in front of a crowd for thirty-four minutes, but today's the day everything changes. And later on, after they fly it, they'll make changes and eventually dismantle the flyer. In 1947 Orville will rebuild it for an exhibit, but he'll only have about sixty percent of this plane. There's a historical society that wants to check the rebuilt plane against this one."

And right then, Wilbur stepped out of the open door of the hangar. "This has gone on long enough. Madam, you should be ashamed of yourself, filling this boy's head with nonsense in order to get him to help in your espionage." He held out his hand to Homer. "Give me the camera, son."

"Espionage?" Louise lifted her cane so it served as a barrier between the man and Homer. "I don't know what you're talking about, but the opera glasses are mine and I'll thank you to leave them alone."

"I overheard everything and though your story is designed to play upon the fancies of a boy, I could hear the elements of truth." He reached over the cane and snatched the opera glasses from Homer's hand.

"Hey!" Homer pushed Louise's cane out of the way and stepped toward the man. "Give that back."

"We've been at pains to keep our invention out of the wrong hands" He brushed past both of them and hurried across the field, waving the opera glasses.

Homer ran after him and caught his coat. "Please, Mr. Wright. I was just funning with her. I didn't think anyone would take me seriously."

Louise hurried after them, focused more on the uneven ground than the man in front of her.

Wilbur shrugged off Homer's hand and shook his head. "We didn't advertise this test flight, so how do you suppose that she knew to come out here today, except through spying?

Louise laughed to hide her discomfiture. This was the sort of thing that it would have been nice for the Time Travel Society to let her know. "You can't think that people aren't talking about this in town, can you?"

"The people in town aren't out here snooping around. Who looks at things up close with *opera glasses*?" Wilbur lifted the opera glasses and mimed snooping.

The moment he looked through the opera glasses he cursed and jerked his head away from the eyepiece. Slowly he put it back to his eyes. His face paled. Wilbur wiped his mouth, lowering the opera glasses to stare at Louise. "Who do you work for?"

"I'm just a woman that's interested in seeing you fly." She could barely breathe for fear of the moment. "You're making history here."

"History." He snorted. "You were talking to the boy about time travel."

Before Louise could think of a clean answer, Homer said, "She disappeared earlier. Utterly vanished. I . . . I think she's telling the truth."

"And if she is?" Wilbur turned the glasses over in his hands. "I look at this and all I can see are the number of inventions that stand between me and the ability to do . . . If I weren't holding it, I should think it impossible."

Louise could not think of a thing to say to the man. He looked as if his faith had been as profoundly shaken as a small boy discovering the truth about Santa Claus. Louise shook her head. "All I want is to watch you fly, once I've done that I'll be gone and you won't have to worry about the pictures I took."

"This is why you were so certain the flyer will work today, isn't it?" There was no wonder his voice, only resignation.

"Yes, sir."

"And what you told the boy, about Orville rebuilding the plane. True? So, we'll be enough of a success that someone builds a museum and sends a time traveler back to visit. That's something, even if I'm not around to see it."

Startled, Louise replayed the things she had told Homer. "Why do you think that?"

"Because everything you said was about my brother. At some point, I'll stop registering on the pages of history." He twisted the glasses in his hands. "Is the future fixed?"

Louise hesitated. "The Good Book promises us free will."

"You have not answered my question." He took his bowler off and wiped a sheen of sweat from his scalp before settling it back in place.

When he looked back at her with eyes as blue as a frozen river, she could see the boy she'd read about. Self-taught and brilliant, he had been described as having a voracious mind. Everything she said would go in and fill his mind with ideas.

"You understand that I'm a only traveler and don't understand the science? If you think about time like a stalk of broccoli, what Mr. Barnes's machine does is it takes a slice of the broccoli and shuffles it to a different point in the stalk. My past is one big stalk. My future is made up of florets. So the only places I can travel back to are the ones that lead to the future I live in. If I tried to go forward, they tell me that the future will be different every time. Which I believe means that you can do things different and wind up in a different stalk of the broccoli, but I'll only ever see the pieces of broccoli that lead to my present." She shook her head. "If that makes any sense to you, then I'll be impressed."

"It makes sense enough." Wilbur lifted the glasses to his eyes again and with them masked said, "I'll thank you not to intimate this to my brother."

"Of course not." Louise shuddered.

"Very good." Wilbur spun on his heel. "Well, find a spot to watch."

"But Miss Jackson's opera glasses . . . " Homer trotted after him.

"I'll give them back after I've flown." Wilbur Wright grinned. "If your history is going to lose track of me, then perhaps the future needs to be reminded."

On the far side of the hangar, the other men were still celebrating the flight. Eighteen minutes and forty-two seconds precisely. She'd recorded their joy but whenever Wilbur looked at her, Louise got the shivers and finally given up to wait out her remaining time out of sight. She leaned against the side of the hangar, studying her watch. Time was almost up.

At a run, Homer rounded the corner of the hangar with the opera glasses in his hands. He relaxed visibly at the sight of her. "I was scared you'd be gone already."

She held the watch up. "Two minutes."

"He didn't want to come. Said that the doubt would be better than knowing for certain." Homer chewed his lip and handed her the opera glasses. "What happens to him, Miss Jackson?"

Louise sighed and remembered all the things she'd read about Wilbur Wright before coming here. "He dies of typhoid when he's forty-seven. I do wish I hadn't said a thing about the future."

Homer shook his head. "I'm glad you told me. I'll—"

And he was gone.

The tall grass of Hoffman Prairie was replaced by a crisply mown lawn of chemical green. Where the weathered hangar had been stood a bright, white replica. Neither the hangar nor the lawn seemed as real as the past. Louise sighed. The air burned her nostrils, smelling of carbon and rubber. The homing beacon in her handbag should bring them to her soon enough.

She leaned back against the barn to wait. A paper rustled behind her. She pulled away, afraid that she'd see a big "wet paint" sign but it was an envelope.

An envelope with her name on it.

She spun around as quickly as she could but there wasn't a soul in sight. Breath fighting with her corset, Louise pulled the envelope off the wall. She opened it carefully and found a single sheet of paper. A shaky hand covered the surface.

Dear Louise,

You will have just returned from your first time travel mission and meeting me, so this offers the first opportunity to introduce myself to you in your present. I wish I could be there, but that would mean living for another forty years, which task I fear would require Olympian blood. You have been such a friend to me and my family and so I wanted you to know two things.

1. Telling me the truth was the best thing you could have done for me. Thank you.

2. We are (or will be by the time you read this) major shareholders in the Time Travel Society. It ensures that your future trips to my past

are without incident, and also will let my children know precisely
when your first trip takes place in your present. I hope you don't mind
that I took the liberty of asking my children to purchase shares for you
as well. I wish we could have presented them to you sooner.

Be well, my friend. And happy travels.

Sincerely yours,

Homer Van Loon

At the bottom of the sheet was a bank account number and then a list of addresses and phone numbers arranged in order of date.

Her eyes misted over at the gift he'd given her—not the account, but the knowledge that she had not harmed him by telling the truth.

In the parking lot, the Time Travel Society's minivan pulled in, barely stopping before Mr. Barnes and the rest of the team jumped out. "How was the trip?" he shouted across the field, jogging toward her.

Louise smiled and held out the opera glasses. "I think you'll like the footage I got for you."

"May I?" He stopped in front of her as long and lanky as she imagined Homer being when he was grown up.

"Of course. That's why you sent me, isn't it?"

He took the opera glasses from her and rewound. Holding it to his eyes as the rest of the team gathered around, Mr. Barnes became utterly still. "Miss Jackson . . . Miss Jackson, how did you get the camera on the plane?"

Dr. Connelly gasped. "On the Wright Flyer?"

"Yes, ma'am. I watched from the ground with the hatcam while Wilbur was flying. I'm quite curious to hear the audio that goes with it. We could hear him whooping from the ground."

"But how did you . . . " Dr. Connelly shook her head.

"I told him the truth." Louise sighed, remembering the naked look on his face at the moment when he believed her. "He took the camera because he understood the historical context."

₪

THE TIME TRAVEL CLUB
₪
Charlie Jane Anders

Nobody could decide what should be the first object to travel through time. Malik offered his car keys. Jerboa held up an action figure. But then Lydia suggested her one-year sobriety coin, and it seemed too perfect to pass up. After all, the coin had a unit of time on it, as if it came from a realm where time really was a denomination of currency. And they were about to break the bank of time forever, if this worked.

Lydia handed over the coin, no longer shiny due to endless thumb-worrying. And then she had a small anxiety attack. "Just as long as I get it back," she said, trying to keep the edge out of her voice.

"You will," said Madame Alberta with a smile. "This coin, we send a mere one minute into the future. It reappears in precisely the same place from which it disappears."

Lydia would have been nervous about the first test of the time machine in Madame Alberta's musty dry laundry room in any case. After all they'd been through to make this happen, the stupid thing *had* to work. But now, she felt like a piece of herself—a piece she had fought for—was about to vanish, and she would need to have faith. She sucked at having faith.

Madame Alberta took the coin and placed it in the airtight glass cube—six by six by six, that they'd built where the washer/dryer were supposed to be. The balsa-walled laundry room was so crammed with equipment there was scarcely room for four people to hunch over together. Once the coin was sitting on the floor of the cube, Madame Alberta walked back towards the main piece of equipment, which looked like a million vacuum cleaner hoses attached to a giant slow-cooker.

"I keep thinking about what you were saying before," Lydia said to Malik, trying to distract herself. "About wanting to stand outside history and see the empires rising and falling from a great height, instead of being swept along by the waves. But what if this power to send things, and people, back and forth across history makes us the masters of reality? What if we can make the waves change direction, or turn back entirely? What then?"

"I chose your group with great care," Madame Alberta. "As I have said. You have the wisdom to use this technology properly, all of you."

Madame Alberta pulled a big lever. A *whoosh* of purple neon vapor rushed into the glass cube, followed by a *klorrrrrp* sound like someone opening a soda can and burping at the same time—in exactly the way that might suggest they'd had enough soda already—and the coin was gone.

"Wow," said Malik. His eyebrows went all the way up so his forehead concertina-ed, and his short dreads did a fractal scatter.

"It just vanished," said Jerboa, bouncing with excitement, floppy hat flopping. "It just . . . It's on its way."

Lydia wanted to hold her breath, but there was so little air in here that she was already light-headed. This whole wooden-beamed staircase-flanked basement area felt like a soup of fumes.

Lydia really needed to pee, but she didn't want to go upstairs and risk missing the sudden reappearance of her coin, which would be newer than everything else in the world by a minute. She held it, swaying and squirming. She looked down at her phone, and there were just about thirty seconds left. She wondered if they should count down. But that was probably too tacky. She really couldn't breathe at this point, and she was starting to taste candyfloss and everything smelled white.

"Just ten seconds left," Malik said. And then they did count down, after all. "Nine . . . eight . . . seven . . . six . . . five! Four! Three! Two! ONE!"

They all stopped and stared at the cube, which remained empty. There was no "soda-gas" noise, no sign of an object breaking back into the physical world from some netherspace.

"Um," said Jerboa. "Did we count down too soon?"

"It is possible my calculations—" said Madame Alberta, waving her hands in distress. Her fake accent was slipping even more than usual. "But no. I mean, I quadruple-checked. They cannot be wrong."

"Give it a minute or two longer," said Malik. "I'm sure it'll turn up." As if it was a missing sock in the dryer, instead of a coin in the cube that sat where a dryer ought to be.

They gave it another half an hour, as the knot inside Lydia got bigger and bigger. At one point, Lydia went upstairs to pee in Madame Alberta's tiny bathroom, facing a calendar of exotic bird paintings. And eventually,

Lydia went outside to stand in the front yard, facing the one-lane highway, cursing. Why had she volunteered her coin? And now, she would never see it again.

Lydia went home and spent an hour on the phone processing with her sponsor, Nate, who kept reassuring her, in a voice thick as pork rinds, that the coin was just a token and she could get another one and it was no big deal. These things have no innate power, they're just symbols. She didn't mention the "time machine" thing, but kept imagining her coin waiting to arrive, existing in some moment that hadn't been reached yet.

Even after all of Nate's best talk-downs, Lydia couldn't sleep. And at three in the morning, Lydia was still thinking about her one-year coin, floating in a state of indeterminacy—and then it hit her, and she knew the answer. She turned on the light, sat up in bed and stared at the wall of ring-pull talking-animal toys facing her bed. Thinking it through again and again, until she was sure.

At last, Lydia couldn't help phoning Jerboa, who answered the phone still half asleep and in a bit of a panic. "What is it?" Jerboa said. "What's wrong? I can find my pants, I swear I can put on some pants and then I'll fix whatever."

"It's fine, nothing's wrong, no need for pants," Lydia said. "Sorry to wake you. Sorry, I didn't realize how late it was." She was totally lying, but it was too late anyhow. "But I was thinking. Madame Alberta said the coin moved forward in time one minute, but it stayed in the same physical location. Right?"

"That's right," said Jerboa. "Same place, different time. Only moving in one dimension."

"But," said Lydia. "What if the Earth wasn't in the same place when the coin arrived? I mean . . . Doesn't the Earth move around the sun?"

"Yeah, sure. And the Earth rotates. And the sun moves around the galactic disk. And the galaxy is moving too, towards Andromeda and the Great Attractor," said Jerboa. "And space itself is probably moving around. There's no such thing as a fixed point in space. But Madame Alberta covered that, remember? According to Einstein, the other end of the rift in time ought to obey Newton's first law, conservation of momentum. Which means the coin would still follow the Earth's movement, and arrive at the same point. Except . . . Wait a minute!"

Lydia waited a minute. After which, Jerboa still hadn't said anything else. Lydia had to look at her phone to make sure she hadn't gotten hung up on. "Except what?" she finally said.

"Except that . . . the Earth's orbit and rotation are momentum, *plus gravity*. Like, we actually accelerate towards the sun as part of our orbit, or else our momentum would just carry us out into space. And Madame Alberta said her time machine worked by opting out of the fundamental forces, right? And gravity is one of those. Which would mean . . . Wait a minute, wait a minute." Another long, weird pause, except this time Lydia could hear Jerboa breathing heavily and muttering *sotto voce*.

Then Jerboa said, "I think I know where your medallion is, Lydia."

"Where?"

"Right where we left it. On the roof of Madame Alberta's neighbor's house."

Lydia had less than ninety days of sobriety under her belt, when she first met the Time Travel Club. They met in the same Unitarian basement as Lydia's twelve-step group: a grimy cellar, with a huge steam pipe running along one wall and intermittent gray carpeting that looked like a scale map of plate tectonics. Pictures of purple hands holding a green globe and dancing scribble children hung askew, by strands of peeling Scotch tape. Boiling hot in summer, drafty in winter, it was a room that seemed designed to make you feel desperate and trapped. But all the twelve steppers laughed a lot, in between crying, and afterwards everybody shared cigarettes and sometimes pie. Lydia didn't feel especially close to any of the other twelve steppers (and she didn't smoke) but she felt a desperate lifeboat solidarity with them.

The Time Travel Club always showed up just as the last people from Lydia's twelve-step meeting were dragging their asses up out of there. Most of the time travelers wore big dark coats and furry boots that seemed designed to look equally ridiculous in any time period. Lydia wasn't even sure why she stayed behind for one of their meetings, since it was a choice between watching people pretend to be time travelers and eating pie. Nine times out of ten, pie would have won over fake time travel. But Lydia needed to sit quietly by herself and think about the mess she'd made of her life before she tried to drive, and the Time Travel Club was as good a place as any.

Malik was a visitor from the distant past—the Kushite Kingdom of roughly twenty-seven hundred years ago. The Kushites were a pretty swell people, who made an excellent palm wine that tasted sort of like cognac. And now Malik commuted between the Kushite era, the present day, and the thirty-second century, when there was going to be a neo-Kushite revival going on and the dark, well-cheekboned Malik would become a bit of a celebrity.

The androgynous and pronoun-free Jerboa looked tiny and bashful inside a huge brown hat and high coat collar. Jerboa spent a lot of time in the Year One Million, a time period where the parties were excellent and people were considerably less hung up on gender roles. Jerboa also hung out in the 1920s and the early 1600s, on occasion.

And then there was Normando, a Kenny Rogers-looking dude who was constantly warping back to this one party in 1973 where he'd met this girl, who had left with an older man just as Young Normando was going to ask her to bug out with him. And now Normando was convinced he could be that older man. If he could just find that one girl again.

Lydia managed to shrink into the background at the first Time Travel Club meeting, without having to say anything. But a week later, she decided to stick around for another meeting, because it was better than just going home alone and nobody was going for pie this time.

This time, the others asked Lydia about her own journeys through time, and she said she didn't have a time machine and if she did, she would just use it to make the itchy insomniac nights end sooner, so she could wander alone in the sun rather than hide alone in the dark.

Oh, they said.

Lydia felt guilty about harshing their shared fantasy like that, to the point where she spent the next week obsessing about what a jerk she'd been and even had to call Nate once or twice to report that she was a terrible person and she was struggling with some Dark Thoughts. She vowed not to crash the Time Travel Club meeting again, because she was not going to be a disruptive influence.

Instead, though, when the twelve-step meeting ended and everybody else straggled out, Lydia said the same thing she'd said the previous couple weeks: "Nah, you guys go on. I'm just going to sit for a spell."

When the time travelers arrived, and Malik's baby face lit up with his opening spiel about how this was a safe space for people to share their space/time experiences, Lydia stood up suddenly in the middle of his intro, and blurted: "I'm a pirate. I sail a galleon in the nineteenth century, I'm the First Mate. They call me Bad Bessie, even though I'm named Lydia. Also, I do extreme solar-sail racing a couple hundred years from now. But that's only on weekends. Sorry I didn't say last week. I was embarrassed because piracy is against the law." And then she sat down, very fast. Everybody applauded and clapped her on the back and thanked her for sharing. This time around, there were a half dozen people in the group, up from the usual four or five.

Lydia wasn't really a pirate, though she did work at a pirate-themed adult bookstore near the interstate called the Lusty Doubloon, with the O's in "Doubloon" forming the absurdly globular breasts of its tricorner-hatted mascot. Lydia got pretty tired of shooting down pick-up lines from the type of men who couldn't figure out how to find porn on the Internet. Something about Lydia's dishwater-blond hair and smattering of monster tattoos apparently did it for those guys. The shower in Lydia's studio apartment was always pretty revolting, because the smell of bleach or Lysol reminded her of the video booths at work.

Anyway, after that, Lydia started sticking around for Time Travel Club every week, as a chaser for her twelve-step meeting. It helped get her back on an even keel so she could drive home without shivering so hard she couldn't see the road. She even started hanging out with Malik and Jerboa socially—Malik was willing to quit talking about palm wine around her, and they all started going out for fancy tea at the place at the mall, the one that put the leaves inside a paper satchel that you had to steep for exactly five minutes or Everything Would Be Ruined. Lydia and Jerboa went to an all-ages concert together, and didn't care that they were about ten years older than everybody else there—they'd obviously mis-aligned the temporal stabilizers and arrived too late, but still just in time. "Just in time" was Jerboa's favorite catchphrase, and it was never said without a glimpse of sharp little teeth, a vigorous nod and a widening of Jerboa's brown-green eyes.

For six months, the Time Travelers' meeting slowly became Lydia's favorite thing every week, and these weirdoes became her particular gang. Until one day, Madame Alberta showed up and brought the one thing that's guaranteed to ruin any Time Travel Club ever: an actual working time machine.

Lydia's one-year coin was exactly where Jerboa had said it would be: on the roof of the house next door to Madame Alberta's, nestled in some dead leaves in the crook between brick gable and the upward slope of rooftop. She managed to borrow the neighbor's ladder, by sort of explaining. The journey through the space/time continuum didn't seem to have messed up Lydia's coin at all, but it had gotten a layer of grime from sitting overnight. She cleaned it with one of the sanitizing wipes at work, before returning it to its usual front pocket.

About a week later, Lydia met up with Malik and Jerboa for bubble tea at this place in the Asian Mall, where they also served peanut honey toast and squid balls and stuff. Lydia liked the feeling of the squidgy tapioca blobs gliding up the fat straw and then falling into her teeth. Alien larvae. Never to hatch. Alien tadpoles squirming to death in her tummy.

None of them had shown up for Time Travel Club, the previous night. Normando had called them all in a panic, wanting to know where everybody was. Somehow Malik had thought Jerboa would show up, and Jerboa had figured Lydia would stick around after her other meeting.

"It's just . . . " Malik looked into his mug of regular old coffee, with a tragic expression accentuated by hot steam. "What's the point of sharing our silly make-believe stories about being time-travelers, when we built an actual real time machine, and it was no good?"

"Well, the machine worked," Jerboa said, looking at the dirty cracked tile floor. "It's just that you can't actually use it to visit the past or the future, in person. Lydia's coin was displaced upwards at an angle of about thirty-six degrees by the Earth's rotation and orbit around the sun. The further forward and backward in time you go, the more extreme the spatial displacement, because the distance traveled is the *square* of the time traveled. Send something an hour and a half forward in time, and you'd be over four hundred kilometers away from Earth. Or deep underground, depending on the time of day."

"So if we wanted to travel a few years ahead," Lydia said, "we would need to send a spaceship. So it could fly back to Earth from wherever it appeared."

"I doubt you'd be able to transport an object that size," said Jerboa. "From what Madame Alberta explained, anything more than about two hundred-sixteen cubic feet or about two hundred pounds, and the energy costs go up exponentially." Madame Alberta hadn't answered the door when Lydia went to get her coin back. None of them had heard from Madame Alberta since then, either.

Not only that, but once you were talking about traversing years rather than days, then other factors—such as the sun's acceleration toward the center of the galaxy and the galaxy's acceleration towards the Virgo Supercluster—came more into play. You might not ever find the Earth again.

They all sat for a long time, listening to the Canto-Pop and their own internal monologues about failure. Lydia was thinking that an orbit is a fragile thing, after all. You take centripetal force for granted at your peril. She could see Malik, Jerboa, and herself preparing to drift away from each other once and for all. Free to follow their separate trajectories. Separate futures. She had a clawing certainty that this was the last time the three of them would ever see each other, and she was going to lose the Time Travel Club forever.

And then it hit her, a way to turn this into something good. And keep the group together.

"Wait a minute," said Lydia. "So we don't have a machine that lets a person visit the past or future. But don't people spend kind of a lot of money to launch objects into space? Like, satellites and stuff?"

"Yes," said Jerboa. "It costs tons of money just to lift a pound of material out of our gravity well." And then for the first time that day, Jerboa looked up from the floor and shook off the curtain of black hair so you could actually see the makings of a grin. "Oh. Yeah. I see what you're saying. We don't have a time machine, we have a cheap simple way to launch things into space. You just send something a few hours into the future, and it's in orbit. We can probably calculate exact distances and trajectories, with a little practice. The hard part will be achieving a stable orbit."

"So?" Malik said. "I don't see how that helps anything . . . Oh. You're suggesting we turn this into a money-making opportunity."

Lydia couldn't help thinking of the fact that her truck needed an oil change and a new headpipe and four new tires and the ability to start when she turned the key in the ignition. And she needed never to go near the Lusty Doubloon again. "It's better than nothing," she said. "Until we figure out what else this machine can do."

"Look at it this way," Jerboa said to Malik. "If we are able to launch a payload into orbit on a regular basis, then that's a repeatable result. A repeatable result is the first step towards being able to do something else. And we can use the money to reinvest in the project."

"Well," Malik said. And then he broke out into a smile too. Radiant. "If we can talk Madame Alberta into it, then sure."

They phoned Madame Alberta a hundred times and she never picked up. At last, they just went to her house and kept banging on the door until she opened up.

Madame Alberta was drunk. Not just regular drunk, but long-term drunk. Like she had gotten drunk a week ago, and never sobered up. Lydia took one look at her, one whiff of the booze fumes, and had to go outside and dry heave. She sat, bent double, on Madame Alberta's tiny lawn, almost within view of the Saint Ignatius College science lab that they'd stolen all that gear from a few months earlier. From inside the house, she heard Malik and Jerboa trying to explain to Madame Alberta that they had figured out what happened to the coin. And how they could turn it into kind of a good thing.

They were having a hard time getting through to her. Madame Alberta's fauxropean accent was basically gone, and she sounded like a bitter old drunk lady from New Jersey who just wanted to drink herself to death.

Eventually, Malik came out and put one big hand gently on Lydia's shoulder. "You should go home," he said. "Jerboa and I will help her sober up, and then we'll talk her through this. I promise we won't make any decisions until you're there to take part."

Lydia nodded and got in her rusty old Ford, which rattled and groaned and finally came to a semblance of life long enough to let her roll back down the highway to her crappy apartment. Good thing it was pretty much downhill all the way.

When Madame Alberta first visited the Time Travel Club, nobody quite knew what to make of her. She had olive skin, black hair and a black beauty mark on the left side of her face, which tended to change its location every time Lydia saw her. And she wore a dark head scarf, or maybe a snood, and a long black dress with a slit up one side.

That first meeting, her Eurasian accent was the thickest and fakest it would ever be: "I have the working theory of the time machine. And the prototype that is, how you say, half-built. I need a few more pairs of hands to help me complete the assembly, but also I require the ethical advice."

"Like a steering committee," said Jerboa, perking up with a quick sideways head motion.

"Even so," said Madame Alberta. "Much like the Unitarian Church upstairs, the time machine has need of a steering committee."

At first, everybody assumed Madame Alberta was just sharing her own time-travel fantasy—albeit one that was a lot more elaborate, and involved a lot more delayed gratification, than everybody else's. Still, the rest of the meeting was sort of muted. Lydia was all set to share her latest experiences with solar-sail demolition derby, the most dangerous sport that would ever exist. And Malik was having drama with the Babylonians, either in the past or the future, Lydia wasn't sure which. But Madame Alberta had a quiet certainty that threw the group out of whack.

"I leave you now," said Madame Alberta, bowing and curtseying in a single weird arm-sweeping motion that made her appear to be the master of a particularly esoteric drunken martial arts style. "Take the next week to discuss my proposition. Be aware, though: This will be the most challenging of ventures." She whooshed out of the room, long flowy dress trailing behind her.

Nobody actually spent the week between meetings debating whether they wanted to help Madame Alberta build her time machine—instead, Lydia kept asking the other members whether they could find an excuse to kick her out of the group. "She freaks me out, man," Lydia said on the phone to Malik on Sunday evening. "She seems for real mentally not there."

"I don't know," Malik said. "I mean, we've never kicked anybody out before. There was that one guy who seemed like he had a pretty serious drug problem last year, with his whole astral projection shtick. But he stopped coming on his own, after a couple times."

"I just don't like it," said Lydia. "I have a terrible feeling she's going to ruin everything." She didn't add that she really needed this group to continue the way it was, that these people were becoming her only friends, and the only reason she felt like the future might actually really exist for her. She didn't want to get needy or anything.

"Eh," said Malik. "It's a time travel club. If she becomes a problem, we'll just go back in time and change our meeting place last year, so she won't find us."

"Good point."

It was Jerboa who found the article in the Berkeley Daily Voice—a physics professor who lectured at Berkeley and also worked at Lawrence Livermore had gone missing, in highly mysterious circumstances, six months earlier. And the photo of the vanished Professor Martindale—dark hair, laughing gray eyes, narrow mouth—looked rather a lot like Madame Alberta, except without any beauty mark or giant scarf.

Jerboa emailed the link to the article to Lydia and Malik. *Do you think . . . ?* the email read.

The next meeting came around. Besides the three core members and Madame Alberta, there was Normando, who had finally tracked down that hippie chick in 1973 and was now going on the same first date with her over and over again, arriving five minutes earlier each time to pick her up. Lydia did not think that would actually work in real life.

The others waited until Normando had run out of steam describing his latest interlude with Starshine Ladyswirl and wandered out to smoke a (vaguely post-coital) cigarette, before they started interrogating Madame Alberta. How did this alleged time machine work? Why was she building it in her laundry room instead of at a proper research institution? Had she absconded from Berkeley with some government-funded research, and if so were they all going to jail if they helped her?

"Let us say, for the sake of the argument," Madame Alberta played up her weird accent even as her true identity as a college professor from Camden was brought to light, "that I had developed some of the theory of the time travel while on the payroll of the government. Yes? In that hypothetical situation, what would be the ethical thing to do? You are my steering committee, please to tell me."

"Well," Malik said. "I don't know that you want the government to have a time machine."

"Yeah, yeah," Jerboa said. "They already have warrantless wiretaps and indefinite detention. Imagine if they could go back in time and spy on you in the past. Or kill people as little children."

"Well, but," Lydia said. "I mean, wouldn't it still be your responsibility to share your research?" But the others were already on Madame Alberta's side.

"As to how it works," Madame Alberta reached into her big black trench coat and pulled out a big rolled-up set of plans covered in equations and drawings, which meant nothing to anybody. "Shall we say that it was the accidental discovery? One was actually working on a project for the Department of Energy aimed at finding a way to eliminate the atomic waste. And instead, one stumbled on a method of using spent uranium to create an opening two Planck lengths wide, lasting a few fractions of a microsecond, with the other end a few seconds in the future."

"Uh huh," Lydia said. "So . . . you could create a wormhole too tiny to see, that only allowed you to travel a few seconds forward in time. That's, um . . . useful, I guess."

"But then! One discovers that one might be able to generate a much larger temporal rift, opting out of the fundamental forces, and it would be stable enough to move a person or a moderate-sized object either forward or backward in time, anywhere from a few minutes to a few thousand years, in the exact same physical location," said Madame Alberta. "One begins to panic, imagining this power in the hands of the government. This is all the hypothetical situation, of course. In reality, one knows nothing of this Professor Martindale of whom you speaks."

"But," said Lydia. "I mean, why us? I mean, assuming you really do have the makings of a time machine in your laundry room. Why not reach out to some actual scientists?" Then she answered her own question: "Because you would be worried they would tell the government. Okay, but the world is full of smart amateurs and clever geeks. And us? I mean, I work the day shift at a . . . " she tried to think of a way to say "pirate-themed sex shop" that didn't sound quite so horrible. "And Malik is a physical therapist. Jerboa has a physics degree, sure, but that was years ago, and more recently Jerboa's been working as a caseworker for teenagers with sexual abuse issues. Which is totally great. But I'm sure you can find bigger experts out there."

"One has chosen with the greatest of care," Madame Alberta fixed Lydia with an intense stare, like she could see all the way into Lydia's damaged core. (Or maybe, like someone who was used to wearing glasses but had decided to pretend she had 20/20 vision.) "You are all good people, with the strong moral centers. You have given much thought to the time travel, and yet you speak of it without any avarice in your hearts. Not once have I heard any of you talk of using the time travel for wealth or personal advancement."

"Well, except for Normando using it to get in Ladyswirl's pants," said Malik.

"Even as you say, except for Normando." Madame Alberta did another one of her painful-to-watch bow-curtseys. "So. What is your decision? Will you join me in this great and terrible undertaking, or not?"

What could they do? They all raised their hands and said that they were in.

Ricky was the Chief Fascination Evangelist for Garbo.com, a web startup for rich paranoid people who wanted to be left alone. (They were trying to launch a premium service where you could watch yourself via satellite 24/7, to make sure nobody else was watching you.) Ricky wore denim shirts, with the sleeves square-folded to the elbows, and white silk ties with black corduroys, and his neck funneled out of the blue-jean collar and led to a round pale head, shaved except for wispy sideburns. He wore steel-rimmed glasses. He had a habit of swinging his arms back and forth and clapping his heads when he was excited, like when he talked about getting a satellite into orbit.

"Everybody else says it'll take months to get our baby into space," Ricky told Malik and Lydia for the fifth or sixth time. "The Kazakhs don't even know when they can do it. But you say you can get our *Garbo-naut 5000* into orbit . . . "

" . . . next week," Malik said yet again. "Maybe ten days from now." He canted his palms in mid-air, like it was no big deal. Launching satellites, whatever. Just another day, putting stuff into orbit.

"Whoa." Ricky arm-clapped in his chair. "That is just insane. Seriously. Like, nuts."

"We are a hungry new company." Malik gave the same bright smile that he used to announce the start of every Time Travel Club meeting. They had been lucky to find this guy. "We want to build our customer base from the ground up. All the way from the ground, into space. Because we're a space company. Right? Of course we are. And did I mention we're hungry?"

"Hungry is good." Ricky seemed to be studying Malik, and the giant photo of MJL Aerospace's non-existent rocket, a retrofitted Soyuz. "The hungry survive, the fat starve. Or something. So when do I get to see this rocket of yours?

"You can't, sorry," Malik said. "Our, uh, chief rocket scientist is kind of leery about letting people see our proprietary new fuel system technology up close. But here's a picture of it." He gestured at the massive rocket picture on the fake-mahogany wall behind his desk, which they'd spent hours creating in *Photoshop* and *After Effects*. MJL Aerospace was subletting ultra-cheap office space in an industrial park, just up the highway from the Lusty Doubloon.

Malik, Lydia, and Jerboa had been excited about becoming a fake rocket company, until they'd started considering the practical problems. For one thing, nobody will hire you to launch a satellite unless you've already launched a satellite before—it's like how you can't get an entry-level job unless you've already had work experience.

Plus, they weren't entirely sure that they could get a satellite into a stable orbit, which was one of the dozen reasons Malik was sweating. They could definitely place a satellite at different points in orbit, and different trajectories, by adjusting the time of day, the distance traveled, and the location on Earth they started from. But after that, the satellite wouldn't be moving fast enough to stay in orbit on its own. It would need extra boosters, to get up to speed. Jerboa thought they could send a satellite way higher—around forty-two thousand kilometers away from Earth—and then use relatively small rockets to speed it up to the correct velocity as it slowly dropped to the proper orbit. But even if that worked, it would require Garbo.com to customize the *Garbo-naut 5000* quite a bit. And Madame Alberta had severe doubts.

"Sorry, man," said Ricky. "I'm not sure I can get my people to authorize a satellite launch based on just seeing a picture of the rocket. It's a nice picture, though. Good sense of composition. Like, the clouds look really pretty, with that one flock of birds in the distance. Poetic, you know."

"Of course you can see the rocket," Lydia interjected. She was sitting off to one side taking notes on the meeting, wearing cheap pantyhose in a forty-dollar swivel chair. With puffy sleeves covering her tattoos (one for every country she'd ever visited.) "Just maybe not before next week's launch. If you're willing to wait a few months, we can arrange a site visit and stuff. We just can't show you the rocket before our next launch window."

"Right," Malik said. "If you still want to launch next week, though, we can give you a sixty percent discount."

"Sixty percent?" Ricky said, suddenly seeming interested again.

"Sixty-five percent," Malik said. "We're a young hungry company. We have a lot to prove. Our business model is devouring the weak. And we hate to launch with spare capacity."

Maybe going straight to sixty-five percent was a mistake, or maybe the "devouring the weak" thing had been too much. In any case, Ricky seemed uneasy again. "Huh," he said. "So how many test launches have you guys done? My friend who works for NASA says every rocket launch in the world gets tracked."

"We've done a slew of test launches," Malik said. "Like, a dozen. But we have some proprietary stealth technology, so people probably missed them." And then, he went way off script. "Our company founder, Augustus Marzipan IV, grew up around rockets. His uncle was Wernher von Braun's wine steward. So rockets are in his blood." Ricky's frown got more and more pinched.

"Well," Ricky said at last, standing up from his cheap metal chair. "I will definitely bring your proposal to our Senior Visionizer, Terry. But I have a feeling the V.C.s aren't going to want to pay for a launch without kicking the tires. I'm not the one who writes the checks, you know. If I wrote the checks, a lot of things would be different." And then he paused, probably imagining all the things that would happen if he wrote the checks.

"When Augustus Marzipan was only five years old, his pet Dalmatian, Henry, was sent into space. Never to return," said Malik, as if inventing more stories would cushion his fall off the cliff he'd already walked over. "That's where our commitment to safety comes from."

"That's great," said Ricky. "I love dogs." He was already halfway out the door.

As soon as Ricky was gone, Malik sagged as though the air had gone out of him. He rubbed his brow with one listless hand. "We're a young hungry company," he said. "We're a hungry young company. Which way sounds better? I can't tell."

"That could have gone worse," Lydia said.

"I can't do this," Malik said. "I just can't. I'm sorry. I am good at pretending for fun. I just can't do it for money. I'm really sorry."

Lydia felt like the worst person in the world, even as she said: "Lots of people start out pretending for fun, and then move into pretending for money. That's the American dream." The sun was already going down behind the cement fountain outside, and she realized she was going to be late for her twelve-step group soon. She started pulling her coat and purse and scarf together. "Hey, I gotta run. I'll see you at Time Travel Club, okay?"

"I think I'm going to skip it," Malik said. "I can't. I just . . . I can't."

"What?" Lydia felt like if Malik didn't come to Time Travel Club, it would be the proof that something was seriously wrong and their whole foundation was splitting apart. And it would be provably her fault.

"I'm just too exhausted. Sorry."

Lydia came over and sat on the desk, so she could see Malik's face behind his hand. "Come on," she pleaded. "Time Travel Club is your baby. We can't just have a meeting without you. That would be weird. Come on. We won't even talk about being a fake aerospace company. We couldn't talk about that in front of Normando, anyway."

Malik sighed, like he was going to argue. Then he lifted the loop of his tie all the way off, now that he was done playing CEO. For a second, his rep-stripe tie was a halo. "Okay, fine," he said. "It'll be good to hang out and not talk business for a while."

"Yeah, exactly. It'll be mellow," Lydia said. She felt the terror receding, but not entirely.

Normando was freaking out because his girlfriend in 1973 had dumped him. (Long story short, his strategy of arriving earlier and earlier for the same first date had backfired.) A couple of other semi-regulars showed up too, including Betty the Cyborg from the Dawn of Time. And Madame Alberta showed up too, even though she hadn't ever shown any interest in visiting their aerospace office. She sat in the corner, studying the core members of the group, maybe to judge whether she'd chosen wisely. As if she could somehow go back and change that decision, which of course she couldn't.

Malik tried to talk about his last trip to the thirty-second century. But he kept staring at his CEO shoes and saying things like, "The neo-Babylonians were giving us grief. But we were young and hungry." And then trailing off, like his heart just wasn't in it.

Jerboa saw Malik running out of steam, and jumped in. "I met Christopher Marlowe. He told me that his version of Faust originally ended with Dr. Faust and Helen of Troy running away together and teaching geometrically complex hand-dances in Shropshire, and they made him change it." Jerboa talked very fast, like an addict trying to stay high. Or a comedian trying not to get booed offstage. "He told me to call him 'Kit,' and showed me the difference between a doublet and a singlet. A doublet is not two singlets, did you know that?"

Sitting in the Unitarian basement, under the purple dove hands, Lydia watched Malik starting to say things and then just petering out, with a shrug or a shake of the head, and Jerboa rattling on and not giving anybody else a chance to talk. Guilt.

And then, just as Lydia was crawling out of her skin, Madame Alberta stood up. "I have a thing to confess," she said.

Malik and Lydia stared up at her, fearing she was about to blow the whistle on their scam. Jerboa stopped breathing.

"I am from an alternative timeline," Madame Alberta said. "It is the world where the American Revolution did not happen, and the British Empire had the conquest of all of South America. The Americas, Africa, Asia—the British ruled all. Until the rest of Europe launched the great world war to stop the British imperialism. And Britain discovered the nuclear weapons and Europe burned to ashes. I travel many times, I travel through time, to try and change history. But instead, I find myself here, in this other universe, and I can never return home."

"Uh," Malik said. "Thanks for sharing." He looked relieved and weirded out.

At last, Madame Alberta explained: "It is the warning. Sometimes you have the power to change the world. But power is not an opportunity. It is a choice."

After that, nobody had much to say. Malik and Jerboa didn't look at Lydia or each other as they left, and nobody was surprised when the Time Travel Club's meeting was cancelled the following week, or when the club basically ceased to exist some time after that.

Malik, Jerboa, and Lydia sat in the front of Malik's big van on the grassy roadside, waiting for Madame Alberta to come back and tell them where they were going. Madame Alberta supposedly knew where they could dig up some improperly buried spent uranium from the power plant, and the back of the van was full of pretty good safety gear that Madame Alberta had scared up for them. The faceplates of the suits glared up at Lydia from their uncomfortable resting place. The three of them were psyching themselves up to go and possibly irradiate the shit out of themselves. Worth it, if the thing they were helping to build in Madame Alberta's laundry room was a real time machine and not just another figment.

"You guys never even asked," Lydia said around one in the morning, when they were all starting to wonder if Madame Alberta was going to show up. "I mean, about me, and why I was in that twelve-step group before the Time Travel Club meetings. You don't know anything about me, or what I've done."

"We know all about you," Malik said. "You're a pirate."

"You do extreme solar sail sports in the future," Jerboa added. "What else is there to know?"

"But," Lydia said. "I could be a criminal. I might have killed someone. I could be as bad as that astral projection guy."

"Lydia," Malik put one hand on her shoulder, like super gently. "We know you."

Nobody spoke for a while. Every few minutes, Malik turned on the engine so they could get some heat, and the silence between engine starts was deeper than ordinary silence.

"I had blackouts," Lydia said. "Like, a lot of blackouts. I would lose hours at a time, no clue where I'd been or how I'd gotten here. I would just be in the middle of talking to people, or behind the wheel of a car in the middle of nowhere, with no clue. I worked at this high-powered sales office, we obliterated our targets. And everybody drank all the time. Pitchers of beer, of martinis, of margaritas. The pitcher was like the emblem of our solidarity. You couldn't turn the pitcher away, it would be like spitting on the team. We made so much money. And I had this girlfriend, Sara, with this amazing red hair, who I couldn't even talk to when we were sober. We would just lie in bed naked, with a bottle of tequila propped up between us. I knew it was just a matter of time before I did something really unforgivable during one of those blackouts. Especially after Sara decided to move out."

"So what happened?" Jerboa said.

"In the end, it wasn't anything I did during a blackout that caused everything to implode," Lydia said. "It was what I did to keep myself from ever having another blackout. I got to work early one day, and I just lit a bonfire in the fancy conference room. And I threw all the contents of the company's wet bar into it."

Once again, nobody talked for a while. Malik turned the engine on and off a couple times, which made it about seven minutes of silence. They were parked by the side of the road, and every once in a while a car simmered past.

"I think that's what makes us such good time travelers, actually." Jerboa's voice cracked a little bit, and Lydia was surprised to see the outlines of tears on his small brown face, in the light of a distant highway detour sign. "We are very experienced at being in the wrong place at the wrong time, and at doing whatever it takes to get ourselves to the right place, and the right time."

Lydia put her arm around Jerboa, who was sitting in the middle of the front seat, and Jerboa leaned into Lydia's shoulder so just a trace of moisture landed on Lydia's neck.

"You wouldn't believe the places I've had to escape from in the middle of the night," Jerboa said. "The people who tried to fix my, my . . . irregularities. You wouldn't believe the methods that have been tried. People can justify almost anything, if their perspective is limited enough."

Malik wrapped his hand on Jerboa's back, so it was like all three of them were embracing. "We've all had our hearts broken, I guess," he said. "I was a teacher, in one of those Teach For America-style programs. I thought we were all in this together, that we had a shared code. I thought we were altruists. Until they threw me under a bus."

And it was then that Malik said the thing about wanting to stand outside history and see the gears grinding from a distance, all of the cruelty and all of the edifices that had been built on human remains. The true power wouldn't be changing history, or even seeing how it turned out, but just seeing the shape of the wheel.

They sat for a good long time in silence again. The engine ticked a little. They stayed leaning into each other, as the faceplates watched.

Lydia started to say something like, "I just want to hold on to this moment. Here, now, with the two of you. I don't care about whatever else, I just want *this* to last." But just as she started to speak, Madame Alberta tapped on the passenger-side window, right next to Lydia's head, and gestured at her car, which was parked in front of theirs. It was time to suit up, and go get some nuclear waste.

Lydia didn't see Malik or Jerboa for a month or so, after Madame Alberta told her weird story about Europe getting nuked. MJL Aerospace shuttered its offices, and Lydia saw the rocket picture in a dumpster as she drove to the

Lucky Doubloon. She redoubled her commitment to going to a twelve-step meeting every goddamn day. She finally called her mom back, and went to a few bluegrass concerts.

Lydia got the occasional panicked call from Normando, or even one of the other semi-regulars, wondering what happened to the club, but she just ignored it.

Until one day Lydia was driving to work, on the day shift again, and she saw Jerboa walking on the side of the road. Jerboa kicked the shoulder of the road over and over, kicking dirt and rocks, not looking ahead. Hips and knees jerking almost out of their sockets. Inaudible curses spitting at the gravel.

Lydia pulled over next to Jerboa and honked her horn a couple times, then rolled down the window. "Come on, get in." She turned down the bluegrass on her stereo.

Jerboa gave a gesture between a wave and a "go away."

"Listen, I screwed up," Lydia said. "That aerospace thing was a really bad idea. It wasn't about the money, though, you have to believe me about that. I just wanted to give us a new project, so we wouldn't drift apart."

"It's not your fault." Jerboa did not get in the truck. "I don't blame you."

"Well, I blame myself. I was being selfish. I just didn't want you guys to run away. I was scared. But we need to figure out a way to turn the space travel back into time travel. We can't do that unless we work together."

"It's just not possible," Jerboa said. "For any amount of time displacement beyond a few hours, the variables get harder and harder to calculate. The other day, I did some calculations and figured out that if you traveled one hundred years into the future, you'd wind up around one-tenth of a light year away. That's just a back-of-the-envelope thing, based on our orbit around the sun."

"Okay, so one problem at a time." Lydia stopped her engine, gambling that it would restart. The bluegrass stopped mid-phrase. "We need to get some accurate measurements of exactly where stuff ends up, when we send it forwards and backwards in time. But to do that, first we need to be able to send stuff out, and get it back again."

"There's no way," Jerboa said. "It's strictly a one-way trip."

"We'll figure out a way," Lydia said. "Trial and error. We just need to open a second rift close enough to the first rift to bring our stuff back. Yeah? Once we're good enough, we send people. And eventually, we send people, along with enough equipment to build a telescope in deep space, so we can spy on Earth in the distant past or the far future."

"There are so many steps in there, it's ridiculous," Jerboa said. "Every one of those steps might turn out to be just as impossible as the satellite thing turned out to be. We can't do this with just the four of us, we don't have enough pairs of hands. Or enough expertise."

"That's why we recruit," said Lydia. "We need to find a ton more people who can help us make this happen."

"Except," said Jerboa, fists clenched and eyes red and pinched, "we can't trust just any random people with this. Remember? That's why Madame Alberta brought it to us in the first place, because the temptation to abuse this power would be too great. You could destroy a city with this machine. How on Earth do we find a few dozen people who we can trust with this?"

"The same way we found each other," Lydia said. "The same way Madame Alberta found us. The Time Travel Club."

Jerboa finally got into the truck and snapped the seatbelt into place. Nodding slowly, like thinking it over.

Ricky from Garbo.com showed up at a meeting of the Time Travel Club, several months later. He didn't even realize at first that these were the same people from MJL Aerospace—maybe he'd seen the articles about the club on the various nerd blogs, or maybe he'd seen Malik's appearance on the basic cable TV show *GeekUp!*. Or maybe he'd listened to one of their podcasts. They were doing lots and lots of things to expand the membership of the club, without giving the slightest hint about what went on in Madame Alberta's laundry room.

Garbo.com had gone under by now, and Ricky was in grad school. He'd shaved off the big sideburns and wore square Elvis Costello glasses now.

"So I heard this is like a LARP, sort of," Ricky said to Lydia as they were getting a cookie from the cookie table before the meeting started—they'd had to move the meetings from the Unitarian basement to a middle school basketball court, now that they had a few dozen members. Scores of folding chairs, in rows, facing a podium. And they had a cookie table. "You make up your time travel stories, and everybody pretends they're true. Right?"

"Sort of," Lydia said. "You'll see. Once the meeting starts, you cannot say anything about these stories not being true. Okay? It's the only real rule."

"Sure thing," Ricky said. "I can do that. I worked for a dotcom startup, remember? I'm good at make-believe."

And Ricky turned out to be one of the more promising new recruits, weirdly enough. He spent a lot of time going to the eighteenth century and teaching

Capability Brown about *feng shui*. Which everybody agreed was probably a good thing for the Enlightenment.

Just a few months after that, Lydia, Malik, and Jerboa found themselves already debating whether to show Ricky the laundry room. Lydia was snapping her third-hand spacesuit into place in Madame Alberta's sitting room, with its caved-in sofa and big-screen TV askew. Lydia was happy to obsess over something else, to get her mind off the crazy thing she was about to do.

"I think he's ready," Lydia said of Ricky. "He's committed to the club."

"I would certainly like to see his face when he finds out how we were really going to launch that satellite into orbit," said Malik, grinning.

"It's too soon," Jerboa said. "I think we ought to wait six months, as a rule, before bringing anyone here. Just to make sure someone is really in tune with the group, and isn't going to go trying to tell the wrong people about this. This technology has an immense potential to distort your sense of ethics and your values."

Lydia tried to nod, but it was hard now that the bulky collar was in place. This spacesuit was a half a size too big, with boots that Lydia's feet slid around in. The crotch of the orange suit was almost M.C. Hammer wide on her, even with the adult diaper they'd insisted she should wear just in case. The puffy white gloves swallowed her fingers. And then Malik and Jerboa lowered the helmet into place, and Lydia's entire world was compressed to a gray-tinted rectangle. Goodbye, peripheral vision.

She wondered what sort of tattoo she would get to commemorate this trip.

"Ten minutes," Madame Alberta called from the laundry room. And indeed, it was ten to midnight.

"Are you sure you want to do this?" Jerboa said. "It's not too late to call it off."

"I'm the only one this suit sort of fits," Lydia said. "And I'm the most expendable. And yes. I do want to be the first person to travel through time."

After putting so many weird objects into that cube, thousands of them before they'd managed to get a single one back, Lydia felt strange about clambering inside the cube herself. She had to hunch over a bit. Malik waved and Jerboa gave a tiny thumbs up. Betty the Cyborg from the Dawn of Time checked the instruments one last time. Steampunk Fred gave a thumbs-up on the calculations. And Madame Alberta reached for the clunky lever. Even through her helmet, Lydia heard a greedy soda-belch sound.

A thousand years later, Lydia lost her hold on anything. She couldn't get her footing. There was no footing to get. She felt ill immediately. She'd expected the microgravity, but it still made her feel revolting. She felt drunk, actually. Like she didn't know which way was up. She spun head over ass. If she drifted too far, they would never pull her back. But the tiny maneuvering thrusters on her suit were useless, because she had no reference point. She couldn't see a damn thing through this foggy helmet, just blackness. She couldn't find the sun or any stars, for a moment. Then she made out stars. And more stars.

She spun. And somersaulted. No control at all. Until she tried the maneuvering thrusters, the way Jerboa had explained. She tried to turn a full three-sixty, so she could try and locate the sun. She had to remember to breathe normally. Every part of her wanted to hyperventilate.

When she'd turned halfway around on her axis, she didn't see the sun. But she saw something else. At first, she couldn't even make sense of it. There were lights blaring at her. And things moving. And shapes. She took a few photos with the camera Malik had given her. The whole mass was almost spherical, maybe egg-shaped. But there were jagged edges. As Lydia stared, she made out more details. Like, one of the shapes on the outer edge was the hood of a 1958 Buick, license plate and all. There were pieces of a small passenger airplane bolted on as well, along with a canopy made of some kind of shiny blue material that Lydia had never seen before. It was just a huge collection of junk welded together, protection against cosmic rays and maybe also decoration.

Some of the moving shapes were people. They were jumping up and down. And waving at Lydia. They were behind a big observation window at the center of the egg, a slice of see-through material. They gestured at something below the window. Lydia couldn't make it out at first. Then she squinted and saw that it was a big glowy sign with blocky letters made of massive pixels.

At first, Lydia though the sign read, *WELCOME TIME TRAVEL CLUB.* Like they knew the Time Travel Club was coming, and they wanted to prepare a reception committee.

Then she squinted again, just as another rift started opening up to pull her back, a purple blaze all around her, and she realized she had missed a word. The sign actually read, *WELCOME TO TIME TRAVEL CLUB.* They were all members of the Club, too, and they were having another meeting. And they were inviting her to share her story, any way she could.

₪

THE GHOSTS OF CHRISTMAS
₪
Paul Cornell

It was because of a row. The row was about nothing. So it all came from nothing. Or, perhaps it's more accurate to say it came from the interaction between two people. I remember how Ben's voice suddenly became gentle and he said, as if decanting the whole unconscious reason for the row:

"Why don't we try for a baby?"

This was mid-March. My memory of that moment is of hearing birds outside. I always loved that time of year, that sense of nature becoming stronger all around. But I always owned the decisions I made, I didn't blame them on what was around me, or on my hormones. I am what's around me, I am my hormones, that's what I always said to myself. I don't know if Ben ever felt the same way. That's how I think of him now: always excusing himself. I don't know how that squares with how the world is now. Perhaps it suits him down to the ground. I'm sure I spent years looking out for him excusing himself. I'm sure me doing that was why, in the end, he did.

I listened to the birds. "Yes," I said.

We got lucky almost immediately. I called my mother and told her the news.

"Oh no," she said.

When the first trimester had passed, and everything was still fine, I told my boss and then my colleagues at the Project, and arranged for maternity leave. "I know you lot are going to go over the threshold the day after I leave," I told my team. "You're going to call me up at home and you'll be all, 'Oh, hey, Lindsey is currently inhabiting her own brain at age three! She's about to try to warn the authorities about some terrorist outrage or other. But pregnancy must be *such* a joy'."

"Again with this," said Alfred. "We have no reason to believe the subjects would be able to do anything other than listen in to what's going on in the heads of their younger selves—"

"Except," said Lindsey, stepping back into this old argument like I hadn't even mentioned *hello, baby,* "the maths rules out even the possibility—"

"Free will—"

"No. It's becoming clearer with every advance we make back into what was: what's written is written."

Our due date was Christmas Day.

People who were shown around the Project were always surprised at how small the communication unit was. It had to be; most of the time it was attached to the skull of a sedated rhesus monkey. "It's just a string of lights," someone once said. And we all looked appalled, to the point where Ramsay quickly led the guest away.

They were like Christmas lights, each link changing color to show how a different area of the monkey's brain was responding to the data coming back from the other mind, probably its own mind, that it was connected to, somewhen in the past. Or, we thought only in our wildest imaginings then, in the future.

Christmas lights. Coincidence and association thread through this, so much, when such things can only be illusions. Or artifice. Cartoons in the margin.

How can one have coincidence, when everything is written?

I always thought my father was too old to be a dad. It often seemed to me that Mum was somehow too old to have me too, but that wasn't the case, biologically. It was just that she came from another time, a different world, of austerity, of shying away from rock and roll. She got even older after Dad died. Ironically, I became pregnant at the same age she had been.

We went to see her: me, Ben, and the bump. She didn't refer to it. For the first hour. She kept talking about her new porch. Ben started looking between us, as if waiting to see who would crack first. Until he had to say it, over tea. "So, the baby! You must be looking forward to being a grandmother!"

Mum looked wryly at him. "Not at my age."

"Sorry?"

"That's all right. You two can do what you want. I'll be gone soon."

■ ■ ■

We stayed for an hour or two more, talking about other things, about that bloody porch, and then we waved goodbye and drove off and I parked the car as soon as we were out of sight of the house. "Let's kill her," I said.

"Absolutely."

"I shouldn't say that. I so shouldn't say that. She *will* be gone soon. It's selfish of me to want to talk about the baby—"

"When we could be talking about that really very lovely porch. You could have led with how your potentially Nobel Prize-winning discovery of time travel is going."

"She didn't mention that either."

"She *is* proud of you, I'm sure. Did something—? I mean, did anything ever . . . happen, between you, back then?"

I shook my head. There was not one particular moment. I was not an abused child. This isn't a story about abuse.

I closed my eyes. I listened to the endless rhythm of the cars going past.

The Project was created to investigate something that I'd found in the case histories of schizophrenics. Sufferers often describe a tremendous sensation of *now*, the terrifying hugeness of the current moment. They often find voices talking to them, other people inside their own heads seemingly communicating with them. I started using the new brain-mapping technology to look into the relationship between the schizoid mind and time. Theory often follows technology, and in this case it was a detailed image of particle trails within the mind of David, a schizophrenic, that handed the whole theory to me in a single moment. It was written that I saw that image and made those decisions. Now when I look back to that moment, it's almost like I didn't do anything. Except that what happened in my head in that moment has meant so much to me.

I saw many knotted trails in that image, characteristic of asymmetric entanglement. I saw that, unlike in the healthy minds we'd seen, where there are only a couple of those trails at any given moment (and who knows what those are, even today?), this mind was connected, utterly, to . . . other things that were very similar to itself. I realized instantly what I was looking at: What could those other things that were influencing all those particle trails be but other minds? And where were those other minds very like this one—?

And then I had a vision of the trails in my own mind, like Christmas lights, and that led me to the next moment when I knew consciously what

I had actually understood an instant before, as if I had divined it from the interaction of all things—

The trails led to other versions of this person's own mind, elsewhen in time.

I remember that David was eager to cooperate. He wanted to understand his condition. He'd been a journalist before admitting himself to the psychiatric hospital.

"I need to tear, hair, fear, ear, see . . . yes, see, what's in here!" he shouted, tapping the front of his head with his middle fingers. "Hah, funny, the rhymes, crimes, alibis, keep trying to break out of those, and it works, that works, works. Hello!" He sat suddenly and firmly down and took a very steady-handed sip from his plastic cup of water. "You asked me to stay off the drugs," he said, "so it's difficult. And I would like to go back on them. I would very much like to. After."

I had started, ironically, to see him as a slice across a lot of different versions of himself, separated by time. I saw him as all his minds, in different phases, interfering with each other. Turn that polarized view the other way, and you'd have a series of healthy people. That's what I thought. And I wrote that down offhandedly somewhere, in some report. His other selves weren't the "voices in his head." That's a common fallacy about the history of our work. Those voices were the protective action that distances a schizophrenic from those other selves. They were characters formed around the incursion, a little bit of interior fiction. We're now told that a "schizophrenic" is someone who has to deal with such random interference for long stretches of time.

"Absolutely, as soon as we've finished our interviews today. We don't want to do anything to set back your treatment."

"How do you experience time?" is a baffling question to ask anyone. The obvious answer would be "like you do, probably." So we'd narrowed it down to:

How do you feel when you remember an event from your childhood?
How do you feel about your last birthday?
How do you feel about the Norman Conquest?
"Not the same," David insisted. "Not the same."

I found myself not sleeping. Expectant mothers do. But while not sleeping, I stared and listened for birds, and thought the same thought, over and over.

It's been proven that certain traits formed by a child's environment do get passed down to its own children. It is genuinely harder for the child of someone who was denied books to learn to read.

I'm going to be a terrible parent.

"Will you play with me?" I remember how much that sound in my voice seemed to hurt. Not that I was feeling anything bad at the time; it was like I was just hearing something bad. I said it too much. I said it too much in exactly the same way.

"Later," said Dad, sitting in his chair that smelled of him, watching the football. "You start, and I'll join in later."

I'd left my bedroom and gone back into the lounge. I could hear them talking in the kitchen, getting ready for bed, and in a moment they'd be bound to notice me, but I'd seen it in the paper and it sounded incredible: *The Outer Limits*. The outer limits of what? Right at the end of the television programs for the day. So after that I'd see television stop. And now I was seeing it and it was terrible, because there was a monster, and this was too old for me. I was crying. But they'd be bound to hear, and in a moment they would come and yell at me and switch the set off and carry me off to bed, and it'd be safe for me to turn round.

But they went to bed without looking in the lounge. I listened to them close the door and talk for a while, and then switch the light off, and then silence, and so it was just me sitting there, watching the grays flicker.

With the monster.

I was standing in a lay-by, watching the cars go past, wondering if Mummy and Daddy were going to come back for me this time. They'd said that if I didn't stop going on about the ice cream I'd dropped on the beach, they'd make me get out and walk. And then Dad had said "right!" and he'd stopped the car and yanked open the door and grabbed me out of my seat and left me there and driven off.

I was looking down the road, waiting to see the car come back.

I had no way of even starting to think about another life. I was six years old.

Those are just memories. They're not from Christmas Day. They're kept like that in the connections between neurons within my brain. I have a sense of telling them to myself. Every cell of my body has been replaced many times since I was that age. I am an oral tradition. But it's been proved that a butterfly remembers what a caterpillar has learned, despite its entire neurological structure being literally liquidized in between. So perhaps there's a component of memory that lies outside of ourselves as well, somewhere in those loose threads of particle trails. I have some hope that that is true. Because that would put a different background behind all of my experiences.

I draw a line now between such memories and the other memories I now have of my childhood. But that line will grow fainter in time.

I don't want to neglect it.

I'm going to neglect it.

I don't want to hurt it.

I'm going to hurt it.

They made me this way. I'm going to blame them for what I do. I'm going to end up being worse.

I grew numb with fear as autumn turned to winter. I grew huge. I didn't talk to Ben or anyone about how I felt. I didn't want to hear myself say the words.

In mid-December, a couple of weeks before the due date, I got an email from Lindsey. It was marked "confidential":

Just thought I should tell you, that, well, you predicted it, didn't you? The monkey trials have been a complete success, the subjects seem fine, mentally and physically. We're now in a position to actually connect minds across time. So we're going to get into the business of finding human volunteer test subjects. Ramsay wants "some expendable student" to be the first, but, you know, over our dead bodies! This isn't like lab rats, this is first astronaut stuff. Anyway, the Project is closing down on bloody Christmas Eve, so we're going to be forced to go and ponder that at home. Enclosed are the latest revisions of the tech specs, so that you can get excited too. But of course, you'll be utterly blasé about this, because it is nothing compared to the miracle of birth, about which you must be so excited, etc.

I looked at the specs and felt proud.

And then a terrible thought came to me. Or crystallized in me. Formed out of all the things I was. Was already written in me.

I found myself staggered by it. And hopeful about it. And fearful that I was hopeful. I felt I could save myself. That's ironic too.

My fingers fumbling, I wrote Lindsey a congratulatory email and then rewrote it three times before I sent it so that it was a model of everything at my end being normal.

I knew what I was going to be doing on Christmas Day.

Due dates are not an exact science. We'd had a couple of false alarms, but when Christmas Eve arrived, everything was stable. "I think it's going to be a few more days," I told Ben.

I woke without needing an alarm the next morning, to the strange quiet of Christmas Day. I left Ben sleeping, showered and dressed in the clothes I'd left ready the night before. Creeping about amongst the silence made me think of Father Christmas. I looked back in on Ben and felt fondly about him. That would have been the last time for that.

I drove through streets that were Christmas empty. My security card worked fine on a door that didn't know what day it was.

And then I was into the absolute silence of these familiar spaces, walking swiftly down the corridors, like a ghost.

The lab had been tidied away for the holidays. I had to unlock a few storage areas, to remember a few combinations. I reached into the main safe and drew out the crown of lights.

I paused as I sat in Lindsay's chair, the crown connected to a power source, the control systems linked up to a keyboard and screen in my lap. I considered for a moment, or pretended to, before putting it on my head.

Could what I was about to do to my brain harm the fetus?

Not according to what had happened with the monkeys. They were all fine, physically. I could only harm myself. We'd theorized that too long a connection between minds, more than a few minutes, would result in an extreme form of what the schizophrenics dealt with, perhaps a complete brain shutdown. Death. I would have to feel that coming and get out, or would have to unconsciously see it approaching on the screen, or just count the seconds.

Or I would fail my child completely.

I nearly put it all away again, locked up, walked out.

Nearly.

I put the crown on my head, I connected the power source, I took the keyboard in my hands and I watched the particle trails in my own mind begin to resolve on the screen, and I concentrated on them, in the way we'd always talked about, and I started typing before I could think again. I hit *activate*.

■   ■   ■

The minds of the monkeys seemed to select their own targets. The imaging for those experiments showed two sets of trails reacting to each other, symmetrical, beautiful. That seemed to suggest not the chaotic accident of schizophrenia, but something more tranquil, perhaps something like a religious experience, we'd said. But of course we had nothing objective to go on. I had theorized that since it turns out we evolved with every moment of ourselves just a stray particle away, the human trait of seeing patterns in chaos, of always assuming there is a hidden supernatural world, was actually selected for. We'd devised a feedback monitor that would allow a human subject to watch, and, with a bit of training, hence alter the particle tracks in one's own head via the keyboard and screen. I had hypothesized that, because the schizophrenic state can be diagnosed, that is, it isn't just interference like white noise but a pattern of interference, there must be some rule limiting which past states were being accessed, something that let in only a finite number. It had been Lindsay who'd said that perhaps this was only about time and not about space, that perhaps one had to be relatively near the minds doing the interfering, and thus, perhaps, the range was limited by where the earth was in its orbit.

That is to say, you only heard from your previous states of mind on the same calendar date.

Which turns out to have been what you might call a saving grace.

It was like being knocked out.

I'd never been knocked out. Not then.

I woke . . . and . . . Well, I must have been about three months old.

My vision is the wrong shape. It's like being in an enormous cinema with an oddly shaped screen. Everything in the background is a blur. I hear what I'm sure are words, but . . . I haven't brought my understanding with me. It's like that part of me can't fit in a baby's mind. This is terrifying, to hear the shapes of words but not know what they mean. I start yelling.

The baby that I'm part of starts yelling in exactly the same way!

And then . . . and then . . .

The big comfort shape moves into view. Such joy comes with it. *Hello, big comfort shape! It's me! It's me! Here I am!*

Big comfort shape puts its arms around me, and it's the greatest feeling of my life. An addict's feeling. I cry out again, me, I did that, to make it happen again, more! Even while it's happening to me I want more. I yell and yell for more. And it gives me more.

Up to a point.

I pulled the crown off my head.

I rubbed the tears from my face.

If I'd stayed a moment longer, I might have wanted to stay forever, and thus harmed the mind I was in, all because I wasn't used to asking for and getting such divine attention.

Up to a point.

What was that point? Why had I felt that? I didn't know if I had, really. How was it possible to feel such a sense of love and presence, but also that miniscule seed of the opposite, that feeling of it not being enough or entire? Hadn't I added that, hadn't I dreamt it?

I quickly put the crown back on my head. I had a fix now, I could see where particular patterns took me, I could get to—

Oh. Much clearer now. I must be about two years old. I'm walking around an empty room, marching, raising my knees and then lowering them, as if that's important.

Oh, I can think that. There's room for that thought in my head. I'm able to internally comment on my own condition. As an adult. As a toddler.

Can I control . . . ? I lower my foot. I stand there, inhabiting my toddler body, aware of it, the smallness of everything. But my fingers feel huge. And awkward. It's like wearing oven gloves. I don't want to touch anything. I know I'd break it.

And that would be terrible.

I turn my head. I put my foot forward. It's not like learning to drive, I already know how all this is done, it's just slightly different, like driving in America. I can hear . . .

Words I understand. "Merry Christmas!" From through the door. Oh, the door. The vase with a crack in it. The picture of a Spanish lady that Dad cut off the side of a crate of oranges and put in a frame. The smell of the carpet, close up. Oh, reactions to the smell, lots of memories, associations, piling in.

No! No! I can't take that! I can't understand that! I haven't built those memories yet!

Is this why I've always felt such enormous meaningless meaning about those objects and smells? I put it all out of my mind, and try to just be. And it's okay. It's okay.

The Christmas tree is enormous. With opened presents at the bottom, and I'm not too interested in those presents, which is weird, they've been left there, amongst the wrapping. The wrapping is better. This mind doesn't have signifiers for wrapping and tree yet, this is just a lot of weird stuff that happens, like all the other weird stuff that happens.

I head through the doorway. Step, step, step.

Into the hall. All sorts of differences from now, all sorts of objects with associations, but no, never mind the fondness and horror around you.

I step carefully into the kitchen.

And I'm looking up at the enormous figure of my mother, who is talking to . . . who is that? A woman in a headscarf. Auntie someone . . . oh, she died. I know she died! And I forgot her completely! Because she died!

I can't stop this little body from starting to shake. I'm going to cry. But I mustn't!

"Oh, there she goes again," says Mum, a sigh in her voice. "It's Christmas, you mustn't cry at Christmas."

"She wants to know where her daddy is," says the dead auntie. "He's down at the pub."

"Don't tell her that!" That sudden fear in her voice. And the wryness that always went along with that fear. As if she was mocking herself for her weakness.

"She can't understand yet. Oh, look at that. Is she meant to be walking like that?" And oh no, Mum's looking scared at me too. Am I walking like I don't know how, or like an adult?

Mummy grabs me up into her arms and looks and looks at me, and I try to be a child in response to the fear in her face . . . but I have a terrible feeling that I look right into those eyes as me. I'm scaring her, like a child possessed!

I took the crown off more slowly that time. And then immediately put it on again. And now I knew I was picking at a scab. Now I knew and I didn't care. I wanted to know what everything in my mother's face at that moment meant.

I'm seven and I'm staring at nothing under the tree. I'm up early and I'm waiting. Something must soon appear under the tree. There was nothing in the stocking at the end of my bed, but they/Father Christmas/they/Father Christmas/they might not have known I'd put out a stocking.

I hear the door to my parents' bedroom opening. I tense up. So much that it hurts. My dad enters the room and sighs to see me there. I bounce on my heels expectantly. I do a little dance that the connections between my muscles and my memory tell me now was programmed into me by a children's TV show.

He looks at me like I'm some terrible demand. "You're too old for this now," he says. And I remember. I remember this from my own memory. I'd forgotten this. I hadn't forgotten. "I'm off down the shops to get you some presents. If I can find any shops that are open. If you'd stayed asleep until you were supposed to, they'd have been waiting for you. Don't look at me like that. You knew there wasn't any such thing as Father Christmas."

He takes his car keys from the table and goes outside in his dressing gown, and drives off in the car, in his dressing gown.

I'm eight, and I'm staring at a huge pile of presents under the tree, things I wanted but have been carefully not saying anything about, things that are far too expensive. Mum and Dad are standing there, and as I walk into the room, eight-year-old walk, trying, no idea how, looking at my mum's face, which is again scared, just turned scared in the second she saw me . . . but Dad starts clapping, actually applauding, and then Mum does too.

"I told you I'd make it up to you," says Dad. I don't remember him telling me. "I told you." This is too much. This is too much. I don't know how I'm supposed to react. I don't know how in this mind or outside of it.

I sit down beside the presents. I lower my head to the ground. And I stay there, to the point where I'm urging this body to get up, to show some bloody gratitude! But it stays there. I'm just a doll, and I stay there. And I can't make younger me move and look. I don't want to.

I'm nine, and I'm sitting at the dinner table, with Christmas dinner in front of me. Mum is saying grace, which is scary, because she only does it at Christmas, and it's a whole weird thing, and oh, I'm thinking, I'm feeling weird again, I'm feeling weird like I always feel on Christmas Day. Is this because of her doing that?

I don't think I'm going to be able to leave any knowledge about what's actually going on in the mind I'm visiting. The transmission of information is only one way. I'm a voice that can suggest muscle movement, but I'm a very quiet one.

■　■　■

I'm fifteen. Oh. This is the Christmas after Dad died. And I'm . . . drunk. No, I wasn't. I'm not. It just feels like I am. What's inside my head is . . . huge. I *hate* having it in here with me. Right now. I feel like I'm . . . possessed. And I think it was like that in here before I arrived to join in. The shape of what I'm in is different. It feels . . . wounded. Oh God, did I hurt it already? No. I'm still me here and now. I wouldn't be if I'd hurt my young brain back then. No, I, I sort of remember. This is just what it was like being fifteen. My mind feels . . . like it's shaped awkwardly, not like it's wounded. All this . . . fury. I can *feel* the weight of the world limiting me. I can feel a terrible force towards action. Do something, now! Why aren't all these idiots around me doing something, when I know so well what they should do?! And God, God, I am horny even during this, which is, which is . . . terrible.

I'm bellowing at Mum, who's trying to raise her voice to shout over me at the door of my room. "Don't look at me like that!" I'm shouting. "We never have a good Christmas because of you! Dad would always try to make it a good Christmas, but he had to deal with you! Stop being afraid!"

I know as I yell this that it isn't true. I know now and I know then.

She slams the door of my room against the wall and marches in, raising a shaking finger—

I grab her. I grab her and I feel the frailness of her as I grab her, and I use all my strength, and it's lots, and I shove her reeling out of the door, and she crashes into the far wall and I run at her and I slam her into it again, so the back of her head hits the wall and I meant to do it and I don't, I so terribly don't. I'm beating up an old woman!

I manage to stop myself from doing that. Just. My new self and old self manage at the same time. I let go.

She bursts out crying. So do I.

"Stop doing that to me!" I yell.

"I worry about you," she manages to sob. "It's because I worry about you."

Is it just at Christmas she worries? I think hard about saying it, and this body says it. My voice sounds odd saying it. "Is it just at Christmas?"

She's silent, looking scared at how I sounded. Or, oh God, is she afraid of me now?

This is what did it, I realize. I make this mind go weird at Christmas, and they always noticed. It's great they noticed. What I grew up with, how I was brought up, is them reacting to that, expecting that, for the rest of the year. This makes sense, I've solved it! I've solved who I am! Who I am is my own fault! I'm a self-fulfilling prophecy!

Well, that's pretty obvious, isn't it? Should have known that. Everybody should realize that about themselves. Simple!

I find that I'm smiling suddenly and Mum bursts into tears again. To her, it must seem like she's looking at a complete psycho.

I tore off the crown. I remembered doing that to her. Then I let myself forget it. But I never did. And that wasn't the only time. Lots of grabbing her. On the verge of hitting her. Is that a thing, being abused by one's child? It got lost in the layers of who she and I were, and there I was, in it, and suddenly it was the most important thing. And now it was again.

Because of Dad dying, I thought, because of that teenage brain, and then I thought no, that's letting myself off the hook.

Guilty.

But beyond that, my teenage-influenced self had been right: I'd found what I'd gone looking for. I'd messed up my own childhood by what I was doing here. That was a neat end to the story, wasn't it? Yes, my parents had been terribly lacking on occasion. But they'd had something beyond the norm to deal with. And I'd been . . . terrifying, horrible, beyond that poor frail woman's ability to deal with.

But that only let them off the hook . . . up to a point.

Hadn't that bit with there being no presents, that bit with the car, weren't those beyond normal? Had me being in that mind on just one day of the year really been such a big factor?

Would I end up doing anything like that? Would I be a good parent?

Perhaps I should have left it there.

But there was a way to *know*.

In *A Christmas Carol*, we hear from charity collectors visiting Scrooge's shop that when his partner Marley was alive, they both always gave generously. And you think therefore that Scrooge was a happy, open person then. But Scrooge doesn't confirm that memory of theirs. When we meet Marley's ghost, he's weighed down by chains "he forged in life." He's warning Scrooge not to be like he was. So were the charity collectors lying or being too generous with their memory of Christmas past? Or is it just that they sometimes caught Scrooge and Marley on a good day? The latter doesn't seem the sort of thing that happens to characters in stories. I've been told that story isn't a good model for what happened to me. But perhaps, because of what's written in the margins there, it is.

■ ■ ■

I sat there thinking, the crown in my hands. I'd been my own ghost of Christmas future. But I could be a ghost of Christmas past too.

Was I going to be a good parent?

I could find out.

I set the display to track the other side of the scale. To take me into the future, as we'd only speculated that some day might be possible. And I put the crown back on before I could think twice.

Oh. Oh there she is. My baby is a she! I'm holding her in my arms. I love her more than I thought it was possible to love anything. The same way the big comfort thing loved me. And I didn't understand that until I put those moments side by side. This mind I'm in now has changed so much. It's hugely focused on the little girl who's asleep right here. It's a warm feeling, but it's . . . it's hard too. Where did that come from? That worries me. She's so little. This can't be that far in the future. But I've changed so much. There's a feeling of . . . this mind I'm in wanting to prove something. She wants to tell me it's all going to be okay. That I have nothing but love inside me in this one year in the future. And I do . . . up to a point.

Oh, there's a piece of paper with the year written on it sitting on the arm of the chair right in front of me. It's just next year. That's my handwriting.

The baby's name is Alice, the writing continues. *You don't need to go any further to hear that. Please make this your last trip.*

Alice. That's what we were planning to call her. Thank God. If it was something different, I'd now be wondering where that idea came from.

Oh, I can feel it now. This mind has made room for me. It knew I'd be coming. Of course it did. She remembers what she did with the crown last year. But what does this mean? Why does future me want me to stop doing this? I try to reach across the distance between her and me, but I can only feel what she's feeling, not hear her thoughts. And she had a year to prepare, that note must be all she wants to tell me. She wants me to feel that it's all going to be okay . . . but she's telling me it won't be.

Ben comes in. He doesn't look very different. Unshaven. He's smiling all over his face. He sits on the arm of the chair and looks down at his daughter, proud and utterly in love with her. The room is decorated. There are tiny presents under the tree, joint birthday and Christmas presents the little one is too small to understand. So, oh, she was born very near Christmas Day. We must make such a perfect image sitting together like this. I don't think I can have told Ben about what I know will be happening to me at this moment on Christmas Day. I wouldn't do that. I'd want to spare him.

But . . . what's this? I can feel my body move slightly away from him. It took me a second to realize it, because it's so brilliant, and a little scary, to be suddenly in a body that's not weighed down by the pregnancy, but . . . I'm bristling. I can feel a deep chemical anger. The teenager is in here again. But I look up at him and smile, and this mind lets me. And he's so clearly still my Ben, absolutely the same, the Dad I knew he'd be when he asked and I said yes. It's not like he's started to beat me, I can't feel that in this body, she's not flinching, it's like when I'm angry but I don't feel allowed to express it.

Is this, what, post-natal depression? Or the first sign of me doing unto others what was done to me? A pushed-down anger that might come spilling out?

I don't care what my one-year-older self wants me to do. She can't know that much more than me. I need to know what this is.

Alice is asleep in her cradle. She's so much bigger, so quickly, two years old! Again, that bursting of love into my head. That's reassuring. Another year on, I'm still feeling that.

But the room . . . the room feels very different. Empty. There's a tree, but it's a little one. I make this body walk quickly through the rest of the house. The bathroom is a bit different, the bedroom is a bit different. Baby stuff everywhere, of course, but what's missing? There's . . . there's nothing on that side of the room. I go back to the bathroom. There are no razors. No second toothbrush.

Where's Ben?

I start looking in drawers, checking my email . . . but the password's been changed. I can't find anything about what's happened. I search every inch of the house, desperate now, certain I'm going to find a funeral card or something. She knew this was going to happen to me, so wouldn't the bitch have left one out in plain sight? Why doesn't she want me to know? Oh please don't be dead, Ben, please—!

I end up meaninglessly, uselessly, looking in the last place, under the bed.

And there's a note, in my own handwriting.

I hate you.

She's deliberately stopping me from finding out. I can't let her.

Alice is looking straight at me this time. "Presents," she says to me. "I have presents. And you have presents." And I can see behind her that that's true.

That rush of love again. That's constant. I try to feel what's natural and not be stiff and scary about it, and give her a big hug. "Does Daddy have presents?"

She looks aside, squirms; she doesn't know how to deal with that. Have I warned her about me? I don't want to press her for answers. I don't want to distress her.

I need to keep going and find out.

I'm facing in the same direction, so it's like the decor and contents of the room suddenly shift, just a little. Alice, in front of me, four now, is running in rings on the floor, obviously in the middle of, rather than anticipating something, so that's good.

Ben comes in. He's alive! Oh thank God.

I stand up at the sight of him. Has she told him about me? No, I never would. He looks so different. He's clean-shaven, smartly dressed. Did he go on a long journey somewhere? He hoists Alice into his arms and Alice laughs as he jumbles up her hair. "Happy Christmas birthday!"

Alice sings it back to him, like it's a thing they do together. So . . . everything's all right? Why didn't she want me to—?

A young woman I don't know comes in from the other room. She goes to Ben and puts a hand on his arm. Alice smiles at her.

"We have to be gee oh aye en gee soon," he says to me.

"Thanks for lunch," says the girl. "It was lovely."

The fury this time is my own. But it chimes with what's inside this mind. She's been holding it down. I take a step forward. And the young woman sees something in my eyes and takes a step back. And that little movement—

No, it isn't the movement, it isn't what she does, this is all me—

I march towards her. I'm taking in every feature of her. Every beautiful feature of that slightly aristocratic, kind-looking, caring face. I'm making a sound I've never heard before in the back of my throat. "Get away from him. Get your hands off him."

She's trying to put up her hands and move away. She's astonished. "I'm sorry—!"

"What the hell?!" Ben is staring at us. Alice has started yelling. Fearful monkey warning shouts.

Something gives inside me. I rush at her. She runs.

I catch her before she gets to the door. I grab her by both arms and throw her at the wall. I'm angry at her and at the mind I'm in too. Did she set me up for this?! Did she invite them here to punish me?! So she could let her anger out and not be responsible?!

She hits the wall and bounces off it. She falls, grabbing her nose. She looks so capable and organized I know she could hit me hard, I know she could defend herself, but she just drops to the ground and puts her hands to her face. I will not make her fight. She can control herself and I can't.

Ben rushes in and grabs me. I don't want him to touch me. I struggle.

"What are you doing?!" He's shouting at me.

I can feel this mind burning up. If I stay much longer, I'll start damaging it. I half want to.

I ripped the crown from my head and threw it onto the ground. I burst into tears. I put my hands on my belly to comfort myself. But I found no comfort there.

But my pain wasn't important. It wasn't! The mistakes I'd made were what was important. What happened to Alice, *that* was what was important.

I got up and walked around the room. If I stopped now, I was thinking, the rest of my life would be a tragedy, I would be forever anticipating what was written, or trying . . . hopelessly, yes, there was nothing in the research then that said I had any hope . . . to change it. I would be living without hope. I could do that. But the important thing was what that burden would do to Alice . . . If I was going to be allowed to keep Alice, after what I'd seen.

I could go to the airport now. I could leave Ben asleep, while he was still my Ben, and have the baby in France, and break history . . . No I couldn't. Something would get me back to what I'd seen. Maybe something cosmic and violent that wouldn't respect the human mind's need for narrative. That was what the maths said. Alice shouldn't have that in her life. Alice shouldn't have me in her life.

But the me who wrote the first note wanted me not to try to visit the future again. When she knew I had. Did she think that was possible? Did I learn something in the next year that hinted that it might be? Why didn't I address that in future notes?

Because of anger? Because of fatalism? Because of a desire to hurt myself? But . . . if there was even a chance it might be possible . . .

I slowly squatted and picked up the crown.

■　■　■

I've moved. I'm in a different house. Smaller. I walk quickly through the rooms, searching. I have to support myself against the wall in relief when I see Alice. There she is, in her own room, making a wall out of cardboard wrapping-paper rolls. Still the love in me. I don't think that's ever going to go. It feels like . . . a condition. A good disease this mind lives with. But what's she doing alone in here? Did I make her flee here, exile her here?

She looks up at me and smiles. No. No, I didn't.

I find the note this time on the kitchen table. It's quite long, it's apologetic. It tells me straight away that Ben and . . . Jessica, the young woman's name is Jessica . . . understood quite quickly after I left her mind and she started apologizing. She apologizes too for not doing anything to stop what happened. But she says she really wasn't setting me up for it. She says she's still working at the Project. She says she's still looking for a way to change time, but hasn't much hope of finding one.

I put down the letter feeling . . . hatred. For her. For her weakness. For her acceptance. That whole letter feels like . . . acting. Like she's saying something because she thinks she should.

From the other room comes the sound of Alice starting to cry. She's hurt herself somehow. I feel the urge from this mind to go immediately to her. But I . . . I actually hesitate. For the first time there is a distance. I'm a stranger from years ago. This isn't really my child. This is *her* child.

The next few visits were like an exhibition of time-lapse photography about the disintegration of a mother and child's relationship. Except calling it that suggests a distance, and I was amongst it, complicit in it.

"You get so weird!" she's shouting at me. "It's like you get frightened every Christmas that I'll go away with Dad and Jessica and never come back! I want to! I want to go away!"

But the next Christmas she's still there.

"Will you just listen to me? You look at me sometimes like I'm not real, like I'm not human!" The mind of the future learned that from her memory of my experiences, I guess, learned that from her own experience of being a teenager with added context. Alice has had to fight for her mother to see her as an actual human being. I did that. I mean, I did that *to* her. I try now to reach out, but she sees how artificial it looks and shies away.

"Do I . . . neglect you?" I ask her.

She swears at me, and says yes. But then she would, wouldn't she?

■ ■ ■

And then the next year she's not there.

A note says the bitch arranged for her to stay with Ben and Jessica, and it all got too much in terms of anticipation, and she's sure she'll be back next time. She's certain of that. She's sorry, and she . . . hopes *I* am too?!

I go to the wall in the hall. I've always used bloody walls to do my fighting. I stand close to it. And as hard as I can I butt my head against it. I love the roaring of the mind I'm in as the pain hits us both. Feel *that*, you bitch, do something about *that*! I do it again. And then my head starts to swim and I don't think I can do it again, and I get out just as the darkness hits.

That was why she "hoped I was sorry too," because she knew that was coming.

I wonder how much I injured myself? She couldn't have known when she wrote the note. She was so bloody weak she didn't even try to ask me not to do it.

I am such a bully.

But I'm only doing it to myself.

There's no sign of Alice for the next two Christmases. When the bitch was *certain* she'd be back next time. The liar. There are just some very needy letters. Which show no sign of brain damage, thank God.

Then there's Alice, sitting opposite me. She wears fashions designed to shock. "Christmas Day," she says, "time for you to go insane and hurt yourself, only today I'm trapped with you. What joy."

I discover that Ben and Jessica are on holiday abroad with their own . . . children . . . this year. And that the bitch has done . . . some sort of harm to herself on each of these days Alice wasn't here, obviously after I left. Is that just self-harm, am I actually capable of . . . ? Well, I suppose I know I am. Or is she trying to offer some explanation for that one time, or to use it to try to hurt Alice emotionally?

"No insanity this year," I say, trying to make my voice sound calm. And it sounds weird. It sounds old. It sounds like I've put quotation marks around "insanity." Like I'm trying to put distance between my own actions, being wry about my own weakness . . . like Mum always is.

I try to have fun with Alice in the ten minutes I've got. She shuts herself in her room when I get too cloying. I try to enter. She slams herself against the door. I get angry, though the weak woman I'm in really doesn't want to, and try to muscle in. But she grabs me, she's stronger than me.

She slams me against the wall. And I burst into tears. And she steps back, shaking her head in mocking disbelief at . . . all I've done to her.

I slipped the crown from my head.

I was staring into space. And then my phone rang. The display said it was Mum. And I thought now of all the times, and then I thought no, I have a cover to maintain here, I don't want her calling Ben . . . I didn't want to go home to Ben . . .

I took a deep breath, and answered.

"Is there . . . news?" she asked. I heard that wry, anxious tone in her voice again. Did I ever think of that sound as anxious before? "You are due today, aren't you?"

I told her that I was, but it didn't feel like it was going to be today, and that I'd call her immediately when anything started to happen. I stopped then, realizing that actually, I did know it was going to be today; Ben said "Happy Christmas birthday" to Alice. But I couldn't tell her that I knew that and I didn't want to tell her I felt something I didn't feel. "Merry Christmas," I said, remembering the pleasantries, which she hadn't.

She repeated that, an edge in her voice again. "I was hoping that I might see you today, but I suppose that's impossible, even though the baby isn't coming. You've got much more important things to do." And the words hurt as much as they always did, but they weren't a dull ache now, but a bright pain. Because I heard them not as barbs to make me guilty, but as being exactly like the tone of the letters the bitch had left for me. Pained, pleading . . . weak. That was why I'd slammed her against the wall, all those years ago, because she was weak, because I could.

"I'm sorry," I said.

"Oh. I'm always sorry to hear you say that," she said.

I said I'd call her as soon as anything happened.

Once as she was off the phone, I picked up the crown and held it in my hands like I was in a Shakespeare play. I was so poetically contemplating it. I felt like laughing at my own presumption at having opened up my womb and taken a good look at where Jacob Marley had come from.

I had hurt my own mother. I had never made that up to her. I never could. But I hadn't tried. I had hated her for what I had done. And I could not stop. And in the future, the reflection was as bad as the shadow. I had become my mother. And I had created a daughter who felt exactly the same way about me. And I had created a yearly hell for my future self, making sure she never forgot the lesson I had learned on this day.

I would release myself from it. That's what I decided.

I put the crown on for the last time.

I'm standing there with my daughter. She looks to be in her late twenties. Tidy now. A worried look on her face. She's back for a family Christmas, but she knows there'll be trouble as always. She's been waiting for it. She looks kinder. She looks guilty. The room is bare of decoration. Like the bitch . . . like my victim . . . has decided not to make the effort anymore.

"Get away from me," I tell Alice, immediately, "get out of this house." Because I know what I'm going to do. I'm going to stay inside this mind. I'm going to break it. I'm going to give myself the release of knowing I'm going to go mad, at the age of . . . I look around and find a conveniently placed calendar. Which was unbelievably accommodating of her, to know what I'm about to do and still do that. I will go mad at the age of fifty-six. I have a finish line. It's a relief. Perhaps she wants this too.

"Mum," says Alice, "Mum, please—!" And she sounds desperate and worried for herself as well as for me, and still not understanding what all this is about.

But then her expression . . . changes. It suddenly becomes determined and calm. "Mum, please don't do this. I know we only have minutes—"

"What? Did I tell you about—?"

"No, this is an older Alice. I'm working on the same technology now. I've come back to talk to you."

It takes me a moment to take that in. "You mean, you've found a way to change time?"

"No. What's written is written. Immediately after we have this conversation, and we've both left these bodies, you tell me everything about what you've been doing."

"Why . . . do I do that?" I can feel the sound of my mother's weakness in my voice.

"Because after you leave here, you go forward five years and see me again." She takes my hands in hers and looks into my eyes. I can't see the hurt there. The hurt I put there. And I can see a reflection too.

Can I believe her?

She sees me hesitate. And she grows determined. "I'll stay as long as you will," she says. "You might do this to yourself, but I know you'd never let your child suffer."

I think about it. I do myself the courtesy of that. I toy with the horror of doing that. And then I look again into her face, and I know I'm powerless in the face of love.

I'm looking into the face of someone I don't expect to see. It's David. Our experimental subject. The schizophrenic. Only now he's a lot older, and . . . oh, his face . . . he's lost such tension about his jaw. Beside him stands Alice, five years older.

He reaches out a hand and touches my cheek.

I shy away from him. What?!

"I'm sorry," he says. "I shouldn't have done that. We're . . . a couple, okay? We've been together for several years now. Hello you from the past. Thank you for the last four years of excellent family Christmases." He gestures to decorations and cards all around.

"Hello, Mum," says Alice. She reaches down and . . . oh, there's a crib there. She's picked up a baby. "This is my daughter, Cyala."

I walk slowly over. It feels as odd and as huge as walking as a child did. I look into the face of my granddaughter.

David, taking care not to touch me, joins me beside them. "It's so interesting," he says, "seeing you from this new angle. Seeing a cross section of you. You *look* younger!"

"Quickly," says Alice.

"Okay, okay." He looks back to me. And I can't help but examine his face, try to find the attraction I must later feel. And yes, it's there. I just never saw him in this way before. "Listen, this is what you told me to say to you, and I'm glad that, from what Alice has discovered, it seems I can't mess up my lines. It's true that you and Alice here fought, fought physically, like you say you and your mum did. Though I once saw her deny that to your face, by the way. She sounded like you were accusing *her* of something, and she kept on insisting it hadn't happened until you got angry and then finally she agreed like she was just going along with it. Oh God, this is so weird—" He picked up some sort of thin screen where I recognized something quite like my handwriting. "I was sure I added to what I was supposed to say there, but now it turns out it's written down here, and I'm not sure that it was . . . before. I guess your memory didn't quite get every detail of this correct. Or perhaps there's a certain . . . kindness, a mercy to time? Anyway!" He put down the screen again, certain he wouldn't need it. "But the important thing is, you only see one day. You don't see all the good stuff. There were long stretches of good stuff. You didn't create a monster, any more than your mum created a monster in you. You both just made people." He dares to actually touch me, and now I let him. "What you did led to a cure for people like me. And it changed how people see themselves and the world, and that's been good and bad, it isn't a utopia outside these walls and it isn't a wasteland, she wanted me to emphasize that, it's just people doing stuff as usual. And these are all your words, not mine, but I agree with them . . . you are not Ebenezer Scrooge, to be changed from one thing into another. Neither was your mother. Even knowing all of this is fixed, even knowing everything that happened, even if you only know the bad, you'd do it all anyway."

And he kisses me. Which makes me feel guilty and hopeful at the same time.

And I let go.

I slowly put down the crown.

I stood up. I'd been there less than an hour. I went back to my car.

I remember the drive home through those still empty streets. I remember how it all settled into my mind, how a different me was born in those moments. I knew what certain aspects of my life to come would be like. I had memories of the future. That weight would always be with me. I regretted having looked. I still do. Despite everything it led to, for me and science and the world. I tell people they don't want to look into their future selves. But they usually go ahead and do it. And then they have to come to the same sort of accommodation that a lot of people have, that human life will go on, and that it's bigger than them, and that they can only do what they can do. To some, that fatalism has proven to be a relief. But it's driven some to suicide. It has, I think, on average, started to make the world a less extreme place. There is only so much we can do. And we don't see the rest of the year. So we might as well be kind to one another.

There are those who say they've glimpsed a pattern in it all. That the whole thing, as seen from many different angles, is indeed like writing. That, I suppose, is the revelation, that we're not the writers, we're what's being written.

I write now from the perspective of the day after my younger self stopped visiting. I'm relieved to be free of that bitch. Though, of course, I knew everything she was going to do. The rest of my life now seems like a blessed release. I wrote every note as I remembered them, and sometimes that squared with how I was feeling at the time, and sometimes I was playing a part . . . for whose benefit, I don't know.

I remember walking back into my house and finding Ben just waking up. And he looked at me, at the doubtless strange expression on my face, and in that moment I recall thinking I saw his expression change too. By some infinitesimal amount. I have come to think that was when he started, somewhere deep inside, the chain reaction of particle trails that took him from potentially caring dad to letting himself off the hook.

But that might equally just be the story I tell myself about that moment.

What each of us is is but a line in a story that resonates with every other line. Who we are is distributed. In all sorts of ways. And we can't know them all.

And then I felt something give. There was actually a small sound in the quiet. Liquid splashed down my legs. And as I knew I was going to, I went into labor on Christmas Day.

Ben leaped out of bed and ran to me, and we headed out to the car. Outside, the birds were singing. Of course they were.

"You're going to be fine," he said. "You're going to be a great mother."

"Up to a point," I said.

₪

THE ILE OF DOGGES
₪
Elizabeth Bear & Sarah Monette

The light would last long enough.

Sir Edmund Tylney, in pain and reeking from rotting teeth, stood before the sideboard and crumbled sugar into his sack, causing a sandy yellowish grit to settle at the bottom of the cup. He swirled the drink to sweeten it, then bore it back to his reading table where an unruly stack of quarto pages waited, slit along the folds with a penknife.

He set the cup on the table in the sunlight and drew up his stool, its short legs rasping over the rush mats as he squared it and sat. He reached left-handed for the wine, right-handed for the playscript, drawing both to him over the pegged tabletop. And then he riffled the sheets of Speilman's cheapest laid with his nail.

Bending into the light, wincing as the sweetened wine ached across his teeth with every sip, he read.

He turned over the last leaf, part-covered in secretary's script, as he drank the last gritty swallow in his cup, the square of sun spilling over the table-edge to spot the floor. Tylney drew out his own penknife, cut a new point on a quill, and—on a fresh quarter-sheet—began to write the necessary document. The Jonson fellow was inexperienced, it was true. But Tom Nashe should have known better.

Tylney gulped another cup of sack before he set his seal to the denial, drinking fast, before his teeth began to hurt. He knew himself, without vanity, to be a clever man—intelligent, well-read. He had to be, to do his job as Master of Revels and censor for the queen, for the playmakers, too, were clever, and they cloaked their satires under layers of witty language and misdirection. The better the playmaker, the better the play, and the more careful Tylney had to be.

The Ile of Dogges was a good play. Lively, witty. Very clever, as one would expect from Tom Nashe and the newcomer Jonson. And Tylney's long-practiced and discerning eye saw the satire on every page, making mock of—among a host of other, lesser targets—Elizabeth, her Privy Council, and the Lord Chamberlain.

It could never be performed.

⁓

RIGHTEOUS-IN-THE-CAUSE SAMSON:
Why is't named Isle of Dogs?

WITWORTH:
Because here are men like wild dogs. Have they numbers, they will savage a lion. But if the lion come upon one by himself, he will grovel and show his belly. And if the lion but ask it, he will savage his friends.

RIGHTEOUS-IN-THE-CAUSE SAMSON:
But is that not right? For surely a dog should honor a lion.

WITWORTH:
But on this island, even the lion is a dog.*

⁓

It could never be performed, but it was. A few days later, despite the denial, Jonson and the Earl of Pembroke's Men staged *The Ile of Dogges* at the Swan. Within the day, Jonson and the principal actors were in chains at the Marshalsea, under gentle questioning by the Queen's own torturer, Topcliffe himself. The other playwright, Thomas Nashe, fled the city to elude arrest. And The Theatre, The Curtain, The Swan—all of London's great playhouses languished, performances forbidden.

The Ile of Dogges languished, likewise, in a pile on the corner of Tylney's desk, weighted by his penknife (between sharpenings). It lay face down, cup-ringed pages adorned with the scratch of more than one pen. The dull black oakgall ink had not yet begun to fade, nor the summer's heat to wane, when Tylney, predictably, was graced by a visit from Master Jonson.

Flea bites and shackle gall still reddened the playwright's thick wrists, counterpoint to the whitework of older scars across massive hands.

Unfashionably short hair curled above his plain, pitted face. He topped six feet, Ben Jonson. He had been a soldier in the Low Countries.

He ducked to come through the doorway, but stood straight within, stepping to one side after he closed the door so that the wall was at his back. "You burned Tom's papers."

"He fled London. We must be sure of the play, all its copies."

"All of them?" For all his rough bravado, Jonson's youth showed in how easily he revealed surprise. "'Tis but a play."

"Master Jonson," Tylney said, steepling his hands before him, "it mocks the Queen. More than that, it might encourage others to mock the Queen. 'Tis sedition."

Recovering himself, Jonson snorted. He paced, short quick steps, and turned, and paced back again. "And the spies Parrot and Poley as were jailed in with me? Thought you I'd aught to tell them?"

"No spies of mine," Tylney said. "Perhaps Topcliffe's. Mayhap he thought you had somewhat of interest to him to impart. No Popist sympathies, Master Jonson? No Scottish loyalties?"

Jonson stopped at the furthest swing of his line and stared at the coffered paneling. That wandering puddle of sun warmed his boots this time. He reached out, laid four blunt fingertips and a thumb on the wall—his hand bridged between them—and dropped his head so his arm hid the most of his face. His other hand, Tylney noticed, brushed the surface of the sideboard and left something behind, half-concealed beside the inkpot. "No point in pleading for the return of the manuscript, I take it?"

"Destroyed," Tylney said, without letting his eyes drop to the pages on his desk. And, as if that were all the restraint he could ask of himself, the question burst out of him: "Why do it, Master Jonson? Why *write* it?"

Jonson shrugged one massive shoulder. "Because it is a good play."

Useless to ask for sense from a poet. One might as well converse with a tabby cat. Tylney lifted the bell, on the other corner of his desk from the play that ought already to be destroyed, and rang it, a summons to his clerk. "Go home, Master Jonson."

"You've not seen the last of me, Sir Edmund," Jonson said, as the door swung open—not a threat, just a fact.

It wasn't the usual clerk, but a tall soft-bellied fellow with wavy black hair, sweet-breathed, with fine white teeth.

"No," Tylney said. He waited until the click of the latch before he added, "I don't imagine I have."

⌒

ANGEL:

Hast sheared the sheep, Groat?

GROAT:

Aye, though their fleece be but silver.
he handeth Angel a purse

ANGEL:

Then thou must be Jason and find the golden fleece. Or mayhap needs
merely shear a little closer to the skin.

GROAT:

Will not the sheep grow cold, without their wool?

ANGEL:

They can grow more. And, loyal Groat, wouldst prefer thy sheep
grow cold, or thy master grow hot?

GROAT:

The sheep may shiver for all I care.

⌒

Tylney waited until Jonson's footsteps retreated into silence, then waited a
little more. When he was certain neither the clerk nor the playmaker were
returning, he came around his table on the balls of his feet and scooped up
the clinking pouch that Jonson had left behind. He bounced it on his hand,
a professional gesture, and frowned at its weight. Heavy.

He replaced it where Jonson had laid it, and went to chip sugar from the
loaf and mix himself another cup of sack, to drink while he re-read the play.
He read faster this time, standing up where the light was better, the cup
resting on the sideboard by the inkpot and Jonson's bribe. He shuffled each
leaf to the back as he finished. When he was done, so was the sack.

He weighed the playscript in his hand, frowning at it, sucking his aching teeth.
It was August. There was no fire on the grate.

He dropped the playscript on the sideboard, weighted it with the bribe,
locked the door behind him, and went to tell the clerk—the cousin, he said,
of the usual boy, who was abed with an ague—that he could go.

～

WITWORTH:
That's Moll Tuppence. They call her Queen of Dogs.

RIGHTEOUS-IN-THE-CAUSE SAMSON:
For why?

WITWORTH:
For that if a man says aught about her which he ought not, she sets her
curs to make him say naught in sooth.

～

Sir Edmund Tylney lay awake in the night. His teeth pained him, and if he'd
any sense, he'd have had them pulled that winter. No sense, he thought.
No more sense than a tabby cat. Or a poet. And he lay abed and couldn't
sleep, haunted by the image of the papers on the sideboard, weighted under
Jonson's pouch. He should have burned them that afternoon.

He would go and burn them now. Perhaps read them one more time, just
to be certain there was no salvaging this play. Sometimes he would make
suggestions, corrections, find ways—through cuts or additions—that a play
could be made safe for performance. Sometimes the playmakers acquiesced,
and the play was saved.

Though Jonson was a newcomer, Tylney knew already that he did not
take kindly to editing. But it was a good play.

Perhaps there was a chance.

Tylney roused himself and paced in the night, in his slippers and shirt,
and found himself with candle in hand at the door of his office again. He
unlocked it—the tumblers moving silently in the well-oiled catch—and
pushed it before him without bothering to lift the candle or, in fact, look up
from freeing key from lock.

He knew where everything should be.

The brilliant flash that blinded him came like lightning, like the spark of
powder in the pan, and he shouted and threw a warding hand before his eyes,
remembering even in his panic not to tip the candle. Someone cursed in a
foreign tongue; a heavy hand closed on Tylney's wrist and dragged him into
his office, shouldering the door shut behind before he could cry out again.

Whoever clutched him had a powerful grip. Was a big man, young,
with soft uncallused hands. "Jonson," he gasped, still half-blinded by the

silent lightning, pink spots swimming before his eyes. "You'll hang for this!"

"Sir Edmund," a gentle voice said over the rattle of metal, "I am sorry."

Too gentle to be Jonson, just as those hands, big as they were, were too soft for a soldier's. Not Jonson. The replacement clerk. Tylney shook his head side to side, trying to rattle the dots out of his vision. He blinked, and could almost see, his candle casting a dim glow around the office. If he looked through the edges of his sight, he could make out the lay of the room—and what was disarrayed. *The Ile of Dogges* had been taken from the sideboard, the drapes drawn close across the windows and weighted at the bottom with Jonson's bribe. Perhaps a quarter of the pages were turned.

"I'll shout and raise the house," Tylney said.

"You have already," the clerk said. He released Tylney's wrist once Tylney had steadied himself on the edge of the table, and turned back to the playscript.

"There's only one door out of this room." And Tylney had his back to it. He could hear people moving, a voice calling out, seeking the source of that cry.

"Sir Edmund, shield your eyes." The clerk raised something to his own eye, a flat piece of metal no bigger than a lockplate, and rather like a lockplate, with a round hole in the middle.

Tylney stepped forward instead and grabbed the clerk's arm. "What are you doing?"

The man paused, obviously on the verge of shoving Tylney to the floor, and stared at him. "Damn it to hell," he said. "All right, look. I'm trying to save this play."

"From the fires?"

"From oblivion," he said. He dropped his arm and turned the plate so Tylney could see the back of it. His thumb passed over a couple of small nubs marked with red sigils, and Tylney gasped. As if through a *camera obscura*, the image of a page of *The Ile of Dogges* floated on a bit of glass imbedded in the back of the plate, as crisp and brightly lit as if by brilliant day. It wasn't the page to which the play lay open. "My name's Baldassare," the clerk—the sorcerer—said. "I'm here to preserve this play. It was lost."

"Jonson's summoned demons," Tylney whispered, as someone pounded on the office door. It rattled, and did not open. Baldassare must have claimed the keys when he dragged Tylney inside, and fastened the lock while Tylney was still bedazzled. The light of the candle would show under the door, though. The servants would know he was here.

It was his private office, and Tylney had one of only two keys. Someone would have to wake the steward for the other.

He could shout. But Baldassare could kill him before the household could break down the door. And the sorcerer was staring at him, one eyebrow lifted, as if to see what he would do.

Tylney held his tongue, and the door rattled once more before footsteps retreated.

"Just a historian," Baldassare answered, when the silence had stretched a minute or two.

"*Historian*? But the play's not three months old!"

Baldessare shook his head. "Where I come from, it's far older. And it's—" He hesitated, seeming to search for a word. "—it's *dead*. No one has ever read it, or seen it performed. Most people don't even know it once existed." He laid fingertips on the papers, caressing. "Let me take it. Let me give it life."

"It's sedition." Tylney grasped the edge of the script, greatly daring, and pulled it from under Baldassare's hand.

"It's brilliant," Baldassare said, and Tylney couldn't argue, though he bundled the papers close to his chest. The sorcerer had been strangely gentle with him, as a younger man with an older. Perhaps he could gamble on that. Perhaps. It was his duty to protect the queen.

Baldassare continued, "None will know, no one shall read it, not until you and Elizabeth and Jonson and Nashe are long in your graves. It will do no harm. I swear it."

"A sorcerer's word," Tylney said. He stepped back, came up hard against the door. The keys weren't in the lock. They must be in Baldassare's hand.

"Would you have it lost forever? Truly?" Baldassare reached and Tylney crowded away. Into the corner, the last place he could retreat.

"Sir Edmund!" someone shouted from the hall.

From outside the door, Tylney heard the jangle of keys, their rattle in the lock. "You'll hang," he said to Baldassare.

"Maybe," Baldassare said, with a sudden grin that showed his perfect, white teeth. "But not today." One lingering, regretful look at the papers crumpled to Tylney's chest, and he dropped the keys on the floor, touched something on the wrist of the hand that held the metal plate, and vanished in a shimmer of air as Tylney gaped after him.

The door burst open, framing Tylney's steward, John, against blackness. Tylney flinched.

"Sir Edmund?" The man came forward, a candle in one hand, the keys in the other. "Are you well?"

"Well enough," Tylney answered, forcing himself not to crane his neck after the vanished man. He could *claim* a demon had appeared in his workroom, right enough. He could claim it, but who would believe?

He swallowed, and eased his grip on the play clutched to his chest. "I dropped the keys."

The steward frowned doubtfully. "You cried out, milord."

"I stumbled only," Tylney said. "I feared for the candle. But all is well." He laid the playscript on the table and smoothed the pages as his steward squatted to retrieve the fallen keys. "I thank you your concern."

The keys were cool and heavy, and clinked against each other like debased coins when the steward handed them over. Tylney laid them on the table beside the candle and the play. He lifted the coin purse from the window ledge, flicked the drapes back, and weighted the pages with the money once more before throwing wide the shutters, heedless of the night air. It was a still summer night, the stink of London rising from the gutters, but a draft could always surprise you, and he didn't feel like chasing paper into corners.

The candle barely flickered. "Sir Edmund?"

"That will be all, John. Thank you."

Silently, the steward withdrew, taking his candle and his own keys with him. He left the door yawning open on darkness. Tylney stood at his table for a moment, watching the empty space.

He and John had the only keys. Baldassare had come and gone like a devil stepping back and forth from Hell. Without the stink of brimstone, though. Perhaps more like an angel. Or memory, which could walk through every room in Tylney's house, through every playhouse in London, and leave no sign.

Tylney bent on creaking knees and laid kindling on the hearth. He stood, and looked at the playscript, one-quarter of the pages turned where it rested on the edge of his writing table, the other three-fourths crumpled and crudely smoothed. He turned another page, read a line in Jonson's hand, and one in Nashe's. His lips stretched over his aching teeth, and he chuckled into his beard.

He laid the pages down. No more sense than a tabby cat.

It was late for making a fire. He could burn the play in the morning. Before he returned Jonson's bribe. He'd lock the door behind him, so no one could come in or out. There were only two sets of keys.

Sir Edmund Tylney blew the candle out, and trudged upstairs through the customary dark.

In the morning, he'd see to the burning.

----

*All quotations are from the Poet Emeritus Series edition of *The Ile of Dogges*, edited by Anthony Baldassare (Las Vegas, NV: University of Nevada Press, 2206).

₪

SEPTEMBER AT WALL AND BROAD
₪
Kristine Kathryn Rusch

Manhattan
September 16, 1920

She didn't want to go to work this morning. Normally, Philippa couldn't wait to leave the tiny two-room walkup she shared with five other women. The place smelled of grease and dirt so old that no amount of bleach would get it out. She had tried to clean the flat when she realized she would have to live like everyone else in this godforsaken century. She scrubbed the place until her hands were raw, and made no difference whatsoever.

Ambition was cold comfort when you shared a mattress with two other women—girls in 1920 parlance—neither of whom had bathed in the last week. The flat had two windows, both of which overlooked the brick building next door. No breezes, no sunlight.

Not that it mattered. She stayed out of the flat as much as she could, coming back to sleep and change clothes. She probably smelled no better than her companions. The bathroom was down the hall, the bathtub foul, and the toilet an atrocity.

She'd been counting the days to September 16, not because that was the day she'd been waiting for, but because she'd be able to go home, real home, bathe, sleep in a bed with Egyptian cotton sheets, and turn on the air conditioning, even if she didn't need it.

For the first time in her entire career, she missed the middle of the twenty-first century. She missed it with a mad passion, realizing that with all the rising sea levels, the incredible population growth, the poverty that no one could quite wipe out, the life she led there was one of privilege, even though she associated more with the upper class here than she ever had there.

Still, she stood at the door of her apartment building, and looked up at the azure sky. A perfect blue, the temperature in the low sixties, promising to be one of those spectacular New York days, the kind that made you wonder why you lived anywhere else. The city, about to enter its ascendancy in American life, glowed under the September sun.

People were walking outside and gazing upward, some even smiling, probably planning a series of errands that would get them out of the office. Folks who worked outside had smirks of superiority; they got paid to be outside.

A few people were probably thinking ahead to lunch, planning to splurge at one of the food carts, and maybe even sit on one of the benches lined up along the streets or head to one of the city's parks, if only for a few minutes. A few snatched minutes that no one would ever get.

She shuddered. She'd been in Manhattan before on a perfect September day. On one of her first jobs, in fact. She'd stood not far from here and gazed upward at a building that wasn't even a glimmer in someone's eye this morning, and watched, at 8:46 a.m., as American Flight 11 crashed into the World Trade Center's north tower.

The same sort of sunshine. Same kind of optimism in the air.

Only then that crisis had been more deadly, using weapons not yet dreamed of, hitting a building impossible to build in this time period, while an entire nation watched on a machine that Philo Farnsworth wouldn't even imagine for another year.

That day had been hard, but she had been prepared. She had watched the footage, read the accounts, talked to others who had also visited September 11th. And that day had been the final test in her training: could she maintain her composure as people jumped to their deaths to escape flames, as buildings pancaked around her, as first responders who wouldn't live out the day ran past her to save as many lives as possible?

She had been, in the words of her instructor, "positively bloodless." He had meant that as a compliment, and she had taken it that way. "Positively bloodless," meant she kept her composure, did her job, and got out with a minimum of notification and a minimum of fuss.

Yes, she had nightmares. Everyone did; it was part of the job. But they weren't debilitating, and she was able to work through the worst of them with the therapist the department had assigned her.

She was, in other words, a stellar candidate, the best of her class. A woman who had since completed dozens of difficult assignments.

A woman who did not want to walk to the corner of Wall and Broad on this beautiful September morning. A woman who did not want to enter the

House of Morgan to take her lowly secretary's desk with its fancy expensive Underwood typewriter, something she had been instructed to be very, very careful with because it was delicate. It wasn't delicate. The damn thing was a tank and it would take a sledgehammer to destroy it.

She would wager, if she had anyone to wager with, that the Underwood would survive today's bombing with nary a scratch.

She sighed, and stepped into the sea of humanity. Only four hours left, and she needed to make the most of them.

Washington, DC
March 23, 2057 (supposedly)

Assistant Attorney General Preston Lane needed a moment to process the information the four people behind him had just presented.

He pivoted and faced floor-to-ceiling window of his office in the Time Department's building. The building was known as the Bubble for a variety of reasons. The first was obvious: its round glass shape looked like a bubble. But the second was because it was protected by time bubble after time bubble after time bubble. "Time bubbles" were the nickname for "time-guards." In some ways, time bubble was more accurate, in that the bubble froze a time period into place.

He worked here instead of the Robert F. Kennedy Department of Justice building (which was a nice, but old building) because the Time Division of the Justice Department, like all time-related government departments, had offices here. The Bubble protected all who served.

The yard outside was in full spring bloom. Cherry trees lined the wall, their blossoms in full pink flower. The green grass, the emerging foliage, all spoke of a fantastic DC spring.

Which hadn't quite arrived in DC yet.

The permanent staff blew smoke up his ass about the yard. *It's enclosed, so it follows its own schedule,* the head gardener told him when he'd asked. *Think of it like a greenhouse.*

A greenhouse with a manipulated timer. He'd gone into the archives shortly after receiving his assignment and looked. This year's cherry blossoms mimicked last year's weather. Last year, the trees had reached full bloom by the end of March, just like they had for the past thirty years. This year, the trees outside the Bubble had returned to their April schedule, the one that had made this city and its cherry trees justly famous.

Plants didn't cooperate inside a time bubble. If you wanted plants to bloom and grow, they actually needed care, just like they would in a greenhouse. If you wanted to pretend that they followed the same schedule as the outside world, you didn't speed up the timeline or import different plants from different time periods. You set the yard's chronometer to its own schedule, and prayed that it worked like the rest of the world.

Which it did not. The world was/is/will always be a messy place. For the plants inside the yard, the world had an unbreakable schedule, and theoretically, the entire staff enjoyed that.

It made his skin crawl. All of this did. The deeper he got into his assignment, the more unhappy he became.

Especially with the Wall Street case.

Before he got appointed to the Time Division, someone on staff had noticed that Manhattan's financial district had been time-guarded from mid-August to mid-September 1920. Time-guards in the United States needed approval from the Time Department. The Secretary of Time had claimed she knew nothing of this, and indeed, there were no records of who or what had installed that bubble.

Plus, the bubble did not conform to government regulations.

Government-formed time bubbles existed throughout the United State's history, and they also existed now. The White House had its own time bubble, as did Congress, the Supreme Court, and the Pentagon. All of the buildings housing the Cabinet had them as well. Not every place could be protected—if someone could easily get to a United States Representative, for example, because the country did not have enough money to protect district offices. The money instead went to time-guarding polling places on each and every election day in the country, no matter how small the election.

Lane did not have the ability to reset time. Officially, no one did. But he suspected someone held that power unofficially, and that someone or those someones existed in the very government he served.

But the answer to that question was above his pay grade.

What happened to Philippa D'Arco, however, was not.

Lane took a deep breath. He'd go out into the yard and walk among the cherry blossoms if he weren't allergic to the damn things. Because he needed to move.

But he couldn't, because he had to finish this meeting. He turned his back on the windows. Wilhelmina Rutger and her three assistants still stood behind him, ignoring the comfortable chairs and the hollow tables that allowed for some selected time viewing.

His wife would be furious. He was supposed to accompany her on some important dinner for her hedge-fund business. She had probably given up on him anyway. She didn't understand the government's mandate: anyone who worked in the Bubble had to take a second oath, vowing to never ever use time travel for personal gain. Even if that gain was keeping peace in a marriage already on the rocks.

He forced his attention back to the problem at hand—not his problem, but the division's problem. They were related, after all.

"Okay, let me see if I get this straight." He had started so many conversations like this in the six months since his appointment. Time travel's complexities made his brain hurt. "D'Arco had ten windows for return and missed all of them, which is, apparently, unlike her. She's also the first investigator we've sent to the September 16th bombing who failed to return."

"Yes." Wilhelmina was petite and blond, with a friendly face completely at odds with her take-no-prisoners personality. "Philippa's body didn't return either, which is our failsafe."

Wilhelmina peered at him, as if she were testing whether or not he actually knew that. He wasn't sure he did. He tried not to look even more creeped out. He hated the way that people just vanished when they stepped into the time chamber, even if the vanishing was only for a moment or two. He didn't want to think about how he'd feel if they came back a few seconds later as a corpse.

"In other words this is extremely unusual." Lane sighed again, and swept his hand at the chairs. "Let's sit."

They did. He frowned at the assistants, having no idea who they were. Wilhelmina always seemed to bring a different set of assistants to every meeting. Lane wasn't sure if that was because she couldn't keep assistants or if her assistants swapped out due to those time complexities.

"Philippa is the first woman we've sent to the Wall Street bombing," Wilhelmina said. "Our previous investigators were all men. The first one arrived just after the time bubble burst, 12:01 p.m. on September 16, 1920, one minute after the bomb went off. He couldn't even get into the bomb site at Wall and Broad. We tried to have our second investigator arrive at 12:02 p.m., and he couldn't do that. He could travel outside the time bubble around the financial district, but he couldn't time-travel inside it within hours of that explosion. We sent our third investigator to Manhattan one month before the explosion with the idea that he would get a job that would allow him to investigate the entire area, and see if the historical record is missing something that we should know."

Lane remembered now. "That last guy is the reason we ended up sending Philippa."

"Yes." Wilhelmina smiled, even though the smile did not go to her eyes. The smile said, *We've had this conversation and you should remember it. All of it. I hate repeating myself. Sir.*

He did remember the conversation now. He had asked her, *Why weren't we aware of the rigid class structure in New York at that time?*

It's not class structure that we're running into per se, sir, Wilhelmina had told him. *It's nepotism. To get hired in the House of Morgan, you need to have some kind of relationship with someone who does work there. And in 1920, we're at the height of the corruption that became known as the Teapot Dome Scandal. Everyone inside the New York Police Department who could hire our man won't now, because he has no ties to Tammany Hall. We—*

He'd cut her off. He had no idea what Teapot Dome was, and didn't want to find out. The same with Tammany Hall. He had some historical expertise, but it wasn't New York in the 1920s. When he accepted the President's appointment as Head of the Time Division in the Attorney General's Office, Lane had hoped to use this job to deal with interesting things, like people traveling back in time to murder someone else's grandmother who just happened to be a federal judge or something.

Instead, he was dealing with protected time periods that hadn't been protected by the proper authorities, and hints and allegations of alleged time abuse. Half his staff was somewhen else at the moment, investigating, prodding, poking, seeing there was a case. Or, as his boss, the Attorney General, liked to say when he brought potential cases to her, the staff was seeing if this was something that would "benefit us in the next election, or is it something that we can leave on the scrapheap of history for the next administration?"

Maybe he should quit, before the cynicism took him out of the game entirely.

"Sir?" Wilhelmina asked.

He'd checked out again. He wondered if he could pretend it was because he didn't understand the time paradoxes.

"No one looked at young women in that period," Wilhelmina said through gritted teeth. She was clearly repeating herself. "If they had jobs, they were clearly from the wrong class and being women, they were considered stupid."

He had no idea how anyone could find women stupid. There had to have been women like Wilhelmina in that day and age. How had anyone believed they were inferior?

"Philippa is one of our best operatives," Wilhelmina said. "She studied the bombing for three months before we sent her back. She's spent a month In Time."

Lane hated that phrase. It came from In Country, military slang for foreign territory, particularly a war zone. But its use here often confused him, because the rest of the world always wanted him to do things "in time" as well, and it meant something completely different. Like "just in the nick of time," which was the only way he'd make that dinner date now.

"Philippa couldn't have been killed in the bombing. She knew where she should stand, what she should do, where the most victims were, the greatest danger. She knew it all. She also knew she could return to us at 12:01, and give us her information. She would have come back, sir. I know it."

Wilhelmina's voice shook as she said that last, not with anger, but with sorrow. Or was it fear? Either way, he'd never heard those two emotions in her voice. Now she had his full attention.

"So what do you want to do?" he asked.

Wilhelmina was authorized to do a lot on her own. The fact that she had come here, with a request that she hadn't yet articulated, meant something was very different.

"I want to send in an investigator, sir," Wilhelmina said.

He frowned. "We already sent in three, not counting Philippa. At a certain point, we have to decide that we have done what we can on this investigation. We only have so many resources."

"We don't leave people in the field," one of the men snapped. Everyone looked at him. He paled. "Sir. Sorry, sir. I mean, after all. She could be in trouble."

Could have been *in trouble,* Lane mentally corrected. But he didn't say it. He continued to address his questions to Wilhelmina. "Do we have information on her after September 16?"

"In a cursory search of the historical record, her alias, which is Philippa Darcy, does not show up. But it doesn't mean anything. Thirty-eight people died that day, and one hundred forty-three were seriously wounded. But that was according to the statistics released long after the fact. No one put up flyers or tracked everyone who had been on the street that day. Even if they had the resources, they didn't have the will. The newspaper reports, for godssake, only listed names and addresses of the lower-class victims, and that was only if they were identified. The authorities didn't even know for certain if the body parts they found matched up to the—"

"I'm aware of the vagaries of the pre-technological age of investigation," Lane said. "I'm asking if Philippa Darcy married or showed up in the public records. Maybe she had done her best to leave a message . . . ?"

The investigators were supposed to send their recall device back if, for some odd reason, they decided to stay in the past. Only a handful of people had ever stayed, and all of those had traveled back just a few years, not more than a century.

"No message, sir," Wilhelmina said. "We checked. But Philippa is in the payroll roster in the House of Morgan for the week before. There is no payroll roster for the week of the 16th, and she isn't on it the following week."

Lane placed his hands on his knees and slid back. "Clearly there's a problem with the time-guard around that time period. What we've been doing hasn't been working, so I don't think sending another investigator into that time-guarded period is the best answer. I think you'll need to come up with a new plan to figure out how this bubble got placed, and who placed it."

One of her assistants slumped, but Wilhelmina's back straightened.

"I'm not asking for someone new to investigate the bombing or that time-guard, sir," she said in a how-dumb-are-you voice. "I'm asking to send an investigator to locate Philippa. I have to believe that she knows something, that she discovered something, and that someone is preventing her return. None of our failsafes have worked, and at least one of them should have. We should have some knowledge of what happened to her, and we have none."

"You automatically leap from this mission didn't go right to someone has harmed her?" It was Lane's turn to use the how-dumb-are-you voice. "For all we know, she could have been standing too close to the bomb when it went off, and she got vaporized. She, her device, the failsafes, everything. After all, as you just pointed out, our information from that time period isn't exactly trustworthy. And I seem to recall that they never did figure out with any certainty what happened that day."

The third assistant grimaced. "There's a lot of evidence to suggest—"

Wilhelmina held up a hand, silencing him. "We do an out-and-back," she said. "A short mission, looking only on that day. We send in someone new. We give him the right credentials. After all, William J. Flynn took a train in from DC the moment he heard about the bombing. We can have our man take jurisdiction for just a few hours."

Lane had no idea who this William J. Flynn was, although he supposed

Wilhelmina had once briefed him on that as well. So many cases, so much to remember. Maybe he would resign at the end of the year. Clearly all of these time paradoxes were taking a toll.

"I thought we already did that," Lane said. "Wasn't that our second investigator?"

She glanced at her assistants. "We had the wrong credentials."

"What?" Lane asked. He knew he hadn't heard this.

"We had legitimate New York police department credentials, but we had given our man a position too high up in the department. They figured out fairly quickly that he was a fraud. Only they figured he worked for former Commissioner Arthur Woods, not that he had come from the future."

Arthur Woods. Another name Lane probably should have remembered. He sighed. He would have to read up on this entire investigation just to refresh his memory. He could either do that, or trust the woman who sat before him.

"How much will this cost the department?" Lane asked.

"It depends," she said flatly. "You can calculate the loss of a human life and the loss of the training we invested into the investigator, or you can figure the price of one more trip into time."

"Possibly losing another investigator," he said.

"Possibly," she said.

"If we do, we both lose our jobs," he said.

"*That's* what's worrying you?" she asked.

"No," he said. "It isn't. What worries me is that we're doing something we don't entirely understand. We're throwing more resources at it rather than investigating the best methods and then taking them. There is no hurry, Ms. Rutger, as you've often told me. If we send in someone today or next week, it won't matter. They'll still go back to the same time period."

She raised her chin ever so slightly. He had gotten through.

"You're right, of course," she said. "In my concern, I had forgotten that. We will conduct a more thorough investigation, and then I will consult with you again."

"Thank you," he said.

Wilhelmina and her assistants left, but he remained seated. Something about this disturbed him greatly. Not Wilhelmina's hurry or even the assistants' passion. In fact, he understood the assistants' passion. They could have been the ones on the front lines. But for the luck of the draw, this conversation could have been about any one of them.

No, something else bothered Lane.

New York's financial district. Three major attacks that he knew of: this one in 1920, the 1993 bombing of the World Trade Center, and the 2001 destruction of the World Trade Center. Plus at least two thwarted attacks, one in 2012 against the Federal Reserve in Lower Manhattan, and another in 2025 against the New York Stock Exchange.

Were they all time-guarded events? If so, were they time-guarded by Homeland or Justice or the Time Department? Or by someone else? Something else? A multinational? A foreign government?

Lane stood up slowly. He had to make a choice here. He could remain the ignorant figurehead, disappointed in the job that they had given him, or he could step into his role as the chief investigator of time irregularities for the Federal Government.

He hated those dinners his wife planned. He used to love investigative work. He'd simply been overwhelmed by his learning curve and, if he were honest, by the fact that he walked through several time bubbles every morning when he came to work. He hated the Bubble, but everywhere he'd worked in DC had a time-guard of one type or another. The problem wasn't the job; the problem was his attitude.

He'd allowed others to dictate policy during his first six months here. Time to change that, no pun intended. Or maybe he did intend to pun. Because it was past time. And he couldn't use the amazing resources at his disposal to start again. So maybe he could use them to solve something huge.

Or, if this wasn't huge, just to make the right decision in the Philippa D'Arcy case.

Whatever that decision might be.

Manhattan
September 16, 1920

Philippa glanced at the clock hanging on the far wall. The incredible clack of typewriters had its own rhythm, a *rat-a-tat-tat-tat-tat-tat-tat-tat bing!* that had become familiar to her. At the desk next to her, the new hire sang "Over There" faintly under her breath, a reprieve from the Tin Pan Alley tunes she had started the morning with. The last few hours of Philippa's last day. She looked at all the girls around her, intent on their typing or fixing their shorthand or stacking already-completed letters in manila folders, and wondered how they would fare.

They might be all right. The large room had no windows, the grillwork making it seem like a prison. All of the girls who worked there wore white shirtwaists and long skirts, their hair in a neat bun. They seemed interchangeable and probably were, to the men who ran the House of Morgan.

Philippa straightened her desk, rolled a sheet of House of Morgan letterhead in the platen of her Underwood, and stood up.

Mrs. Fontaine looked up from her desk. It faced the rows and rows of desks.

"You do not have permission to stand," she said. She was twice the age of the girls and twice their weight. She ran a tight office, but a fair one. She pretended to be an ogre, but the girls loved her, because she understood what it was to be young and employed and a little bit terrified.

"I'm sorry," Philippa said. "I'm afraid I need a personal moment."

Technically, the girls weren't to leave their desks until their thirty minute unpaid lunch break. But Mrs. Fontaine understood that women couldn't always sit that long, particularly at certain times of the month. She claimed she got her girls to do five times the work the girls in other financial houses did, because she allowed them "personal moments."

Mrs. Fontaine nodded. "Make it quick."

Philippa wouldn't make it quick. Not that it mattered. After noon today, she would no longer be employed at the House of Morgan.

She would make one more tour around the building, and try to see if there was something unusual. Then she would return to her desk and prevent some of the girls whom she'd befriended from taking their usual lunch. They would be safe inside their windowless room, but on that street, near the Curb Market, the Sub-Treasury, the New York Stock Exchange annex, and all of the other buildings, people would die, lose limbs, have their lives forever changed.

Technically, she wasn't supposed to prevent that. Technically, she was supposed to go about her business. But there was no way of knowing what the girls would have done without her, so trying to play that game didn't work. She had to live with herself, and even though, in her real life, in her real time, these women were long dead, they were alive now, she'd been their friend, and she owed them.

She slipped a steno pad into the pocket of her long skirt, and stepped away from her desk. She smiled a thank you to Mrs. Fontaine, then headed in the direction of the women's necessary. The one great thing about the

House of Morgan was that it had bathrooms and they were clean. Not that she needed to use one.

She waited until she was out of Mrs. Fontaine's sight, then pulled the steno pad from the pocket of her skirt. She hugged the pad against her chest and then wandered, making certain she looked lost.

It had worked every time she had done this in the past. Some man would ask her where she needed to go, she would give an answer, and he would point her in the right direction. The younger men would ask her name, and give her a bright smile. The older men would sometimes put their arm around her and guide her to the correct floor.

She didn't want either to happen today. She needed to do her last tour unescorted. Then, if she didn't find anything, she would slip onto the street and run to the Sub-Treasury building.

She couldn't get their mission off her mind either. Right now, as she patrolled the inside of the House of Morgan, workers at the Sub-Treasury building were transferring a billion dollars in gold coins and bullion to the federal assay office across the street.

She had no real idea how they were doing this; her reading told her that the workers were using a wooden chute, and after the bombing, a U.S. Army battalion would arrive to protect the gold.

Initially the Time Crimes Division believed someone was trying to steal the gold. After the first investigator discovered that no gold got stolen, someone suggested that the time-guard had put into place to *prevent* the gold from getting stolen, and had been successful.

But that didn't make sense either, because the gold would be a lot easier to steal after the bombing than before. Hell, she could figure out how to do it: she could time travel into the Sub-Treasury or next to the chute in the assay office at 12:01 in the chaos. With the right kind of manpower and weaponry, the gold would disappear.

But it didn't; it wouldn't; it never would. It would remain.

The fact that she was even thinking of heading to the Sub-Treasury building showed just how desperate she was to get some information, any information, before she left 1920 at 12:02 p.m. She had already been to Sub-Treasury courtesy of a nice young guard, who had thought her harmless. A different nice young guard had shown her what he could in the assay office, and there, she found nothing out of the ordinary.

Not that she knew what she was looking for. Something. Something had to be here, besides this bombing.

Something had to be so important that changing it threatened The Way Things Were.

She walked up a marble staircase to the private meetings floor. She'd been called into a few of these conference rooms. She'd sat on a wooden chair in the back and taken notes.

Today, if someone asked where she was going, she had a half-plausible lie based on that previous experience. She knew that Junius Spencer Morgan the younger, the heir to the throne, was having a meeting in one of the rooms facing Wall Street. She'd seen photographs of the aftermath, although she wasn't sure which room he was in. If someone stopped her, she would tell them she was going to relieve the secretary handling that meeting.

But no one stopped her. She went up staircase after staircase to floor after floor and she was about to give up, when she noticed one of the doors to the maintenance area stood open.

She'd tried that door in the past, and it had been locked. This time, she slipped inside.

Four men were leaning together, gesturing and whispering. They appeared to be arguing. They didn't notice her.

They didn't look like maintenance men. They were too clean for one thing. People who did physical labor in this decade had a layer grime on their clothes and skin that just couldn't come off in a weekly bath. Their clothes were off too. A little too shiny, a bit too new. And one man wore shoes that had a metal ridge she had never seen before. Or, rather, that she hadn't seen in a very long time. Or, rather, that no one would see for many many years.

The men all looked at her at the same time. One man flushed red.

"Can we help you?" asked the man wearing the odd shoes. He had dark eyes and skin that wasn't quite white. She wouldn't have noticed that a month ago, but after living here, in a world where everything was defined by skin color, last name, education, and accent, she noticed.

Her heart started pounding. Her planned lie about Mr. Morgan seemed wrong, somehow.

"I saw the open door . . . " she said.

"Christ," hissed the man who flushed. "She saw us. No one was supposed to see us."

His teeth were white. Even. Perfect. So were the teeth of the first man who spoke. So were her teeth. People here remarked on that.

These men didn't belong here any more than she did. And, she would wager, no one in the Time Division knew about them.

She backed out of the room, slammed the door closed, and ran for the stairs. With one hand, she lifted her skirt enough so that her own boots didn't catch, and with the other, she put the steno pad in her pocket. Then she reached for the railing. The steps were slick, and she had to slow down some.

She heard footsteps behind her. She sped up just as someone grabbed her. He smelled of cologne. Not Bay Rum. Cologne. Nothing from this time period. It was too subtle, too complex. And the hand that covered her mouth had had a manicure.

She bit his palm. He cursed, but didn't let her go. Instead, he dragged her up the stairs. She struggled, but couldn't free herself. Her feet banged on every step, jarring her all the way up her spine.

Surely, someone on the lower levels heard that. Surely, someone would come investigate. Surely, someone would do something.

She elbowed the man, then tried to hit his face with her fists. When he pulled her onto the upper floor, she levered herself up on his arm and kicked him on his shins. He didn't even flinch. He continued to drag her. One of the other men joined him, and they flung her into that room.

She slid along the floor on her skirt, and nearly slammed into the wall. The men peered down at her.

"What do we do with her?" asked the man who had flushed.

The man who had dragged her reached down, and pulled her lips back so that he could look at her teeth like she was a horse. She tried to bite him again.

"Feisty bit of business," one of the other men said.

"Who are you, really?" the man who dragged her asked.

"Philippa Darcy," she snapped, using the name she used in this period. "I'm expected in Mr. Morgan's office."

"It's eleven-thirty," one of the men said to the others.

The man who dragged her grinned. "Then I'll wager that Mr. Morgan won't mind if you don't show up. He probably won't even notice."

"He *will*," she said, keeping to the game. "He'll notice. He'll send someone searching for me."

"Nice try, honey," said the man who dragged her. "But you girls aren't that important to anyone in the House of Morgan. No one except your boss even knows your name."

"What do we do with her?" the man who flushed asked again.

"We can't send her home for another thirty-one minutes," said the man with the shoes.

Her heart rate increased. They knew. They knew about the bomb; they probably knew that she didn't belong here.

"What's really going on?" she asked.

"Ah, honey," said the man who dragged her. "That's above your pay grade. It's strictly need-to-know."

She struggled to her feet. Damn the skirt. Her legs caught in its folds.

"I think I need to know," she said, with more bravado than she felt.

"And you will know," the man who dragged her said. Then he grinned. "All in good time."

And all of the men laughed, as if he had told a particularly witty joke.

Washington, DC
March 23, 2057 (supposedly)

Lane was deep in his research when his assistant peeked her head in the door. He nearly snapped at her, but thought the better of it. Her lips were in a thin line, her hair slightly out of place. She looked frazzled, and one reason he had hired her was because she was the most unflappable person he had ever met.

"The Attorney General just called a meeting downstairs," she said. "He says it's urgent."

"I thought nothing was urgent in the Time Division," Lane said.

"Apparently," she said, "this is."

Manhattan
September 16, 1920

At 11:55 a.m., Charles Gage took his seat at the back of Fred Eberlin's New Street restaurant. The place smelled of frying meat and spilled beer. The table was sticky, and even in the middle of the day, the electric lights were on. They weren't very powerful, and they barely cut the gloom.

The waiter who had greeted him didn't want him to sit so far back.

"Wouldn't you rather have a seat up front by the window, sir?" he asked as Gage strode toward the back of the restaurant. "You can watch all of New York go by without moving a muscle."

"Not today," Gage said. Today, if he sat by that plate glass window, or any plate glass window within six blocks of Wall Street, he ran the risk of serious injury, maybe even death.

Even sitting this far back was a risk. But he wanted to be inside the time-guard. Within the hour, the police would block off sections of Wall Street, and he wouldn't be able to get in unless his paperwork was perfect.

He didn't want to rely on perfect paperwork. He wanted to rely on outsmarting whatever it was that had set up the time bubble in the first place.

The waiter sighed loudly. "The specials are on the board up front, sir, but I suppose I can recite them for you."

"I'd rather have a sarsaparilla," Gage said. He'd acquired a taste for the damn things on another job, ten years ago his time, but only a year before this one. He had a hunch that whatever the Coca-Cola Company used to make the drink was bad for him, but he didn't care. It was a taste he couldn't get anywhen else. If, of course, he had time to drink it.

He pulled out his pocket watch. He'd set it to New York time the moment he arrived. He couldn't get to Washington, DC, on September 16, so he'd had to settle for Philadelphia which, for some reason, wasn't time-guarded at all. He took a train to Manhattan, and arrived at Penn Station at 9:00 a.m. Then he'd walked down the island, and stopped near the Equitable Life Insurance Building, which, at thirty-eight stories, was currently the tallest building in the city, if not the world.

He'd loitered outside for as long as he could, watching the cutthroat operatives of the outdoor Curb Market trade the junk stocks and bonds that the regular markets sneered at. Part of him was fascinated to see history in action. The Curb Market's annex was nearly finished, and these traders would move inside within the year. But for the moment, they acted like street vendors, waving their tickets and shouting to be heard.

But he couldn't simply observe them. He needed to keep an eye on the street. He was watching for a touring car with a New Jersey license plate. He was also looking for some sort of old wooden wagon being pulled by an elderly horse. The horse would end up in pieces all over Wall Street, as would the wagon. The touring car would end up on its side.

Smart money believed that the car rear-ended the wagon, which had probably come from the DuPont Powder Works with a load of dynamite. Manhattan had banned the transport of explosives on its streets during the daylight hours, but that didn't mean that companies followed the rules.

He saw the touring car, recognizing its plate—NJ24246—and realized that the man who claimed to the chauffer in the news reports looked nothing like the man driving. Then Gage saw a brand new wagon being pulled by an elderly horse. He wished he could take video, but he didn't dare. He was already attracting enough attention by standing outside the Equitable Building.

He'd slipped through the crowds and made his way to the restaurant where he sat now, wondering if the things he had seen had any meaning whatsoever.

Not that he was here for the bombing. He wasn't. He was here to find Philippa D'Arco, or Darcy as they called her. Her image was stamped— literally—inside his mind. One of those chips that the investigators for the Justice Department used on occasion. He knew what she looked like when she walked, talked, laughed, as if he had known her well. He wouldn't be able to miss her any more than a lover or her own family would have.

If Gage saw her. If he found her.

He wasn't entirely sure she was still here. He had telephoned the House of Morgan that morning, and asked if she was working. He'd been told that secretaries did not receive personal calls while at work, and then someone had asked his name.

"I'm her father," he had lied. "Her mother's gravely ill. I would like to speak to her."

"You may do so during her regular luncheon," the young man who had answered the phone told him. "All female secretaries take luncheon beginning at noon."

"But she is in the office?" Gage pressed.

"She signed in at 7:45 a.m., sir. Good day." And the young man had hung up.

So Gage had three pieces of information to take back with him. Philippa D'Arcy had shown up to work. The chauffer on the touring car did not look like his photograph in the papers from the hearings. And the wagon that might or might not have been carrying the dynamite was brand new.

The waiter set down a tall glass with the greenish brown liquid foaming inside. Gage picked it up, hoping for one sip before all hell broke loose—

And then the world went white. A sound, louder than anything he'd ever heard, shook the building. The air turned fire hot, then evaporated, and his lungs ached. He dove under the table. Too late. Already shards of glass had slid their way here.

Everything went deadly quiet. Nothing. Not a single sound. Almost as if all of New York held its breath at the same moment.

And then someone moaned.

The waiter was crouched against the back wall. The two customers who had been sitting near the window were sprawled on the floor. Another waiter leaned against the counter, still clutching a plate of food.

Gage stood, ran his hands over his suit, checking to see if he was uninjured. He was. He knocked some glass shards out of his hair, picked up his hat, and shook it off as well.

The screams were beginning, as were the cries for help.

He took a deep breath, tasting smoke, blood, and something acrid, but at least there was oxygen again. He steeled his shoulders, and stepped into what he knew would be the hardest few minutes of his life.

He had to step over the injured, pass the dumbstruck, avoid the helpless, and head for the door. It had been blown open by the force of the explosion. A young man sprawled on the steps, bleeding from a gash in the head. His trembling right hand reached for a spiked rail that had ripped through the shoulder of his suit.

That had to be George Lacina, who worked at Equitable Life Assurance, the man whose comment to *The New York World* had set off all sorts of alarms in 2057. Lacina said that he later noticed that all the buttons on his coat had come off, and his watch was ten minutes slow.

Almost as if time had stopped. Or gone backward. Or rippled.

All signs of a time-guard.

Gage glanced at his pocket watch. It appeared to have stopped. But as he looked at it, the second hand moved. He needed to do the same.

It was easier said than done. Hundreds of people poured out of buildings, hurried down stairs, and ran away from the financial district. Some of them bleeding, many of them covered in glass or plaster, all of them looking terrified.

He had to go upstream, pushing through them all, careful not to fall or he would be trampled to death. All the while his feet slipped on blood or severed limbs or body parts he couldn't identify.

A woman on fire screamed as she ran past him. A man tackled her from the side, wrapping her in a coat.

Gage pretended he didn't see, reminded himself it was history. When that didn't work, he lied to himself that it was a virtual simulation—and he'd been through hundreds of those. Thousands. He couldn't help these people. They were more than a century dead, and for most, this was the worst day of their lives. But he couldn't reach out, couldn't do anything.

He had to find Philippa.

He reached the House of Morgan, pushed his way up the narrow steps toward the open doors. People still poured out, but he didn't see her among them. He caught some of the women who looked unhurt.

"Philippa," he said. "Where's Philippa?"

Mostly they shook their heads, then shook him off. One heavyset older woman frowned at him, said, "She went . . . necessary. But . . . an hour ago."

Only she was gone before he could parse out what that meant. Or what he hoped it had meant. Philippa had gone to the ladies room an hour before and had never come back.

If she was a smart little time traveler, she would have vanished by now, safe back in 2057, inside the Bubble, making her report. But he was here because she hadn't done that. Her body hadn't shown up, her chip hadn't activated, her failsafe device hadn't returned.

He knew his chip would survive a blast—he'd been through half a dozen of them, not to mention the fact that everything was tested for all kinds of conditions—so he doubted her equipment had failed.

He kept grabbing people, asking, "Philippa?" and getting no response.

Except from a red-haired young man, wearing shirtsleeves, and ripped pants.

"Thought I saw her upstairs," he said, voice trembling. "Lordy, I hope she's all right."

Gage nodded, kept moving, found the stairs, tried to ignore what he saw. Couldn't ignore all of it. The young man held into place by something large—a bit of wall, maybe?—pinning his skull to his teller cage. The man with the broken leg trying to help another man bleeding from the face. The woman ripping pieces of her skirt and using them to tie off oozing wounds.

Above the trading floor, the glass dome that marked this part of the House of Morgan creaked. People screamed and dove for the walls. He didn't. He knew it wouldn't collapse.

Junius Morgan, carrying a wounded man toward the door. His face was scorched, his clothing blood-covered, but he seemed determined.

All of these people were heroes. Gage wasn't. He couldn't be. He had to keep searching for Philippa.

He explored several floors, saw more wounded, but no more dead, avoided some of the dazed victims, and kept searching. He didn't see her and no one seemed to know where she was.

He spent nearly two hours inside the House of Morgan, exploring each room, seeing all the damage—which was much more considerable than the papers ever made it out to be—and he found no trace of her.

It was as if she had followed instructions and vanished. Only she hadn't.

Finally, when he walked out of the bank, exhausted and covered in dirt and blood, he braced himself. Time to assume his identity as a Pinkerton, pretending he'd been hired by the Equitable Company, since the House of Morgan was unofficially using William J. Burns's International Detective Agency.

He would find Philippa, or the parts of her, or what became of her, if he had to stay here for the next year to do so.

Washington, DC
March 23, 2057 (supposedly)

The conference room, bunkered under the building, was an unassuming little space, modeled on the White House's Situation Room. Bunkered, time-guarded with all the latest gadgetry, but so shielded that no one could travel in even from inside the Bubble itself.

Lane hated the little room. It looked like something out of time itself. Rectangular, with blond wood paneling, matching table, and the most uncomfortable blue chairs in the world, the room was always stuffy and tension-filled.

He was the last person to arrive, and as he pulled the door open, he had only seconds to prepare. No one had warned him that he faced not only the Attorney General, but Cabinet Secretaries from Treasury and Time as well. And, off in a corner, as if he were monitoring the meeting instead of participating in it, Brandon Carnelius, the Chairman of the Federal Reserve.

Lane had barely gotten the door closed when the Attorney General said, "You need to recall Charles Gage from 1920."

Kayla Huntingdon was not known for her diplomatic skills, something that had gotten her into trouble with Congress more than once. Sometimes Lane wondered how she ever made it through her confirmation.

"We lost an operative," Lane said. "And we've found some anomalies."

"We know," said Noah Singh. He ran Treasury. He *was* known for his diplomacy, not that it showed at the moment. "Recall him anyway."

Lane knew better than to remind Singh that he did not work for Treasury. Annabelle Tsu, the Time Secretary, nodded. "We have decided. We're going to leave the time-guard in place."

"We didn't create it," Lane said. "I've researched. It didn't come from the government."

"Not technically," Singh said. "But you needn't worry about it."

Lane looked at Huntingdon. He realized from the set of her full mouth that she was furious. She had not been informed about something. Tsu's long red fingernails tapped on the tabletop. Apparently she hadn't been informed either.

"You want to tell me what's going on?" Lane asked. He'd directed the question at his boss, Huntingdon, but he didn't care who answered.

"Technically, you don't have the security clearance," Singh said. "We've decided to bring you into this, since you might run into an anomaly, as you call it, again, and we need you to be prepared."

Huntingdon looked down, her blond hair covering her face. Lane had seen her do that before. It was a deliberate move so that no one could see her expression. Yep, she was pissed. And he had a hunch he was about to be.

"I'm not sure that you're aware of the fact that the Federal Reserve System was founded in 1913," Singh said.

"I know my history," Lane said.

"Let him speak," Tsu said quietly.

"And worked with other central bankers in other nations during the various wars. The Fed's powers expanded after the Great Depression, the Great Recession, and of course, the recent Currency Crisis," Singh said. He sounded like every bad professor Lane had ever had.

"Let me cut through the bullshit for you," Huntingdon said. "Somewhere along the way, these so-called financial geniuses figured the only way to control monetary policy was to change it. By going backwards."

"What?" Lane blinked. No one was supposed to alter major historical events just because they hadn't worked properly. Or what this generation thought of as properly. "They can't do that. It's not legal."

"We started our policy before it was illegal," Carnelius intoned from his corner. As if that made it right. There were laws in place to cover such things. Otherwise someone could go back in time and do something that wasn't a crime then, but was now, and be completely immune from prosecution.

Lane started to say that, but Tsu shook her head. Tsu, who looked as angry as Huntingdon.

"Forgive me, sir," Lane said to the Fed Chair, knowing he was out of turn. "But we're all forbidden from messing with Time."

"Yes, we are," Singh said, taking the focus off Carnelius. "The Fed knows that now. But they started before the rest of us. Interestingly enough, they had time travel devices long before anyone else did. And they did things that they've been trying to clean up ever since. You're probably most familiar with the Flash Crash of 2010? That was an error on the part of the time travelers from the International Monetary Fund, who are tied into this as well."

"I don't understand," Lane said.

"Someone," Huntingdon said, "and no one will say *who* . . . " and with that she looked at Carnelius, "tried to use a time device in 1920. And then tried to cover it up. Which why all the original detectives from the Bureau of Investigation to the New York Police Department to the private detectives had no real idea what happened, because *all* of their theories were true."

Lane got cold. A messy cover-up led to conflicting time stories, which led to bad investigations, which lead to chaos that often cost lives. Like it had in this instance.

"We cannot investigate the so-called bombing without making matters worse," Huntingdon said. "So call off your people. And when you hit a similar time-guarded moment related to something financial, check before you send investigators into the past."

"Wouldn't it be easier if we knew what periods to avoid?" Lane asked Huntingdon.

Her lower jaw moved slightly before she responded. "It would. And yet, apparently, the Fed is not in the business of making our lives easier."

Carnelius shook his head slightly, as if no one understood him.

Lane filtered several responses before he said the one thing he felt he had the right to say, "We've been working on the Wall Street Bombing for nearly a year of our time. We've used a lot of resources. Why has this just come up now?"

"Because," Carnelius said, "one of your operatives stumbled on some of ours."

"Who?" Lane asked. "And when?"

"In 1920. Miss Philippa—Darcy? D'Arco? She stumbled on my people. The moment they found out who she was, they sent word to us."

Time didn't work that way, but the language didn't keep up. They'd found out in 1920, but when had they discovered it in 2057? Or had they? How had word gotten back? Lane didn't know, and he had a hunch everyone would say he didn't have the right to ask.

"When can we get her back?" he asked. That at least, would be a victory. He wouldn't have lost an investigator to this ridiculous operation.

"They won't give her back," Huntingdon said, the frustration clear in her voice.

"See here, Kayla. It's not quite like that," Singh said.

"She can't come back," Tsu said. "She knows too much."

"She's ours now," Carnelius said. "You don't need to worry about her. We'll take good care of her."

"Like you took good care of Wall Street in 1920?" Lane snapped.

"Prescott," Singh said. "Some respect."

"Yes, respect would've been nice, wouldn't it?" Lane said as he got up. "Thirty-eight dead, hundreds more injured, in what history considers the worst act of terrorism on American soil until a bombing in Oklahoma City in 1995? All caused by some idiots mishandling time travel for the Federal Reserve."

"Technically, it wasn't us," Carnelius said. "We're not the only Central Bank with time travel capabilities."

"Oh, that makes it so much better." Lane spread his hands on the tabletop and looked at Huntingdon. "I'm going to tender my resignation."

"And I'll have to refuse it," she said. "With this kind of secret, you have just become a lifer in the Time Division."

Lane's breath caught. He felt a moment of terror that he then suppressed. "You can't do that. I serve at the whim of the President."

"And at whose whim does the President serve?" Tsu muttered.

"Enough," Singh said. "This meeting is over. And it never happened."

"Of course not." Lane felt dizzy. "Just like I never lost an investigator."

"You didn't lose her," Carnelius said. "You simply transferred her to a better paying job."

"I did nothing of the sort," Lane said. "I want that on the record."

"What record?" Huntingdon asked. "This meeting never happened."

Lane tilted his head back. His brain hurt. And this wasn't even a time paradox. It was a political one, with real repercussions on real people's lives.

"When will you return her to us?" he asked.

"We won't," Carnelius said. "She's ours now. Forever."

That would have sounded ominous outside of the Bubble. Inside it, it was damn near terrifying.

"I suppose you won't tell me what that means," Lane said.

"It means she's elsewhen." Carnelius stood. "And that's all I'm going to say."

Manhattan
September 1, 2088 (supposedly)

"You've got to be kidding," Philippa said. She sat on what looked like air, a clear chair that was more comfortable than anything she felt in weeks. "I have to stay here?"

"Not here, exactly," said the man who had dragged her. His name was Roland Karinki, and he worked for the Time Unit in the Federal Reserve.

At the moment, they were in the Manhattan Fed, in a room that literally vanished in the clouds. "You're free to leave this job, to do whatever you want."

"But I can't go home," she said.

"If by that you mean 2057, no, you cannot. It's forbidden to you now. But we can use your services here or in the distant past. We have a lot to do."

She tried not to look panicked. She tried not to *be* panicked. Her training had warned her that she might get stuck out of her time. It wasn't supposed to bother her. She was positively bloodless, after all.

But she didn't feel bloodless.

"I liked 2057," she said. "No, I loved 2057."

"I believe you," Karinki said. "At least you're not trying to lie to me by saying that you're leaving behind friends and family. I know Time Division forbids both of those."

"Not friends," she said, although if she were being truthful, she had not been encouraged to have good friends.

Which made her wonder about all those girls she'd worked with in the House of Morgan. Had they made it out safely? Were they badly wounded? Would she ever know?

"You'll like it better here," Karinki said. "I promise."

"Promises from a man who grabbed me and tossed me into a room, then took me out of my life. Great. How do I know I can trust you?"

"Because," he said, "I have orders from your boss. Do you recall Prescott Lane? He left a file for you, which you can view at your leisure."

She narrowed her gaze. "I know nothing about 2088. You could have faked it."

"I could have," Karinki said. "But I didn't. *We* didn't. And we will help you adjust."

She leaned her head back, and thought for a moment. She was somewhen else. That was what she wanted when she woke up this morning in that wretched two-room flat, with two smelly girls beside her on a flea-ridden mattress. And she had a hunch the food would be better than it had been in 1920. The attitudes would be better as well. And then there was the matter of comfort.

Maybe she was positively bloodless. Because she could feel herself transitioning to the new when.

"I need a hot shower," she said. "Some new clothes. And a bed in place that has climate control."

"That's easy," Karinki said. "How about dinner?"

"Sure," she said. "Alone. In my new apartment. With all kinds of information at my fingertips about the last thirty-one years. I won't make decision until I know what my options are."

"Fair enough," he said, and then extended his hand. "Welcome to the future."

She looked at his palm. It was clean, but it had bite marks on the fleshy part that he hadn't yet cleaned up.

"It sure as hell better be nicer than the past," she said.

"Time periods are never one thing," he said. "You should know that."

She did know it. Maybe better than he did.

Maybe better than anyone.

She looked out that window at Lower Manhattan. Sunlight reflected off the Equitable Building struggling to survive between skyscrapers she couldn't identify. Through the buildings' canyons, she saw the Upper Bay, Battery Park, and a clean Statue of Liberty. Saw New Jersey in the distance.

"What month is it?" she asked.

He grinned. "September."

She looked outside again, but not down this time. Up, like people on the sidewalks in 1920. She saw a clear blue September sky. The kind that promised one of those spectacular New York days, the kind that made you wonder why you lived anywhere else.

"I'm staying in Manhattan," she said. "I don't care when. But I do care where."

He studied her for a moment, then nodded. "We can arrange that."

"Good," she said. "Because I wouldn't work for you any other way."

₪

THOUGHT EXPERIMENT
₪
Eileen Gunn

Ralph Drumm, Jr., as we all know, devised the first practicable method of time travel, in our timestream and in countless others. He was an engineer and a good one, or he would not have figured it out, but in one significant way, he simply had not thought things through.

It was mere happenstance that Ralph even had the time and inclination to consider the matter, that day in the dentist's chair. It wasn't as though he needed any dental work: Ralph had always had perfect teeth, thanks to fluoride, heredity, nutrition, and a touch of obsessive-compulsive disorder. Most of the time, all he needed from the dentist was a quick cleaning, and he was done, but this time he opted for a little something extra: whitening. Ralph had always thought his perfect teeth would surely be more perfect if they were whiter.

The whitening process took an hour and a half, and it was not as much fun as the advertising brochure promised. But Ralph had a great fondness for thought experiments, so he set his mind to figuring out how to disassociate himself from the dentist's chair. Being an engineer, he thought it through in a very logical and orderly way.

It was Ralph's genius to intuit that time travel is accomplished entirely in your head: you just need some basic software development skills, plus powers of concentration that work in all four dimensions. It seemed simple enough, merely a matter of disassociating not only his mind, but also his body. A trick, a mere bagatelle, involving a sort of n-dimensional mental toolbar that controls the user's timeshadow. The body stays behind, where it started, and the timeshadow travels freely until it alights in another time and place, where it generates a copy of the original worldline, body and all, in the timestream.

Ralph wondered why nobody had ever thought of it before. He was about to test it when the hygienist came back and started hosing out the inside of his mouth. Better leave this until I get home, Ralph thought. Even if it didn't work, it was a wonderful theory, and it certainly whiled away ninety minutes that would otherwise have been entirely wasted, intellectually.

At home, Ralph got to work. He set up a few temporal links on the toolbar in his head: first, an easy bit of pre-industrial England. He should fit in there rather nicely, he thought, and they'd speak English. After that, he planned an iconic weekend in cultural history, and a couple of exciting historical events it would be fascinating to witness. Then, focusing the considerable power of his mind, he activated the first link.

Wessex, 1440

The weekly market looked like a rural food co-op run by the Society for Creative Anachronism. People wearing homespun clothing in dull tones of brown and green and blue walked around with baskets, buying vegetables from similarly clad peasants who sat on the ground. In one area, a tinker was mending pots; in another, a shoemaker was stitching clunky but serviceable clogs.

The smell was a little strong—body odor, horse manure, wet hay, rotting vegetation, cooking cabbage—but Ralph felt right at home. He'd devised himself a costume that he thought would look nondescript in any time period, and carried a pocketful of Roosevelt dimes, figuring silver was silver, and Roosevelt did look a little like Julius Caesar.

He looked around nervously, but no one had noticed him materialize, even though he was right in the middle of the crowd. It was as if he'd been there all along, he thought. Ralph was unaware of the most basic tenet of time travel, as we understand it now: that the traveler's arrival in a timestream changes both the future and the past, because his timeshadow extends for the length of his life. His present is his own, but his past in this timestream belongs to another self, with whom he is now entangled.

Ralph, our Ralph, was hungry, despite the unappetizing stink. There was a woman selling pasties from a pot, and another selling soup that was boiling on a fire. Neither of the women looked very clean, and each of them was coughing a lot and spitting out phlegm on the ground. Ralph decided that the soup was probably the safer choice, until he noticed how it was served: ladled into a bowl that each customer drank from in turn. Next time, he'd remember to bring his own cup.

He noticed a man grilling meat on wooden skewers. Just the thing. There was a small crowd around the charcoal-filled trough: a couple of rough-looking men, an old woman, some younger women with truculent expressions on their faces, and a handful of children. A quartet of buskers was singing a motet in mournful medieval harmony. A girl-child of about twelve watched him solemnly and with interest as he approached. Ralph hoped he hadn't made some dreadfully obvious mistake in his clothing, so that he looked a foreigner, but no one else seemed to be paying any attention to him.

As he waited his turn, the child's unblinking stare made him nervous. He was afraid to meet her eyes, and gazed earnestly at his feet, at the ash-dusted charcoal blocks, at the meat. He quickly made his way to the vendor and handed him a dime. The man gazed at it in disbelief, and then looked at Ralph with a canny mixture of greed and suspicion.

"Geunne me unmæðlice unmæta begas, hæðenan hund!"

It was a salad of vowels, fricatives, and glottal stops. But Ralph had realized it would be hard to get a handle on the local dialect, and figured he could get by on charm and sympathy until he worked it out. He smiled, and gestured in sign language that he was deaf.

The vendor stepped back suddenly and, with an expression of fear and revulsion pointed at Ralph and shouted "Swencan bealohydig hwittuxig hæðenan, ellenrofe freondas! Fyllan æfþunca sweordum!" The crowd turned toward him, and started in his direction. They did not look friendly. They were shouting words he could almost understand.

Ralph jabbed desperately at the next link on his mental toolbar.

Bethel, New York, 1969

His heart pounding, Ralph found himself in a farmer's field, in a sea of mud and rain and under-clothed young people. It's okay here, he thought. The vibe was totally mellow, and so were all the people, who were slapping mud on one another and slipsliding around playfully.

The rain was soft and warm, and when it let up, someone handed him a joint. He took a toke and passed it on. How did he know, he wondered, to do that? And why was it called a toke? Time travel was really an amazing groove . . .

A beautiful longhaired boy gave him a brownie, and a beautiful longhaired girl gave him a drink of something sweet and cherry-flavored from a leather wineskin. "You have such a cosmic smile," she said. "Have a great trip, man." She kissed him, evading his hands gracefully and moving away, her thin white caftan clinging damply to her slim body.

Then the music started, and Ralph was pulled like taffy into the story of the song. He was the minstrel from Gaul, the soldier from Dien Bien Phu, the man from Sinai mountain. What did it all mean, he wondered briefly, but then he left meaning behind, and fell into the deep, sugar-rough voice of the singer. He was music itself, pouring out over the crowd, bringing together four hundred thousand people, all separate and all one, like the leaves of a huge tree stirred by a kind breeze, moving gently in the humid, muddy, blissful afternoon.

Time passed. Someone put a ceramic peace symbol on a rawhide thong around his neck. His clothes were muddy and he took them off. Set after set of music played. The sun went down, and it got dark.

The smell was rather strong here, too, he thought: body odors again, and the stink of the overflowing latrines. It was too humid, really, and something had bitten him on the butt. He put his clothes back on, rather grumpily. Ralph was starting to come down, and he was feeling just a little paranoid. Maybe Woodstock wasn't such a good idea . . .

Then the music suddenly stopped, and the lights went out. On stage, people with cigarette lighters scurried about. Finally, a small emergency generator kicked in, and a few dim lights came back on. Arlo Guthrie grabbed the mike, and the crowd cheered him expectantly, though a bit mindlessly. "I dunno if you—" he said. "I dunno, like, how many of you can dig—" He shook his head. He seems a bit stoned, Ralph thought. "—like how many of you can dig how many people there are here, man . . . " Arlo looked around. "But I was just talking to the fuzz, and, hey!—we've got a time traveler here with us." The audience laughed, a huge sound that echoed in the natural amphitheater that sloped up from the stage. Arlo pumped his fist. "We're historic, man! Far fucking out! We! Are! His*toric*!"

Then he shrugged apologetically. "But, can you dig this, the n-dimensional timefield effect has short-circuited the electrical system. We're going to have to call it off. Y'all're gonna have to go home. Sorry about your weekend, people. Good luck getting outta here . . . "

It was dark, but Ralph could sense, somehow, that four hundred thousand people had all turned their heads toward him. He panicked, and stabbed randomly at his mental toolbar.

Wessex, 1441

Damn! He'd hit the Wessex button again. He was back at the market, a year later. Ralph was an engineer: he was, he thought, the kind of man who thinks things through, so he had programmed his mental toolbox not to send him back to the same timespace twice, for fear he'd meet himself, so he knew he was exactly a year—to the second—from his previous appearance. As we know now, of course, that worry was irrelevant, but it adds a certain predictability to his visits to Wessex.

This time, Ralph thought, he would be more circumspect, and wouldn't offer anyone money. It might be that Franklin Delano Roosevelt (or maybe Julius Caesar) was not welcome on coins in this place. Or maybe the sight of a silver coin itself was terrifying. He wouldn't make that mistake again. Maybe he could beg for some small local coins.

Or—that's it!—he could sell his peace symbol. As long as he didn't have to talk to anybody, and could get by on grunts and nods and smiles, he was sure he'd be okay. Thank God he'd put his clothes back on.

Ralph staked himself out a small space and sat down on the ground. He smoothed the dirt in front of him and put the ceramic medallion down in the center of the smooth space.

People walked by him, and he tried to attract their attention. He coughed, he waved, he gestured at the peace medallion. People ignored him. He would have to work harder, he thought, since he wasn't willing to say anything. But he was an engineer: sales had never been his strong point.

So Ralph stood up. He held the medallion out to passersby. They turned their heads away.

Ralph was getting hungry. He thought about the salespeople he knew. They didn't give up: rather, they ingratiated themselves with their potential customers. He looked around nervously.

He noticed a buxom young woman in the crowd, staring at him intently. She was quite a bit older than the girl who had watched him so carefully last time he was here. She was very pretty—maybe he could include her in his sales pitch, and then, after he sold the medallion, he could buy her something safe to eat.

Ralph smiled at her with what he hoped was his most engaging smile and dangled the medallion, swinging it in her direction and then holding it up as though she might like to try it on.

Almost instantly, a crowd formed. Aha! he thought with a grin: the language of commerce is universal. But then he noticed that they were muttering in a very unpleasant tone, picking up stones and glancing in his direction. Whatever they were saying, it sounded like he was in a mess of trouble.

Ralph was getting a little queasy from this rapid temporal disassociation.

He didn't know what is now common knowledge: that the reverse-Schrödinger effect, which creates the dual timeshadow, causes info-seepage from the newly generated parallel self, adding data at a subconscious level.

Superimposition of the time-traveling Ralph over the newly generated stationary Ralph, fixed in the timestream both forward and back, generated a disorienting interference pattern. The traveling Ralph (TR) influenced the stationary Ralph (SR), and vice-versa, though neither was quite aware of the other. Each of them thought he was acting of his own free will—and indeed each one was, for certain values of free.

At any rate, the crowd was ugly, and Ralph didn't feel so good. So, of his own free will, Ralph bailed, whacking the toolbar without saying goodbye to the young woman or, really, paying much mind to where he was headed.

Washington, DC, 1865

Ralph looked around groggily. He was in a theater filled with well-dressed, jolly-looking people, sitting in an uncomfortable seat that was covered in a scratchy red wool. It was anything but soft: horsehair stuffing, probably. The stage in front of him was set as a drawing room. It was lit by lights in the floor that illuminated the actor and actresses rather starkly: a funny-looking, coarsely dressed man and two women in elaborate crinoline dresses.

"Augusta, dear, to your room!" commanded the older of the two actresses, pointing imperiously into the wings, stage right.

"Yes, ma," the young woman said, giving the man a withering glance. "Nasty beast!" she said to him, and flounced off the stage.

The dialog sounded a bit stilted to Ralph's ears, but the audience was genially awaiting the older woman's comeuppance. *Our American Cousin*, he thought abruptly, that's the play—it's been a hit throughout the war.

He glanced up at what was obviously the presidential box: it was twice the size of the other boxes, and the velvet-covered balustrade at its front, overhanging the stage, had been decorated with red-white-and-blue bunting. Just then, President Lincoln leaned forward through the drapery at the front of the box and rested his elbow on the balustrade, to catch the next bit of dialog.

Ralph was dumb-struck, and who would not have been? Medieval England, Woodstock, these had been interesting enough places to visit—but seeing Abraham Lincoln—an iconic figure in American history, an instantly recognizable profile, in the flesh, alive, moving, a real human being, on the very day that the long war had come to a close, with a startlingly cheerful smile on his face as he anticipated a famously comic rejoinder—was to Ralph an intensely moving experience.

He held his breath, frozen, as, at the back of the box, unknown to its occupants, he saw a stunningly handsome man—John Wilkes Booth, he was sure—move in against the wall. Booth pulled out a handgun and drew a bead on the president's head. Without thinking, Ralph leaped to his feet. "Mr. President! Duck!" he shouted.

The gun went off. There were screams and shrieks from the box. A large young man in the presidential party wrestled with Booth, as Lincoln pulled his wife to one side, shielding her. A woman's voice rang out, "They have shot the president! They have shot the president!" Lincoln clutched his shoulder, puzzled but not seriously hurt. Booth leaped for the stage, but strong men grabbed him as he landed, and brought him down.

Oh, cripes, Ralph thought. I've really done it now. This would change the future irrevocably! He would never find his way back to his own time, or anything resembling it. And, panicking, he hit the mental button a third time.

Wessex, 1442

Ralph looked around at the damned medieval street market. This time, before he could say anything, an attractive, dark-haired woman grabbed his upper arm firmly, pulled him close to her, and spoke into his ear. "Keep your mouth shut, if you know what's good for you," she whispered urgently. She looked remarkably like the young woman he had seen before, but a bit older and a lot more intense.

She took him by the arm, and led him through the fair. Toothless old women in their forties offered her root vegetables, but she shook her head. Children tried to sell her sweetmeats, but the young woman pushed on. Without seeming to hurry, without drawing attention to herself or him, she quickly led Ralph to the edge of the fair. People who noticed them smiled knowingly, and some of the men gave him a wink. The woman led him behind a hayrick, a seductive look on her face.

Behind the huge mound of hay, the noise of the fair was diminished, and, for the moment at least, they were visible to no one. The woman's flirtatious manner had vanished. She pushed Ralph away from her and glared at him. Ralph was a little afraid: didn't people in medieval times hit one another a lot? This woman was *mad*.

"Ralph, you idiot!" she said in a low but exasperated voice. She's not speaking Middle English, Ralph thought. Momentarily he wondered: was she a medieval scholar of modern English? Uh . . .

She looked at him sternly. "People here are smarter than you think! You have to take some precautions! You can't just show up and expect everyone to ignore you."

"What?" said Ralph, brilliantly.

"You dunderhead," she said. "You're lucky you weren't burned at the stake. They were waiting for you, or someone like you. Any old time traveler would do."

"What's your name?" Ralph asked.

"I'm Sylvie, but that's not important."

"It's important to me," said Ralph.

She shook off his attention. "Come with me. Don't say a word, don't even open your mouth."

"But how did you know?" said Ralph. "How do you know I'm a time traveler? Why do you speak a language I can understand?"

"Oh, for Pete's sake," said Sylvie. "You were the first, but you're not the only. Historians of time travel come here all the time, to see where you landed on that very first trip. The locals are getting restless. They flayed those travelers they identified, or they burned them, or they pressed them to death with stones. We couldn't let that happen to you, especially before you told us how it worked."

"How on Earth would these yokels have ever noticed me?" he asked.

"Your damn teeth," she said. "Your flawless, glow-in-the-dark, impossibly white teeth." She handed him a rather ugly set of yellowish fake teeth. "Put these on now." Ralph did.

Sylvie then gestured toward a nearby hovel. "Over there," she said. "Inside. It's time for you to explain to me how time travel works." He went where she told him to, and did what she said. How could he not? He was smitten. Fortunately for Ralph, Sylvie was likewise smitten. Many a woman would be, as he was a handsome man with good teeth, and he gave up his secrets readily.

Sylvie then traveled forward, to a time before she was born, and told her parents the secret of time travel. Her parents, who became the most famous temporal anthropologists in history, educated a few others and, when baby Sylvie came along, brought her up to leap gracefully from one century to the next. More gracefully, in fact, than her parents themselves, who vanished in medieval England when Sylvie was twelve. She was, in fact, looking for them when she came upon Ralph that very first time.

Ralph and Sylvie were married in Wessex in 1442, Ralph's dental glory concealed by his fake teeth. Sylvie, inveterate time-traveler that she was, convinced him they should live in the timestream, giving them a sort of temporal immortality. And this is where Ralph, who was, after all, an engineer, not a physicist, failed to anticipate the effect of his actions.

Time does not fly like an arrow, it turns out. It just lies there, waiting for something new to happen. So when Ralph Drumm showed up—completely inappropriately—in the past, that past changed—the past healed itself—so that he had always been there. He acquired ancestors, was born, grew to adulthood—to Ralph's exact age in fact—and his body just happened to be in the exact place where Ralph's time-shadow showed up.

Time travel changes the past as well as the future: time is, in fact, an eternal present when viewed from outside the timestream.

So, as Ralph and Sylvie moved from time to time, they created more and more shadows of themselves in the timestream. As they had children—one, two, three, many—and took them about, the timeshadows of the Drumm children were generated and multiplied. Each shadow was as real as the original. Each shadow lived and breathed . . . and bred.

Although they were innocent of any ill intent, Ralph and Sylvie Drumm changed the flow of the stream of time in a way more profound than could be accomplished by any single action, no matter how momentous its apparent effect. Their genetic material came to dominate all of human history, an endless army of dark-haired, blue-eyed Caucasians with perfect teeth. They looked the same. They thought the same. They stuck together.

And this is why we, the last remnants of a differentiated humanity, are waiting here today in Wessex, in 1440—to defend our future from the great surge of the Drummstream. This time, they will not escape us.

₪

NUMBER 73 GLAD AVENUE
₪
Suzanne J. Willis

"What time does the clock have, Charlie?" Mary looked left, dark, bobbed hair brushing her shoulders. She heard him mutter then carefully shut the doors, locking the timepieces away, before walking around to face her, his little tin feet clicking softly against the wooden floor.

"Twelve May 1923. Six p.m."

She looked down at Charlie as he packed the powders and glass vials, which were no bigger than her thumbnail, into the black leather doctor's bag, before climbing in and settling into the spare space at the side. At twelve inches tall, he just fit inside, with a whisker of room between his head and the bag's brass clasps. "Comfortable?" she asked.

"I'll be better when we've arrived. Let's get going." He clapped his hands together then waved as she shut him in.

Mary walked down the street. Silver waves of time flowed around her in a shimmering cascade as the buildings, the path, the people disappeared or grew or shrank into their new lines as required. Each step carried her quite gradually from 1852 to 1923, the bag clenched firmly in her hand, and she gave a little shiver. *It's so different*, she thought. All the beautiful clean lines, the geometric shapes of the buildings fronted with sunbursts and arching curves: the simple luxury of it all. Visiting the twenties—whether from the past or the misty future—never ceased to amaze her. There was something so fresh and almost, well, bouncy about it. It was an era in which Mary felt revived, which was no easy feat given that she and Charlie were constantly scissoring back and forth between the decades, centuries, epochs.

It had been so long now, Mary had quite forgotten how their journey back and forth through time was supposed to end. She shook that thought away; better to let these things work themselves out.

The air stilled and she looked around. Horse-drawn carriages had given way to automobiles, sleek and chrome, slinking down the road. A shiny brick-red model passed by, the jaguar in mid-leap on the hood shining under the late afternoon sun. The driver whistled at Mary and tipped his hat as she smiled back.

"What is that infernal racket?" came Charlie's muffled voice from inside the bag.

Mary listened for a moment. There it was—the unmistakable sound of jaunty pianos and sexy, snaking trumpets. She realized she was tapping her foot.

"It's jazz, Charlie, you old stick-in-the-mud. And *I* quite like it."

He mumbled a reply.

"It's strange, though. Today doesn't *feel* terribly important. There's usually someth—"

"Number 73 Glad Avenue," was the exasperated response from the bag.

"Right you are, Charlie."

Number 73 was set on a huge expanse of land fronting the river. Geraldine, their employer for the evening, led Mary into the front room that overlooked the lawn rolling down to the river bank, a dark emerald in the dying light.

"And here's the bar." Geraldine pointed to the buffet unit in the corner. "Walnut, with marble top, if I'm not mistaken? And chrome trim."

Geraldine nodded. "We had it shipped all the way from New York, you know. There's not another one like it in the world."

"It's beautiful. And quite perfect for what we have in mind. I hope I don't seem immodest, but you couldn't have chosen a better hostess. You and your guests are in for a treat," Mary smiled. "I do so love a good party, Geraldine."

"You don't appear to have brought much with you, dear," Geraldine pointed at the black bag.

"There's not a lot I need, as you'll see." Mary opened the clasps and brought out a miniature replica of the walnut and marble unit, placing it in the center of the real one.

Geraldine looked shocked. "But how could you know?"

"Ah, now, a magician never reveals her secrets." With that, she pulled Charlie from the bag and stood him up behind the little bar, where he looked for all the world like a china doll with twinkling blue-glass eyes and impressively thick moustache. Mary smoothed his ginger hair.

"He's just adorable," Geraldine said.

"And quite the star of the show, as you'll see. I'm fine to see to things here, if you'd like to get ready for your guests. Of course, we do require payment up front . . ."

"Oh, naturally, yes." Geraldine rummaged through the drawers of a dark bureau on the other side of the room. For the sake of discretion, Mary turned and walked over to the tall, arched windows. She looked at the long wooden jetty. A woman sat at the end, silhouetted against the sunset-flamed river, her toes skimming the water.

"Beautiful at this time of day, isn't it?"

Mary smiled. "It's like something out of *The Great Gats—*" she stopped herself. *That's not until 1925!*

"From what, dear?"

"Oh, nothing. Who is that sitting on the end of the jetty?"

"That's my older sister, Freya. She's a funny thing, keeps quite to herself and . . . but I'm rattling on, here you go." Geraldine held out a gold pocket watch; it swung gently on the end of its chain and caught the last rays of the sun. "It hasn't worked for years, but it does pain me to part with it. It was my grandfather's. Still, you come so highly recommended." She paused, glancing at Mary suspiciously. "If you don't mind my saying so, it does seem like an odd price . . ."

With a beatific smile, Mary reached out for the watch. As metal and flesh came into contact, the watch shivered, its gold sparking in the gathering dark. She shifted it in her hands: it warmed to her touch. *Click.* The cover sprang back to reveal the ornate hands slowly journeying around its pale face. The second hand was missing.

"Well, now, look at that. It seems to be working after all. Even has the right time." She waved her free hand at Geraldine, dismissing her confusion. "Which means *you* must go and get ready."

Once Geraldine was gone Charlie stretched and yawned on the bar, blinking his glassy eyes. He jumped into the bag, rummaged about then jumped out again with several vials. He began to mix the powders and fluids together in a bell-shaped bottle, humming softly to himself.

The jetty drew Mary's gaze again. Freya was walking along it towards the shore, leaving a trail of silvered footprints shining like old stars.

Mary smiled at the women—*flappers*, she remembered—in their feathered headpieces and beaded frocks; at the men in their razor-sharp suits as they lit cigarettes in long holders for their paramours. Her own close-fitted dress was black, long-sleeved, innocuous; the only feature was a row of silver buttons down her back. But the colors the flappers wore! And the fabrics! The delicate, diaphanous skirts; the trailing ribbons from dropped waists; the long strings of jewels, darlings, the jewels.

The parquetry floor shook and the chandeliers tinkled as the guests shook and shimmied and stomped to the jazz band, its piano, trumpet, and Sharkey Malone's whiskey-voice jumping across the night. No one looked lonesome in a corner, or was without one of Charlie's fabulous gin martinis or old-fashioneds. Everything was going to plan.

"I would honestly love to know how that little barman doll works. He seems so like-life . . . lifely . . . um, *real*." Geraldine had crept up behind Mary and slung an arm around her shoulder. Her voice was a little slurred and her headpiece of peacock feathers and jet sat askew.

"He's always a hit. But now, I think, would be a good time for the main event, seeing as the band's about to break." She signaled to Sharkey Malone, who pulled a worn little hipflask from his pocket and toasted in reply. "If you'll just get everyone to—"

"Darlings. My lovely katty-kits. No, wait—my kitty cats . . . " Geraldine giggled and swayed as all eyes turned towards her. She waved a hand at Mary, who felt a little thrill run through her. *This* was what she had been waiting for.

"Ladies and gentlemen, if you'd like to form an orderly line in front of the bar, we have a rather special treat for the evening, courtesy of the lovely Geraldine," Mary smiled winningly.

The crowd cheered as she walked to the bar and stood beside Charlie. Tiny ruby glasses, about twice the size of a thimble, were stacked on the right of his little bar. On the left were the bell-shaped bottle and two chrome cocktail shakers. The booze, she knew, would be on the shelf underneath.

"You really are an old pro, aren't you, Charlie?" Mary whispered to him. He replied with a wink.

"Whiskey or gin?" asked Mary of the first guest, a plump woman with a fur-trimmed neckline and tight rings that made her fingers look like sausages.

"Whiskey, thanks, honey."

At this stage of the evening Charlie could relax a little. People were drunk enough not to notice that his movements were fluid, less like a spring-powered automaton. It was exhausting to keep that act up all night, she knew. He deserved to have a little fun with his favorite part of the night.

He poured the whiskey into the shaker, over crushed ice, followed by a shot of something shimmering that looked like liquid violets.

"Hang on a minute, honey. That's not anything that's *stronger* than booze now, is it? If you get my drift." The plump woman looked concerned.

"Madam, I assure you we serve nothing dangerous."

"Now who's the old pro?" whispered Charlie under his moustache. The shaker frosted over as he gave it a quick, expert shake. He lifted it high in the air, straining the beverage into one of the ruby glasses. A fine mist wafted from the liquid as it waterfalled into it; the sound of children's laughter splashed up from the drink.

"Now isn't that just the strangest thing?" The woman's pink-painted lips curved into a smile, her chubby cheeks shining. She held the glass up to the light; crimson sparkles shone on the wall behind it.

Mary smiled back. "Now if you'd like to make your way to the lawn?"

The plump woman stood aside for a man in a brown fedora.

"Whiskey or gin?"

They streamed to the bar, full of laughter and disinhibition. Mary watched Charlie pass another tiny glass of violet liquid to a smiling, swaying man, reveling in their abandonment.

Geraldine waved at Mary as the last guest wandered outside. "Bottoms up, darlings!" she cried, downing the drink in one mouthful as Mary switched off the lights.

Charlie wiped out the cocktail shakers as he looked out the window. "Admiring your handiwork?" Mary asked.

"It never gets dull, does it? I mean, I never quite know how they're going to react . . . "

"Look," she whispered. The crescent moon was slung low on the horizon, refusing to illuminate the garden with more than a wan glow. Geraldine laughed, a raucous guffaw from her belly. As it rang out, the laughter vapourized into yellow light, like boiling water into steam. It broke off into tiny pieces that flew up into amber lanterns that Mary had earlier strung through the trees, around the ironwork fencing, along the edges of the lawn. Luminous, the lanterns lit the party with the light of a worn-through sunset. Silhouettes of the ants and insect wings forever frozen in the amber filled the grounds.

"Beautiful as ever," Charlie sighed. "It does seem sad, though, that they don't ever remember it."

"Perhaps. But it doesn't mean that it doesn't change them, that they don't carry it with them." Laughing softly, she pointed toward the plump woman who had taken the first drink. All her flapper frippery had fallen off, discarded on the damp grass. She stretched, her body elongating, the soft white flesh stretching and curving around the changing bones. An unseen vessel tipped over her head, spilling shining liquid until she was coated head to foot in chrome. Naked, unadorned, she arched her back in an imitation of the Diana lamps and ashtrays of the day.

"Amazing, isn't it, what people can do when you take back just a little time from them?" Mary never grew tired of the endless shapes, the form and formlessness that rested under the layers of time that humans wore like a shell. She wondered what would happen if it was age, the strangely complicated effect of time, that was stripped away. But the drink took back time itself, bringing out all the possibilities that the years steal away.

"So that's how you do it, then."

Mary jumped. The arrival of the owner of that low, sweet voice meant that they had a problem on their hands.

Charlie froze, the tiny white towel swaying in his hand.

Freya, in cloche hat and almond-colored wrapover coat, walked from the shadows, smiling. She looked like she was holding a secret inside her, beating like a second heart. Mary reached up to smooth down her hair, something she only did when she was unsettled.

"I don't believe you've had one of Charlie's drinks . . . "

Freya laughed. "I don't know that I will, in any event." She moved to the window; Mary felt a small electric shock as Freya's arm brushed hers. They stood together and looked onto the changing quicksilver shapes in the flickering shadows. Mary was surprised that Freya didn't seem shocked by any of it.

"Geraldine always was a scattered girl. Never too sure what she wanted." Freya pointed to her sister, who was filled with light from within, illuminating the network of veins, arteries, capillaries under her skin. The light dimmed and she laughed as a monkey tail poked out from the waistband of her skirt and wound around her waist. The guests giggled and chattered, jazz dancing through the trees. A man looked down as his body transformed into a series of geometric, frosted glass panels separated by thin lead welds. His friend leaned down to peer through the glass, seemingly unperturbed by the snowy wings that had grown where his ears should be.

Geraldine laughed and swung her tail—quite flirtatiously, Mary thought—at a woman whose skin had turned a mottled sea-blue. Delicate leafy sea dragons swum around her wrists and wove through her hair as it drifted as though tugged by the tide and unseen currents.

"We don't allow people to witness our parties if they aren't prepared to participate." Charlie sounded a lot less amiable than usual and Mary noticed he was holding an icepick, its point gleaming. She shook her head at him, not wanting to have to take Freya's time by force. That was a messy business at best and could turn ugly. "Easy, Charlie. Easy," she whispered.

"But I *have* seen one before. Don't you remember?" Freya looked surprised, then took a step backwards as she glanced at Charlie's icepick. "You told me to be patient because you'd come back and I would discover things way beyond what I had seen that night." She held her left hand out to Mary, palm upturned.

The skin of her wrist was pale, the veins cobalt underneath. Between the delicate layers was a watch hand, pointing toward her palm.

Mary recognized it instantly. "That's the second hand from your grandfather's watch," she said.

"So you do remember!"

Mary shook her head. "I'm afraid not. We've never met before, but . . . things that have happened in your past may be going to happen in our future, see?" *Why am I telling her this?* she wondered.

Charlie scowled as her words spilled out.

She hurried on. "So you had better tell your story so we can see exactly what's going on." *And how on earth we're going to deal with it*, she thought.

Freya looked nervously at Charlie, the icepick still in his hand. Mary frowned. "Put it *away* Charlie."

Grumbling, Charlie reluctantly stowed the weapon under his counter.

"I was only seven," Freya began "when my grandparents had a party, just like this one. The world in 1889 was a lot different to the world now—it was all propriety and manners and rules—it was claustrophobic, especially for a child. I couldn't sleep and lay in bed, listening to the party downstairs. And then I heard your voice, Mary, calling for everyone to line up for the evening's special treat—just like you did earlier tonight. I crept to the top of the stairs and I, I saw . . . it was just like tonight, people changing into things I'd never dreamed of. Can you imagine what that was like for a child?"

A loud bang on the window made them all jump. An enormous peacock, still with human legs, lay sprawled on the grass, shaking its head.

"Amateur," muttered Charlie.

"I wanted to join them," Freya went on "and I crept out from my hiding place, made it to the first landing. That was when you saw me, Mary. You walked up the stairs towards me and I thought you were so lovely, so different. But as you got closer, I felt very peculiar . . . sort of still from the inside out."

Mary glanced across at Charlie, who shrugged his shoulders. "You introduced yourself, held out your hand and when I shook it, the stillness filled me up entirely and we shone then, Mary, you and I, like a shooting star. 'Here she is,' you called quietly downstairs. And then you leaped up, Charlie, nimble as you please, to say hello."

"And the watch hand?" he asked.

"My grandfather's watch was there on the bureau. You fiddled about with it for a bit, then asked me to hold out my arm. You told me not to look and that it would feel a bit like a bee sting. When it was done, you said that it would remind me to wait for you. To wait for my new life. And I've been waiting ever since."

Charlie began polishing the cocktail shakers, even though they were already clean. "And now that we're back, what is it you want?"

Freya looked surprised. "To come with you, of course."

The shaker clattered to the floor. "We're not taking applications, here! This is a two-man gig."

"But I've been waiting *my whole life*. It's already happened, don't you see? My past, your future, it must all lead to now. You talk about taking people's time, but I've given all my time just waiting, knowing you'd come back."

Mary turned toward the window, unable to look at Freya's hopeful face. Geraldine's guests were scattered across the lawn in little groups; some dancing, others with their arms, or fins or wings, wrapped around one another singing. They were all having the night of their lives, in exchange for just a little of their time.

"You know, Charlie and I have traveled an awful lot and seen some amazing things. This is a magical decade to be living through. You should be out there enjoying it, not wanting to come along with the two of us." She turned to face Freya, who was twisting her hands anxiously. "Listen to that wonderful jazz. Doesn't that make you want to forget everything and just *be*?"

In a shadowy corner of the garden, the band played, their instruments now part of them. The fat bellied bassist *was* the double bass, the trumpeter's trumpet sprouted from his lips. Sharkey Malone, of course, was still Sharkey Malone, but with every gravelly note he sang, a bronze honey-bee flew from his lips and there was just a glimpse of the piano keys that had taken the place of his teeth. "When I hear it, it makes me think of timeless things, like I can see into forever. I'm not like them." She looked mischievously at Charlie. "And I'll prove it. I'll have one of your special drinks, please. Gin," she stated, before Charlie could ask.

Mary sighed, relieved, then smiled at Charlie, who was making a double for Freya. This would fix the whole issue once and for all. A drink, a transformation, a blissful forgetting would leave them in the clear. No matter what Freya said, she didn't belong with them.

"One more question. What do you do with the time that you take back?"

"When we know that," said Charlie "it'll be time to go home."

Freya lifted the tiny glass, the violet liquid shining. "To tomorrow," she said, then downed it in one shot. She glided outside, where she was joined by a swarm of dragonflies, their wings shimmering Lalique-green and plum, which had previously been a rather prim man in a pinstripe suit.

"So that's that, then," said Charlie. "I think we better—"

"Go while we have the chance?"

"Couldn't have said it better, old girl."

Mary and Charlie whisked around the room, collecting bottles and glasses and packing them into the black bag. She snapped the case shut and picked it up as Charlie climbed up onto her shoulder.

They went out onto the lawn, for their traditional last walk-through of a party. To their left the plump woman who had become a chrome goddess lay sleeping, like a fallen statue. The dragonflies buzzed about in a man-shape, hovering around the amber lights. And the band played on, a sad, sweet dirge.

> Ain't no sun, my autumn girl
> Ain't no moon or rain
> Got an empty home, an empty heart
> Since the sunrise stole you away . . .

"Well, bugger me . . . "

"Charlie! Language."

On their right was a giant willow tree; at its base stood Freya, her eyes dark and sparkling.

Mary stared, her eyes wide. "You've not changed one bit. And that was a double dose. How?"

"I told you, I'm not like them. I'm all still inside. Only after I had that drink, this happened."

Mary and Charlie looked down at Freya's wrist. The watch hand was moving, now, ticking away second by second. They reached out and rested their forefingers gently over it. Freya's time pulsed through them and it felt like exaltation.

Mary clasped her hand. "Time is indeed the fabulous monster in us all. The difference is in what you do with it. Best you do come along with us, after all."

They set out for the jetty, stretching out across the darkened river that held the night reflected.

On the shore sat Geraldine, propped against a fig tree and snoring softly. Her dark locks lifted gently in the breeze, rippling and shaking as they parted to reveal glossy black feathers. With a fierce beating of wings, the sky was filled with ravens from her hair.

Freya bent to kiss her sleeping sister, then followed her new companions waiting on the jetty. Mary sat on the edge, Charlie still on her shoulder.

"What time does the clock have, Charlie?"

He swung from her shoulder and began to climb down her back, deftly unclasping the square silver buttons that ran the length of her spine. As he undid the last one, the doors of her back opened wide. She heard Freya gasp as she looked inside and wondered what it must be like to see it for the first time; a giant hourglass in the center, surrounded by carefully hung fob watches, alarm clocks, chronographs, and wristwatches, with a stone sundial sitting at her left hip. They softly ticked and swung, the silvery river of time swirling and twisting around them and shivering the sand in the hourglass.

"Twenty-one July 1969, 2:56 a.m." He shut the doors, then gave Mary a wink before hopping into the bag.

"Now that *does* feel like a celebration," Freya said.

"You just wait," replied Mary.

The air around them quivered and flowed as they walked toward the end of the jetty . . .

ꖴ

THE LOST CANAL
₪
michael moorcock

1
Martian Manhunt

Mac Stone was in trouble. He heard the steady *slap-slap-slap* of the P140 auto-Bannings and knew they'd licked the atmosphere problem. That gadget could now find a man, stun him, or kill him according to whatever orders had come from Terra. If necessary, the bionic "wombots" it carried could follow him into space. The things worked by popping in and out of regular space the way you bunch up a piece of cloth and stick a needle through it to save time and energy. Human physiology couldn't stand those instant translations—in and out, in and out through the cosmic "folds"—but the wombot wasn't human; it moved swiftly and easily in that environment. Flying at cruising speed for regular space-time, the wombot could cross a million miles as if they were a hundred. The thing was a terrible weapon, outlawed on every solar colony, packing several features into one—surveillance, manhunter, ordnance. If Mac were unlucky, they'd just use it to stun him. So they could take their time with him back at RamRam City.

Why do they want me this bad? He was baffled.

They had him pinned down. In all directions lay the low lichen-covered Martian hills: ochre, brown, and a thousand shades of yellow-gray almost as far as he could see. You couldn't hide in lichen. Not unless you could afford a mirror suit. Beyond the hills were the mountains, each taller than Everest, almost entirely unexplored. That was where he was heading before a wombot scented heat from his monoflier and took it out in a second. Four days after that, they hit his camp with a hard flitterbug and almost finished him off. Nights got colder as the East wind blew. Rust-red dust swept in from the desert, threatening his lungs. It whispered against his day-suit like the voices of the dead.

If they didn't kill him, autumn would.

Mac plucked his last thin jane from his lips and pinched off the lit end. He'd smoke it later. If there was any "later." The IMF had evidently gotten themselves some of the new bloodhound wombots, so compact and powerful they could carry a body to Phobos and back. Creepy little things, not much bigger than an adult salmon. They made him feel sick. He still hoped he might pick the site of his last fight. He had only had two full charges left in his reliable old Banning-6 pistol. After that, he had a knife in his boot and some knucks in his pocket. And then his bare hands and his teeth.

They had called Stone a wild animal back on Mercury and they were right. The Callisto slave-masters had made him into one after they pulled him from a sinking lavasub. He'd been searching for the fabled energy crowns of the J'ja. The rebel royal priests had been planning to blast Spank City to fragments before the IMF found the secret of their fire boats and quite literally stopped them cold, freezing them in their tracks, sending the survivors out to *Panic*, the asteroid that liked to call herself a ship. But the J'ja had hidden their crowns first.

So long ago. He'd been in some tough spots and survived, but this time it seemed like he'd run out of lives and luck.

You didn't get much cover in one of the old flume holes. They'd been dug when some crazy twenty-second century Terran wildcat miners thought they could cut into the crust and tap the planet's plasma. They believed there were rivers of molten gold down there. They claimed that they heard them at night when they slept curled within the cones. Someone had fallen into a particularly deep one and sworn he had seen molten platinum running under his feet. Poor devils. They'd spent too long trying to make sense of the star-crowded sky. Recently, he'd heard that the inverted cones were used by hibernating ock-crocks. Mac hoped he wasn't waking anything up down there. He doubted the theory and did his best not to think about it, to keep out of sight and to drop his body temperature as much as he dared, release a few dead fuel pods and hope that the big Banning bloodbees would mistake him for an old wreck and its dead pilot and pass him by.

"You only need fear the bees if you've broken the law." That familiar phrase was used to justify every encroachment on citizens' liberty. Almost all activities were semi-criminal these days. Mars needed cheap human workers. Keep education as close as possible to zero. The prisons were their best resource. Industrial ecology created its own inevitable logic.

Sometimes you escaped the prisons and slipped back into RamRam City, where you could live relatively well if you knew how to look after yourself. Sometimes they just let you stay there until they had a reason to bring you in or get rid of you.

And that's what they appeared to be doing now.

Slap-slap-slap.

Why were they spending so much money to catch him? He knew what those machines cost. Even captured, he wasn't worth a single wombot.

Wings fluttering, big teeth grinding, the flier was coming over the horizon, and, by the way it hovered and turned in the thin air, Mac's trick hadn't fooled it at all. Good handling. He admired the skill. Private. Not IMF at all. One guy piloting. One handling the ordnance. Or maybe one really *good* hunter doing both. He reached to slide off the pistol's safety. Looked like he was going down fighting. He wondered if he could hit the pilot first.

Stone was a Martian born in the shadow of Low-Canal's massive water-tanks. The district had never really been a canal. It had been named by early explorers trying to make sense of the long, straight indentations, now believed to be the foundations of a Martian city. But it was where most of AquaCorps's water was kept. Water was expensive and had to be shipped in from Venus. Sometimes there would be a leakage, and, with kids like him, he could collect almost a cup before the alarms went. His mother lived however she could in the district. His father had been a space ape on the wild Jupiter runs, carbon rods rotting and twisting as they pulled pure uranium from the Ki Sea. He'd probably died when the red spot erupted, taking twenty u-tankers with it.

When he was seven, his ma sold Mac to a mining company looking for kids small enough to fit into the midget tunnelers working larger asteroids and moons able to support a human being for a year or so before they died. His mother had known that "indentured" was another word for death sentence. She knew that he was doomed to breathe modified methane until his lungs and all his other organs and functions gave out.

Only Mac hadn't died. He'd stolen air and survived and risen, by virtue of his uninhibited savagery, in what passed for Ganymedan society. Kru miners made him a heroic legend. They betrothed him to their daughters.

Stone was back on Mars and planning to ship out for Terra when his mother sent word that she wanted to tell him something. He'd gone to Tank Town with the intention of killing her. When he saw her, the anger went out of him. She was a lonely old woman lacking status or family. He'd only be doing her a favor if he finished her off. So he let it go. And realized that she'd been holding her breath as he held his, and he turned and laughed that deep slow purr she knew from his father. This made her note his tobacco-colored skin, now seamed like well-used leather, and she wept to read in his face all the torments he had endured since she'd sold him. So he had let her die believing a lie, that they enjoyed a reconciliation What he said or thought didn't mean much to the Lord she believed in.

After that, he'd started stealing jewels with a vengeance. Good ones. Big ones. He'd done very well. Hitting the mining trains. Fencing them back through Earth. Generous, like most thieves of his kind, and therefore much liked by the Low-Canal folk who protected him, he'd done well. He was one of their own, accepted as a Martian hero with stories told about him as V-dramas. Only two people had made it out of the Tanks to become famous on the V. Mac Stone was one, and Yily Chen, the little Martian girl he'd played hide-and-go-seek with as a kid, was the other. Yily now operated from Earth, mostly doing jobs the corps didn't want anyone to associate directly with them. Her likeness had never been published. He remembered her for her lithe, brown body, her golden eyes. He'd loved her then. He couldn't really imagine what she looked like now. No doubt she'd become some hard-faced mother superior, pious and judgmental, like most tankers who grew up staying within the law, such as it was. She had put Tank Town behind her. He'd elected to stay. But he'd been sold out once again, this time to the Brothers of the Fiery Mount, whoever they were. They put him back to work on Ganymede with no idea he had family there.

Then some war broke out on Terra for a while. It couldn't have come at a better time. It destroyed the old cartels and opened the planet up to real trade. And everyone wanted to rearm of course.

By the third month of Stone's return, his clan, riding a wave of similar revolutions through the colonies, had conquered a significant number of exec towers and looted a museum for a heliograph system they'd been able to copy. Communications. Codes. Bribes. Clever strategy. Guerilla tactics. By the sixth month, as they prepared for the long tomorrow, they had won the moon and were doing business with four of the richest nations of Terra and New Japan.

Meanwhile, over at the freshly built Martian Scaling Station, the "black jump" was opening up the larger universe hidden in the folds of space-time through which the wombots traveled. They'd begun to realize that they were part of a denser, mostly invisible cosmos. Until recently, the "cosmic fog" had obscured so much from the astronomers. The discovery brought about new power shifts and unexpected alliances. With the right start, they said, some of those worlds could be reached in days! Now it didn't matter if Terra was dying. Was that really the prevailing logic?

Mac knew that he and the human race were at some sort of crossroads, poised at last on their way to the stars. They might find an unbeatable enemy out there. Or beatable enemies. Or they could learn to negotiate. The game Mac knew best wasn't necessarily the best game. For now, however, he needed capital to play with the big guys, and he was never going to get that kind of money in one piece. Not while he remained an outworld Martian wolfshead. He knew enough about those odds. He knew who the men were who owned the worlds. All of which was to his advantage. His equal share of the Ganymede profits wasn't large enough and he didn't like his public profile getting bigger. He'd made his ex-brother-in-law boss and quietly returned to Mars and his old trade. He—or really the pseudonym he'd chosen—developed a serious reputation. He was credited with any number of unsolved cases. No one knew what to expect from him. Few knew his face or his real name. A fist diamond had paid to have every mugshot and most records wiped. He began to build his pile. The first thing he needed was a good ship of his own. He went into water brokerage. He had a half share in an atmosphere factory. He was earning that ship when he'd been, he assumed, betrayed. He wondered if that had anything to do with the sneaky little Venusian lep who had come to see him with a suspicious offer a week or two before his arrest.

To his surprise, because it was a special private prison, they took him straight to Tarpauling Hill. Or meant to. Escaping his escort had not been difficult. Escaping a planet was going to be harder.

This was his eighth Martian day on the run. There were no real maps of the hinterland. He knew the Interplanetary Military Force. They let their big robot Bannings loose if they thought that someone was hiding in an area. He could have stayed in RamRam City, hidden in the tanks, but it would get expensive in terms of human lives. He'd had to lead them into wild, unpopulated country or they might have killed half Low-Canal's population. Out to the wide valleys and high mountains of the Monogreanimi, where, it was said, the old high queens of Mars still dreamed in the deep ice.

Mac was trying to find one of the legendary "blow holes," sunk by Mars's last race, who had been seeking air for the shelters in which they'd taken refuge from the Long Rain, the incessant meteor storms pulverizing the planet. The falling meteors had destroyed almost every sign of the dozen or so major civilizations who had once ruled a Mars almost as lush as Venus.

Mac hated Venus. He hated her fecundity as well as her unpredictable gas storms, which regularly wiped out hundreds. Terran Venusians went crazy just to survive the extremes. He hated native Venusians, the smelly little green people nicknamed leprechauns by Terrans. He hated Terrans, too. And he really hated Mercury. Mars, he could not help loving. He loved her vast, tranquil deserts, her hills and high wild mountains where nothing breathed. Once he'd longed to make her self-sustaining again. He'd dreamed of bringing in enough water to make her bloom as she had in the days when the few surviving pictograms and engravings had been created. When she still had seas. There were other legends of how she had been, but these could all be traced back to myths created in the twentieth and twenty-first centuries.

All Mac wanted was the reality. To see the canals running again while sun and moons illuminated blue forests and small fields of brass-colored crops. To settle down on a few acres of land, growing enough to sell and sustain himself. Then maybe a family. To make a new Mars, a peaceful Mars where kids could grow. That's what he'd dreamed. That's what had kept him alive all these years. He let out a brief, not particularly bitter, laugh. Now the best he could hope for was a quick death.

He wondered if he could gain any time by giving himself up in the hope that he'd find another chance of escape. It would avoid what was probably an inevitable death out here. He had to take control of his own determined soul, which would rather fight and die than wait for another chance. But that was all he could do. He got hold of himself and, disgusted by his chosen action, he snarled and pulled a big white silk scarf out of a leg pouch in his leathers.

He was tying this to the barrel of his Banning when he felt something moist, cold, and scaly slip around his ankle and give it an experimental tug.

He yanked free. It took a tighter hold. It seemed patient. It knew he couldn't escape. He'd done his best to keep clear of the wombot's sensors, but his movement had already alerted the thing. It chickled out a challenge. Again, he tried to yank his leg away.

The wombot spit a bubble of death syrup all over the nearby rocks. They weren't going to waste valuable gas or darts on him unless they had to. At least he wasn't going to need a white flag. Now he knew that they wanted him dead rather than alive.

Below Mac, the ground powdered. The tentacle tugged harder and the area beneath him broke open, dragging him down a fissure, scraping every inch of his day suit. The suit's circuits wouldn't survive another attack. Suddenly, it was inky-dark. He heard the odd rattle and boom of the thing's heart-lung. He forgot the native name someone had guessed at, but it was without doubt an ock-croc.

Mac Stone prepared himself for death.

2

To Destroy the Future

He was still trying to point his pistol when the fissure became a tunnel, thick with something caked around its sides. The worst stink in creation. Croc dung! Threat of death really did sharpen the memory. That's what it coated its long burrow with. The Martian *wanal* or ock-croc was the only large predator left. These giant tentacled reptilian insects drove deep burrows using old blow-holes or wells, they weren't particular. They hibernated for years, woke up very hungry. The first hatchling typically ate all its siblings and sometimes its parent. Then it ate whoever was still hibernating. Although not radioactive themselves, they preferred areas still "buzzy" and lethal to humans. If the crock didn't eat Stone right away, the chances were he'd soon die painfully of radiation poisoning.

"Oh, damn!" He couldn't do anything with his holstered gun. The thing seemed to know precisely how to catch him so he did it the least damage. He had to be many meters down now, the Banning long since passed out of sight and was no longer his main fear. A bionic wombot might follow him, but so far he felt relatively sanguine about that. The chances were the crock would also eat the wombot, built in explosives and all! The thought gave Mac a brief moment of satisfaction.

The tunnel opened into a pit occupied by a huge pulsing head with six round eyes the size of portholes, which slowly retreated from him as a single tentacle—one of many—dragged him deeper.

Mac did all he could to slow his descent into the pit, where its own green-yellow luminescence revealed the croc's enormous carcass. A nightmare of snakelike waving arms with a long snout full of dagger-size needles for teeth, the wriggling body a black blob of scaly horror. More tentacles snared him so that he couldn't move any part of his body without making things worse. He was resigned to what must happen next.

He heard a double click as the thing disconnected its jaw, ready to swallow him. Then he thought he heard human speech. One tentacle released his right arm. If he could only get hold of his gun, he might not kill the crock but he'd give it the worst attack of indigestion it had known in all its long, quasi-reptilian life. He made one last lunge. His fingers clutched for the butt.

As his Banning came loose, something else fell out of the air and rattled on the rock. He looked down, and saw a tiny blue flickering of flame. Voices seemed to jeer inside his head.

He felt horribly cold. At this rate, he'd freeze to death before the crock ate him. The questor had found him just as he was making camp. He'd had to move fast. When the Martian night caught him without his Hopkins blanket, it would be over anyway. The *wanal* only had to wait for him to lose a little more heat. They were famous for their cunning patience. Once, there had been a dozen varieties of the creature. Mac had seen pictures of them in the old hunting cubes of the Sindolu, the extinct nomads of the Northern hemisphere, from whose encampments a few artifacts had been miraculously preserved. The *wanal* they had feared most had massive mandibles and ten tentacles. This was that kind of *wanal*.

It reached out for him again, giggling its nasty pleasure. Then it hesitated. Something red and dripping was thrown to it over the edge of the pit. Then a sharp command came from the darkness and it backed off, peering hungrily from him to the meat.

Snagging the hard case containing the flickering blue flame, Mac pocketed the thing and made haste to clamber as best he could up the other side of the rough pit. The slippery shale made climbing difficult, but he virtually levitated himself out of there. He took the case with the flickering flame out of his glove and put it on the palm of his hand. It made a small hiss. What in the nine inhabited worlds was it? He sensed danger, glanced to his right.

Mac glared in utter disbelief at a bulky "noman" staring down at him from illuminated eyes, hooked hands resting on its metal hips. A type of robot he'd never seen. It looked local. Like something he'd come across in the Terran Museum of Martian artifacts. Only that one had been about a foot high and carved from pink teastone. The archeologists thought it was a household god or a child's toy.

Just above the faceless noman, a pale green pillar fizzed like bad Galifrean beer. Then it coalesced into a figure that Stone was surprised to see was human. A bronzed man in the peak of physical condition, wearing less than was considered seemly even on Jambock Boulevard. Except for the little signs of regular wear and tear on his leather harness, the man looked like something out of a serial V-drama. At his right hip was a big old-fashioned brass-and-steel pistol. Scabbarded on his left was some kind of long, antique sword. For a wild moment, Stone wondered if he had been captured by those crazy re-enacters who played out completely unlikely battles between invented Martian races. He'd seen groups of them in Sunday Field on vacation afternoons.

The guy in the green pillar fizzed again and broke up a few times before he stabilized long enough to say clearly: "You can't fight me. I'm not actually here. I'm a scientist. I'm from Earth like you. I came to Mars millennia ago, long before the meteor storms. I'm projecting this image into my future. It's interactive."

He smiled. "I'm Miguel Krane." Evidently, he expected Mac to know the name. He had an old-fashioned accent Mac associated with Terra. "We call this little device a chronowire. It sends images and sounds back and forth across time. It is the nearest we've been able to come to time travel. Living organisms get seriously damaged. We discovered to our cost that people and animals can't travel physically in time. The *wanal* won't bother you now. Her old responses are still reachable in her deep sub-conscious. In our time, we domesticate and use her ancestors to find lost travelers. Their natural instinct is to eat us, but thousands of years of training changed their brains. We found her down here with our explorer noman. We sent her for you. In case of any problems, we fed her some sleepy meat. I'm sorry about the crude robot, too. Believe it or not, he's code-activated! We have to work through remote control with what we can find. In this case, very remote! What do you want to know from me?"

Mac shuddered as he scraped gelatinous stuff from his battered day suit. He looked around. A manmade room. Two doors. A kind of stone box at his feet. He was surprised how warm it was. "You're not fooling me. Time travel? How the hell could you have gotten from Terra to Mars thousands of years ago? Before anyone had space travel?" He looked around at the cavern. Ingeniously reflected light. The walls were bright with luminous veins of phosphorescent ore and precious stones sparkling like stars. If he kept his knife he might be able to dig out a few long diamonds and get away. Assuming he could dodge this madman.

The man in the projection shrugged. "Malfunctioning matter transmitter. Lost control. I traveled backward to Mars. One way. You've probably heard of me. Captain Miguel Krane? Haven't you read my books? About my life on Mars? I'm surprised you don't know them. They didn't appear under my name, but I dictated them myself."

"I don't listen to books much."

The man in the green pillar seemed thrown by Mac's illiteracy. But Mac could read forty-seven interplanetary languages and write fluently in most of them. He had taught himself for purely practical reasons. He wasn't a scholar. He was a thief. He would have been insulted to be thought of as anything else.

For his own part, Mac was uneasy, still checking for his gun, reassured by the feel of a knife in his boot. Miguel Krane's voice was amused, but Mac didn't like to hear it in his head like that. Too creepy.

Yet Krane had been instrumental in saving his life. Somewhere over their heads, on the Martian surface, a wombot was still searching for him with the objective of covering him with jelly that could seep through his skin and eat his bones from the inside out. He was in no doubt about his preference. He'd take his chances here.

"Those chances aren't much better, Stone." Krane's voice was still amused. "Let's just say you'd be dying for a good cause."

Mac laughed. "When I hear words like that, I reach for my Banning. Where *is* my gun, by the way?"

"Look for yourself. I didn't take it. Neither did the noman. Want to know why I sent the *wanal* after you?"

"I guess." Mac looked down into the pit where the nasty thing was finishing its bloody meal. He saw his gun some way up, where it had lodged on a shelf of rock.

"Do you recall a lep coming to see you a few weeks ago?"

"Yeah. Little green man about so high. One of those freaks from Venus. Had some sort of deal. I wouldn't go for it. I didn't like the smell of it. Thought he was lying. Too dangerous." He was on his belly, stretching for the Banning.

"So you told him."

"Was it him fingered me to the IMF?"

"Not exactly, but you didn't do yourself any favors turning him down before you listened."

"He was lying. I know leps. I didn't want to know what his pitch was. I used to get crazies like him all the time, offering to cut me in on some fantasy in their heads."

"The poor little guy was scared out of his wits. He'd found one of our time seeds and he thought we were magic. Ghosts of ancient Martians or something. Still, he did what I told him to do and he only once looked inside the bag. That nearly killed him. He almost dropped it and ran. The lep wasn't just bringing my message. He had a bag of indigo flame sapphires with him."

"A *bag*?" Stone laughed. The rarest jewel in the system, indigo flame sapphires couldn't be cut, polished, or broken up. They had extraordinary properties. There were three known existing sapphires. One was in the Conquest of Space Museum on Terra, one was in the hands of United System President Polonius Delph—he was the richest man in seven worlds, or had been until he'd paid cash for his jewel. The other had been stolen soon after its discovery. Maybe Delph had it. "There's no such thing."

"There is. And Delph wants them. He thinks you've got them on you. They tortured Gunz, the man I sent after the lep. He told them you had them."

"Oh, great! So I was set up by a Venusian leprechaun who was set up by a V-Image! That's why they've been willing to spend so much money hunting me down. They just want to know where those mythical jewels are. They don't care if they kill me. It's just as easy to interrogate a fresh corpse using a couple of ccs of dreme . . . You remind me of my mother!"

"I can only guess what strange patchwork of information comes through the time seeds. We scatter them into our future, more or less at random. Often they are destroyed or are recalled, damaged. Enough land unharmed to broadcast back. We aren't talking *linear* time as you imagine it, but *radiant* time. From what I understand of your world, Delph isn't the only one who wants the sapphires. He has rivals in the Plutocracy. Another mysterious collector? Or those rivals are competing for the presidency or they think they can ruin him. As you know, it's a vicious circle in politics. You can't get to be president unless you have the wealth and you can't make really massive sums until you're president. It was much the same in my day."

"Your day?"

"That depends where you're counting from." The more he listened, the more Stone recognized the tone coming through the old accent. Miguel Krane spoke with the economical style of an army man. "Or which planet. So. Was this particular scenario set-up by the IMF in order to trick you into giving up the jewels? No. The Interstellar Military Force has nothing to do with us. That was not an IMF ship pursuing you. Probably it's Delph's. I know you don't have the sapphires. The lep was too scared to keep them. He brought them back and left them with the noman."

In spite of this denial, Stone grew cautious again.

"Then who *are* you with?" he challenged. "And why are you so interested in me? Someone's spending a great deal of dough on hunting me down. A real pro, that's for sure. So—really—who are you?"

"My military experience was in Korea, in the middle of the twentieth century," said Krane. "I'm a scientist. Later, I worked on a matter transmitter for the Pentagon. I tested it on myself. It went wrong. I was dragged back to old Mars instead. The Karnala—the clan I fell in with—have access to ancient knowledge and technology left behind by an earlier intelligent race, the Sheev. This machine is some of it. We call it a 'memory catcher' in Karnalan. This is the most sophisticated type.

"What is it? It's an interactive device that can communicate across time. We've been studying them for years. We're not sure we're using the technology appropriately, but we've rigged it so it works for us, after a fashion. We have clear visuals and, when we get over language and other problems, can exchange information or even casual ideas! The Sheev scientists were masters of time. Many believe they abandoned Mars for past eras or the future of another planet, wherever conditions were ideal! Some think they had colonies on ancient earth or in our future! But that is unlikely. This is about the best use we've found for their technology. And it's to ask of *you*, Mac Stone, something that I would do myself if I weren't merely an ethereal image in your world."

"So you want to make a deal. Isn't that usually the size of it? What can I do for you that you don't want to do yourself? Isn't that usually the deal?"

Krane's image smiled. There was a sense of rapport between the two men. "Usually."

"Okay," said Stone. "What's the score? Oh, and don't forget to tell me more about those indigo flame sapphires. Presumably they come into your deal at some point. Let's hear it. I have plenty of time to listen."

Krane did not smile in reply. "Unfortunately," he said, "you haven't."

3

The Star Bomb

"There was a war," said the bronzed Terran. "We weren't ready for it. We thought we'd earned an era of peace. But we had enemies who hated all we stood for. A tribe that had hidden itself underground years earlier, after my people had defeated it. We have our own technology, but that earlier race— the Sheev—developed horrendous weapons. They never used most of them because everyone got scared at the same time. So the weapons, with many of the scientific instruments that helped make them, were locked away by common consent. We didn't know about one particular cache. Our enemy discovered it. An n-bomb probably powerful enough to destroy a whole planet. They planned to use the underground Ia canal to float it under our city, Varnal of the Green Mists, and blow us up. Meanwhile, our scientists found out about it. Thanks to many of the enemy's own people rebelling against their leaders, who were perceived as reckless, we defeated them. Only when we were discussing terms did we learn about the n-bomb and where it was. It would shortly be directly under Varnal, and would blow within hours.

"We got our best people down there. They could find no way of stopping the thing from detonating. All they could do was adjust the timer—which they set about doing. By unlocking seven wards in sequence, the timer could be advanced but not neutralized. So the first thing our scientists did was to set the timer to detonate close to a million years into our future. The maximum the timer allowed. We figured that would be more than enough time to find a solution. I thought that Mars would no longer be highly populated by then. We would work on the problem until we had it licked. A million years—plenty of time! The second thing we did was to move the bomb away from the city. We did this by floating it further on down the canal until it was under a barren, uninhabited part of the planet. Are you familiar with the Ia trans-Martian canal and its story?"

Stone jerked his thumb at the roof. "All the old canals have dried up. There's nothing left of them apart from traces of their beds. And no records, of course. Pretty much everything was lost during the great 'four-millennia cannonade,' when asteroids and meteors pounded Mars to dust, down to most of her farthest shelters. There are a few freak survivals. Nothing much. The canals were deep and wide once, designed to get the most from dwindling water supplies. The meteors leveled them. But this Ia canal? It was underground?"

"My clan's ancestors planned to build this great underground canal, protected from all foreseeable danger, completely encircling the planet, with branches serving other local systems. The canal was named for an ancient water goddess, Ia. Ia would connect to a series of hubs serving other canal systems. Its creators thought that it would, through the trade it would stimulate, bring peace to the entire planet. Ia would circle Mars from pole to pole, where the melting icecaps would continuously refill it. The project was abandoned long before my time."

"Abandoned? What happened?" In spite of his circumstances, Stone found the story engaging. "It sounds a great idea."

"During construction at the Pataphal cross-waterway intersection, after hundreds of miles of the Ia system had already been built, a terrible disaster struck. A whole section of the great Nokedu Cavern floor, which had been tested and found solid, fell away. Hundreds were killed. More of the cavern kept falling, until it formed a massive chasm, miles deep and far too wide to bridge. Black, unfathomable, the Nokedu Falls dropped deep into the planet's heart. The entire project was abandoned. It was considered folly to attempt another submartian watercourse. No more would have been said had not an extraordinary phenomenon occurred maybe a month after the project was closed for good. A guard reported seeing the canal slowly filling with water!

"Some freak of natural condensation created a system which had the effect of filling the Ia canal with enough water to float a good-sized barge. But of course, at Nokedu the water again rushed into the great chasm. Damming didn't work. It became pretty clear that the water had to circulate. Several expeditions had been made into the Nokedu Deep to find the cause of the phenomenon. The expeditions were lost or returned without success. The water supply remained continuous. Then, about five hundred years in your past, a quake dislodged the bomb."

Mac played dumb. "What—and sent it down the falls where it could explode harmlessly?"

"You don't seem to understand. The Sheev originally planned war against nearby planets, especially Terra. The bomb was too powerful. It was never meant to be detonated on *Mars*. Even in space, it had limited useful targets. It was a *star-bomb*, intended to be launched at another planet and turn that world to cosmic dust!"

"And that's what's down there somewhere now?" Stone jerked his thumb toward his feet. "Ticking away as we speak. When's it due to go off?"

"In just under seven hours," said Krane.

"Great! So you simply made your problem *our* problem?" Mac didn't try to disguise his disgust. Fear began to tie his insides together.

"Not deliberately. We only recently learned that Mars was still populated—or repopulated. This wasn't the first time we've tried to contact someone like you or to defuse it. This was the closest we could get to you on this time-line."

"If you know the future, you know what will happen."

"This is the *furthest* we can get in time. We get nothing back if we go further . . ."

Mac was silent, thinking that over. He was familiar with Gridley's theories of radiant time. "So there might not be any future for us?"

The image shimmered as Krane picked up some kind of yellow gossamer scroll on which symbols sparkled. "Our best minds have worked on the problem ever since we knew about it. We have at last determined how to neutralize the n-bomb."

Mac still didn't speak. He just wanted to hear Krane's pitch.

"Okay. So where do *I* come into it?"

"We need you to do the neutralizing."

"For what?"

"To save your planet. Research says you're a Martian, even more than I am. You're a survivor."

"Except that there are easier ways to live."

"That's why you'll get the sapphires."

"A *bag* of indigo flame sapphires?"

"What the lep tried to show you. What Delph heard about."

Mac grinned. "It's a sweet incentive. If you're right, I haven't a chance of getting out of this alive. I might as well take the lot of you—or them—with me. You're all as crooked as I am."

"Except that's not your style, Stone. You're a Martian. You were born on Mars. You don't want Mars to die like that. Not blown to bits."

"Okay. Let's assume you're right. How would I get down to this canal and do what I need to do to the bomb."

"It's not quite so simple," said Krane. "The bomb moved, as I told you. After the quake it actually floated down the canal. Until it hit whitewater. Happily the casing is very strong and relatively light. By luck, it eventually caught between some rocks above the falls. Water currents coming in from three sides actually held the thing steady. It's still there."

"Rapids? That's why your robot can't reach it?"

"One reason."

"Is it hard to dislodge?"

"That, unfortunately, *isn't* a problem. It should dislodge relatively easily."

"So? Where exactly is it?"

"It's pretty much on the brink of that chasm," said Krane. "Where the water of the Ia rushes over the broken canal floor and gushes down into we don't know what. Into the heart of the planet."

"On the brink of hell, in other words."

"Pretty much," said Krane. "But you'll have help. Look over to your left. At the noman's feet."

Stone saw a large steel-and-slate chest, about a meter square. It had some odd markings stenciled on the side.

"Look inside," said Krane. So Stone bent and lifted the catches, opening the lid which eased up on its own. Inside was soft kalebite packing used for delicate scientific instruments. He picked this off carefully. The contents looked unexpectedly sturdy. He reached in both hands and took it out.

"It looks like a big helmet. Like one those old Terran firefighters had."

Krane said: "It's a Gollowatt'n battle hat. They once fought the Kolvini through the Martian catacombs and never once saw the light of day." Quickly, he described the helmet's intuitive features. "Modified for your use. It'll let you see in the dark for a start. Heat pictures. And there's a sensor which tunes to your own eyes so you can use them as super-sensitive binoculars. There are extra-powerful lights for when you need to do fine work, such as on the bomb itself. There's a set of force-tools you can project and use. But it's a lot more than that. There are a million neurolinks so the helmet works intuitively according to the wearer's normal responses. We built a detector into it, too, if it survived the journey."

"Force-tools?"

"They're modified and mostly intuitive, tuned to your brain so you only have to visualize the problem, not the tool itself. Best make appropriate head movements."

"Okay." Stone was dubious. "So what's the magic word?"

"There is none. The helmet was made for a Gollowat'n medic, believe it or not. That's why it was built with an empathy conceptor, so the medic could work on a wounded soldier or an injured civilian at the scene, usually in a battle situation. Empathy was a Gollowat'n middle name. The greatest doctors on seven worlds. They're porcine, of course, but close enough to humans for the helmet to work pretty well. It should be compatible with your suit. The noman will make any adjustments you need."

"It's no more than a couple of planets at stake." The helmet was light and felt unexpectedly organic. It shifted like flesh to his touch. It had a faint, pleasant smell, like brine. He lifted it over his head and brought it slowly down, fitting it like a hat. Then it seemed to flow over his skull and snuggle around his throat, his forehead. His suit suddenly buzzed recognition codes. Rounded blinkers fitted over his eyes but he could see well. If anything, his eyes were sharper. For a moment, his cheekbones itched and he saw an uncomfortable series of cherry-colored flashes. Then a wash of dark red, almost like blood, gave way to enhanced clarity of vision.

The noman extended its arms, touching him gently here and there. His suit settled more comfortably on his body. He was surprised how healthy the thing made him feel. Maybe Gollowat'n medics had to be healthy in order to empathize with their patients. He had a sudden thought.

"This bomb? Is it sentient?"

"Not much," said Krane.

"So what do I have to do to turn the timer off?"

"You have to open a series of locks. Numbered right to left in what they call G-script. We coded them to a particular melody in a particular time signature. It's a tune, with each note representing a complex number. Do you know the old Earth tune 'Dixie'? Just whistle it to yourself. That number should cancel out the existing sequence and effectively baffle the bomb's key and register. The locks will snap off and it will probably simply go dead in your hand."

"And if it doesn't?"

"Well, it will still be live."

"And ready to blow."

"Yes. I'm assured there is very little chance of this going wrong, Mac Stone. Our people worked it out. Essentially, all you have to do is memorize that simple little tune. *Oh, I wish I was in the land of cotton—*"

"There is a problem." Stone was almost embarrassed.

"What's that?"

He flushed. "I'm tone deaf," he said.

4
Dancing in the Dark

"Then try to remember the intervals." Krane seemed bitterly amused, like a man who believes he's thought of everything only to be told of one obvious unconsidered fact. "The helmet should help you. We've entered the code and the helmet should translate it automatically."

Stone shrugged. "And if I succeed, I come back here and you give me the sapphires?"

"The whole bag. I promise."

Stone didn't have much choice now. He had to make a decision. Believe this strange Earthman or not? He laughed his long, low purr and tested the helmet's responses. He pulled the casque down a little more firmly, settling the bond with his suit. Somehow he knew what to do next. He blinked to make the lights come on. Then he lay down on the side of the pit, fishing up his gun. The *wanal* made an unpleasant noise but went on eating.

Stone wiped slime off the barrel of his Banning and shoved it back in its holster. "What now?"

"The helmet's programmed to help you find the bomb. If you leave this chamber, you'll be at the top of a flight of stairs leading to a wide walkway. It runs beside the canal. All the Sheev waterways were made like that and their successors copied them." There was a warm, Terran voice speaking to him now. Was this what Miguel Krane really sounded like? "There's a numbering system still based on Sheev. The Sheev system used predominantly eleven. One, two, eleven, eleven, twenty-two and so on.

"The Ia was rediscovered by the last Martians. They followed us. They built cities where they could shelter from the meteors. Air enough and water. They cultivated plants that grew well in the hydroponic fields. They built the atmosphere factories. They traded up and down that stretch of the canal. They sustained their particular civilization for another thousand years or more. When the meteor storms had passed, as you know, the whole planet had been pulverized. Almost all trace of Martian life was wiped out, except for things that lived below ground. They never really came back to the surface."

Mac wondered what his own chances were. As he found the wide, black steps that led downwards, he thought of those ancient Martians who had built them back when the planet was still a world of gentle seas and green hills, of endless forests and big skies, before humans had evolved at all. And then came the Five Ages. The ages of the humanoid Martians. And then the meteors. The Martians would ultimately grow lonely as the remaining scraps of their culture were buried by the rusty Martian sands. They elected to find solitude below the surface and fade into death surrounded by the massive black stones of their eerie necropolis.

For all he was a loner, Stone found it hard to understand their mind-set. From the moment he burst out of his mother's womb, he'd had to fight to remain alive, and had relished every second he won for himself, grateful for whatever air he could drag into his gasping lungs, for every sight and sound that told him that he still lived. Mac Stone had a human brain and he was proud of his Martian heritage. He didn't care whose lives he was saving or what reward he would receive. Mars was all he cared about. His battered flitboots echoed down wide steps of black pearl marble, as smooth and as stately and as beautiful in their subtle curvature as they had been on the day they were finished. He hardly noticed their grandeur. He thought of the big reflective tanks he had played among as a little boy and what so much water could do for the Low-Canal.

He breathed vanilla air which reminded him of the shows he'd watched as a kid on the big public V-drome screens, sometimes as real as life, sometimes better, and he wondered if this was like that. Was this his life starting to replay at faster-than-real speed as his brain got ready to die? Was he already dead, remembering the high moments, the fine moments, of his wild life before he'd been sold? When he and Yily Chan would scamper like scorpions in and out of the blackness cast by the vast tanks and at night chase the flickering shadows cast by Phobos as she came sailing from the west, shreds of darkness skipping before her like familiars, spreading a trail of shades behind her . . . Oh, that raw intemperate beauty! Alive or dead, Mac swore he was never again going to leave Mars.

The noman had thoroughly repaired and recharged his day-suit. Mac felt pleasantly warm as he reached the bottom of the stairs and stood on the edge of the great canal and looked out over it. He was stunned by the amount of water the planet was keeping secret! It could have been an ocean, with no far shore visible. To his left and right, the canal was endless. From what he could tell, much of it followed an old watercourse, but other parts were hollowed out by something that had sliced easily through the dark Martian granite and decorated it with deep, precise reliefs showing half-human creatures and unlikely beasts. Machinery of alien design and mysterious purpose. There were walkways cut into the canal walls, allowing animals or machines to drag boats beside them. Characters etched into the granite counted off *glems*, close to a meter, in what Stone knew as "Dawson," named for the script's first Terran translator.

He moved his head to his right. In the helmet's crisp illumination, he saw black water rippling, making its rapid way toward the falls, which had to be miles away, and yet were already distinct. A distant roar. At a discreet sound from the helmet, Stone turned right keeping the water on his left as the walkway widened, revealing the dark bulk of buildings, low houses, all abandoned. This had been a busy, thriving port. People had traded down here and been entertained, had families and lived complex lives. Mac wished that he had time to explore the town. Unlike the canal itself, the settlements along the bank were on a human scale and in different styles. This was where the last humanoid Martians had lived. The place had a bleak atmosphere. Mac saw no evidence for the legends he'd grown up hearing in the Low-Canal of enduring pockets of Martians still living down here.

They were not the last native Martians. Those were the *raifs*. Never wholly visible, they flitted around the Low-Canal settlements—the so-called mourning Martians, whose songs sometimes drifted in from the depths of the dead sea-bottoms and whose pink-veined outlines were almost invisible by noon. They drifted like translucent rays, feeding on light. Their songs could be heartbreaking. Storytellers insisted they were not a new race at all, but the spirits of the last humanoid Martians, forever doomed to haunt the Low-Canal.

Stone had never felt quite so alone. The buildings were thinning out as he walked, and his helmet showed him an increasing number of great natural arches, of stalagmites and stalactites forming a massive stone forest beside the whispering waters of the Ia canal. Some had been carved by ancient artists into representations of long-since-extinct creatures. Every so often, he was startled by a triangular face with eldritch, almost Terran, features. Mac, used to so much strangeness, felt almost in awe of those petrified faces that stared back at him with sardonic intelligence.

Nothing lived here, not even the savage crocs. Nothing flew or scampered or wriggled over the smooth marble, amongst the stone trunks of stone trees whose stone boughs bent back to the ground. The only noise came from the rushing water, and even that was muted.

He thought he heard a faint rustle from within the stone forest. He paused, and heard it again. A sound. Nothing more. He couldn't identify it. But he did know that he probably shouldn't be hearing that sound. Maybe some remnants of a civilization did still live down here after all?

He moved his jaw, his ears. As Krane had promised, the helmet responded intuitively and amplified some of the outside sounds while filters dampened others. All he heard was the steady flow of the canal waters. Had he imagined something? When it came again, he knew what it was. A biped in shoes was following him. Or keeping pace with him, out there in the endless caves. Louder. There it was. A light, steady footfall in step with his own. When he stopped, it stopped. It came from the seemingly endless stone archways on his right. His laugh was almost demonic. He reached to loosen his Banning in its holster and bent to feel for his knife, still in place. He recalled boyhood tales of fierce monsters down here, of horribly disfigured mutants who lived off human flesh. Until now, he'd believed none of them.

Another step. Stone blinked to turn off the helmet's lights. He crept as silently as he could into the nearest stone arch. The faintest scuttling sound came next. Carefully, he drew his blaster, dialing a swift instruction with his thumb. When he leveled the gun, it shot out a group of tiny light bursts, like so many brief, brilliant stars slowly arcing through that natural crypt, throwing a shadow against the curving stone pillars. A human. He *was* being followed. Somebody sent by Krane? Unlikely. The lep? Certainly not that noman. One of Varnal's ancient enemies? He now had a charge and three-quarters left in his Banning. Logically, there was only likely to be one other person in the catacombs—whoever had chased him down here in the first place. They would be very well armed!

He snarled into the blackness. "Listen, I don't know what you expect to get from me. If it's sapphires, not only do I not have them, I don't know where they are. And if you have any idea that I'm lying, I ought also to tell you that I'm on a mission. If I'm stopped, Mars will be blown to bits, and you with her. Now I don't much care for what they've done to Mars, but I was born on this planet, and I'd like to spend a few more years here. So whatever you're after, mister, maybe you should back off. Or show yourself. Or just come into the open and fight. I'll take whatever option you like."

No answer came out of that cold blackness, just the echo of the water whispering on its way to oblivion.

Keep moving.

Crunch!

A stunshell went off where he had been moments earlier. Only an amateur would have missed him. A suspicion became a thought in Stone's mind.

It had to be the same hunter who had been trailing him since RamRam City. He should know who it was by now. If it was a bluff, he'd been bluffed by a pro. Yes, there was no doubt. Someone was playing a game, maybe searching for his weaknesses.

With that, Stone snapped the helmet lights back on. There it was! A human shape fluttering amongst the stalagmites. He switched the light off, listening. Then, very quietly, he left the wide path. He passed among those great natural arches, seeking whoever hunted him. By the way they darted through the darkness, he couldn't help wondering how long they had lived on Mars. He recognized that same characteristic movement. A habit of approaching everywhere from the side or from behind. A habit of caution. The anticipation of attack. So this wasn't some Terran bounty hunter after his hide. This was a Martian.

Stone knew all the Martians likely to be offered the job and this wasn't their style, no matter how high a reward he had on his head. Except—

Again, he brought his lights into play, and this time he got more than a glimpse. A red-and-black night-suit. Carrying extra air. Two Banning 22-40s. Every bounty hunter had a signature.

Could it be Yily Chen? Or someone working with Chen?

Crunch!

Now he knew they didn't really want him dead. It had to be Chen. They had just been pretending up there before the ock-croc got him. They had wanted him to think he was as good as dead. Or maybe they'd wanted to get him down here where they could take their time with him?

"If that's you, Yily, why are you after me? You're on Terra. I'm on Mars. We were never at odds."

Her voice hadn't changed as much as he'd expected. A sweet, light, lilting brogue came back out of the darkness. "Maybe the price was never high enough, Mac."

"I don't believe you."

"Okay. Then you tell me why somebody wants you alive and doesn't want me to talk it over with you?"

"You wouldn't torture me. I know it. Not me."

"Maybe. Circumstances change, Mac. Times change."

"Very true. But *you* don't. *I* don't. We're Martians. You're more Martian than I am. You don't have anyone they can get at you through. Same with me. We have identical reasons for keeping free of ties."

"We're different, Mac. Fundamentally. I'm a hunter. You're a thief. Sometimes hunters are commissioned to find thieves."

"So who gave you the job? Who wants you to bring me in?"

"Can't you guess?"

"Delph. And he has most of the money in the universe. But not enough to pay for me."

"Maybe so much money that I got curious. I wanted to know what he wanted which is worth such a lot. A bag I'm not supposed to look in. And which you don't have. I know you don't or you'd have used it as a decoy by now. I've hunted you for nearly a week, Mac. I've almost killed you half a dozen times. I've given you a chance to try all the angles. And you've tried them."

"What? You were testing me?"

"I guess."

She stepped out into the open, into the beam of light, a quick, boyish figure. Not at all what he'd imagined. She held her helmet in her left hand, one of her guns loose in the other. Her brown, curly hair framed an impossibly beautiful triangular face with heavily slanted golden eyes. Her brows were thin and sloping, her lips red and bright as fresh blood. Few of those she hunted ever saw that face. Her clients rarely saw Yily Chen at all. She just delivered her "commissions," like packages. She'd been his sister. He'd played with her every day as a young child. For all he remembered her as smart and pretty, Mac could hardly believe how truly beautiful she had become.

"Hello, Yily. What are you really after?" He lifted his visor.

"Hi, Mac." She smiled and holstered her pistol. "You're a hard guy to fool. And hard not to kill, too. I guess I wanted to know what Delph needs so bad from you that he'd let me name my price."

Now he had a good idea what this was all about. He holstered his own Banning. She slipped her gun into its sheath and went back to drag something from the shadows. A bulky pack. She knelt to check the harness.

"And did you find out?"

Mac wondered why he remained so wary of her. The answer was probably simple. The strongest man, usually able to keep control of his emotions and stay cool, would find it hard to resist that beauty.

"Sure I did." She straightened her back. She moved toward him, half smiling, looking up from under heavy lids, her voice husky. "But I couldn't trust him to pay."

Stone caught himself laughing. "I last saw you twenty years ago, stealing water from the tanks."

She grinned. He remembered that grin from when he had chased her through the bazaars of the Low Canal and she had mocked him for his clumsiness. She boasted then that she had true Martian blood from a time when the great Broreern triremes had dominated the green seas swelling under a golden sun in the autumn of the planet's long history. Stone could easily believe her. Cynics said Yily's mother was a Terran whore and her father a Martian prison guard. But, with that glorious light brown skin, her beautifully muscled, boyish frame, that curly hair, her long legs, those firm, small breasts, her sardonic, golden eyes, no one who saw her ever believed she was anything but a Mars woman reincarnated.

There were very few career possibilities on Mars for a girl of Yily's background and looks. She had chosen the least likely: first as Tex Merrihew's sidekick, learning the bounty hunter's trade, then as a fixer on her own account. Mac wondered if Yily Chen had other reasons for helping him. She was known to be clever and devious. Was her word as good as they said? "So what are you proposing, Yily?"

"A partnership, maybe."

"I didn't know you liked me that much."

"I don't like Delph at all. I don't like what he's done to Mars or what he *will* do if he gets what he wants. What *does* he want, Mac?"

"He believes I have a bunch of indigo flame sapphires."

"A *bunch?*"

"A bunch."

She was silent. He could almost hear her thinking.

"What was that about a bomb?" she said.

He saw no reason not to. So he told her all he knew.

When he had finished she said: "Then I guess I'd better help you."

He asked why.

She grinned. "Because I'm a Martian, too." She bent and picked up her heavy pack. "And I'm not tone deaf."

5
Whistling Dixie

They came to the falls, increasingly communicating through their filtered helmet radios. The sound was deafening. An eerie pink light glared up from the chasm's depths.

"Some say that's Mars's core down there." She didn't elaborate.

"Have you been here before?"

"Once. Guy jumped bail on Terra. Thought he had immunity here. He did, but they framed him anyway because the judge in Ram owed the judge in Old London a favor. So I was in for double reward. A share of the bail money if I brought him in alive. Well, it turned out he had friends here. Archeologists. Academics. They crack easily. They told me how they'd found evidence for what they called the lost canal. You know the story?"

He nodded. "Guy's out in the desert. He beds down for the night. Wakes up suddenly. He hears water. He listens more carefully. Running water. It's the ghost canal. A kind of mirage, leading travelers astray so they die of thirst convinced there's water all around them."

"They told him about a cave system. Legends said it was a way in to another world. Some argued it came out on Terra, in Arizona somewhere. Some thought ancient Mars. Others linked it to the discoveries of the so-called 'hidden universe' obscured from our astronomers by drifting clouds of cosmic fog." She shrugged. "You don't have to break many fingers before they put two and two together. I found the cave, found this place, found him, hauled him up, took him in and took the money."

"Why didn't I ever hear of that entrance?"

"Because I destroyed it. Didn't want those archeologists to be embarrassed again. My guy had two reasons not to talk. He might escape and hide out down here. And he knew what I'd do to him if news of the falls ever reached the surface. They sent him to Ceres. You don't live long there. As far as I know, he died with the secret."

The falls mesmerized them. They both found themselves walking too close to the edge, drawn by the vast, rearing walls of water spraying blue and gold, emerald and ruby, in that strange light. Old light, thought Mac without knowing why. Light which appeared to be pressed down by the cavern's impenetrable blackness. Mac saw all kinds of shapes in there. Faces from his past. People he had hated. Nobody he had loved. Men with weapons. Women wanting his money or contempt or both. Cruelty ran through interplanetary society like a fuel. Not his drug of choice. Peace. Why was he thinking like this as the pink flume blew into a million shapes and offered to hold him like a baby, safely, safely . . . ?

"*Stone!*"

Her strong hand grabbed his arm and yanked him back from the edge. "Damn! I thought you could look after yourself." Her anger was like a slap across his face. He swore. Those eyes, those glaring eyes! What had they held in that moment when she raged at him?

He shook his head. "Don't worry. I'm sorry. It won't happen again."

She was frowning now, peering through her distance glasses out across the raging falls and pointing. "What's that?"

A flash of electric lime green. An obviously unnatural color. Nothing like anything surrounding it. He switched over to the helmet's optics and brought it in sharply as instruments reported distance and size. She adjusted her own glasses to check it out.

About one-and-a-half meters square, the star bomb lay balanced between a rough circle of rocks. Almost peacefully, white water whirled around it. Contrary currents held it in suspension. Any one of the currents could alter course slightly and take the bomb over the brink from where it would never be recovered. And would ultimately detonate, splitting the planet apart.

The falls bellowed, echoing through the vast cavern whose roof lay beyond sight in the glittering darkness. According to the helmet, its walls held deposits of gold, silver, diamonds, and many other metals now very rare on Terra. Stone could imagine what would become of the place once the likes of Delph found out about it. He scanned the falls as far as he could see, pointing out a possible pathway through to it, where a great slab of black granite formed a canopy on which tons of water fell by the second. The rocks beneath the canopy were given a little potential protection, at least for part of the way. Some of the rocks disappeared behind another great massing of fallen debris. They formed a blind spot. Neither Stone nor Chen could see what danger might be waiting for anyone who tried to cross beyond that point. There didn't seem to be a better route anywhere else.

"We'd best rope up." She lowered her heavy pack to the walkway. "We can't work on that thing out there. We're going to have to fetch it."

"I could try firing a grapnel from my Banning." He showed her the tonkinite hook on his belt. "It's attached to fifty meters of spiderwire. But even if it was a good idea, there's no way we could do it from here. We need to be sure we have the bomb securely held. We can't make mistakes. We need to switch over to gravity equalizers. They should hold off the worst of the force from the water. Does your suit have equalizers? Doesn't matter. We'll use mine. Both of us will probably have to go out there for at least as far as that route takes us."

They had little left to discuss. First, they tested the GE potential. This took the power of anything threatening them, and, using the threat's own energy, converted it into a force field theoretically capable of equalizing any outside pressure. The idea behind the technology was brilliant, but there had been more than one infamous GE accident. You didn't get any second chances. They contacted Miguel Krane. He assured Stone that the helmet had been tested for all environments, particularly for the power of the falls. He was surprised to learn that Yily Chen was involved, but he saw no problem in both of them using the suit. "One or a dozen, it can theoretically protect against a considerably stronger power. Of course, we haven't allowed for human error. Just remember, it only takes one break in the circuitry and you'll both be swept over those falls in a blink." He suggested that they have her suit run on low power as a backup. "You'll have to decide between you if that would work." Krane sounded a little uncertain.

Soon they were ready. They roped up using, Mac's spiderwire. It was unwise to rely on their helmets' intercom. They would rely as much as they could on visual signals. Even with everything turned to minimum input they could still hear the heavy beating of the water against the rocks, the yelping gush of the canal as it spilled over into that bottomless gorge. Together, they inched out over the slippery causeway, hands, feet, elbows, and knees on full suction, allowing them to gain traction with every limb. The vast weight of water, even though not the full mass, smashed against their force converter, allowing them to move forward. They were tiny specs caught above those gigantic liquid walls. Able to see less than a meter ahead, they clung together, taking careful steps, often crawling on hands and knees, blinded by the screaming spray surrounding them. More than once, Stone lost his balance. She remained surefooted and caught his cord before he followed his momentum down into the hungry core of the planet. He calculated that she'd saved his life at least seven times in as many minutes.

Above them, the wild spray boomed and shrieked. Their heads rang under the hammer blows of the surging current. Once, she was almost swept over the rim. He held on with hands and feet as he extended the field, hauling her back, kicking an impossible surge of power out of his equipment and falling backwards as something caught his shoulder. Recovering, he saw that debris was also being carried down the falls, effectively doubling their danger. They watched for larger objects as much as possible, another eye on their chronometers, which were telling them roughly how much time still remained before the bomb was due to blow. Forty minutes. They reached a place where the water was suddenly quiet and even the sound seemed muted. For a moment or two they rested, gratefully recovering their strength in calm water forming little pools beneath the huge canopy of granite. They made up some of their lost time.

Once or twice, Stone looked back toward the bank, now invisible to him. Was all their effort worthless? Wouldn't it be better to accept the impossibility of their mission? He began to think Krane was mad. If there were a threat, then inevitably they would die. Death was the future of all people, all planets, all universes. Their struggle was symbolic of the futility of living creatures who fought against their own inevitable extinction. What were a few more years of existence compared to the longevity of a cosmos? In those terms, the whole history of their species lasted for less than a fraction of a second. And then, sheltering beside him under the protection of the energy equalizer, she looked up for a second, and, obscurely, he understood that the effort always would be worth it. Always had been worth it.

They emerged eventually from the overhang. They saw the gaudy lime-green box glittering on the far side of a rocky cleft. Stone could see no obvious way down to it. For a moment, it seemed that they had come this far only to fail. Then Yily nodded and signaled that if he held on to the spidercord, she might be able to swing down and snag the box. But it would mean switching over to her own untested equalizers. Whether her suit had enough capacity was uncertain. She shrugged and began tying herself on.

The falls coughed and grumbled, always treacherous.

Stone grew concerned that there wouldn't be enough spiderwire. He had trouble gauging the distance properly. He braced himself. He would have to switch off as soon as he could after she switched on, conserving power and maintaining stability for split seconds. He raised his hand and gave the signal. They knew a sickening few moments while the switch took place and then she was dropping out of sight before coming back into view, a far smaller figure than he had expected.

The blue and red of her suit was just visible, flashing on and off as she fell through a sickening weight of water. Her relative gravity, thanks to the converter, gave her extra resistance, and she stretched out her arms and clasped the n-bomb to her, swinging free over the rosy abyss. She cried out her triumph in a wild yell, her body curving back into the trajectory. He thumped the control and brought her up to where he perched, hanging on with everything but his nails and teeth. He was laughing like a fool as she swung to stand beside him, counting out with elated blows on his arm the measure to activate his helmet's converter so both were again protected. He could feel her elation as he hugged her tight.

They had the star bomb!

Now, somehow, they had to follow the steps back to the sheltering rock. Inch by inch, they crossed the exposed falls, feet feeling for holds as the minutes slipped by, and they dared not waste a moment trying to see how much time they had before the bomb did what it had been designed to do. The climb back to the walkway seemed to take longer than the whole rest of the mission. Increasingly, the strain on the equalizer became greater. Little bubbles of energy flinched and disappeared into the wavering field.

Stone was almost convinced they had run out of time and strength. He gasped his surprise when, suddenly, his boots stood on the smooth granite and the bomb was on the ground before them. Manhandling it to the relative quiet of the stone arches, they were at last able to turn off the equalizers. The suit crackled and zipped, revealing flaws which moments later would have meant sudden death.

Stone triumphantly announced their success to Krane over the radio. The Earthman seemed less than overjoyed.

"You have twenty-seven minutes left," he said. "Do you think you can do it, Stone?"

Yily grinned and began to whistle.

"What's that?" Krane asked.

"It's not doing anything," she said. "'Yankee Doodle,' right?"

But, even when the correct tune had been relayed back to them by Krane, only four of the eleven locks protecting the n-bomb snapped open. They needed seven in sequence. "The Yellow Rose of Texas" snapped open two more. "Moonlight On the Wabash" made two snap back. She tried different keys and speeds, new sequences. Two more. One more. But after that it was no good. She was embarrassed. "My grandma came to Mars in the *Revival Follies*. We used to sing them all before the dope took her."

"This is getting dangerous," Krane told them. "Something has jammed. Stop!" Oblivious of his growing concern, they kept trying and kept failing as the minutes and the seconds died. "You've got to stop!" Krane told them. "Unless every lock is undone in order, the bomb can't be neutralized. It took us years to work out those codes. We encrypted everything in easily remembered traditional tunes. We—we haven't time to work out the codes again! If anything, we've complicated the situation. We have eight minutes left."

Mac hovered over the bomb, trying different force tools on the remaining locks. "This is hopeless. We could explode the thing at any moment." He watched the most recently tried force tool fade from his glove.

"I guess neither of us is musical enough. Time for Plan B." She reached with both hands into her pack and pulled out a large square metal container. Quickly, she dragged off the box's covering, revealing a compacted canister covered with government warnings, which, as she stroked it with her gloved fingers, began to expand, flopping and twitching like a living thing until it lay in her lap like a long, khaki-colored barracuda. "I'd better set this now."

Stone recognized the unactivated B-9 wombot. He guessed her plan but he said, "What are you going to do with that?" It was his idea too.

But she wouldn't stop. "I'm a lot lighter than you."

"Give me your big scarf," she said. "Hurry! And some of those tools might prove useful here. I'll tell you what to do. We need that spiderwire. Can you disconnect it from your suit?"

"I can try."

So he dragged out his long, white scarf. She began to wind the thing around her waist. No clocks or numbers on the bomb told them how much time they had left. They had only their own chronometers. "Seven minutes."

He was still planning to do the thing himself. "Now," he said, "get those magnets situated. The scarf will be useful. It won't bear any serious strain, but it'll keep the bomb in position while we spiderwire it to the wombot. Leave those ends free. Screw drill might help."

The thing grew firm in her hands as she helped give the cables a few more turns. "Okay," he said. "More magnetic clamps. As many as we have between us." The bomb was settled on the ground, the wombot beside it. At his count, they seized the bomb, rolled it, and bound it with the wire while they fixed the eight magnetic manacles she normally used for heavy-gravity truants. They held the wombot squarely on the bomb. Six minutes. He took a deep breath.

Then, while he was still thinking about it, she had straddled the whole contraption, binding herself to it with the scarf and the remaining spiderwire, leaving her limbs free. There wasn't time to argue. Stone grew more and more unhappy. He realized that he couldn't take over. Too late to start arguing.

Soon she had the whole contraption firmly beneath her, the wombot now fighting like a fish to be free. He gripped it hard as he could with his numbed hands. Then she began powering up her suit.

He couldn't find any more words. He felt sick. He had an unusual set to his jaw as he watched her first switch her own equalizer to run and then eased the bomb but not the wombot, outside her suit's circle of power. She tapped in codes on her arm. Wouldn't she need a helmet? There was a faint flash and she winced. Not a suicide mission! Don't say it was that! The sound of the falls still drowned any noise they made without using the radio. The powerful bionic drone jumped in her hands and lifted over Stone's head with Yily still clinging to it. It bucked and pirouetted and bucked again. He yelled for her to let go, that he would catch her.

"I have to test it first," she said. "There isn't much time."

"Maybe we should say goodbye." Suddenly calm, though scarcely reconciled, he stepped back.

"Maybe." And then she released the wombot.

It leapt into the air, looped once, with her hanging on for dear life, her e-suit flickering and flashing. The wire secured the bomb. She was held only by a few magnetic clamps, spiderwire, and her own strength. But Stone could have sworn he saw her grinning.

The contraption began to move in a straight line. Out over the Nokedu

Falls—out through the distant spray, gold and silver in the pink light—and, to Stone's utter horror, *down!*

Down flew Yily Chen. Down she flew! Out of sight as she was dragged by the wombot into that vast rosy chasm and those wild, dancing, deadly waters. Stone had never known so much fear before. Never so much fear than when he saw her vanish. "Oh, God!" He tried to get his radio back on but there was no reception. "Oh, Yily!" He felt ill. He scanned the gold-flecked air with his enhanced eyes. Nothing.

The Nokedu Falls shouted its beautiful, monstrous laughter.

Then, triumphantly, the wombot leapt like a salmon up the falls, into the air above the canal, and seemed to hover for a moment with Yily flying behind it, going through some weird contortions, maybe to gain altitude. Up she came, then back, hurtling almost directly toward him. He dove clear of the thing as it seemed to home on him. Was he the nearest heat? Had he really been the target all along? Then here she came, just in time, jumping clear of the flying bomb, down onto the walkway as the wombot performed a perfect turn and flew like a radium ray straight and true back along the way they had first come—and then vanished from normal space-time. Now it would push through the folds of unseen space, seeking maximum heat, blinking up to the surface through the rock until it hit thin air, still skewering through the folds of space-time, on its way to Sol.

He rolled over as she switched off her suit and fell, laughing, into his arms.

Then Stone did what unconsciously he had wanted to do since he'd first chased the tousled, brown-skinned Martian girl playing hide-and-go-seek in and out of the deep shadows of the tanks. He took her in his arms, tossed away his helmet, and kissed her full on her blood-red lips. She kissed him back with a passion, biting his tongue and grinning as he responded.

Up in RamRam City, a scummer lying on his back, high on jojo juice, saw a quick blossom of brightness appear in Sol's northwest quadrant, a crimson flower against dull orange, and had no notion how lucky he was to be alive or what that brief moment had earned.

Soon Stone and Yily followed the long walkway of polished black granite beside the wide canal and up the great staircase to the chamber where he had first met Krane. The Earthman was gone, but on a hook extending from the deactivated noman's right arm was a soft gray ratskin bag, and when Stone poured the contents into her open palm Yily gasped.

Stone lit the last three inches of his jane, drew deep, smiled, contentedly watching her as she laid them out, side by side on the bag: Seven perfect flame sapphires, pulsing with constantly shifting shades of indigo. Each was a different world. Each was utterly fascinating, ready to reflect and amplify your secret dreams. Should you wish, you could live in one forever.

"Yeah," said Stone happily. "Quite a sight."

Epilogue

They knew what would happen, of course, when the mining companies and the archeologists discovered a plentiful supply of water. That water would still be contaminated by centuries of leakage from an alien super-bomb and would have to be filtered, probably not very thoroughly. That wouldn't be much of a problem, especially with expendable prison labor working down there. Stone guessed what the exploiters would do with the great calm waterway perpetually pouring into a bottomless canyon to be captured and recycled, by some mysterious process, back into the canal again. Power.

"It'll all go," said Yily Chen. "It'll be sensationalized and sanitized. People will run boat tours to the safe parts. There'll be elevators directly down to the falls. Tourist money will bring a demand for comfortable fiction. Guides will play up invented legends and histories. Art critics will explain the grandeur of her design, the beauty of her reliefs, the ingenuity of her architects and engineers. She'll give birth to a thousand academic theories. Crazy theories. Cults. Religions. And that won't be the worst of it when people like Delph start tearing out the metals and the precious jewels . . . "

"No," he said. "It doesn't have to happen. We can keep it to ourselves. Just for a while."

It was what Yily wanted too. She smiled that sweet, sardonic Martian smile. "I guess I was planning to retire," she said.

So they bought Mars. She only cost them two indigo flame sapphires, sold to a consortium of Terran plutocrats. For the pair, Stone and Chen got the mining companies, a couple of ships, RamRam City and other settlements, the various rights of exploration and exploitation, the private prisons Stone had known so well and subsequently liberated so promptly.

Later, it might be possible to create on Mars a paradise of justice and reason, a golden age to last a thousand years where their Martian descendants could grow up and flourish. But meanwhile, for a few good months, maybe more, they had the lost canal to themselves.

Ⴎ

ABOUT THE AUTHORS

Charlie Jane Anders (charliejane.net) writes about science fiction for io9. com, and she's hard at work on a fantasy novel. You can find her work in the *McSweeney's Joke Book of Book Jokes*, *Best Science Fiction of the Year 2009*, *Sex for America*, and other anthologies. She's also contributed to *Mother Jones*, the *Wall Street Journal*, the *San Francisco Chronicle*, *ZYZZYVA*, *Pindeldyboz*, *Strange Horizons*, and many other publications. She organizes the Writers With Drinks reading series. With Annalee Newitz, she co-edited the anthology *She's Such a Geek* and published an indy magazine called *other*. She wrote a novel called *Choir Boy*, which won a Lambda Literary Award and was a finalist for the Edmund White Award.

Dale Bailey lives in North Carolina with his family, and has published three novels, *The Fallen*, *House of Bones*, and *Sleeping Policemen* (with Jack Slay, Jr.), as well as a collection of short fiction, *The Resurrection Man's Legacy and Other Stories*. He has been a four-time finalist for the International Horror Guild Award, a two-time finalist for the Nebula Award, and a finalist for the Bram Stoker and the Shirley Jackson Awards. His fiction has appeared in *Alchemy*, *Amazing Stories*, *Asimov's*, *Clarkesworld*, *The Magazine of Fantasy & Science Fiction*, *Lightspeed*, *Nightmare*, *SciFiction*, and *Tor.com*, among other places. "Death and Suffrage," his International Horror Guild Award-winning novelette, was adapted for film by director Joe Dante as part of Showtime Television's anthology series, *Masters of Horror*. He has two books coming out next year, *The End of the End of Everything: Stories* and *The Subterranean Season*.

Best known for her "The Company" series, **Kage Baker**'s notable works include the novel *Mendoza in Hollywood* and "The Empress of Mars," a 2003 novella that won the Theodore Sturgeon Award and was nominated for a Hugo Award. In 2009, her short story "Caverns of Mystery" and her novel *House of the Stag* were both nominated for World Fantasy Awards. Baker died on January 31, 2010. Later that year, her novella *The Women of Nell Gwynne's* was nominated for both Hugo and World Fantasy Awards, and won the Nebula Award. Based on extensive notes left by the author, Baker's unfinished novel, *Nell Gwynne's On Land and At Sea*, was completed by her sister Kathleen Bartholomew and published in 2012.

Elizabeth Bear was born on the same day as Frodo and Bilbo Baggins, but in a different year. When coupled with a childhood tendency to read the dictionary for fun, this led her inevitably to penury, intransigence, and the writing of speculative fiction. She is the Hugo, Sturgeon, Locus, and Campbell Award-winning author of about a hundred short stories and twenty-six novels—the most recent of which are *Steles of the Sky* (Tor) and the *One-Eyed Jack* (Prime Books). Her dog lives in Massachusetts; her partner, writer Scott Lynch, lives in Wisconsin. She spends a lot of time on planes.

Paul Cornell—a writer of science fiction and fantasy in prose, comics, and TV—is one of only two people to be Hugo Award-nominated for all three media. He's written *Doctor Who* for the BBC, *Action Comics* for DC, and *Wolverine* for Marvel. He's won the BSFA Award for his short fiction, an Eagle Award for his comics, and shares in a Writer's Guild Award for his television work. His latest urban fantasy novel is *The Severed Streets* from Tor. He lives in Buckinghamshire with his wife and son.

Eileen Gunn is a writer and editor. Her fiction has received the Nebula Award in the United States and the Sense of Gender Award in Japan, and has twice been nominated for the Hugo Award. Her first short story collection, *Stable Strategies and Others*, was nominated for the Philip K. Dick and World Fantasy Awards, and short-listed for the James Tiptree, Jr. Award. A new collection, *Questionable Practices: Stories by Eileen Gunn* was published earlier this year by Small Beer Press. She was the editor/publisher of the edgy and influential *Infinite Matrix* webzine (2001-2008) and also edited, with L. Timmel Duchamp, *The WisCon Chronicles 2: Provocative Essays on Feminism, Race, Revolution, and the Future*. Gunn has had an extensive career in high-tech advertising. Originally from the Boston area, she now lives in Seattle with her husband, typographer and book designer John D. Berry.

Mary Robinette Kowal (maryrobinettekowal.com) was the 2008 recipient of the Campbell Award for Best New Writer and a Hugo winner for her story "Evil Robot Monkey." Her debut novel *Shades of Milk and Honey* (Tor, 2010)—a "fantasy novel that Jane Austen might have written"— was nominated for the Nebula Award for Best Novel. The fourth novel of her Glamourist Histories, *Valour and Vanity,* was published earlier this year and a fifth, *Of Noble Family,* will appear next year. Her short fiction has appeared in *Strange Horizons, Asimov's,* and several "year's best" anthologies. A professional puppeteer and voice actor, she lives in Portland with her husband Rob and nine manual typewriters.

Yoon Ha Lee's first short fiction collection, *Conservation of Shadows*, was published in 2013. She lives in Louisiana with her family, used to design constructed languages as a hobby, and has not yet been eaten by gators.

Ken Liu (kenliu.name) is an author and translator of speculative fiction, as well as a lawyer and programmer. A winner of the Nebula, Hugo, and World Fantasy Awards, he has been published in *The Magazine of Fantasy & Science Fiction*, *Asimov's*, *Analog*, *Clarkesworld*, *Lightspeed*, and *Strange Horizons*, among other places. He lives with his family near Boston, Massachusetts. Ken's debut novel, *The Grace of Kings*, the first in a silkpunk epic fantasy series, will be published by Saga Press, Simon & Schuster's new genre fiction imprint, in April 2015. Saga will also publish a collection of his short stories.

Sarah Monette lives in a 108-year-old house in the Upper Midwest with a great many books, two cats, one grand piano, and one husband. Her Ph.D. diploma (English Literature, 2004) hangs in the kitchen. She has published more than fifty short stories and has two short story collections *The Bone Key* and *Somewhere Beneath Those Waves*. She has written two novels (*A Companion to Wolves* and *The Tempering of Men*) and four short stories with Elizabeth Bear, and hopes to write more. Her first four novels (*Melusine, The Virtu, The Mirador, Corambis*) were published by Ace. Her latest novel, *The Goblin Emperor*, published under the pen name Katherine Addison, came out from Tor in April 2014. Visit her online at www.sarahmonette.com or www.katherineaddison.com.

Michael Moorcock, widely acknowledged as one of the premiere masters of SF and fantasy and selected by *The Times* of London as one of the fifty greatest British writers since 1945, is the author of dozens of works of SF, fantasy, and mainstream fiction, such as the Elric sequence (starting with *The Stealer of Souls*), the Corum Seres (starting with *Knight of Swords*), and the Hawkmoon series (starting with *Jewel in the Skull*). He has received the World Fantasy Award for life achievement and was named an SFWA Grand Master in 2008. Moorcock's first independent novel in nine years, *The Whispering Swarm*, will be published later this year. It is the first in a trilogy that is both fantastical and autobiographical. He lives in Texas.

Tom Purdom has been publishing science fiction since 1957 and writing about music since 1988. He currently reviews for *The Broad Street Review* (www.broadstreetreview.com). Purdom has written non-fiction about subjects as varied as arms control and interior decorating for magazines such as *Kiwanis* and *American Education* and institutional clients such as the University of Pennsylvania and the United States Air Force. His science fiction credits include five novels and a multitude of highly praised shorter works. Purdom's literary memoir, *When I Was Writing*, can be found online at www.philart.net/tompurdom/wiwone.htm.

USA Today bestseller and Hugo Award-winner **Kristine Kathryn Rusch** writes more time travel stories than she usually admits. *Gallery of His Dreams*, her breakthrough novella, which was nominated for every award in SF, has just been re-released by WMG Publishing. Her time-travel novel, *Snipers*, appeared in 2013. She'll write more in that series after she finishes a eight-book saga for her Retrieval Artist series. WMG Publishing will release the remaining six books in that saga one per month starting in January of 2015. Rusch writes much more than time-travel stories—other science fiction, fantasy, mystery, romance—and is the former editor of *The Magazine of Fantasy & Science Fiction*. She lives and works on the Oregon Coast.

A prolific writer of novels, short stories, TV scripts, and screenplays (most notably, *The Crow*), **John Shirley** (john-shirley.com) has published over three dozen novels and eight collections. Among his novels are *Doyle After Death*, *Demons*, the seminal cyberpunk works *City Come A-Walkin*, and the *A Song Called Youth* trilogy of *Eclipse*, *Eclipse Penumbra*, and *Eclipse Corona*. His collections include the Stoker and IHG Award-winning *Black Butterflies* and *In Extremis: The Most Extreme Stories of John Shirley*. As a musician Shirley has fronted his own bands and written lyrics for Blue Öyster Cult and others. In 2013, Black October Records released a two-CD compilation of Shirley's own recordings, *Broken Mirror Glass: The John Shirley Anthology: 1978-2012*. His latest novel is historical fiction: *Wyatt In Wichita* (Skyhorse).

Born and brought up in New Delhi, India, **Vandana Singh** (users.rcn. com/singhvan) now lives near Boston where she teaches at Framingham State College. Her short fiction has appeared in periodicals including *Clarkesworld*, *Lightspeed*, *Strange Horizons*, and *The Third Alternative* and anthologies such as *Clockwork Phoenix*, *Solaris 2*, *Steampunk Revolution*, and *Trampoline*. Some of her work has been reprinted in *Year's Best Fantasy & Horror, Year's Best Science Fiction, Year's Best SF*, and *Twenty-First Century Science Fiction*. Her collection, *The Woman Who Thought She Was a Planet and Others Stories*, was published in 2008. She has also published two books for children and coedited *Breaking the Bow: Speculative Fiction Inspired by the Ramayana* with Anil Menon.

Steve Rasnic Tem is a past winner of the Bram Stoker, World Fantasy, and British Fantasy Awards. His two books from 2012 were the novel *Deadfall Hotel* and the noir collection *Ugly Behavior* (New Pulp Press). Three Tem collections—*Onion Songs* (Chomu), *Celestial Inventories* (ChiZine), and *Twember* (NewCon Press)—were released in 2013. Another collection, *Here With the Shadows,* was published in February 2014 (Swan River). Southern gothic *Blood Kin* (Solaris) is his latest novel.

Genevieve Valentine's first novel, *Mechanique: A Tale of the Circus Tresaulti*, won the 2012 Crawford Award and was nominated for the Nebula. Her second novel, *The Girls at the Kingfisher Club*, a 1920s retelling of the Twelve Dancing Princesses, was published by Atria earlier this year. *Persona*, a near-future political thriller, will be published by SAGA Press in March 2015. Her short fiction has appeared in *Clarkesworld, Strange Horizons, Journal of Mythic Arts, Lightspeed*, and other periodicals, as well as anthologies *Federations, The Living Dead 2, After, Teeth*, and more. Her story "Light on the Water" was a 2009 World Fantasy Award nominee, and "Things to Know About Being Dead" was nominated for a 2012 Shirley Jackson Award. She is a coauthor of pop-culture book *Geek Wisdom* (Quirk Books).

Suzanne J. Willis is a Melbourne based writer and a graduate of Clarion South. Her short stories have appeared or are forthcoming in *Luna Station Quarterly, Schlock Magazine, Postscripts*, and anthologies by Fablecroft Publishing and Kayelle Press. "Number 73 Glad Avenue" has been podcast by StarShipSofa, and Suzanne is currently working on a novel detailing Mary, Charlie, and Freya's adventures, in addition to weaving more short stories. She can be found online at suzannejwillis.webs.com.

回

ACKNOWLEDGMENTS

"The Time Travel Club" © 2013 Charlie Jane Anders. First publication: *Asimov's*, October-November 2012.

"Mating Habits of the Late Cretaceous" © 2012 Dale Bailey. First publication: *Asimov's*, September 2012.

"The Carpet Beds of Sutro Park" © 2012 Estate of Kage Baker. First publication: *The Best of Kage Baker* (Subterranean Press).

"The Ghosts of Christmas" © 2012 Paul Cornell. First publication: *Tor.com*, 19 December 2012.

"Thought Experiment"© 2011 Eileen Gunn. First publication: *Eclipse Four: New Science Fiction and Fantasy*, ed. Jonathan Strahan (Night Shade Books).

"First Flight" © 2009 Mary Robinette Kowal. First publication: *Tor.com*, 25 August 2009.

"Blue Ink" © 2008 Yoon Ha Lee. First publication: *Clarkesworld*, Issue 23, August 2008.

"The Man Who Ended History: A Documentary" © 2011 Ken Liu. First publication: *Panverse Three*, ed. Dario Ciriello (Panverse Publishing).

"The Ile of Dogges" © 2006 Elizabeth Bear & Sarah Monette. First publication: *Aeon 7*, May 2006.

"The Lost Canal" © 2013 Michael Moorcock. First publication: *Old Mars*, edited by Gardner Dozois & George R. R. Martin (Bantam).

"The Mists of Time" © 2007 Tom Purdom. First publication: *Asimov's*, August 2007.

"September at Wall and Broad" © 2013 Kristine Kathryn Rusch. First publication: *Fiction River: Time Streams*, ed. Dean Wesley Smith (WMG Publishing).

"Two Shots from Fly's Photo Gallery" © 2009 John Shirley. First publication: *He Is Legend: An Anthology Celebrating Richard Matheson*, ed. Christopher Conlan (Gauntlet Press).

"With Fate Conspire" © 2013 Vandana Singh. First publication: *Solaris Rising 2: The New Solaris Book of Science Fiction*, ed. Ian Whates (Solaris).

"Twember" © 2012 Steve Rasnic Tem. First publication: *Interzone*, #239, March-April 2012.

"Bespoke" © 2009 Genevieve Valentine. First publication: *Strange Horizons*, 27 July 2009.

"The King of Where-I-Go" © 2005 Howard Waldrop. First publication: *SciFiction*, 7 December 2005.

"Number 73 Glad Avenue" © 2013 Suzanne J. Willis. First publication: *One Small Step: An Anthology of Discoveries*, ed. Tehani Wessely (Fablecroft Publishing).